World Without End

G. Lloyd Helm

Credits

Cover Artist: Christine Young
Editor: Sheryl Lynn Gerety

Printed in the United States of America

Dedication

This book is dedicated to Michele, who believed.

Prologue

Joshua Gordon, The Creator, was fifty-eight years old when he felt himself beginning to die. He was of medium height with graying hair, brown-gold eyes, a face pleasantly marked with smile wrinkles and a body with a tendency toward plumpness in the middle. The feeling was just an odd little twinge at first; a sort of pinching at the base of his neck, producing a barely perceptible weakening in his legs, gone almost before noticed, not to be thought of again until the pinching became stronger and the weakness more pronounced. His medicos said the condition was a genetic defect, accelerated neuro-myelitis, but when Gordon began questioning what the hyphen bearing Latinate gobbledygook meant, they hemmed and hawed, provoking him so he lost his temper.

"You mean you have not the foggiest notion on God's green earth what is wrong with me! Am I right?"

"Take it easy Dad," Joshua's son Lucian said, putting his hand on his father's shoulder. Lucian, the very image of his father at the same age, had driven Joshua to the doctor, pushed the wheelchair Joshua did not really need down the hospital corridors.

"No sir! It does not!" the young doctor protested. "We know the sheathing around your nerves is growing thinner, at some places it has thinned to nothing. Without sheathing, the signals traveling along your nerves are diverted or scrambled."

"In other words, I have a short circuit in my electrical system because the insulation around my wiring isn't any good?"

The doctor smiled at his question. It was so typically Gordon and the doctor had been a fan of Joshua Gordon's books since he was a child. "Yes sir. Pretty accurate description," he said.

"So, why is it happening, and what can be done about it?"

Now the doctor was not so quick to reply. "I can't answer those questions, Mr. Gordon. We don't know what causes it yet, and because we don't know we don't--"

"Yeah, OK." Gordon said holding up a hand to stop the doctor. "How long?"

"Mr. Gordon, it's--"

Gordon held up his hand again. "Just go ahead and say it. A year, a day, an hour-and-a-half, what?"

The doctor hated what he was about to say, he knew the reaction he was going to get, but there was no avoiding it. With a mental shrug he said, "We don't know."

Gordon opened his eyes wide in disbelief just as the doctor had seen him do on countless talk shows. He knew it *always* preceded the skewering of some pretentious asshole.

"You don't know?" Gordon said softly.

"No sir."

Obviously holding in an explosion Gordon said, "Then get me a doctor who knows something."

The doctor blushed. "Your privilege and I recommend it, but they will all tell you the same thing, Mr. Gordon. They will say it differently, but it will boil down to the same thing. There are several related genetic conditions and we have no cure for any of them. There is an experiment going on now in Scotland where some Vets are trying to re-grow or create new myelin sheathing in dogs born without the sheathing, and there are several genetic studies going on, but there is no way of knowing what sort of success they are having. And as to how long--it depends on the rate of degeneration. Your onset was late in life, which may be good-"

"But it may be bad."

"Yes."

"So I could live another sixty years, or I could suddenly collapse with the galloping shakes and kick over in the next couple of minutes."

"You probably will not live another sixty years..." the doctor said with an earnestness which pinked Gordon in his twisted, ironic wit and caused him to smile despite the situation.

"Can't ever tell Doc," he said. "Can't ever tell."

~*~

The ravens circled like a column of black smoke rising on the updrafts from the furnace hot desert floor. They would have descended hungrily to the body lying spread eagled beneath them, but the red bird that circled below them, between their sky and Lord Lucian's earth, would not let them approach.

The body lying on the sand belonged to John Fisher. He was not quite dead, but the ravens would not have minded had they been able to get at him. Fisher's body was well muscled but showed signs of abuse with bruises around his wrists, the skin of his face red and peeling with sun exposure; still he would have made a delicious feast for the ravens if the red bird would let them reach it.

The red bird, the size of a large cardinal, descended, perching itself on Fisher's chest. It pecked at the rawhide neck lacing of the hunting shirt the man wore, saying, "Time to wake up John. I can't chase Lucian's messengers off much longer. If you don't wake up they're going to have you for lunch." After a moment the bird hopped to Fisher's bearded chin and pulled several of the ragged dusty hairs from it then hopped into the air, once more placing itself between Fisher and the ravens.

Fisher opened his sea green eyes and sat up. The sun was a blazing orange ball hanging in a washed out blue cloudless sky. He shook his head and tried to bring his tattered mind into some kind of order. The simple gesture didn't work. A jumble of memories rolled and tumbled, but none of them would hold still long enough for him to really get a look. They all seemed to be thickly wrapped in cobwebs. Fisher squeezed his eyes shut so hard he saw yellow and green phosphene spots; opening them he found nothing had changed. He swallowed almost lacking saliva. The heat had already dried much of the moisture out of his body.

Where am I? And how the hell did I get here?

No answer was forth coming. He was sure there was memory in his brain somewhere, but he couldn't quite seize it.

One way or another I gotta get out of this sun. I'm already burned and drying out. I need to find some shade or I'm done for. He looked around. A little behind him was an outcropping, an island of boulders in a sea of sand. Among the rocks some gray green plants, more like desiccated sticks than living things, poked up. Some of the boulders were large enough to cast considerable shadows, at least until the sun rose more toward the meridian.

Fisher pushed himself unsteadily to his feet and started toward the shade. The sand was hot. It burned his feet right through his--

He glanced down and found his feet clad not in shoes, but in boots-- high topped moccasins really. They looked worn but sturdy, and the tops came well up his calves to keep the sand out. His pants legs were tucked into the boot tops. They were dusty gray and made of some heavy woven cloth like canvas. He was also wearing a long-sleeved hunting shirt which might once have been tan, but was so sweat stained and dirty the color was hard to determine. It hung almost to his knee. The neck was open, but it could be closed with a thong which crisscrossed over the opening.

"What am I, an Indian?" Fisher asked aloud. Then thought *No, I'm Scots-Irish.*

He shook his head again and long hair flopped into his view. He reached up and found his hair at shoulder length. He had a beard, also not right, but he put thinking aside for the moment. He had to get into the shade.

The sand, soft and yielding, made walking difficult. Fisher's legs felt very heavy, but after a little he made it to the boulders to sit down in the shade. For the sake of sanity he blanked out his mind for a while. The thought surfaced anyway--I wonder if this is a dream? But it didn't seem dream-like.

Everything was too clear. The tightness in his throat, thickened with thirst, had none of the detached-from-reality feeling his dreams usually had.

A little sound diverted his attention outward. He didn't see anything, the desert appearing lifeless. The sound again, came from above. He looked up. Perched on an outcrop of looming boulder was the bright red bird, a cardinal the size of a raven perhaps? It was a bird the like of which Fisher thought he had never seen before, or at least he couldn't remember that he had.

The bird cocked its head to the right to study Fisher with a steady stare. The black bead eyes were so penetrating Fisher could feel them stabbing deeply.

"What are you looking at?" Fisher asked.

"John Fisher," the red bird answered. "A man with a purpose."

Fisher's mouth fell open in surprise and, after a moment of shocked gasping, he fainted.

~*~

Lucian smiled. That smile was not out of place, but the doctor observed that it seemed to contain a bit more satisfaction than might be expected under the circumstances. Apparently Lucian Gordon was not heart broken to hear his father's death sentence. Later, while he didn't buy a bottle of Dom Perignon to celebrate, he did pour himself a stiff drink of good whiskey by way of congratulation--sort of. He lifted the glass in a toast to himself, saying, "Here's to ya, Pop," then he slugged down the Glenury Royal so fast he didn't taste it.

He set the glass down and wiped his stinging, watering eyes; perhaps these tears were the bite of the whisky? Perhaps emotion. One way or the other he didn't need to make that call. The old man had only a few more windings of this mortal coil, whereupon Lucian was going to come into considerable money and property. Of assets, though, he had plenty. He cared more that *he* would be alive; the Great Joshua Gordon would be dead.

Perhaps, he thought, with his father safely planted beside his mother, the long shadow of his father's literary career would fade leaving Lucian to receive the praise and acknowledgement he deserved. Perhaps if there were no new Joshua Gordon creations on the shelves, the book buying public might soon discover there was more than one Gordon who could write.

Unfortunately, while Joshua Gordon had given his only son money, love, and an education, he had not gifted him the one thing Lucian wanted more than anything in the world, the creative spark. Lucian's writing wasn't all that bad. Many people had told him his work was good. It was literate, and lucid, and even, sometimes, witty, but somehow...it just had no breath of life. Even Lucian recognized it. Immersed in jealousy, still he knew that compared to his father's work, his stories were a waste of paper and ink. They had no power to move the heart or prick the mind to rebellious thought. Such inability was no sin! There were a lot of other authors who were not Joshua Gordon. Authors who sold. Their books didn't sit on the shelves until the covers began to curl, not like his. He ran his fingers through his hair, tugging hard at handfuls of it to release his thoughts.

Lucian poured himself another drink, a generous portion then sat down at his desk. Dazed, he looked around his office. His eyes found the life-size oil painting of his mother that hung opposite his desk. His office was a beautiful place, but the portrait was the only thing in the room he truly cared about. To him all the rest was just so much slag.

On the shelf right behind the desk were four books with Lucian Gordon's name on the spines. Lucian clenched his jaw. They served to remind him how much he hated his father. But for the name of Gordon, they would not have been published. Though the name had not helped them sell. People had picked them up, Lucian imagined, flipping through the first few pages, thinking "*This isn't Joshua Gordon's usual style.* Looking at the authors name they had said, "Ah, the son. Too bad some of the old man's talent didn't rub off on the kid."

But Joshua's overshadowing talent was not the only reason Lucian Gordon hated his father. Lucian knew in his heart of hearts that

TUCHINARA and the other books of the Forneria series had been the cause of his mother's death. They mattered more than wife, or children, or anything else in the world to Joshua. He had been touring, promoting *TUCHINARA,* when Lucian's mother collapsed and died. The doctors said a brain aneurism, but Lucian was certain it was neglect. She would never have died if his father had been home.

Now, the old man was dying, betrayed by his own body, and the irony did not escape Lucian. His mother's body had betrayed her by the bursting of a blood vessel. Now his father was dying because his body was betraying him. Poetic justice.

The old man dead--the thought darkened Lucian's satisfaction. *Dead, but not dead to the world, because of the world Joshua Gordon had created!* Lucian threw his empty glass across the room, the crystal shattering explosively, spraying sparkling shards across the carpet. *But they'll be under my control. They'll come to me in his will.* The literary property of Joshua would become the property of Lucian. Books – Worlds would be under his control. Worlds his father had created to be sure, but with the old man dead, those worlds should also die.

Maybe I should just take over where the old man leaves off, Lucian thought bitterly. He rose to meet his mother's eyes. *Take over where the great Joshua Gordon leaves off. Why not? I can imitate pop's style perfectly--used to be a standard line in all my reviews--"too much like Joshua Gordon". No! I refuse to live in his shadow! I'll let them die. No new printings, no new books. No more Forneria! I'll just let it dry up completely.*

Lucian crossed the room to the liquor cabinet pouring a fresh libation in another beautiful tumbler. He brought the glass to his mouth and sipped then smiled, lifted the glass again and said, "Here's to you, Pop. And hurry up with your dying."

PART ONE

One

The sun rose higher and the shadow Fisher had been lying in shrank away to nothing. The baking heat once more brought him awake. He opened his eyes with the thought, *Man what a dream*, just trickling from his unconscious into his conscious mind, but the washed out desert blue of the sky stopped it dead.

"Awake again, I see," a voice said.

Fisher sprang up and looked around, eyes rolling like a horse about to bolt. His vision grabbed at the red bird sitting on the boulder whereupon his mind spun.

"Gently," the bird said. "Just step over into the shade and get hold of yourself."

Fisher blinked, feeling the scratchiness of his dry eyeballs. "I'm thirsty."

"I don't wonder. You'll have some water in a little while, but first you need to get oriented. Right now you still think this is some kind of weird dream..."

Right you are, thought Fisher, but he did not say it. He moved up into the shade of the island of boulders and sat down.

"Much better," the bird said.

"I'm still thirsty."

"Patience."

"This is crazy. I must be crazy," Fisher said to himself.

"Lots of others think so too. Most people think prophets are crazy," the bird said cocking its head to the right as though to get a look at Fisher from a different angle.

"Prophet?"

"It's what they call you."

"They?"

"The people."

"What people?"

"Those people," the bird said and flipped its black beak toward the far off mountains. A cloud of dust which might have been raised by an errant breeze showed against the blueness of the mountains.

Fisher shaded his eyes and stared at the little tan smudge of dust. "Who are they?" he asked. A tingle of apprehension ran from the back of his neck up over his scalp.

"You'll find out as we go along. For right now think of them as the people you have come to save?"

"To save?" Fisher looked at the bird.

"Yes, to save. It's why Gordon sent you here. Your purpose. You are here to save the world."

"Huh?" Fisher said.

The red bird shook its head and rolled its black bead eyes. "Now there's an intelligent response," it said and disappeared into thin air.

Two

Joshua Gordon, philosopher, poet, fantasy novelist, professor at Rathmer College, Los Angeles, California, read up on myelitis of all sorts and became quite the lay-expert on it. But all his reading boiled down to one thing. He was going to lose control of his body and he was going to die with this disease, barring some unforeseen miracle and no doubt about it.

Gordon didn't expect any miracles. It wasn't the way God worked, or at least not in Gordon's experience. According to various scriptures of the world there was a time when miracles were a fairly common occurrence, but Gordon didn't put much stock in scriptures of any stripe. He was an Episcopalian by upbringing and a Christian in practice, but had little use for churches. Mostly he thought they were filled with bigots of one sort and another who spent more time seeking reasons to *not* love their fellow men than practicing what Jesus preached, but he didn't hold the bigotry against them much. It was the way the author of this novel (of which he, Joshua Gordon, was the hero) had written them, so it wasn't exactly their fault. Still, it did bother him. People hated one another on such slim pretexts as skin color or national origin, or what god they prayed too and the stupidity of that was mind boggling.

That said, Gordon knew his beliefs in the Great Author God and his belief in the rightness of what Jesus preached were in conflict and he didn't care. He agreed with Emerson's comments on foolish consistency and small minds when it came to conflicting beliefs.

So--Gordon didn't expect a miracle in this world which, perversely, was why he began looking to commit a miracle in the world of his own creation. *I have to hand my world over to someone so it'll continue to live,* he thought. *I can't let it go static like all those other scribblers who had the temerity to create worlds only to go and die without finding a way to let those worlds continue to live. Gods should take care of their creatures, or they shouldn't create them.*

Then the miracle Gordon didn't expect happened--sort of. Medical science didn't suddenly come up with a cure, nor did some creature with a hot line to the Creator lay hands on him, shout "HEAL!" and zip zap shabam Joshua Gordon was whole again. But for some unexplained reason the degeneration of his "insulation" stopped. He didn't get better, but he didn't get worse either. "In remission," the doctors said.

Gordon was cynical enough to translate "remission" as "Stay of Execution," but he was happy with the stay all the same. It gave him a little extra time to finish committing his miracle before he made his final bow.

I just wish the faulty wiring had remitted before it put me in this wheel chair. But, once again, he fell back on the "hero in a novel" theory and figured his Author would wind up the whole story to the satisfaction of his readers, and if it meant Josh Gordon in a wheel chair so be it.

Three

John Fisher watched the dust cloud grow closer and wished it would hurry. Thirst tortured him; the red bird had said they would give him water. He could not believe he was putting any stock in anything the red bird had told him, but he really had no choice--he would play along. *This has to be some kind of dream. A very realistic dream, but a dream nevertheless. If it isn't, I'm insane and off in some delusion, so I might as well believe the creatures here. After all, Poe's delusions made pretty good stories; maybe I can get a story or two out of this.*

The dust cloud resolved itself into a train of ten tall covered wagons each with a two wheeled tank attached behind. The wagons were pulled by huge, shaggy, camel-like creatures. *Dromules. Draft animals are called Dromules.* He didn't know where the knowledge came from but it was there. Fisher rose from the shrinking shadow of his boulder and waved at the driver of the first wagon in line.

The driver, a fellow wearing a hat with a brim as broad as a roof, but who otherwise looked as though his beard and hair were the heaviest part of him, drew hard back on the reins and stared at Fisher for a long time.

Other drivers from the wagon train, also wearing broad brimmed hats, were leaning out to see what was going on.

"Could I have a drink of water?" Fisher asked at last.

"So you are real? Thought you was a heat wiggle. You a demon?"

13

Fisher ran what the driver had said through his mind a couple of times, trying to make some sense out of it. He failed. "I'm no demon, I don't think," he answered at last.

The driver looked him over some more then said, "If you ain't a demon then what are ya?"

"Just a thirsty human, I guess."

"Name of...?"

Fisher didn't understand.

"What's your name pilgrim? If you're not a demon give me your name."

"John Fisher."

The man tilted his head down to strain the sight of Fisher through his eyebrows, and sift away any falsehood. "That your true name?"

Fisher blinked hard, trying to understand what was going on and not succeeding. "It's the only name I have. I guess it is my true name."

"Humph," the driver grunted. "Well, if it ain't, it's not the smartest handle you coulda hung on yourself," he said then he turned a little and said, "All right Mandy, he seems harmless. You can put down the pistol. Gimme a water skin."

A woman, as leathery looking as the driver and wearing a bonnet to shade her face, poked her head out of the curtain blocking the entrance to the wagon. "You sure Ez?" She asked. "This ain't the place for a man. 'Specially one calls hisself John Fisher."

"Just gimme the water bag," he said, not taking his eyes off Fisher.

She disappeared back through the curtain and reappeared a moment later with a heavy bag made of a whole goat skin.

"Come on John Fisher," the driver said, pulling a cob stopper from the mouth of the bag.

Fisher moved to the wagon's side and lifted his hands to take the bag. It was heavy and hard to maneuver. When the driver let the weight down into John's hands, the mouth of it flopped over. A gush of water poured forth.

The driver was off his seat and onto the ground in a blur of movement, and a cloud of curses. He grabbed the neck of the bag and held it

14

up to stop the spilling. "What'n the hell is wrong with you, fool? Don't you know water's worth more 'n gold out here? Mandy," he hollered. "Bring a cup. This misbegotten son of a turd beetle spilled half a dram!"

"What?" Mandy screamed. Her head popped out of the wagon curtain. "Anybody so stupid deserves to go thirsty. Put the cork back in and leave him sit here."

"Just bring a cup, dammit!"

Mandy glared at the two men then shook her head and grumbled something Fisher didn't understand, turning back into the wagon. In a moment she re-appeared with a wooden pint cup. It was clear she wanted to fling it at someone's head, but instead she climbed down the high side of the driver's box and held the cup while Ez poured it full.

Fisher drank greedily. The water was tepid and had a strange taste, but that didn't slow him down. He drained every drop and held the empty cup out in a silent plea for it to be filled again.

Ez didn't look happy about it, but he filled the cup.

Fisher drank the cup empty then held out the cup.

Ez waited a long time before he filled it again. When he finished pouring, he put the cob stopper back and banged it tight with the heel of his hand.

Fisher wanted more, but the stopper didn't look as though it were going to come out again--ever.

Mandy climbed up on the wagon, and Ez handed the water bag to her then turned back. "Climb on up Brother Fisher," he said, "'Les' you gonna flap your wings and fly. We ain't got all day."

Four

From the first instant Joshua Gordon set eyes on John Fisher he loved him. There was no sex in it, or at least none Joshua could ferret out. *Maybe buried so deep I could never find it without years of therapy*, he thought, and let the thought go almost without knowing it had been there. But when Joshua saw the tall, straight young man with his tangle of crisp black curls sitting in his masters level creative writing class, it was like greeting some lost part of himself. He shook off the feeling as best he could because he did not want to give any advantage to the young man.

Gordon prided himself on scrupulous even-handedness with his students. His grading scheme was so simple and fair, he lost most of the-would-be class within the first few weeks. His opening lecture to his basic writing classes, his only lecture was, "There are two grades in this class. All of you right now have "A's". To keep your "A" all you must do is turn in one thousand words of creative work, be it fiction or fact, OR one hundred lines of poetry per class period, which accumulated, means three thousand words per week, or three hundred lines of poetry. Your submissions don't have to be good, just regular. First drafts are almost never good anyway. Writing is re-writing and all those other clichés you have heard or will soon hear." Most kept up with the requirement for the first two weeks, but the six thousand word mark was somehow magic. Class attendance dropped off wonderfully after it passed and the pile of 'Withdrawn' slips grew heaping.

16

But the advanced class was not as easy. It required some skill in the use of the English language and some familiarity with the forms of fiction and poetry. Most who signed up for the advanced class were those who had stuck out the basic class and moved on. John Fisher was not one of those. He was an unknown and Joshua determined not to let the young man get by easily.

After the first assignment Gordon knew there was more than just the look of this John Fisher he was going to love. The short story had been wonderful and needed only a few changes to be publishable. He noted those changes and handed it back with a note saying, "Submit this to the *Rathmer Literary Supplement*," then he waited for the submission to come in. It didn't.

A couple of weeks passed when Gordon, having waited in vain, told Fisher, "I've been looking for your story. The deadline is coming up in a couple of days you know?"

Fisher had dropped his eyes and blushed.

"What's wrong, John?" Gordon asked.

"Well, sir, I just...*The Lit.* pays in copies sir."

Joshua didn't understand what the problem was. The *Rathmer Literary Supplement* was a fairly prestigious college publication. Many, who had published for the first time in *The Lit.*, had gone on to much wider publication.

"You can't eat copies sir," Fisher continued with a practical but smart-alecky turn to his voice.

"Ah, I see. Have you submitted it to a cash market then?"

"Yes sir, the day after I got it back from you. I made most of the changes you suggested and sent it off to *Future*."

Gordon was surprised Fisher would submit at all, much less to *Future*. *Future* was a premium market and not easy to break into for an unknown. He said as much to Fisher and was not surprised when Fisher blushed again.

"A form reject slip, right?" Gordon asked.

Fisher's eyes came up to meet his. "Oh, no sir. They called yesterday. They want to buy it."

Gordon's mouth fell open. After a little he closed it up and asked, "Have you sold any thing else?"

"No, sir. This is the first time I've submitted anything."

"You mean this was your first story?"

"Well, no. I've written a lot of stories, but it was the first one I thought was good enough to maybe sell. And you liked it so I gave it a shot."

Gordon ran his eyes over his student for a long time, trying to decide if the kid was for real. At last he decided either the kid was for real or the damnedest actor he had ever met.

"So, you're a pro now, John. Are you going to continue here in class?"

Fisher suddenly looked spooked. "Did I violate some school policy or something, Professor? I didn't mean too."

"No, no. I just thought since you were now officially a professional you'd drop out to write full time."

"I don't intend to drop your class, sir." He blushed again. "I'm sorta using this class as a kind of free editorial service, if you don't mind."

Gordon blinked and ran it through his mind again then he burst out laughing. Fisher blushed deep scarlet thinking Gordon was laughing at him, but Gordon clapped his hand on the younger man's shoulder in comradely joy. "Not to worry, Brother Fisher. Not to worry! You are welcome to use and abuse me and this class in any way you want so long as you keep writing."

After a few more classes and a couple more stories--good, but perhaps not as good as the first one--Gordon talked to Fisher again. "Any more sales, John?"

"No, sir. Not yet."

Something in the younger man's voice and demeanor told Gordon things were going even less well than Fisher was letting on. "One of the hardest things for me," Gordon said, "was my first couple of rejections after I had sold a story for a pretty good chunk of money. I couldn't figure out how they could turn me down when I had just sold to a really big mag. Don't let the rejects get to you. They hurt like a bastard for a while, but you'll get over it. Just keep working and keep submitting. You'll do OK."

Fisher studied Gordon's face looking for any mockery in it, but found none. "Thanks, Professor. I'll try to keep my future success in mind for the next 'Thanks but no thanks'."

Gordon laughed. "You are far too young to be so cynical," he joked, "and I think anyone that world weary ought to call me Josh--or Joshua if you must--since we are colleagues."

Again Fisher studied the older man, looking for mockery. He smiled when he saw none, and stuck out his hand. "OK, Joshua. I may still slip into the 'sir' mode once in a while. Old habits are hard to break."

"Military?"

"Yes, sir."

Gordon smiled. "Glad to be out?" he asked

Fisher answered with a smile of his own, and said, "Sorta. I didn't mind much except not having time to write."

Gordon looked close into the young man's eyes, seeking some hint the student was telling the professor what he wanted to hear. He found no such hint.

"I had no real gripe with the service, though. I traded a few years for the chance to go to school and write full time. I figure I did OK in the swap."

"Sounds like," Gordon said.

Maybe that was when I began thinking of doing more than reading the kid's stories, Joshua thought later when he needed an assistant. *Anybody willing to trade years of work for the chance to write might be just the kind of person I want.*

Fisher continued to write and submit and come to Gordon's class. Professor and students talked often and it was nothing odd for Gordon to have students visit his home, but Fisher was different than all the others. He visited more and became almost like family. His talent grew as the class nurtured it. The trouble was few magazines seemed ready to publish such a talented newcomer. Fisher was in no danger of becoming wealthy on what the buying markets paid. There were too many rejects in proportion to sales, and too many of those rejection notices told Fisher his work was good. They often ended with, "...this is just not right for our readers."

"What am I doing wrong, Joshua?" Fisher cried out over coffee one late evening.

"Years ago I heard of a Chinese magazine, when it rejected any work, sent a note something like, 'We would not shame such a wonderful writer as yourself by publishing your superior story in our miserable magazine.'"

Fisher lifted an eyebrow and allowed a bitter smile to cross his lips. "And your point is?"

"My point is you are not doing anything wrong. You are just too new to the game for these guys to have categorized you yet. You are carving out a niche for yourself. Be patient. They are learning, just like you're learning. Pretty soon you'll be selling more."

"Meantime, I guess I'll just let the rent slide another week," the younger man said with a disgusted shrug. He slouched deeper into his chair and stared moodily at his coffee cup.

"Is it really so bad?"

Fisher snorted. "Naw, the wolf isn't quite at the door, but he is sniffing around the front gate."

Gordon was still a year away from his death sentence so he had not yet thought to commit his miracle, or even to need an assistant. He only knew this talented young man needed help. "If you are a little short, I could help out, John."

Fisher glanced at the other trying to read his face and not succeeding. "You offer to pay rent for all your students, do you Joshua?"

The barb went deep, because the same thought had occurred to Gordon when he examined his own motives, but he kept the thought off his face and answered, "No, only the ones with cute asses."

Fisher nearly choked on the sip of coffee he had just taken, and Gordon nearly choked laughing.

"You are a cruel man, Gordon," Fisher said with a grin when he quit coughing.

"I pride myself on it."

"And probably a closet buggerer too."

"Not since I was a Boy Scout."

Fisher nearly choked again.

After a little Gordon turned serious. "I mean it, John. If you need help with eating money or rent money, just say so. I have it if you need it. No strings."

John Fisher looked at his mentor for a long time before he shook his head. "No, Joshua. Not now anyway. Thanks for the offer, but I don't know when I could pay you back."

"I didn't really mean it as a loan. More like a grant."

"Oh, well, then--the answer is definitely no. Those are the worst kind of debts."

"It wouldn't be a debt, son."

"Maybe not to you, but it would be to me, so thanks, but no thanks."

Gordon wanted to push the point further, but something told him not to, so he let it drop with, "OK. But if you need help just let me know."

"I'll keep it in mind."

But Fisher never asked for help. Though it frustrated Gordon to see his young protégé labor through hard times alone, it won him admiration to go along with the love.

Five

Fisher rode inside the wagon with Mandy and a younger woman, hardly more than a girl. Neither Ez nor Mandy bothered to introduce him. All three sat atop heaps of what looked to Fisher like sticks. *They have to be more than just sticks though. Why would anybody haul wagon loads of sticks across this desert?* He considered asking Mandy or the girl, but Mandy seemed to be still hostile and when he said hello to the girl, she cringed back and looked suspiciously at him.

He was still thirsty, but not like before. He glanced from time to time at the half dozen water skins like the one from which he had drunk which hung from the arched ribs holding up the canvas cover.

The jounce and sway of the wagon were hypnotic as Fisher sat inside and the heat was thick. It made Fisher drowsy and soon he found his chin bouncing off his chest as his head bobbed. He scooted around so his back was against the side of the wagon and let himself drift off. In a moment the hazy reality of dream held him.

A smiling man in a wheel chair. Fisher knew the man. It was Joshua Gordon, his father--no. Not father. Something less, or perhaps more.

Fisher's head snapped up as he started awake. Joshua Gordon was the man I worked for, he thought. But it didn't make sense. He had no memory of Gordon as a man in a wheel chair when he was awake save as memory of the dream. Here, in the back of this hot stuffy wagon, Gordon was not a man. He was the Creator. The red bird had said Gordon had sent Fisher to this world to save it. Gordon, the Creator who was his father, but not exactly.

"Could I have some more water, please?" He asked after a while.

"No," Mandy snapped then she softened a little. "We'll be stopping soon. We'll probably get all we want to drink then, so just be patient."

"Probably?" Fisher asked.

Mandy looked hard at him as though trying to search out some trick. "The spring may be dry. Great Lucian, his name be praised," the twist of her mouth belied the praise "has caused the sun to burn fierce this summer. A lot of wells and springs out here are dried up ain't never been dry before."

Fisher blinked at the name Lucian. He recognized it as he recognized the name Gordon. There were two memories. One waking and one sleeping. The dream memory was of a man about his own age who looked rather like the man in the wheel chair. The waking memory was of Lucian as a god of this world; he had somehow wrested control of it from Gordon; he had no right to praise.

"Why praise so cruel a godling?" Fisher asked, puzzled.

Mandy's eyes opened wide in fear and surprise, and the girl gasped and tried to shrink down among the sticks. "You are Fisher, or a Fisherite for sure, ain't ya?"

"I am John Fisher," he answered. "Him who is sent by Gordon to wrest the world from Lucian's hand."

Fisher blinked at this last. They weren't exactly his words, but they had fallen out of his mouth, and they seemed right.

"Maybe he's one of Lucian's demons, Momma" the girl said, her voice breathy. "Maybe he's trying to make us say something bad about Great Lucian so's he can gobble us up."

"I am no demon, child. Only a human like you."

"You ain't gonna be a living human for long you keep bad mouthin' Great Lucian," Ez's voice came through the partly open curtain. He had been listening over the jingle of the wagon harness.

"I do not fear Lucian," Fisher said, still not knowing where the words were coming from. "Gordon is my maker and protector."

"That how come you was way out here without a dram to drink or even a hat to keep the sun off?" Ez asked with a twist of sarcastic disbelief in his voice.

Fisher thought for a moment then answered, "I am here because it is the will of Gordon the Creator."

"Well that's convenient," Ez said. "Maybe we'll let Great Lucian's servants figure it all out when we get to Barstow in a few days," he cackled at his own joke.

The name Barstow tickled familiarities in both Fisher's memories. It was a town in the Mojave Desert in the place where Gordon was in a wheel chair, and a wagon caravan center and fortress here.

"Betcha they'll even be happy to pay for the very joy of figuring it out too," Mandy added and echoed the other's laughter.

Six

Almost simultaneous with the thought of a new book, a last book, Joshua Gordon wanted John Fisher to be his co-author, to assist him in the book's creation. If Gordon the Creator was going to cause a miracle, he wanted his heir apparent to see it--even, he hoped, participate in it. He wanted to hand Forneria over to someone who could become the creator-god for that world, which was not going to be as simple as just hiring someone to write to the formula Gordon had established. He wanted the heir/creator to know Forneria in its most intimate detail and *know* that it was a physical place as surely as the state of California was a physical place. He thought of Forneria as a slightly altered form of California and had even borrowed a piece of the name and skewed pieces of the Golden state's history to fix it more firmly in his mind.

The trick was to get John to go along with the program. That was where the mystical part of it all reared its ugly head. How was he going to convince John that Forneria was "real" and that it existed both inside the creator's mind and outside in physicality? All the great religions of the world had dealt with this same problem and all had come up with different solutions. Buddhists believed that all was illusion, even the physical world. Taoist's believed that the Tao was everything. Christians believed God created everything and was in everything but that the physical world was separate from the creator. Since Joshua had been raised in Christianity that was the way he leaned. He was the god-creator of Forneria and existed inside it but also existed separate from it. And, truth be told, he had no idea how it was going to work, or if it was even possible. It was going to be like alchemy. No one new why the philosopher's stone turned lead to gold but they knew it did.

Then, too, there was Lucian, which was a complication Gordon, as the Creator, however reluctantly, must deal with.

Gordon was not ignorant of his son's desires as far as Forneria went. Lucian wanted the manuscripts, the copyrights, the books, everything. But most of all he wanted to have created Forneria, a preposterous, impossible, empty desire. One could not will the spark of creation to another from whom it was missing. Gordon wrote his first Forneria story as a child. Forneria and the creatures in it belonged to Gordon. Lucian did not love the books or the characters in them. He wanted only to control them.

Preposterous! If one could not possess creatures who were figments of Gordon's imagination, they simply weren't for sale. To Joshua Gordon, Forneria was not just a literary property; it was real and populated by living creatures so far as he was concerned. Even should he wind up in a padded room because of the conviction of his belief. He so loved them that any successor must love them as well. Lucian might think of Forneria as an interdependent world, at least on some level. He was sure the thought of Lucian as possessor of power over the Forneria books caused a solid lump of arctic stone to roll down his throat and land with a thud in his stomach.

But when Joshua Gordon thought of John Fisher as possessor of power over Forneria, there was a comforting warmth in the thought. A shared belief in the life of created creatures was in John Fisher. It showed in his work. When he wrote into being a character or a place it became alive, certainly in his own mind. The trick, the task, the accomplishment was to let said belief leak through the stories to infect the reader. The reader had to come to believe, at least for a few moments, the creation was real; the creatures and worlds created in the book did truly exist. They existed on some other plain than the reality of this world, to be sure, but they existed none the less.

That Gordon had such ability could be measured: his readers believed in the life of his creations; his books were still so popular they remained in print long after they might have been remaindered. L. Frank Baum in the OZ stories had it. Louis L'Amour had it in his westerns. Dostoyevsky had it in *The Brothers Karamazov*. Tragic, machismo-flogged Hemingway had it. Others had it, as well. So long as readers still believed, even for just a little while, in the reality of those creations, those creations continued to live.

John Fisher had the same strange ability. It was not fully developed yet, but it was there none the less. It was what Gordon was counting on for his miracle.

The night Joshua Gordon announced his retirement and his reasons for it to his advanced writing class, he asked John Fisher to stay after class. When the room was empty Gordon, who had habitually prowled the front of his class rooms even when he wasn't lecturing, settled himself on his desk. He had almost no control over his legs anymore--they tingled rather like they were "asleep," but though he habitually kneaded his thighs when the tingling was in them, there would be no pins and needles awakening. The feeling came and went as though it had a mind of its own.

Fisher sat in the student desk directly before his mentor, unconsciously "sitting at the master's feet."

Gordon said, "I know you don't want to be beholden to anyone, John, and I don't want you to think this is going to be an offer of that kind."

Fisher's attention sharpened but he kept his mouth shut.

"What I want," Gordon continued, "is for you to come to work for me as a sort of assistant."

Fisher started to say something but Gordon stopped him.

"Let me finish then you can talk, John."

The younger man nodded his assent.

"I am going to write a last book while I am still able, but I have no idea how soon this myelitis is going to incapacitate me. I'm already vascillating in and out of the ability to work a word processor. Some days it is just like old times and I can fly right along, but other days, like today, I hardly have enough control to pick up a spoon or walk across the room. I am spending some time in a wheel chair. It seems like my legs are failing faster than my hands and brains, thank God, but the time is coming when even my hands won't work, which is why I want to hire you. I want you to help me finish up the Forneria stories."

Fisher almost stopped breathing. He covered his shock by bringing his hands up from his lap, steepling his index fingers and laying them against his lips. He said nothing because he wasn't sure he could say anything. This was an honor he had never expected. It was going to make some complications too, although John wasn't sure yet how crazy this might become; assistantships to best selling authors, especially those who had been given death sentences, had by definition to be complicated one way and another.

"I know it is rather a lot to ask, but you came to mind the minute I thought of doing a final book."

The younger man thought hard, weighing this invitation against his pride. Was Gordon really asking for help or was this some trick to give Fisher the money he had offered before? Fisher didn't think it was since Josh was really sick.

After a time of silent staring into Gordon's eyes, Fisher found his voice. "Sir--Joshua, I can't believe you would think of me like..."

"I know you don't want to be beholden to anyone, but that isn't what this is. This is a real legit job. And I know it is sort of a step down to..."

"Step down?" Fisher said, surprise making its way through his phlegmatic mien. "It's an honor! I mean, God! There are about a thousand or so people who would kill to be your assistant, but you're asking me....."

"It's not such big an honor, I promise." Gordon said dryly. "I could be a whirling son of a bitch before, especially where my work was concerned. It'll be worse now because of the disease. Frustration and such. Sometimes I just explode for no apparent reason."

"Yeah," Fisher began, with an ironic half grin, "like you're so totally stable about everything else."

Now it was Gordon's turn to grin. "But at least if you were my assistant you'd get paid and rather well for enduring my tantrums. And it isn't going to be charity or any such thing. You'll earn every nickel you get."

Fisher wiped his hand over his chin, almost as though he had already bitten deeply at Gordon's juicy offer. "Sounds better than barely getting paid for putting up with the conniptions of the drunk in my cab last night. Bet I wouldn't have to hose you off either like I had to do to the back of the cab."

Gordon had not known his protégé was driving a cab to make ends meet. The thought of it made him sad. When did the boy have time to sleep? But he didn't let any of his thoughts show. "Can't ever tell," he said, only half joking. "I have no idea what this myelitis is going to do to me down the line."

"Will I have time to work on my own stuff too, or are you going to be a real slave driver?"

"I should smack you down for that crack, but I won't. You'll have time for your own work, if you don't mind working between midnight and six a.m.," he said, dead pan.

Fisher grinned. "More time than I get now."

Gordon sighed his relief, but he wasn't fully at ease. "There is one more thing. I think it would be better if you came to live at my house for the duration. It'll probably cramp you some, I know, but..."

Fisher was shaking his head, "No problem, no problem. I'm on the verge of getting evicted from my rat hole anyway. I've been sorta half looking for another place. This deal could solve a couple of my problems at one swipe."

"We have a deal then?" Gordon asked, carefully keeping the triumph out of his voice.

Fisher thought a further minute on the offer then stuck his hand out. "I guess we have a deal. When do you want me to start?"

Gordon gripped the offered hand. "How about now? I need a ride home."

Sorry Joshua, I don't have a car."

"That's alright. I drove in, you can drive home."

~*~

The trouble started a little while after John set foot in the house as Gordon's assistant.

Lucian had a habit of showing up unannounced just before bed time on what Gordon called "Good night Poppa," visits. In his more cynical moods Gordon wondered if the visits were more to let Lucian judge how far his father's disease had progressed.

"Luke, this is John Fisher," Gordon said.

Lucian swept his eyes over the tall young man standing beside his father's wheel chair. Instinctively Lucian did not like this Fisher. He felt a threat from him radiating like a static charge waiting to be released.

"John used to be a student of mine – guess he still is in a way. I've hired him to help me finish the last of the Forneria stories."

Fisher examined the younger version of Joshua Gordon who stood before him and felt a distinct chill. Lucian was a handsome fellow. Probably attracts women in droves, John thought. "Happy to meet you, Luke" he said, and stuck out his hand.

Lucian looked at the extended hand and did not take it. "When did this happen?"

Joshua's jaw tightened. "It would be polite to at least acknowledge the greeting, Luke," he said.

Lucian ignored both admonition and extended hand. "Since when did you decide to do another book, Dad? And why? You probably won't have the strength to finish it anyway."

Fisher flinched at the hardness of the son's observation.

"Which is why I hired John," Gordon said. "He is going to assist me."

"And what kind of credentials does he have?"

Gordon's demeanor suddenly became prickly. "He's right there in front of you. Why don't you ask him?"

"I'm asking you."

Joshua ran his eyes over his son. He had expected some reaction, probably negative, but not like this. "I think maybe you better go home, Luke," he said. "Come back when the manners you were taught surface."

Lucian hesitated a moment before turning on his heel and stalking out.

"Not a good thing, Joshua," Fisher said.

"You are a master of understatement, Brother Fisher. I figured he would be a little upset because he didn't get to hire me an assistant, but I didn't figure it would be this bad."

Fisher glanced down at Gordon, not sure whether to feel put out, or worried, or what at Lucian's reaction. He had thought this assistant business might have its difficulties. He didn't figure they would start so soon or that they would originate with Joshua's son, Lucian.

"How much trouble is this going to be, Joshua?"

"Second thoughts?"

Fisher hesitated for a time and finally said, "Yeah, probably. How much trouble is this going to be?"

"Truth is, I don't know. I don't see how it is going to be more than an inconvenience, but I really don't know. You can back out right now if you think this is going to be more grief than you can handle, but I have no way to judge how much grief it really is going to be."

"Let me think it over a while, OK?"

Joshua raked his bottom teeth over his top lip for a moment. "OK. Think about it as you move in here. Sleep on it. But I'm going to need an answer pretty soon, John. I'm running out of time."

Seven

The drowsy heat of the late afternoon blanketed the caravan. The sway and clink of the moving covered wagons lulled Fisher's thoughts away from trying to figure why anyone would haul a load of sticks across the desert and into sleep. His head bobbed on his neck.

Mandy and her daughter Em watched Fisher as though he were a somnolent rattlesnake.

Could this really be John Fisher, they wondered? Could this be the man whom Great Lucian was willing to pay a thousand pieces of gold for? Surely though, one so wanted would not go around announcing himself to strangers in the desert....

For that matter, what was he doing in the desert? The last thing Mandy had heard of John Fisher he had been on the verge of being killed by a mob down in Los Angeles. He had stood up on the rim of the dead fountain in the plaza and proclaimed Lucian was an evil god who wanted only to subjugate all the people in order to destroy the world. He was even supposed to have said Great Lucian was really the errant child of the ancient god called Gordon. But no one believed in Gordon now. Gordon was dead or departed or had never existed. Even these travelers, once called the chosen of Gordon, no longer believed in him. After all, how could anyone believe in a god who let such a thing as the Dry happen? And even if, by some stretch of the imagination, such a god might allow such a thing as the Dry to happen, he surely would not allow his own child Lucian to persecute the chosen in such a way.

But in Mandy's heart of hearts--beneath the wrinkled, leathery skin; beneath the sagging infant scored breasts which had last given suck to the fear ridden girl-child staring fixedly at the sleeping stranger; behind the eyes, cloudy with sun induced cataracts and red streaked with dust irritation, there was a glimmer like a single sun spark reflected from a dark sea. A wish...a hope John Fisher was speaking the truth when he said Great Lucian's days of dominion on the earth were numbered.

Fisher was supposed to have said he was sent by Gordon to defeat Great Lucian and to open the water gates of heaven to allow the sweet rain to fall once more...

"Gee up, Anna Bell," Ez shouted to the lead beast who pricked up her ears and leaned hard to the right in her harness. "Gee up, Black. Hup! Gee up droms!" he called and the off lead Dromule leaned hard to the right in his harness. The calls to the animals became a chant in which Ez called out the name of each beast and continued to do so until the team turned a large right curve around a group of scraggly trees in a green depression which looked totally out of place amid the scrub and Joshua trees.

The wagonneer behind Ez began his own chant which brought his team into a leftward curve. Each wagon following turned to follow one wagon or the other's lead so the wagons ended in a large circle with the oasis in the center.

Fisher woke with a start when the wagoneers began their chants, struggling to drag the half remembered dream into his consciousness. It would not come clear. Again he had seen the man in the wheeled chair and another, younger man who bore him a strong resemblance. They were Father and son and for some reason the younger man was furious with the elder.

Dread and anxiety accompanied the memory. A knot of fear beneath Fisher's heart told him the younger man, the son, was angry enough to do the father hurt, and Fisher could not let such happen. But there was nothing else. Fisher could not call up more of the dream. Had there been such a confrontation?

And did I step in?

The sway and rattle of the wagon ceased.

"Where are we?" Fisher asked.

"Boron Springs," Ez answered.

"Is they water, Ez?" Mandy asked. Fisher caught the scratch sound in the woman's voice and he realized she was as thirsty as he was. *She hasn't drunk since this morning*, he thought. *In this heat she must be nearly dead with thirst.*

"Don't look like it," Ez answered, moving himself off the high seat and climbing down the side.

"Oh Mercy, Oh Mercy, Oh Mercy...." the girl lifted her hands toward heaven and begged the darkening blue of the sky. Her voice was the whisper of desiccated leaves moved by the wind from a furnace door.

"Hush em," Mandy said, but it was like an after thought.

"But Mama, I'm so thirsty..."

"We still got water in the skins and the tank."

"She's dry Mandy," Ez called up from the sink which used to be Boron springs.

"Oh Mercy, Oh Mercy, Oh Mercy..." the girl began her despairing chant again. This time Mandy did not stop her. The elder woman looked as though she were on the verge of joining in the plea.

"How far till the next water?" Fisher asked.

The old woman blinked as though she had forgotten Fisher's presence then said, "They's a alkali seep another day east. The water ain't good, but we got Sweetenin' by the wagon load," She jerked a sort of nod at the piles of sticks they were sitting on, "but if it's dry all the Sweetenin' in the Tehatchapi ain't gonna help."

Sweetening. The word bubbled up like a spring in Fisher's memory. The sticks leached alkali and other poisonous minerals from water. It could even leach salt from sea water if there was need. The people close to the sea used to have little need of it. Springs of water used to burst from the coastal mountain earth and run down the canyons in rills, but no longer. The Dry had eaten up the springs and streams. Great Lucian's Dry. And no rain. Great Lucian's Dry had even stopped the rain. "Sweetening" was now worth more than its weight in gold, and it became more valuable by the day as the meadows where it grew were harvested then re-cut before the plants could truly recover. Once men had bought and sold it as a common commodity, now the price was blood and life and spirit. Buy "Sweetening" to make sea water or alkali spring water drinkable, or sell your soul to Great Lucian for the water his army controlled.

"But are you wagoneers not servants of Great Lucian?" John asked. "Did you not tell me so when you shared your water and your wagon with me? Why has your god treated you so cruelly? Why has he made this spring here dry?"

Mandy turned flat, dusty eyes upon him and even the girl, Em's, plea faltered for a moment. "We are believers, not servants...but we cut and sell Sweetenin' just as our people have always done. We could sell to Great Lucian's army, but they do not pay enough. In order to live we must sell at the highest price and others, even Fisherites, pay more."

Fisherites. There was that word again. They had used it when he first joined them. John did not understand it. Why was this group of people called after his own name?

A clacking which made John think of rattling bones called his attention. At the front of the wagon, on the seat where Ez had been sitting, perched the large red bird that spoke to him when he first found himself in the desert. Fisher glanced back at the two women. They were stopped mid-gesture--mid-breath; frozen between moments.

"Now is the time, Savior," the bird said with the same taunting voice as before.

"Time for what, bird? And who are you? And what have you done to these people?"

"I told you before; I am a messenger from the Creator. He put me here to help you along toward your destiny..."

"To save the world..."

"Very good. You still remember our last conversation."

"But I don't understand it any more now than I did before," Fisher said testily.

The red raven cocked its head first right then left as though listening. "Lucian's messengers are arriving to report what happens. You had best get busy so they will have something to report."

"But, what? What am I supposed to do?"

"Relax," the bird said as it spread its wings and lifted from the wagon seat with the night breeze. "You'll know what to do and when it needs doing if you'll just relax" And with a squeak of pinions through dry air the bird was gone. The world returned to normal. The women did not seem to notice any time had passed.

Perhaps no time did pass, Fisher thought, instantly putting the thought aside.

Another squeak and flap of wings called John forward to look out the front opening of the wagon. The desert sky was brassy yellow on the western horizon. Half way up the sky stars were beginning to shine through. A flock of ravens, conventional black rather than red, had settled in the scraggly trees, making a raucous squawking, cawing noise of excited conversation.

Ez and some of the other men tried to chase the ravens away by throwing stones and curses at them....

"Damn carrion eaters..." Fisher heard. "We ain't done yet! Get outa here!"

The ravens sifted the air with their spread wings, only putting forth enough effort to dodge the missiles before settling again, continuing their rudely interrupted discussions.

John climbed down the high driver's box. He walked to the men who had clustered along the edge of what had been the water hole. He was careful to walk around the sandy depression though he could not have said why.

The wagoneers had turned their backs on the dry sink as though not looking at it might make the water return. Better to throw stones and try to chase the shiny black birds away; feel as though they were doing something to defeat fate or the desert rather than admit they were despairing, afraid, and at the mercy of Lucian.

"Fisher..." one of the ravens called, not as clear spoken as the red raven but understandable.

John looked around to see if anyone else had heard the raven speak, but if they had they did not show it. They did not freeze between moments as when the red raven had spoken, but they did not seem surprised.

Perhaps they don't think it odd for ravens to talk, he thought.

"You are not welcome in Forneria, Fisher," the raven continued. "You have brought hurt to these fools..." The rest of the flock squawked and laughed in agreement.

"What have I to do with dry water holes?"

"It is because of you they are dry."

"Lucian dried up the water, not me."

The shiny black ravens sent up an agitated cawing and clacking. The chief raven hurried to say "Great Lucian, his name be praised, is god of all you see. He will never surrender to you or him who sent you. Be gone. Your life is worthless. You are powerless."

"I am thirsty, and so are these who so mercifully helped me. Why has Lucian been so cruel as to make this well dry? These have done him no harm."

"Their Sweetening is an affront to the ever merciful Great Lucian."

"Without it they cannot live..."

"If they submit to him who is god of all they can live. If they hand you over to the army in Barstow, they can live."

"I will hand myself over to anyone, even you bird, if Lucian will open the water gates of earth and heaven. I will do it now if you wish."

The ravens flapped and laughed. "Not yet, Fisher. Not yet. You have not suffered enough."

The brassy sun was gone and a thickening twilight made the ravens difficult to see.

"Then let me suffer," Fisher said, "but let these who were kind to me drink."

"Not yet, not yet, not yet..." the birds cawed, "Not yet, not yet, not yet..."

Fisher looked over the darkening desert sand then turned away from the mocking ravens, walking toward Ez and Mandy's wagon. Raven voices rose in triumph at his retreating back, but stuttered and cackled to silence when, rather than walk around the empty sink, he walked directly across it, and in his foot steps bubbling, gurgling springs of water rose.

Eight

Days passed. Fisher waited for Gordon to give him copy to read through, correspondence to answer, or anything to file, a fact to verify. Nothing came his way. John did small chores around the house. He swept up a little and straightened the books in the library shelves, and dusted same, but he had yet to do anything he would have considered "assisting with a book."

At last Fisher approached his mentor and asked what was going on.

"What do you mean, John?"

"I mean I am beginning to feel like I'm taking money under false pretenses. So far I haven't done anything worth while."

Gordon, less and less able to get the chill out of his bones though the temperature was a comfortable 75 degrees, was sitting in his wheel chair in the living room before a blazing fire. He rubbed at his chin thoughtfully and unconsciously kneaded his thighs then said, "I'm sorry John. I'm just so used to doing things for myself I forget I have help. I never used to let anyone see my rough drafts, but I guess I am going to have to change that."

John thought about what Joshua said and it bothered him some. He did not want to be beholden. At the same time he knew what Joshua was talking about. After a just-too-long silence he said, "I understand. It would be hard for me to open my work up to anyone, and I haven't been at this nearly as long as you have."

"Thank you for that, and I promise I will try to mend my ways, but understand, there is going to be more for you to do in a little while, John, and it isn't going to be as pleasant as dealing with my little story."

A deep gut chill touched Fisher. "What do you mean?" he asked.

Gordon rocked himself a little to the left and brought out a legal sized manila envelope which he had been sitting on.

Fisher recognized the envelope. It had come in the morning mail. He had slit it open and given it to Joshua without much thought about what was in it.

"This is a notice from a lawyer," Gordon said, "Lucian's lawyer. It isn't really a legal document or any such thing, more like a courtesy to me. It says Lucian is beginning a court case to have me declared incompetent to take care of myself, or, more importantly, to take care of the business end of my writing."

"Son of a bitch!" Fisher said then apologized, "I'm sorry Boss; I know he's your son."

Gordon chuckled bitterly. "He takes after his father in the 'son of a bitch' department."

They were silent for a time then John asked, "So then, where does it leave us? Leave me?"

"This is because I hired you of course. Lucian is afraid I am going to turn too much over to you. He wants all the Forneria stories under his control. He has for a long time, so he is doing this to try to get complete control."

"But why? I mean they would come to him any way when you die..." He reddened a little at the indelicacy but Joshua chuckled darkly again.

"Not to worry son, I'm well aware I am on my way out of this world in the relatively near future."

"OK then, what is Lucian up to if what I said is true?"

"I wish I knew. Maybe he wants to be sure I know he is the one in charge and I have to be alive to know it, at least by his lights."

Fisher blinked. "I think I don't understand what you mean."

"I mean Lucian holds no belief in an after life. So if I'm dead, I won't know he is in charge since there is no after life."

Fisher looked speculatively at his boss. "You believe in an after-life?" he asked.

"Probably."

"Probably? Isn't much of an answer."

"No it isn't but it is the best one I've got. The point is Lucian wants to rub my nose in his control of my stories. He can't create his own so he wants to control mine."

"So then, I'm back to my original question. Where am I in this?"

"Right in the middle of what could turn into a very ugly court case if you are willing to stay."

"I don't see how it is really going to affect me much, Boss. I'm only an employee. If the worst happens, I'm just back on the street, right?"

"Yes, I suppose," Gordon said but he didn't sound convinced. After a moment he tried to steeple his fingers and lay them against his lips but had trouble with even such a simple movement now.

His fine motor control seems faded today, Fisher thought. *I wonder if the lawyer's letter had something to do with that.*

At last Gordon succeeded and sat thinking. John did not disturb him. Gordon liked the patient silence of the young man. It was as though they had established some mental or emotional link--Fisher sensed what Gordon was thinking, but more impressive to Gordon was how Fisher always seemed more ready to listen than to talk.

Gordon lowered his fingers and said, "Have you ever considered the Author as God, John?"

Fisher's consciousness spun round the question. The direction was so unexpected he first thought he had misunderstood. "The Author as God?" he asked.

"Yeah. It's not so foreign an idea. Been around a pretty long time."

What brought this on? If Joshua Gordon wanted to talk about God or what ever, it was fine with him.

"You mean," Fisher began," somebody who writes a story is like God to the people in the story? Like God is the author of the Adam and Eve story?"

"More or less."

Fisher shrugged. "I guess it is sort of true if you believe in a Creator God."

"But does the world an author creates have some real existence somewhere besides on the pages of the book I mean?"

John leaned back in his chair and thought about the idea for a while, steepling his fingers like Gordon had only without the difficulty. "Seems like I remember Robert Heinlein kicking the idea around. I kind of liked it, but I didn't much like the way he left it."

"Did you ever consider how we might be creatures in some divine tale...?"

"The Divine Comedy--"

Gordon lifted his shoulders in a fractional shrug. "Only without the cynical implications."

Fisher moved his eyes over the figure in the wheel chair for a few minutes not sure where this was going. "OK, suppose you tell me what this is really all about and what it has to do with this lawyer letter."

Gordon drew in a deep breath and let it out slowly like a man squeezing the trigger of a rifle. "I don't know what I'm hesitating for," he said. "You are already convinced I'm nuts--but don't tell Lucian. It might be misunderstood in court, if you know what I mean..."

Fisher nodded and grinned.

"Ya see," Gordon continued, "I do believe some--maybe all, but at least some--stories create a reality in some other plain of existence. I know there is a world called Forneria out there somewhere. I'm its God or at least its Creator. The creatures on it are my creatures."

John narrowed his eyes trying to decide if this was some joke or if Gordon was serious. If he was serious, maybe Lucian was right. Maybe the old man really did belong in some kind of a care facility...

But then again, being a little nuts was not necessarily a bad thing for an author. Maybe it was even desirable, or perhaps unavoidable was more like it. Anybody who would spend time scratching out stories on paper had to be a little whacked to begin with.

Gordon shivered and pulled the blanket tighter around his shoulders though the room was almost stifling.

"Would a toddy help take the chill out of you, Boss?" Fisher asked.

Gordon lifted an eyebrow at being called Boss. John had just started doing it. "I don't think anything could take the chill out of me John, and you don't have to call me Boss."

John shrugged. "Seemed appropriate, and you haven't ever tasted one of my toddies. Guaranteed to take the chill out of a corpse."

Joshua snorted a short laugh. "My Doctors would probably have apoplexy, but with that kind of a guarantee I can't pass it up. Bring me one."

"Your wish is my command, oh great one," Fisher said with a mocking bow, trying to lighten the mood.

"Be careful of volunteering. You can't ever tell where it might land you," Gordon said.

Fisher lifted *his* eyebrow, but said nothing else, only went to fix the drinks.

Joshua watched Fisher go through the door. He wondered; should he continue as he had contemplated? It might very well convince young John Fisher he was indeed nuts, but Gordon knew he could not begin using John in the story without John's knowledge. The Savior in this story had to be a volunteer. He couldn't shove him into the story because sooner or later the Savior was going to take over the Godship of Forneria.

Fisher returned with the steaming toddies and placed one on the fold-down tray table of Gordon's wheel chair. "Can you handle this like it is or do you need one of these?" the younger man showed Joshua a straw still wrapped in its sanitary paper sleeve.

"I'd like to say, 'real men don't use straws,' but you'd probably better skin it and put it in the drink."

Fisher grinned slightly, tapped the straw out of its wrapper, and put it into the toddy then settled himself back into the same chair as before.

Gordon first inhaled deeply of the steam rising from the glass in front of him then carefully drew a taste up the straw. Flavors of orange honey, lemon peel, spice rum a little thinned with hot water spread over his tongue. The combination of the aroma and the taste did indeed seem to warm him and he was glad.

"OK," he said after savoring the toddy, "back to the author as God."

"OK."

"Suppose as how once upon a time, God created the heavens and the earth and the earth was without form and void."

"Genesis, only there is no once upon a time there."

"Don't be too literal in all this, and don't worry about philosophy. Just go with the flow of the story as a story."

"OK."

"So God creates this world and it is sorta formless like an idea for a story in your head, but you think it's a pretty good idea so you start kicking the idea around in your mind and maybe doodling with it on paper. Pretty soon you, God, have created Eden and Adam and Eve and such, but when you read it, you say to yourself it needs some dynamic tension or it is going to fizzle pretty fast. So you, God, think back to another story you wrote and remember it came out pretty well, but you always felt like you hadn't used one of the major characters to the fullest so you bring him back in your new story...."

"Are we talking about Satan here? Fallen Angel and leader of the rebellion in heaven before the creation?"

"Clever boy! Clever boy!"

"OK, old Nick dressed as a serpent comes into the story and the story does get more interesting," John agreed.

"Also more complicated, because you the Creator have put your creatures, all of them, into a mess from which they must be extracted at some point down the line. So, like a good author, you continue to tell the story adding more characters and more sub-plots, but all concerned with the basic theme of how to extract your world from the mess you have put it into for the sake of making it an interesting story. You try out several scenarios for bringing the whole thing to a satisfying conclusion but, like say Dumas, your story keeps getting bigger and more complex and some of the things you try don't work out so well. You are kinda tired of the story so you decide to just end it with some big catastrophe."

"Like the Flood maybe?"

"Yes, like Noah's flood. But the flood doesn't work out quite like you had hoped because you have been publishing this thing serially in Cosmic Tales and it has become wildly popular."

"Like the Sherlock Holmes stories?"

"Exactly. Your readers are clamoring for more, and when you wash the world away the readers are outraged so you find yourself jiggering up a way to continue on with the story. But you still have the same basic problem. If you just let Noah and company repopulate the world and make a new Eden, you're back with the same sweet but boring story you started out with. Now you have written yourself into a corner because you've written all these characters with a basic flaw which is passed on from generation to generation so you do just what you did before."

"You let Satan come back into the story to capitalize on the flaw and make the story interesting again but also more complicated," John said, nodding.

"Exactly. And it wouldn't be so bad except as you have gone along creating the nice round characters and these great plots for them to be in, you have fallen in love with them and the world you have created. Washing them all away again or some other device to bring this story to an end just ain't gonna serve. You must find some way to save these people--to get around the flaw you wrote into them--even the people who you killed off for the sake of the plot. You can't leave them dangling out there because you have made it clear there are

45

'buffets and rewards' for your characters outside of the lives you gave them in the story. So you have to have some way to save them. Enter, THE SAVIOR."

"Hey," Fisher said delightedly, now caught up in Gordon's story. "Jesus as plot device. I had never thought of such a thing."

"It has been used several times since the original author first used it," Gordon said dryly, pleased he had brought Fisher along in the story just as he had intended.

"Yeah, I guess it has. Saviors of one sort and another show up in a lot of places, like westerns, where the tall stranger rides into town to save the people from the evil cattle baron."

"Right. Which brings me to the real reason I brought you into my house."

Fisher experienced a sudden foreboding, of recognizance in the pit of his stomach, but he tried to ignore it. "I think I don't understand again," he said.

Joshua looked at Fisher for a long silent time on the edge of committing an act of intimacy very dangerous to his own interests. At last he drew in a breath and said, "Forneria needs a savior. I want you to be him."

"Savior?" Fisher asked. He could not believe Gordon was really asking what he thought he was asking.

"Yes." The other answered.

Fisher scratched his chin and had a sip of his toddy, trying to compose what he was going to say into a form which would not offend the man before him, but Gordon spoke before Fisher could get his mind around what he wanted to say. "And now you are thinking the old boy's cheese has really slipped off his cracker, and what the hell am I going to tell a judge if this gets into court? Right?"

Fisher opened his mouth to answer but no words seemed appropriate so he closed it again and shrugged his assent.

"OK then, lets come at this from another direction. Something a little more mundane. How about if I ask you to allow me to model a character in my latest novel after you? I want to make him look like you and talk like you and, if I do a good job of writing him, think like you —"

"Is that what you meant then?" Fisher countered, stopping Gordon.

Joshua ran his eyes over his young assistant. "If you want to view it that way, yes. But I fear you may find something deeper in it when the process actually begins."

He really believes this. He's completely bug house and he thinks if he uses my name and description in his book I'll somehow actually be there in the story. On the other hand, what does it matter what he believes so long as the story gets written. It won't hurt me any to let him use my name and face, and it might help him to finish this book before he dies, which is really all he wants.

"Look Boss," John began. He wanted to couch this in terms which would not wound the old man. "I'm going to take a position of complete agnosticism on this. I'm not sure I believe in any afterlife. I'm not sure if there is some Creator God, or if what an author creates ever really exists on any plane except the plane of the page the story is printed on. I'm not sure if this is just some ploy to test me or a joke or what, but if you want me as a character in your book. I'm willing. I'll even try to pretend to be Jesus the Christ to your God the Father, if you want, but it's the only commitment I can make on this."

Joshua Gordon nodded his head. "OK. Good enough, but..." a corner of his mouth lifted in a dangerous smile, "...just to make sure you are convinced I'm certifiably nuts if something happens and you begin to be...uncomfortable with your role as Savior, let me know. I intend you to have some input into this story since you are going to be so intimate with it."

The implications of Gordon's statement did not escape Fisher. To at least to some degree, he was going to be a collaborator on Joshua Gordon's last novel.

Nine

Fisher was as astonished by the bubbling water as anyone. He had not consciously made a decision to walk back across the sink rather than around it. He had just turned and walked away from the birds.

The people of the wagon train were stunned into fearful silence at first then Ez, too practical and too thirsty to be kept from the water by fear, dropped to his knees and buried his face in one of the bubbling footprints.

After a little Ez sat back on his heels, a look of wonder glowing on his sun leathery face. "It's water all right," he said, wiping crystalline drops from his beard with his forearm. "Sweet as honey and cold as ice."

The others still hesitated for a moment, but when Ez stuck his face back in the deepening water, their thirst overcame their fear and they dropped to their knees too and began drinking.

Fisher watched the thirsty people drink for a time then knelt and began drinking himself. He could hear the small sucking noises of drinking humans and dromules, and the lapping of dogs around him, and another odd ticking sound, but he was too thirsty to worry much about it at first. At last he realized what the sound could be. The ravens had flapped down to the edge of the pool and were drinking. They dipped their bills into the water than lifted them toward the sky and clacked them open and closed to let the water run down their throats. Even Lucian's messengers were taking advantage of the miracle. They not only drank but waded into the water to bathe, splashing and fluffing out their feathers.

Fisher sat back on his heels and all sounds of drinking ceased. He found all eyes, human, raven, dromule, and dog turned on him. Twilight had thickened toward darkness making the creatures looking at him only silhouettes against the dark turquoise of the sky, but he could see they all expected him to say something. He did not have any idea what was expected, but after a moment he asked, "Have all had enough?"

Silhouette heads nodded.

"Even Lucian's messengers?"

"We should have shooed 'em off," someone mumbled.

"No," Fisher said firmly. "All who live should share the water of mercy. Gordon the Creator intended all his creatures, even ravens, should taste of his mercy."

The ravens squawked and flapped. "Great Lucian will hear of this, Fisher. That other name is forbidden!"

"The other name, Gordon," John said, "is the name of He who created you. Who created Lucian? How can the creature forbid the Creator?"

The birds set up an ear-punishing squawk.

"Silence!" Fisher commanded and they fell silent. "Go to your master and tell him what has happened here. Tell him John Fisher was sent by the Creator to bring the cruelty of Lucian's Dry to an end."

A confused clacking and flapping came from the ravens as they rose back to the trees, but they did not leave.

Em, who had prayed for mercy only a little before asked, "Have you truly come to end the Dry?"

Fisher lifted his hand and swept it over the water which had now formed a broad pond.

"But why?" someone asked.

Fisher blinked and thought a moment. He did not truly know why, but he found himself saying, "Because Gordon wishes it," and knew it was true.

"And where has Gordon been in the years before now? Was it not dry enough then?" a voice from the now barely seen people asked.

There was a murmur of mixed agreement and outrage. The ravens added their voices to the noise.

Fisher was once again overcome with the feeling he had back when he first awoke. A feeling of being wrong. Being in the wrong place and being the wrong man. Something else was his; some other place, some other people, but he could not bring them into focus.

"There was no *before*," John began. "Time was *not* until today. All this-- all of you--were created from the mind of Gordon. Until I saw your dust this morning you did not exist. This world did not exist. I did not exist....No. I did, but not here. I am from the other place. The Creator's place."

The wagoneers glanced one at another, turning their eyes only a little as if afraid to be caught. And all were thinking, *This Fisher is a mad man just as we have heard, and those who follow him must be mad also. This Fisher is a devil come to steal our souls or our belief, or our pasts.* But they also remembered only a half hour ago they had been thirsty, this seep dry. Now they had all drunk their fill of the cold sweet water of the springs. Where there had been despair there was now hope. Hope bubbled forth from the footsteps of a mad man.

When the moon rose, full and yellow, the people brought water bags to fill. They left children to watch the bags while some adults formed bucket lines to fill the tanker wagons the train hauled and others tended to the droms and made meals. Most of them, adults and children alike, made a point of not looking at or speaking to Fisher. Ez was one of the exceptions. He stepped to where Fisher sat and said, "John Fisher, how can what you said be true? I existed before we found you. I remember myself as a child. I remember my mother and father, my grandmother?"

Fisher thought about the words for a time then shook his head and answered, "Perhaps you are right, Ez. Perhaps I am the one who did not exist. I am confused. I do not remember my parents or anything else before I woke near where you picked me up...." and even as he said it he knew it was not quite true. He remembered some, but not from this world.

"Maybe it is the heat," Ez said. "Heat makes strange things happen. Makes you see water where it ain't..." he glanced at the pond which had ceased growing when it had filled the depression where the spring had existed before,

50

"And makes you think maybe strangers you find in the desert might be come to save us from the Dry." The old man paused for a time, still staring at the dark water then said, "Em will have food ready soon. Come and eat."

"Thank you." Fisher lifted his hand to clap the other man on the shoulder, but when he touched Ez, the man shied back as though Fisher's touch was hot iron. Ez was ashamed to be afraid of this stranger who had brought enormous benefit to the wagoneers, but he was. "I am sorry, John Fisher," he mumbled as he rose and backed away.

Don't know as how I blame you. I'm beginning to think I might like to get away from me too.

~*~

Fisher, who had slept beneath Ez's wagon rather than go into the stifling heat inside it, came awake at the soft clink and rattle of droms' harnesses being hitched to wagons. The eastern sky was pale yellow and the breeze which had been like the exhalations of a blast furnace the previous day, felt as though laden with ice crystals. He crawled from beneath the wagon. Mandy, whose back was too him, tended to a black iron kettle and a coffee pot hung over a mesquite fire.

"Good morning," Fisher said.

The old woman jumped and turned to face him. Her eyes showed such fear of him it was as though she thought he were a tiger about to devour her

"I am sorry. I didn't mean to startle you," he said.

Mandy got herself under control then quickly bowed her head to him. Gone was the harridan who would yesterday have left him stranded in the desert for spilling a few drops of water. "Good morning sir," she said.

"The breeze is cold this morning. How could it be so hot yesterday evening and so chilly this morning?"

"The way of the desert, sir. Would you have some coffee, sir? It isn't real coffee but it isn't too nasty. We wouldn't have it atall if you hadn't tread

51

up water for us last night, sir...." Mandy realized she was jabbering on and snapped her mouth shut.

Fisher looked in the direction of the pond which had bubbled up from his foot steps, not really expecting to find it, but there it was; a clear bluish spring which had formed a lakelet of perhaps ten yards diameter. Lucien's messengers were gone but the spring was well and truly where it had been the night before. "I thought I had dreamed it," he mumbled to himself.

"Sweetest water I have tasted in years, sir," Mandy said. She turned and poured some steaming brown liquid into a formed leather cup, perhaps the same one Fisher had drunk from the day before. She offered it to him. "Spring used to be right brackish because of all the alkali here abouts, but don't taste a bit of it now. Sweet as the mountain springs used to be."

As he took the cup he felt the slight tremble of her hand.

Ez making a final check of the harness came around the heads of his lead droms. He glanced up to see Fisher holding the steaming cup. "I was just gonna come wake you, John Fisher," he said, but a small narrowing of the eyes told John this was a lie. Not a lie meant to hurt or fool but meaning Ez too feared this stranger underneath whose footprints bubbled sweet water. But he didn't want to show it.

Fisher ignored the lie and nodded at Ez. "Have you had your coffee yet?" he asked.

"T' isn't coffee, John Fisher...."Ez began.

"I told him, Ez...." Mandy said.

"It's more like sagebrush tea, but it will push out the morning chill."

Fisher squatted beside the fire and sipped at his tea. It did taste rather like sage. Not bad. "How long until we reach Barstow, Ez?" he asked.

"Now, with plenty water, we should make her in a couple or three days."

"And what will you do when we get there?" Fisher asked.

Ez studied Fisher for a long time before answering, "Ain't sure, John Fisher. Just ain't quite sure. Thought to sell ya to Great Lucian's troopers, but it wouldn't hardly be hospitable fer me to do it now, what with you bringin' the spring back to life and all."

"I would think," Fisher said with a small crooked smile, "hospitality not withstanding, it would be a good idea for you to turn me over to Lucian. The messengers implied as much last night."

Ez studied the man across the fire from him. "And if I did, what would you do, John Fisher?"

"I do not understand what you mean."

"A man who makes sweet water bubble up in his tracks is a man not to be trifled with." A grin split Ez's beard though he tried not to smile.

Fisher smiled in return. "Do not worry, Ez. I came to save the people of Gordon's world, not punish them. I think you should sell me in Barstow."

Both Ez and Mandy stopped cold at the suggestion. At last Ez seemed to realize day-light was almost upon them. He shook himself, stood up, removed his broad brimmed hat, and glanced up at the lightening sky. "Gonna be another scorcher," he said. "Best get moving."

Ten

Fisher snapped awake and sat up. He stretched out his right hand and found the bedside table with the lamp on it – right where it belonged. He snapped on the light, relieved to see his room in Joshua Gordon's house. Fisher threw back the covers and in his boxers and T shirt padded across the carpet to the door which connected his room with Gordon's. He carefully opened it and peeked through, not wanting to disturb Joshua if he was asleep. Gordon looked up from the computer. "Did you call me, Boss?" Fisher asked.

"Didn't say a word."

"What time is it? Shouldn't you be asleep?"

Joshua looked down at the box clock on the corner of his desk. "It's three fifteen."

"And you really should be in bed."

Gordon lifted his eyebrows and his shoulders minutely. "I've pretty much given up sleeping so, if I'm gonna be awake anyway, I might as well work."

Fisher paused a moment then said, "Well, don't wear yourself out." He started to head back to his room but turned back. "Is it this thing with Lucian keeping you awake? Is it bothering you?"

"It bothers me but it's not why I can't sleep." Fisher looked his question into Gordon's eyes and Joshua went on after a moment. "I just feel like I'm running out of time here. So I'll just go back to Forneria."

A chill ran down Fisher's back. It was déjà vu only more urgently so.

Joshua saw the look pass over his protégé's face. "You OK? You look kinda strange."

"Yeah, yeah, I'm OK--just a dream I was having when I thought I heard you call me. You said Forneria and it made me feel--I don't know--weird."

Joshua glanced at his computer screen then back at John. "What kind of dream was it?"

John shrugged. "Just my usual. Lost in some desert or something and you mentioned Forneria. It just made me feel kinda odd and out of place is all."

Joshua studied the younger man for a moment. "Dreaming of Forneria, are you? That's probably good. I dream of it. I told you it exists out there somewhere, but it exists in my mind for sure. Maybe we have some kind of leakage between us."

John felt another shiver but said, "I don't think so. Forneria may be real for you, but I'm not so sure I believe it, dream or no dream."

"This Lucian mess worrying *you*?"

Fisher shrugged. "The idea of coming between a father and son bothers me. I mean, my father died when I was just a baby and I always sorta wished I'd had a chance to know him. I feel like a rat breaking up something I wanted but never had."

Gordon sighed. "You haven't come between Luke and me. You are just the proximate cause."

""Proximate cause. Huh? Well, it still isn't too comfortable."

"More second thoughts? Are you ready to give it up?"

Fisher studied Gordon for a moment, feeling there was more here than he understood. "No, I'll hang in a while." He turned for the door again and Joshua looked down at his computer screen for a moment.

Gordon said," Come back here for a moment. I want to ask you something--or maybe tell you something. Whatever. "Fisher came back in and went to the desk. "Have a seat." Gordon said and indicated a wingback chair near the window. Fisher sat down.

"What's up?" he asked.

"I've done something I should have asked you about before I did it, but I didn't so--anyway--If you don't think you can 'bear the burden' as it were, tell me and I will change it."

"OK, now you *are* beginning to scare me a little," Fisher said grinning.

"I'm serious John. This is important."

"Oh, sorry. Guess I'm a little punchy. What is it?"

"I had Ed Chance, my attorney, change my will a few days ago."

"Your prerogative, your will, right?"

"Right. But I should have asked you first because it concerns you?"

Fisher felt a sudden drop in his stomach as if he had just gone over the top of the first rise in a roller coaster. He looked into Joshua's eyes then dropped his gaze. "OK, what is it? You decide to leave me the dog or something?" He asked lightly.

Gordon noted the light tone and decided it was going to be useful considering the weight of what he was about to drop on the young man. "I don't have a dog, so--I left you Forneria."

Fisher laughed and started to stand up. "I thought you were going to be serious. I'm going back to bed."

"I am serious. I had Edmund Chance change my will to leave you all the Forneria copyrights and the royalties to the books until the copyright runs out."

Fisher subsided back into the chair. "But why in God's name would you...?"

"To keep them out of Lucian's hands."

"Why would you want...? No wait, I sorta understand after the little-set to the other night, but it just seems petty. And maybe just a little nuts. Why would you want to keep them out of Lucian's hands? Did you cut him out of the will completely?"

"No. Everything else goes to him except for a couple of things going to some charities."

Fisher shook his head as though trying to settle the idea into his brain. "It makes no sense, Joshua. Why would you give the copyrights of your books to an almost complete stranger just to keep them out of your son's hands?"

"Because Lucian hates the stories – or rather he hates me and knows the Forneria stories are precious to me. He wants to control them and destroy them."

"OK now, you said something like that before, but I'm telling you it really sounds like paranoia.

"If it weren't true, it would be paranoia, but it is true. Lucian has a thing about those stories and has had for a long time. He somehow blames them--me for writing them--in his mother's death--among other things."

Fisher looked a long time at Gordon trying to read his face. "I don't think I understand."

"It is the kind of logic a little child could use. See, Elizabeth, my wife, died of a massive aneurism out of the blue. She had never been sick or had any health problems more than a cold, but when I was on the book tour for the first book, *Tuchinara,* a vessel in her brain ruptured and she died. I was in Iowa when word reached me. I closed up and flew home the instant I heard, but ever since then Lucian has hated the Forneria stories and me for writing them. Every time I wrote another one and went away to sell it--did the talk shows, all of it--he would beg me to stay home, but I didn't. So it grew worse and worse, and by the time he was in college--well.

"And then he tried his hand at writing too, which didn't go well."

"Couldn't get published, huh?"

"No, the trouble was he did get published. First crack out of the box." Joshua shook his head sadly. "The book was not good. The only reason it was published was because of me and my name. If Luke had sent it in under a pen name, it never would have had a chance. The company thought they could use the book to try to muscle me into changing publishers. I refused to be muscled and I think it made him hate me even more. The company didn't publish anything else of his. He tried some other places with other books with similar results and they all tried to muscle me, but when they found out I wouldn't be bullied, they dropped him."

"I can't believe anyone could be so low down," Fisher said.

"Believe it. Publishing is a cut throat business and most of the time it matters more who you know than how good you are."

"But," John began and was stopped by Gordon's slightly raised hand. "You have been remarkably lucky, John. Remarkably. Add luck to your talent and no publisher in the country can turn you down."

Fisher laughed a bitter little chuckle. "You're wrong. Plenty have turned me down."

"But some haven't, and when a few more don't and your name gets better known, even fewer will turn down any bit of trash you want to turn out.

"Looking offended Fisher started to say something but was cut off by Joshua continuing. "Not that you would turn out trash, but there are those who will and if they are well known enough they will get published. It is why Lucian was published."

"What a shame. I never thought you could get killed by good luck, but I guess you can."

Joshua inclined his head. "The whole mess soured Luke. He was not terribly talented in his writing, but small talent can often be overcome by large determination and lots of work. Once he had the luck to begin with, he just could not make himself buckle down to really learn how to tell a story. All of it has its part in why he hates the Forneria stories. Somehow he feels I continued to write them just to affront him. I tried to explain I wrote them because I loved the stories and the characters and the world, but he just wouldn't buy it."

"OK. I understand, but why leave the stories to me? Why not leave them to a library or a foundation or something? Why me?" Joshua's eyes searched Fisher's face, considering whether he should be candid. At last he decided to open the box only a little. "I want to leave them to you because I think you love Forneria too. I want you to take the copyrights and the royalties and after the Great Author writes me out of this book, I want you to write more stories. I want you to keep Forneria alive."

Eleven

A day and a half after leaving the restored spring Ez noticed a dust cloud staining the eastern sky., "If I was to be a betting kind of fella, I'd bet it is a troop of Lucian's Cavalry coming out to meet us," Ez called back into the depths of the wagon.

Fisher picked his way over the piles of Sweetening and stuck his head up beside Ez who pointed toward the yellowish cloud that boiled up ahead of them.

"Must be a lot of them to make such a cloud," Fisher said.

"Yep."

"The ravens said Lucian would get me."

"Filthy beggars," Ez said.

"You are going to turn me over to them--the Cavalry I mean?"

"When first I saw you, I thought we might sell you. Then I found out you was Fisher. I thought to maybe really turn a profit, but then you went and filled up Boron springs when we was thirsty...."Ez shook his head making his broad hat brim wiggle up and down. "If it wasn't for the birds, I believe I'd have let ya walk away, but ain't no way we can fight no Cavalry. So I reckon there's no choice but to turn you over to 'em. But I ain't gonna ask for nothin'. "

"Is there not a reward for turning me over to Lucian?"

Ez glanced at Fisher from the corner of his eye. "There's supposed to be, but I wouldn't try to collect it even...well, you know."

Fisher found one corner of his mouth turning up in a sardonic half grin. He might be a total stranger in this desert with memories not his own yet his all the same, and he might not understand what was really happening here, but he understood Ez. The wagoneer wasn't going to ask for anything from the troopers because he knew he probably wouldn't get anything anyway, promised reward not withstanding.

The wagoneer cut his eyes toward Fisher and seeing the half grin answered with a grin of his own.

"I'm going to go sit down and wait," Fisher said and started back into the wagon.

"Shouldn't be too long," Ez said.

Mandy had been taking better care of Fisher since the waterhole and now she had taken the moments of his absence from his place to straighten the blanket which had been draped over a sheaf of the Sweetening to make a more comfortable chair. When Fisher sat down again, Mandy brought one of the water skins from where it had been swaying with the movement of the wagon and handed it to him. "You best drink all you can, sir," she said. "Them troopers ain't likely to want to part with any water."

Fisher accepted the bag. "Thank you. I'll try not to spill any this time," he said.

Mandy blushed beneath her deep tan at remembrance of her reaction the first time she set eyes on Fisher, and the blush brought a sudden realization to him. Gordon loved these creatures and the love had somehow devolved onto Fisher.

"I'm sorry," Mandy said. "It was just we were so thirsty...."

"I understand." He unstoppered the bag, careful this time to hold it just beneath the top so the neck didn't flop over. He drank his fill of the tepid water then put the stopper back into the neck and banged it tight with the heel of his hand. He handed it back to the old woman and said, "May you never thirst again Mandy nor any of you who have helped me."

Mandy blinked at the wish then bowed her head beneath it.

"John Fisher," Ez called. "Best come up here. The troopers are most on us." The horse troop was formed up in two lines with supply wagon and water tanks pulled by dromules at the back of the column. The harness of their horses and wagons jingled as they walked along while the men's equipment clattered. Puffs of dust rose up from each hoof and the puffs combined into a cloud which covered the troopers in a yellow gray coat. When the lead trooper lifted his hand to halt the column, the cloud drifted over the wagons and set dogs, droms, and people sneezing and snorting.

"I am Captain Mortemer Fay of Fort Barstow," the troop leader said to Ez. "I am ordered to take one calling himself John Fisher into custody."

Fisher stood up. "I am John Fisher." He turned and began climbing down the side of the driver's box.

"You be easy with him, Captain," Ez said. "When we were thirsty, he gave us water."

The Captain looked uneasy but shifted in his saddle, his posture becoming arrogant. "The messengers squawked some such nonsense, but they are notoriously unreliable--as are Sweetening hauling Travelers." The Captain said *Travelers* as though it were a vulgarity.

The insult fairly snatched Ez up from his seat. His pulling on the reins made his droms snort and saw at their bits.

"Don't, Ez." Mandy, who had been watching from behind the wagon seat reached up to her man.

"Mandy is right, Ezra. Don't," Fisher said looking up. "You have tasted the water. What does it matter if fools do not believe in the well?"

The Captain looked sharply at Fisher who smiled back.

"Bind his hands with a long rope," the Captain said. "He can walk behind the troop like a dog. And bind his mouth too."

A trooper jumped to do as the Captain said.

As his hands were being tied, John looked at the crowd of Travelers who had left their wagons to come forward.

"Remember me," Fisher said. "And remember Gordon who created you all."

There was a rumble from the small crowd and a tiny spark of fear came into the Captain's eyes. "Bind his mouth fool!" he snapped. "That name is forbidden."

"Yes, sir!"

When the rope was attached to Fisher's wrists, the cavalry column wheeled and started off at a trot which pulled Fisher off his feet. Suddenly there was a flash of red and the squeak of wings through dry air at the front of the column. All the horses spooked and reared. The riders hung on sawing the reins until they once more had control of their mounts.

Fisher rose to his feet and stood waiting until the horses were quieted. The troop Captain once again spurred his horse trying to make the troop start off quickly so as to drag their captive behind them. Again Fisher was pulled to the ground, but again the flash of red and the sound of wings spooked the horses. They reared and bucked--some of them so fiercely their riders were thrown, the troop Captain among them.

The wagoneers could not help but burst out laughing at the fallen troopers, but out of fear of the troopers, they quickly brought the laughter under control.

The unhorsed troopers did their best to control the still dancing and rearing horses, but even those who had control of their animals did not try to mount again. They stared from their fallen Captain to their prisoner then to the wagoneers doing their best to suppress their laughter.

The Captain picked himself up storming and swearing at his horse and at his men, but when he turned his anger toward Fisher who was smiling and waiting patiently, the torrent of words dried up. He stared at his gently smiling prisoner for a long time with clouds of wonder passing through his eyes. After a moment he removed his hat and dusted himself a little. It was more symbolic than useful since it would take a good deal more than one swipe to shake the dust loose from his uniform.

"Mount up!" the Captain called and put his foot into his stirrup then swung up into the saddle.

The troopers did as they were commanded, and when they were mounted, the tension throbbed in the air.

The Captain lifted his hand ordering, "At a walk, Forward Ho!" The troop started off at a gentle walk which was not taxing to Fisher's walking speed.

Fisher had seen this same situation before somewhere, the familiarity overwhelming his senses. But, as with other memories which seemed to be *his but were not his* he could not recall its source.

The wagoneers kept watch as the dust cloud formed around the horse column until the cloud was nothing but a stain on the eastern sky. "Wonder how come he called me Ezra?" the Traveler thought aloud.

"Yor name, ain't it?" Mandy asked rhetorically.

"Only one ever called me by it was my Momma though."

Twelve

Barstow was another familiar yet strange memory to John Fisher. He knew the name and knew he had been to the city before, but this was not the city he recalled. This city was a huge walled fortress made of adobe brick, almost the same color as the desert from which it had been pressed. There were trees and grass, but all growing things looked heat blasted except the starburst-topped cactus trees. From Fisher's experience of déjà vu he suddenly knew these were called Joshua trees but once again did not know how he knew.

The troop led Fisher through the winding streets of the town. Small knots of people gathered here and there to watch the prisoner being paraded, but none of them seemed anxious to stand too long.

At last the troop reached a large, ugly central building made from stacked and mortared stone rather than mud brick. The heart of Fort Barstow.

The Captain raised his hand, called a halt then commanded his troopers to dismount. The Captain hauled Fisher in closer to him, coiling the rope with which his captive had been bound. He did not look at the prisoner, perhaps afraid of what he might see.

Fisher did not resist. He used the moments to look around him and to look at the troopers still standing beside their horses. *John Wayne*, the thought materialized, but he could not connect the name with anything.

An ironbound door, substantial enough to withstand much battering, swung open and five troopers marched out. Four were armed with rifles resting on their shoulders. The fifth wore a pistol belt and a sword. This one saluted the troop Captain, waiting until the salute was returned before dropping his arm.

"This is a strange one Lieutenant," the troop Captain said. "Handle him carefully until we get further word. Make sure he has separate accommodations from the other prisoners."

"Yes sir," the lieutenant said taking the coiled rope. "We have a nice private room all set aside."

"Very well then. Carry on.'

The Lieutenant did a smart about face and the four enlisted men fell in behind him with Fisher in their midst, still harnessed to the lieutenant by the rope leash.

The outside glare made the inside of the building seem totally dark, but the lieutenant marched on confidently. Fisher squeezed his eyes shut hard, trying to make his eyes adjust faster, failing miserably. His eyes were still so dazzled he almost fell down the stairs behind the escort.

At the bottom a lamp was burning. The Lieutenant picked it up without a pause, continuing to the end of the corridor. There was a solid wood door which had a spy slide cut into the top of it. The lieutenant unlocked the door with the key sticking out of the lock, swinging the heavy door open. He stepped aside as the four riflemen escorted Fisher into the cell then did a smart about face and marched out. The lieutenant stepped into the cell to untie Fisher's wrists. But he left the gag in place.

"Welcome to Fort Barstow," he said coldly. "Most just call it Hell. Honey bucket's there," he pointed toward a dark corner, but Fisher could not see anything but more darkness. "Keep it covered," the lieutenant went on. "Water bucket there. Don't get 'em mixed up," he laughed. "If a jailer opens the slide in the door, you stand at attention. If a jailer calls your name, answer up. Any questions?" He did not wait to see if there were any, just turned on his heel and pushed the heavy door shut. Fisher heard the grating of the lock being turned and listened to the retreating tread of the escort. In a moment he was alone in the silent darkness of Hell.

Thirteen

Joshua called his attorney the day following the heads up from Lucian's attorney. Two days later official notice of the competency hearing was delivered. Gordon telephoned Whittaker, Belhaven, and Chance, Attorneys at Law and instructed Edmund Chance to do everything in his power to block and delay the hearings.

"If you can keep the paper flying back and forth long enough, Ed, the whole thing will be moot. I'll be too dead to be examined for competency and too dead to care even if I could be examined."

"A little cynical even for you isn't it, Joshua?"

"To accuse me of being cynical is just a Pollyanna way of denigrating realism."

Chance laughed. "I suppose it is."

"You said my will was pretty much bullet proof, right?"

"Pretty well, yes. I mean these new provisions you put in might make it subject to challenge, but I don't think a challenger would win. Of course it will depend on the competency hearing too, but assuming the hearing goes our way, it would be pretty hard to make a case to vacate a will from just changing one thing. It isn't like you suddenly decided to leave your whole estate to the dog or the Moonies or something."

"I may get to that point if Lucian gets any snottier," Gordon said with a bitter chuckle.

"Don't even joke about such things," Chance said with a quake in his voice meant to be comic but might have been real.

"Is there anything further you need from me to go forward with this?"

"Not at this time. One of the means for delaying this is we will submit our own psych evaluation to the court so you are going to have to undergo an examination by a shrink working for us at some point."

"Can the evaluation be done here? It is difficult for me to get out now, even with John's help."

"I don't see why not."

"Fine. When is this going to happen?"

"I'll let you know. We have to contact our tame psychiatrist and set it all up."

"All right then. Keep me posted."

"I'll let you know what is happening as soon as something happens."

"Thanks, Ed."

After a moment, Chance said, "Don't let this worry you too much, Joshua."

"I'll try not to, Ed, but I won't lie to you, it is on my mind a lot. Good bye."

Gordon hung up the phone and sat looking at it for a moment, thinking he should probably get a speaker phone. But he was less inclined to do such things on days when he could control his hands better, and this was one of those days. He almost felt as though he could get out of his wheel chair today.

After staring at the phone for a little while, he picked up the receiver, pressed the buttons, listening to the familiar non-tune they played as he dialed Lucian's number.

The phone rang three times before Lucian picked it up.

As soon as Lucian said hello Gordon asked, "What will it take for all this competency nonsense to go away, Luke?"

"And a good morning to you too, Father."

"Good morning--now answer my question."

"Fire your boy and forget about this new book."

Gordon had known what his son's reply would be, but it hurt him all the same.

"Why? A new book will keep me amused until I shuffle off the mortal coil."

"Maybe because I don't want some opportunist to alienate my dear Poppa's affection," Lucian said sarcastically. "Or maybe I don't want some lousy new Forneria book coming out to confuse the issue when your will is executed."

"It won't be lousy. Besides, the Forneria stories are not going to be a problem for you. I'm not leaving them too you." The silence coming down the phone to Joshua was like dripping acid.

"You still there Luke?" he asked after a time.

"Who gets them?"

"You'll know when the will is read."

"Ah," Lucian said, "your curly haired paramour. I never figured you for a queer, Pop. But it would explain why there were never any women after Mom."

"You know better."

"The courts won't. Just more ammunition for the competency suit."

Joshua drew a deep breath and let it out then asked, "Why do this, Luke? Almost everything else of mine is going to come to you. Why do this?"

"You already know the answer. I want the Forneria Stories. In fact, if you want this competency thing to go away, I'll make you a deal. You keep everything else or give it all away--even to your new buddy Fisher. Just leave me the Forneria stories. The rest of it is nothing to me. I'll have papers drawn up and have them on your desk by this afternoon. How about it?"

"You know I won't, so why ask for it?"

"Because I know those stories are the only thing really precious to you out of your whole estate. Hell, those stories were more precious to you than Mom or me."

"That isn't true."

"Of course it is. If it wasn't, we wouldn't be having this conversation."

"But they are just stories. Pulp fiction even. They aren't even considered literature!"

"Then give me the original drafts and sign the rights over to me so we can forget all this lawyer business."

Joshua held the phone to his ear without speaking for a time then said, "If I do, what will you do with them?"

"I'll let them all go out of print, and if I can figure out a way to do it, I'll make sure they are never reprinted under any circumstance. I will burn the original drafts. I will do everything in my power to utterly wipe out any memory of them."

There was such venom in Lucian's voice a chill ran through Joshua. "That is totally insane you know? Totally. Obsessive," he said.

"You're a fine one to talk. You're the one willing to go to court over this."

"It's never going to happen you know? I'll never let it happen."

"We'll see."

"Yes, I suppose we will. Good bye Lucian." Gordon didn't wait for his son to say Good bye before hanging up the phone.

~*~

The computer screen was like a huge hypnotic jewel that had captured Fisher's mind, but the screen itself was not the fascinator.

It was three in the morning and he had been working on a story of his own when the in-house network alert had beeped. He minimized his story screen and opened the message from Joshua to find the chapters of the new book with the note at the top saying "Read through these and let me know what you think."

The words of the chapter on the screen shook him to his core; even on the fifth reading. *I told him I would play the savior in the book, but these words and these stories are my dreams.* He had always dreamed wild dreams, but now he was

69

looking at a perfect recapitulation of his dreams since moving into Joshua Gordon's house.

John rose from the computer, threw on a robe, and headed down the hall. At Gordon's door he stopped. It was three a.m. The boss was probably asleep. Besides, Fisher kept telling himself, this was crazy! How could he know my dreams?

Fisher almost turned back to his room, but he still wanted to see Joshua, so he carefully opened the door, hoping Gordon was awake, but not wanting to disturb him.

"Come on in, John," Gordon was sitting up in the fancy automatic bed he had ordered. "I've been waiting for you since I sent the pages."

"Waiting? It's three in the morning. You should have been sleeping."

"I wanted to prepare myself for the little chat we are about to have."

Fisher studied Gordon for a moment. "You know what I want to talk about?"

"I believe so, but I want to hear it from your perspective before I say anything else."

"The pages you sent me--"

"Yes. But remember, I asked your permission to make you a character in the book."

"Character? OK, but apparently there is more. As a character is one thing, but this is more than being a character. Somehow you are tapping into my subconscious mind and taking my dreams. I'd call it dream logic or coincidence if the story and the dreams weren't so perfectly matched."

Gordon seemed a little confused by what his protégé was saying. "What about your dreams?" he asked.

"I think you know more about them than I do at this point. I am half wondering if you drugged me with some psycho-hypnotic and planted the dreams in my mind. Post hypnotic suggestion or something."

Again Joshua looked confused. "Tell me about these dreams," he said.

"What is there to tell? You already know them. You wrote them perfectly in the pages you sent me. The desert, the wagons, the prison, the red bird, the water, everything to the smallest detail of how Ez's hat brim bounced as the wagon full of Sweetening bounced."

"Well, well," Joshua said. "Well, well. This is not precisely what I expected, but..." he made an attempt at a shrug. "I don't know what I did expect really. I put you in the story to try to make sure you had a real stake in it, so if I should kick off before it is done you could finish it. But I never expected you to be 'in it,' if you know what I mean."

"You mean you're not...I mean the dreams aren't...you didn't drug me or something?"

Gordon thought a moment then said, "If I had, I wouldn't tell you and you wouldn't believe me if I denied it without some kind of proof. Well, I have no proof. But as God is my witness, I have not drugged you or hypnotized you or made a voodoo doll or anything."

Now it was Fisher's turn to think and study Joshua. There was no way he could believe the other. No way. And yet he did. "Boss, I don't know if I can trust you or not. I'm pretty gullible, but I think you are telling the truth."

They looked at one another for a long time. "All right then," Fisher began, "if you're not doing it, how is it happening?"

Once more there was silence as they studied one another. After several moments Joshua said, "Maybe we are all part of the great cosmic unconscious Jung talks about, or the Buddhist Universal life force. Or maybe it is happening because the great Author/Creator of this world has decided it will make an amusing story."

John could see no hint of levity in Joshua. "Maybe. Or maybe we are just so much in harmony you are somehow tapping into my dreams without meaning to."

Joshua again took a long time considering and studying John before he said, "And there is something else. You already know that I believe Forneria is a real place." John shrugged and nodded. "Maybe my belief is like an infection that has spread to you. Maybe, at least in your subconscious mind, you now believe it too.

They were silent for a long time.

"So the question now is what happens next?" Fisher asked.

"What do you want to happen? Since it seems to be your dreams I've invaded, I think you ought to get the choice. I could scrap this whole idea and start again or..." he stopped.

"Or what?"

"Or just scrap the whole idea of a last book. It has been very hard for me to get even the few pages I sent you, and with all this competency hearing business--maybe I should just forget it and get on with dying."

Without as much as a thought Fisher said, "No. You need to keep working. It'll keep you alive."

"Question is do I want to keep living?"

The question stopped Fisher cold. Until now it had been dreams and scribbles and legal troubles that affected him only on the surface; that could be walked away from with a simple, "I quit," but now the decision had real life and death consequences which he began to roll over in his mind. He thought a long time and Joshua did not interrupt, knowing this decision was going to be crucial.

At last John said, "Yes, you do. If not for yourself then for the sake of your creatures, just like we talked about before. You brought them to life so you owe them something--even the creature who is me in Forneria."

Fourteen

After the Guard Captain and the escort left Fisher in the dark, he pulled the gag off, felt his way to a wall, and sat with his back against it. He was tired from walking behind the horses and thirsty, but not enough to begin the search for the water bucket. Gradually his eyes adjusted to the dimness. The cell was a stone box with a straw strewn, packed earth floor and a hewn plank ceiling. Faint streaks of light seeped between the ceiling planks to relieve the total darkness he had at first perceived. There was no other light source, no window or flickering torch. The cell was dry, for which John was grateful, thinking how much worse the place would be with dank slimy walls. But the dryness had its hardships too. Every movement he made, even the smallest, stirred up a cloud of dust, a mix of the powdery earth floor and pulverized hay. The dust made it hard to breathe and seemed to take forever to settle down. It made him thirstier.

The two buckets sat side by side, one covered, one not. The uncovered bucket had a dipper/cup made from a small gourd hanging by the crook in the handle on its side. Fisher went to it and dipped up a drink. The water was stale and brackish as though it had been sitting in the bucket for a long time, but even so it tasted better than the water from the Travelers' water skins. He sipped from the dipper and listened to the sounds of the prison.

At first, Fisher had thought his prison was silent. After the sounds of the escort's steps died away, he could hear nothing save his own breathing and the tiny sounds of his own movements. But after he had become accustomed to those noises, others began to be heard. There were creaks and groans created by the clash of wood and stone. There were rustles and squeaks of mice--and other creatures John did not even want to think about--and there was a sound mixture he could not put a name to. It was a sound which somehow made him feel more sad and desperate. A sound so small it could not really be heard deliberately with the ears, but was heard with the heart when the ears stopped trying to listen.

At last--perhaps it was hours later or perhaps only moments--Fisher could no longer stand the noise of Hell and he cried out. "Is there anyone else here?"

His voice echoed off the stone walls of his cell and for a while he could hear nothing except the ringing his own voice had set off in his ears. But after a time he thought he could hear something which might be whispery voices. He turned his head slowly from side to side trying to discover the direction the sound was coming from and at last decided the sound was behind him coming from the wall he was leaning against. He turned and put his ear to the wall.

"....I heard only the one cry," a whispery voice said. "And I could not understand it. Was it words or just a sound?"

A second voice, just as whispery, answered the first. "It was probably just a cry. Poor wretch probably stepped on a scorpion or some such."

"Hello?" Fisher said, not so loud as to make his ears ring again.

"Did you hear?" the first voice asked.

"Someone said hello," the second voice answered.

"If you can understand me, stranger, speak again," the first voice said.

"I can hear you," Fisher answered with wonder in his voice. "I can hear you."

"Was it you who cried out?" the second voice asked.

"I shouted to ask if anyone could hear me."

"Loud doesn't work here. Quiet is much better. You are against a wall, yes?" the first voice asked.

"Yes."

"When you speak, speak directly to the wall. If you can aim your words at one of the mortar joints between the stones, it helps sometimes."

"But sometimes not," the second voice added.

"Who are you," Fisher asked, "and why are you here?"

"I am Noah Simons," the first voice answered. "And I am here because I am a Fisherite."

"I am Thomas Pitney. I am here because I am a fool who knew better than to stand around listening to Fisherites, but did so anyway. And who are you, stranger, and to whom did you cause offense to get sent to Hell?"

Fisher almost told them his name, but suddenly thinking better of it he said, "I am Theo Waters, and I do not know why I am here."

"Perhaps you are here because of your name," said the second voice with an ironic twist. "Great Lucian, our Protector, wishes to bring all water under his control."

"Thomas, your soul is scarred with cynicism," Noah Simons said.

"I understand none of this," Fisher said. "I am a stranger from a far country and I do not know this Lucian."

John could almost feel the stunned silence echoing from the other two. "It must be a far country indeed if you do not know Great Lucian," Thomas said.

"Is Lucian not worshipped in your land, Theo Waters?" Noah asked.

"We worship Gordon, the Creator, the maker of all. Why would you worship any other God?"

"Why indeed," Noah said.

"Noah! Shut your foolish mouth!" Thomas said. "You could be talking to a guard sent to spy on us."

"Then the damage is already done, so I will go on. What will they do to me? Put me in prison?" Noah said with a bitter chuckle.

"Put you on the gallows, fool!" Thomas answered.

"Then it will be a short drop, a quick snap, and I will fly to Gordon's arms, relieved of the burdens of this life."

"And what makes you think so, fool?"

"John Fisher told me so and I believe him."

"Then you truly are a fool. Fisher is gone. He is dead or departed, maybe to this land of Theo Waters' where they worship Gordon, and you rot in Fort Barstow."

Fisher listened to this exchange and wondered. *Was I here in this world before I woke in the desert? They talk like I was, but I don't remember.* He said, "Tell me about this Fisher. Perhaps I should follow him too."

"Why not?" Thomas said. "You already are receiving the consequences of the sin, why not commit it."

"Ignore him, Theo Waters. He is bitter and afraid. John Fisher is a man sent by Gordon the Creator to save Forneria from Lucian who has stolen it from him."

Fisher's head spun round. This was so like something in his mind, half remembered like a faded dream drawn back by the words. Suddenly he remembered. The red bird had talked about his being the one who had come to save the world.

"And how will this Fisher do such a thing?"

There was silence from the whispering wall.

"Hello," Fisher said. "Are you still there, Noah? Thomas?"

"I do not know how John Fisher is going to save us," Noah said at last.

"Because he is dead," Thomas added.

"He is not! We aren't sure," Noah said like a man trying to convince himself of something despite the evidence of his eyes.

"Tell me about this Fisher," John said.

There was silence again for a long time before Noah began by saying "Holy and honored be the name of Gordon who created all...

"John Fisher was born thirty years ago in a little town called Flower on the other side of the mountains to the west. He was brought up in the old ways believing in Gordon the Creator though not many still worshipped

Gordon even then. When he was a young child, a vision came to him of one of Gordon's servants who told him he should preach against Great Lucian who was trying to steal the world from Gordon. He began to preach against Lucian then but he was mostly ignored. Who pays attention to a child's words? But he continued and would not be silenced and finally some listened and believed. They began again to worship Gordon, to pray to Him for relief from what came to be called Great Lucian's Dry. This did not sit well with the army of Great Lucian, but they were afraid to kill Fisher lest those who had listened and believed his words might rise up. But they did take him and imprison him for a time then had him banished to this side of the mountains. He was never to return to his home in Flower on pain of death.

"Some of us, a few dozen including families, who had listened to Fisher and believed in Gordon followed Fisher into the desert. We wandered for a time but ended in a valley we called Paradise because it had a spring flowing through it. Despite Lucian's Dry, Paradise Spring still flowed and watered Paradise Valley. We built a temple there and began to worship Gordon. Life was good. We hunted and grew food and began to be a community. Some, those who had not been officially banished, would leave from time to time and return to the land to the west of the mountains where they would preach about Gordon and tell about Paradise. They told the people of the west Great Lucian was not a merciful God, that he hated them and Forneria and wanted only to see it all destroyed.

"At first the preachers were ignored, but soon they began to cause restlessness in the people. People, who worshipped Lucian before the Dry, when he seemed a merciful God, began to turn away and cry out to Gordon the Creator to save them. Fisherite preachers began to be jailed. Those with the largest followings were banished, others they killed.

"In Paradise we raised up our voices in prayer for Gordon to send us relief, for him to grant us strength to fight, but John Fisher said Gordon would not. Fisher said Gordon was a benign Creator, not like Lucian, a bloody handed devourer. Many left Paradise then. They wanted Fisher to be a war leader, but he was not."

"He was a cowardly weakling," Thomas Pitney said.

"He was no coward, Thomas," Noah said, not in sharp defense but in quiet assurance. "He did not flinch from any danger."

"What happened to him?" John Fisher asked.

"After the rising at Santana they sent a thousand troops to Paradise to take him, as though they were laying siege to a fortress or seeking a gang of bandits..."

Fisher could hear the disgust in Noah's voice.

"A few of us tried to resist at first, but John Fisher said no. He always preached we should resist by not resisting until the time came to resist."

"Gibberish," Thomas said.

Noah ignored him. "When the troops rode into Paradise, John Fisher came out of his house into the square beside the spring. He asked them what they wanted. They had been ordered to take John Fisher prisoner. John said to the people gathered there, 'Do not resist. I will go with these men, but I will return. Remember, Gordon is the Creator. Serve him.' Then he submitted himself to the troopers."

Fisher waited for more, but neither voice continued. "Where did they take him? What happened then?" He expected Noah's voice to answer, but instead it was Thomas.

"They took him to Los Angeles, tried him for sedition against Great Lucian, found him guilty and sentenced him to death."

"So he is dead?" Fisher asked.

"When the day of execution came the executioners went to take him from his cell in Fort Bouchet, and although they searched the fort from turret to cellar, he was not found."

Fisher silently pondered this before asking, "When did this happen?"

"A month gone." Thomas said.

Fifteen

Ed Chance's "Tame Shrink" showed up a few days after the court papers had been served. He was a short little gnome of a man with a bald head and thick glasses that made his eyes look huge. His name was Dr. Alex Erdinger. With hardly a word he gave Gordon a cursory physical examination then said, "If I were you, Mr. Gordon, I would get myself a full time nurse." Joshua didn't like the idea. "I have an assistant already." Erdinger glanced at John who was standing in a corner of the room. "And does this assistant know nursing? Can he administer an injection? Take blood pressure? Give a bed bath?"

"I don't need any of those things," Joshua said.

"You will," he said, "sooner or later."

"All right. Can you recommend someone?"

"Yes, several. I'll send some information packets over when you want them."

"That would be helpful. Thank you." Erdinger put away his stethoscope and blood pressure cuff. "Shall we continue?" he asked. "I don't want to tire you too much."

"Doctor, I just want to get this finished. Let's go ahead. Do you mind if John stays?"

79

"However you would be more comfortable, Mr. Gordon," Erdinger said, smiling for the first time. His voice was remarkably deep considering his size.

"I'm afraid there is no way for me to be more comfortable, but having John here will be convenient. He can fetch and carry if we need him too."

Doctor Erdinger glanced at John who felt like a horse at auction and said, "You're welcome to stay then, Mr. Fisher." Doctor Erdinger picked up a briefcase from where it had sat beside his doctor's bag. He laid it on a bedside table and opened it. From the briefcase he removed a small tape recorder which he laid on the table then closed the brief case and put back beside his other bag.

"What, no electrodes? No implements of torture?" Joshua said.

"Nope, only a little tape recorder," the doctor answered.

John continued to stand in the corner, arms crossed. He wanted to observe without being observed.

"I'm disappointed," Joshua continued. "I thought you would bring an electro-shock machine at least."

"Next time, if you don't give me satisfactory answers this time," he answered, sitting down without so much as a pause to acknowledge the joke.

Maybe it wasn't a joke, Fisher thought, but let the thought go.

Erdinger turned the tape recorder on and shoved it toward Joshua.

"Joshua Gordon interview, May 6, 2005. Alexander Erdinger interviewer," the doctor said. "Also present Mr. John Fisher, assistant to Mr. Gordon." He paused for a moment then looked from one to the other and said, "Good morning gentlemen."

"Good morning, Doctor," Joshua said. "Ask any thing you want. I'll do my best to answer it."

"This is going to be more like a friendly conversation between us, Mr. Gordon, not an inquisition."

"OK. But if we are going to be friendly, you had better call me Josh, or Joshua if you must."

"Very well, Joshua. And you may call me Alex--"

"Alex," Joshua said then, "And the young fellow in the corner is John."

Erdinger nodded at John and as quickly disregarded his presence. "Very well then, Joshua, tell me why your son wants you declared *non compos mentis*?"

"I thought you weren't going to ask questions," Gordon said.

Erdinger shrugged. "We have to start the ball rolling somewhere."

"True enough," Joshua said. He hesitated for a moment then began by saying, "The easy answer is he wants me declared incompetent because I changed my will."

Erdinger lifted an eyebrow. "I was under the impression the suit was filed before the will was changed."

Now it was Joshua's turn to lift an eyebrow. "You are very well informed."

Erdinger shrugged again.

After a moment Joshua said, "The hard answer is, my son and I have been, if not estranged then certainly at odds for many years, since he was a child in fact. I think he did it because I hired John which threatened Luke's power over me. He didn't like it because he was looking forward to having control over me and my work."

The psychiatrist studied Joshua and John for a moment. "Is that why you cut him out of you will? Because he wanted to control you?"

"I didn't cut him out of my will, only changed it a little."

"You didn't cut him out of the will in favor of..." he looked at John but did not say his name, "in favor of someone else?"

"No. I only changed a couple of things. All the rest of my estate will go to Lucian."

"And what was it you changed?"

Joshua scanned the psychiatrist's face. "You already know the answer I'm sure so let's get to the real crux of this."

Erdinger nodded his assent and said, "OK, what is the crux of this?"

"I made it so Lucian could not get his hands on anything having to do with a certain literary product; specifically anything to do with my Forneria stories. I named each one in the will and said specifically what should go to John."

"Which begs the question, why?"

"The obvious answer is because I wanted to."

"Which doesn't really explain it does it? Why did you change only the copyrights? Why not cut Lucian out completely if you were upset with him over something?"

Joshua turned the question over in his mind for so long Erdinger thought he would refuse to answer, but as he was formulating another question Joshua said, "Because I love my son and understand him. I wanted him to have everything else."

"But not these books."

"Right."

"Again, why?"

"Because he told me he wants them only to make sure they are destroyed. He wants to wipe out all memory of them." After a moment of consideration the doctor said, "Be a pretty big job wouldn't it? I mean the memory of the books will be around so long as there is a copy anywhere in the world. How could he assure they would all be destroyed?"

"He can't really. As you said, so long as there is a copy, but within a couple of generations the books will become scarce and within a hundred years or so the books will be collector rare, which will effectively make it extinct except for a very few copies. And sooner or later even those will probably be lost or destroyed."

Erdinger noticed the sadness in Joshua's eyes when he spoke of his books disappearing, but he also noticed an avidity which made the sadness more than a melancholy regret. "It will happen even if you leave the books to your assistant, won't it?" he asked.

"Maybe, but I doubt it. At least not in his lifetime. I am hoping John will continue the series. I brought him in to assist me on this last book I am writing in hopes he will continue after I am gone."

Erdinger glanced at John but saw only his stony face and protectively crossed arms. "You'll forgive my saying it all sounds rather petty and just a little obsessive. I mean, what difference will it make to you when you are dead?"

"Whoa! That's a little cold, doc?" John said, suddenly leaning forward.

"Yes it is, and I would like an answer."

Joshua laughed. "Doctor, I have a confession to make. I am a weak man, weak in my faith. I was raised in the Christian faith, and I should believe there is an afterlife. I should believe I will be rewarded for my virtue somehow or punished for my sins. But as I sit here on the edge of the great unknown, I have more than a little difficulty believing there will be a divine handshake or kick in the rear when I depart this mortal coil, so I am trying to hedge my bets. I have always been one who likes to keep as much of my life in my own hands as possible, and this way lets me steal a little of the power from God – if he exists. If I preserve the Forneria stories, I will have some control. Even if I am not here, if my works continues to be read it is a form of immortality."

"Immortality? Is that what this is really about," the doctor asked with a frown, "literary legacy?"

"Yes," Joshua answered, "and Lucian's desire to rob me of it."

"May I say something Doc?" Fisher asked.

"Certainly."

"It would seem to me what the boss is talking about is probably the sanest thing I have heard in a long time. And Lucian wanting to stop it sounds like the nuttiest. Why would a son be so obsessive about his father's literary legacy he would want to destroy it? Even though we three agree as to how really destroying it would probably be impossible or, at the very least, difficult."

Erdinger noted how Joshua glanced at the younger man with something like admiration in his face. He wondered if there was something else going on between them. Was it possible Gordon was "keeping" Fisher? He did not see how there could be anything sexual in such a relationship, what with Joshua's incapacity, but the ingenuity of human sexuality had surprised many people many times. But did it matter if there was some hidden sexual element to this partnership?

Erdinger filed the thoughts in the back of his mind and said, "I agree it does seem a little--odd. Is there some kind of hidden logic to it? Does Lucian have some reason for wanting to hurt you like this?"

"Yes, I'm afraid he does. His mother..."

"Crap," Fisher said with some force. Joshua stopped what he had been going to say.

Erdinger looked back and forth between them. "Please, John, let him finish," he said.

"Fine, but it is absolute garbage. I told him it was crap the first time he said this."

"Said what, Joshua?"

"I was about to say Lucian blames me for the death of his mother. He blames the first of the Forneria books because I was away promoting it when Elizabeth died. If I had been at home..."

"You could not have done a damn thing," Fisher said. "You said the aneurism came out of no where. No signs of any kind."

Erdinger waited for Joshua to say something but when he did not, he asked, "Could you truly have done something to save her if you had been here?"

Joshua looked down as though the question shamed him then shook his head. "No. I doubt if anything outside of a major emergency room could have helped her and maybe not then. But I...it makes no difference to Lucian. In his child's eyes..."

"How old was he then?"

"Eight."

"Was he alone with her when she died?"

"No, no. He was in school or rather on his way home. The maid found Elizabeth in the kitchen. Elizabeth was preparing dinner. Lucian came in a few moments after the EMT's arrived. Apparently he saw them working on her before the maid took him out."

"He blames you," the doctor said.

"Yes."

"But he also blames himself, you know? He wasn't there when it happened so he blames himself, and it is probably why he is taking this out on the books. It's displacement. He can't hold himself responsible and continue living so he displaces the anger and guilt onto you and onto the books as the reason you were not there to help her."

"I know," Joshua said.

"Same thing I told him doc," John said.

Erdinger looked at Fisher with a new curiosity. Fisher shrugged. "Psychology 101," he said.

The doctor smiled at the modesty even as he recognized its falsity. "You should have listened to him Joshua. Psych 101 is very informative," he said to lighten up the mood again.

The hard look on Fisher's face did not change but a flush went up his neck. Joshua, still determined to take blame onto himself, said, "You can add to the rest, I was a lousy father. Luke was mostly raised by hirelings. Strangers."

"So, with all of it you feel guilty..."

"Because I am."

"But not guilty enough to let him punish you by letting him have the stories."

Joshua looked hard at Erdinger. "No, not guilty enough."

The men fell silent for a time then Erdinger asked, "Could you not avoid all this by simply selling the copyrights to Mr. Fisher or someone else?"

"I suppose I could, but it would be just business, and this is more than business. It would not be--*organic* to sell them. They have to be given--it is hard to explain.

The psychiatrist knew there was something else beneath all this explanation. "I have a feeling," he began, "an intuition if you will. There is more involved in this than you have told me thus far. Do you want to tell me more about it?"

Joshua tried to shrug, but was not able to manage it very well. "I don't think I can. It is more mystical than I can explain. And also, if you had not already noticed, I have a sort of an obsession with these particular stories.

More than just the fact they are *mine* in the sense they make money for me. I love the stories and the characters in the stories and it is almost like Lucian is threatening my children when he tells me he wants to destroy the books, even if it is probably impossible."

"On that particular point," John began, "I think the boss is a little nuts, but don't quote me."

Erdinger smiled. "I have worked with artists of several types and I can say with some authority they are all nuts when it comes to their creations; this doesn't mean they are *non compos mentis*. It just makes them artists."

"What would constitute *non compos*?" Gordon asked.

"Oh, giving away the house to a stranger. Or talking with people who aren't there, and not being able to keep up with a medication schedule or pay your bills on time. "

"I don't do any of those things, though I have been known to talk to myself sometimes."

"If you didn't, it might be grounds right there. Most people talk to themselves one way or another."

The three fell silent. After a few moments Dr. Erdinger said, "It is my opinion Mr. Gordon, Joshua, you have nothing to worry about. The psychiatrist for your son may want you to take some tests which seem remarkably easy or remarkably stupid. I could have done the same, but I decided to check you out this way first. I don't think we need the tests. You seem as *compos mentis* as anyone, considering the circumstances."

"Thanks doc," Joshua said. "Are we done then?"

"I believe we are. I will send the list of nurses over via e mail if I may."

"Fine and thank you."

"Very well. Interview ends at eleven fifteen a.m." He reached up, shut off the tape recorder and put it back in his brief case.

"Well, seemed easy enough," Joshua said.

"Don't let the ease of it throw you," Erdinger said. The light gleamed off his glasses making it hard to see his eyes. "I work for you and Ed Chance.

Unless you were just a blithering idiot, totally and obviously out of your mind, I was going to draw the conclusion you were competent to take care of your own affairs."

"Ah. Then do you have doubts?"

"I am satisfied enough to swear to my findings in court."

"Should be sufficient," Joshua said. "Thank you for your time."

"You are quite welcome and good morning to you."

"Can you find your way out or should I send John with you?"

"I can manage."

Sixteen

John Fisher sat on the floor of his cell, knees drawn up, leaning against the whispering wall. He had not found out much about this place. The Fisherites, apparently named for him, were scattered and disheartened because of his arrest. Many presumed he was dead, if not by execution then by stealth, at Fort Bouchet. Fisher, his forehead resting on his knees, reran the short history since he found himself in the desert. *What the hell am I doing here? And what the hell is this other life I remember? And why did my walking across a dry water hole make it fill up? Did I just happen to be there when it happened? Would the water have come bubbling out sooner or later even if I wasn't there? Or if just anybody had walked across?*

The view slide in the door banged open and John looked up. The flickering light of a torch came through the slide and eased the darkness of the cell. "On your feet," a gruff voice commanded.

John did as he was told. "When can I get out of here?" he asked.

"When the colonel says so."

"But I haven't done anything."

"And I should care, why?" the guard laughed. It was not a merry sound.

"I want to know why I'm in here."

"You must have pissed somebody off about something," the jailer answered still with his mocking laugh. The view port slammed shut. After a few moments, John resumed his seat.

"Theo, are you still there?" came the voice of Noah Simons whispering through the wall.

"Yes, Noah, I am still here."

"When I heard the jailer," Noah said, "I thought they had come to question you."

"They are welcome to question me," Fisher said.

"Then you are a fool," Thomas said. "The questions they ask will probably cause you pain."

Fisher thought for a moment. "Have you two been questioned?"

There was so long a silence John said, "Are you still there?"

"I am here, Theo," Noah answered.

"As am I," added Thomas.

"Have you been questioned," Fisher asked again.

"I have," Noah said.

"It doesn't bear thinking on," Thomas answered.

They sat quietly for a time until Fisher said, "Tell me of Lucian."

"*Great* Lucian, blessed be his name," Thomas said quickly. "You must never speak his name without the honorific. Men lose their tongues for the omission. He is the god of Forneria now. Those who first worshipped him were the Corani from the south. When they came to conquer, Great Lucian came with them."

"It was two hundred years past," Noah added. "Those who helped the Corani were given much by Great Lucian. Those who didn't were killed at first but later that stopped. Great Lucian said, 'Worship me and I will give all you ask,' so many left off believing in Gordon the Creator."

The spy slide in the door of John's cell snapped open again. "Stand up, prisoner," the guard commanded. John did as he was told.

There was a grating sound as the lock on the door was released. The jailer and four uniformed troopers stood in the passage. "Colonel wants to have a talk with you," he said with a nasty smile. "Come along."

The colonel was a large blond fellow. His hair was long and he wore a drooping moustache and pointed goatee. He stood with his hands behind his back and ran his blue eyed gaze over the prisoner. Fisher stood before the colonel with his hands bound behind his back in unconscious mimic of the officer. "You don't look strong enough to pull a man off his horse, but Captain Fay says you did." John continued to gaze at the officer. He did not blink or show any emotion. "What is your name?"

"You know my name, sir. The captain knew my name, and I am sure he told you." The colonel examined his prisoner and found no trace of fear or defiance.

"Fisher. You claim to be John Fisher, but it cannot be true. Great Lucian told us you would be no more trouble."

"I make no trouble for your god or you. I only want to be left alone to think on why Gordon sent me here."

The colonel stared into Fisher's face for a long moment then turned and walked back to his desk and picked up a piece of paper. "His name is forbidden you know?" he said off handedly, not seeming to mind the use of Gordon's name. He nonchalantly studied the paper he had picked for a moment then looked at Fisher once more. "Says here you called water from a dry waterhole. Is it true?"

"No sir. I did nothing save walk across the place where the water had once been."

"And the water just started bubbling up in your footprints." It was not a question.

"Yes."

"And you did nothing to call the water?"

"No. Only walked across the dry place."

"Do you know Great Lucian has decreed all water will be under his control?"

"No sir, I didn't know."

The colonel was silent for a long time, looking at Fisher as though he were under a microscope before saying, "I think you are a Fisherite pretending to be Fisher in order to stir up the masses against Great Lucian."

Fisher shrugged. "Believe what you will. I am who I am."

A soft rumbling, the sound of a billion, billion tons of earth rubbing against itself set Fort Barstow to vibrating, snatching all thoughts from the colonel's mind. He looked to the ceiling then toward the corner of the room. The rumbling grew and the walls began to tremble and sway. The wheel shaped chandelier in the center of the ceiling began swinging wildly. "Earthquake!" the colonel cried, "earthquake!" He ran for the door, forgetting his prisoner and everything else accept his terror of the trembling earth. John Fisher was left standing, hands still bound behind his back, before the desk. The floor and walls of the building swayed and danced, stealing all reliance on the steadiness of earth. John managed to turn and take a step after the colonel, but the temblor threw him to his knees. He struggled to rise but a voice said, "Relax. Be patient. It'll be over soon." Fisher looked around and found the red bird standing on the floor in front of him. "The building is going to collapse!" John said, panic in his voice.

"Relax," the bird said again. "The building is going to collapse and when it does you are going to walk out of here without a scratch. You won't even be dusty. "As though on cue cracks began to appear in the walls and quickly widened. Fort Barstow gave one final groan of resistance and began to fall apart. John lowered his face to the floor, trying to protect his head as best he could. Walls crumbled all around. Beam's fell from the roof and crashed like great stiff wooden waves. No matter what the bird had said, John was sure he was a dead man, but after an eternity of shaking and terror, the ground began to settle. In moments the vibrations ceased. Earth became solid again while building stones, dust and tiles continued to crash and roll. Quiet slowly returned. Fisher sat up. All around him was ruin. Heaps of broken masonry, beam's, paper, furniture lay all about, but the bird had been right. John was not even dusty though a yellow brown dust cloud covered the whole scene.

"I told you," the bird said.

"Who are you?" Fisher asked. "Are you a hallucination? Am I drugged or something?"

"I'm not a hallucination," the bird said. "You are the only one can see me like this, but I am not a figment of a drugged mind."

"Then who are you and why do you keep showing up when I am in trouble?"

"I'm Joshua, or an avatar of him, rather. I'm here to help and advise you as you go about saving Forneria from Lucian."

Some of this made sense to John, but some of it was--"How did I get here? I don't belong here," Fisher said.

"You volunteered."

"Why don't I remember? I think I would remember volunteering."

"You will, by and by, a little at a time--usually just as you need the knowledge. And I'll be here to help you--for a while."

"For a while?"

"Yes, but now it is time to get on your feet and go out to let people know you are alive."

Fisher shook his head, trying to organize all he had heard, and to clear the last of the fear out. He struggled to his feet as best he could with hands bound behind him then picked his way through the rubble without any idea where he was headed. After some minutes of stumbling along he reached an area free of debris, stopping to look around. Buildings everywhere were collapsed, but the dry fountain in the center of the plaza was remarkably intact considering the shaking it had just taken. There were people climbing out of and around the ruins. A few were turning back to begin digging for others who might be buried.

"It is you!" a voice shouted. John turned toward the sound. A man dressed much like Fisher, and equally clean considering, was running toward him. There was something familiar about the man, or rather about his voice. "I knew you were alive!" the man said, looking deep into Fisher's face. Then he threw his arms joyously around John and kissed his bearded cheek. "I knew Lucian could not defeat you!" Suddenly John knew. This was Noah, to whom he had been talking through the echoing walls of his cell. He had known this one before.

"Noah, please untie my hands," he said.

"Yes, yes! Of course!" Noah stepped behind John and struggled with the knots jabbering his joy all the time. "When Lucian took you prisoner, I knew he could not hold you. Gordon the Creator would never allow it! I told them all! I told them you were alive and would be free again. Where have you been?"

"In the desert with the Travelers," he answered, chaffing his wrists to get the circulation rushing back into his hands.

Noah's gush of joy stopped short "The Travelers?"

"Come, Noah, we must help these people."

"But how did you escape from Fort Bouchet, the very heart of Great Lucian's power."

"Doesn't matter. I am here now and we must help the people buried in the rubble."

Noah stood for a moment with his mouth open then said, "Yes, yes! Of course, of course." He turned to look for a starting place. There was a woman twenty meters distant who was struggling to roll large chunks of masonry away from a pile. Noah went to help her. John turned back to the ruins of the building he had just walked out of. It was nothing but a heap of broken gray stone mixed with brick, roof tiles, and dust. He almost turned away when a flash of color, out of place in the rubble, caught his eye. He moved closer and found it was the blond hair of the colonel dully reflecting the sunlight despite a layer of dust. At first John thought the man was dead, for there was a bright red splash of blood on his face. His lower body was covered with stone leaving his torso, arms and head exposed. He was bleeding from a cut on his brow. John knelt beside the colonel and the man opened his eyes.

"You're alive," John said with just a touch of surprise. The colonel's eyes rolled toward the voice. There was conscious intelligence in them, but there was also pain.

"My legs are broken," he said through teeth clinched against the pain. There was blood at the corner of his mouth also. Without a word John turned and began moving rubble off the trapped Colonel.

The man watched with open dismay. Only a few moments before he had been questioning this man with intent to find a reason to execute him, now the same man was trying to dig him out of the ruins of the collapsed fort.

In a few moments another came to stand beside John.

"Leave him there," the man said. His voice was familiar. "He is a colonel in Great Lucian's guard."

Without stopping John said, "Thomas, it is Gordon's way to help those in need of help, no matter who they might be."

Thomas was surprised when Fisher called his name. "Do I know you, stranger?"

"We met in the dungeon with the whispering walls." Fisher said without straightening from his task. "I am John Fisher."

"John Fisher? Theo Waters--I should have guessed."

The colonel groaned.

"Are you in great pain, Colonel?" Fisher asked.

The colonel did not answer. His eyes had rolled back, but he was still breathing. Some small red bubbles showed at his nostrils.

"He is finished, Fisher," Thomas said. "His ribs are probably stove in."

Fisher did not stop lifting and tossing rubble away, nor did he answer Thomas in any way. After a time Thomas joined him.

They worked steadily for half an hour. In every direction, just like them, others were digging in similar piles of rubble. Dust slowly settled in the still air, and the sun beat down toward desert noon. Cries for water resounded around them.

Fisher heard the cries and after a time straightened from his labor, stretched his back, and looked around. His eyes fell on the dry fountain in the keep court yard. It was a simple round basin three meters in diameter with a rippled pyramid rising from the center. Sitting right on top of the fountain like a carved decoration was the red raven.

"They need water, Savior. Give it to them," the bird said.

"How?" Fisher asked.

"All you have to do is ask."

"Ask who?"

"Don't be dense. You know who. Just ask and it will be given."

Fisher nodded and walked toward the dry fountain. Thomas stopped his work and straightened to watch.

When John reached the fountain he looked up toward the red bird then lifted his arms above his head. "Father Gordon, we need water for these people who are suffering. Hear their cries for mercy and grant them relief."

A rumbling like an after shock of the earthquake began, but there was no shaking of the ground. A sudden gush of water burst from the top of the pyramid in the fountain, cascaded down the side, and began to fill the basin at the bottom.

John looked around for something to carry water in but found nothing. At last he removed his long hunting shirt dipped it in the water and pulled it dripping from the pool. He carried it quickly back to where Thomas was still standing over the colonel.

Fisher knelt beside the injured man and, using his shirt wiped the blood and dust from the colonel's face.

The soldier opened his eyes and John said, "Open your mouth." The colonel did so. John lifted the shirt and squeezed it until some of the water dribbled into the man's mouth. "May you never thirst," he said.

"Thank you," the colonel breathed, more bloody bubbles coming from his nose. "Thank you." The light of life went from his face and when Fisher saw the soldier was dead, he wept.

Seventeen

After the psychiatric exam, Joshua's myelitis seemed suddenly to worsen from a major inconvenience to a painful affliction so that sitting up, even in his fancy bed, became almost more than he could endure. The need for a full time nurse was now so clear the hunt began.

The list of nurses Dr. Erdinger sent included ten names, seven of which were male or female copies of Erdinger himself. By number seven John could see Joshua was almost out of patience and said, "Boss, why don't you just pick one? They are all qualified."

Joshua's eyes blazed. "They all look like Erdinger! If I must have one, I at least want one who is a little bit decorative!" John threw up his hands and escorted the next one in. Numbers eight and nine would have been better if they *had* looked like Erdinger. Number eight was a huge male with gorillas not too far back in his family tree while number nine looked like number eight's female other half. After seeing number nine, Joshua said, "Enough, John. I'm tired. Is number ten out there?"

"Wasn't when I brought nine in. I'll go check." The living room where the others had waited was still empty, but just as John turned to go back to Joshua's room, the door bell rang. Fisher turned and frowned at the door. He had posted a sign on it saying candidates should simply walk in and be seated so either this one could not read or this was not a candidate. He went to the door and opened it to find a tall, leggy blond with an oval face, close cropped hair, and sapphire blue eyes. John took a moment to close his mouth and gather his wits before asking, "Are you here to interview for the position." She smiled dazzlingly and said, "Yes." John stepped back and allowed the woman to come into the house. "My name is John Fisher. I'm Mr. Gordon's assistant."

"Katharine Zabriski." She shifted a small black bag from her right shoulder to her left hand and stuck out her right. John shook the offered hand and found the grip strong but gentle.

"This way please," he said as they headed down the hall. He began to explain what the job involved, ending by saying, "He is stubborn as an iron fence post and won't admit he is hurting, but he is on the edge of despair right now and he is hurting like hell. From what I understand the pain is generalized and not a whole lot can be done about it without completely knocking him out, which he won't hold still for. Says if he only has a little while left he wants to experience it all. I don't think he even sleeps much now. I've never found him asleep even in the middle of the night."

Katherine nodded her understanding. "That is probably why Dr. Erdinger asked me. I am a pain management specialist.

When they reached the door, John said, "If you'll wait here a moment please."

The look on Fisher's face told Gordon something interesting was about to happen. John said, "Boss, you ain't gonna believe it. You want decorative? Her name is Katherine."

"Well don't just stand there, get her in here."

John opened the door and invited her in. "Katherine Zabriski, this is Joshua Gordon."

Gordon lifted his hand with difficulty, and Katherine grasped it. "Forgive me for not standing, Miss Zabriski."

"Quite all right, Mr. Gordon, and you must call me Katherine."

"And you must call me Josh, or Joshua if you must."

"Are you in pain, Joshua?"

"Less now than a few minutes ago, Katherine."

She smiled, setting her bag on the side of the bed. "Dr. Erdinger made sure I was well supplied with pain killers. Would you like something?"

"I don't want anything to knock me out. I don't have enough time left to be wasting any unconscious."

"A small dose of morphine should help you without totally knocking you out."

"Morphine, eh. Fine, I'll try it once, but if it spaces me out too much, I won't do it again."

"Very well," she said and gave him the shot. "We'll be better able to judge dosage after we see how the drug affects you."

Without ever formally pronouncing the words "You're hired," Katherine Zabriski, RN, came to work for Joshua Gordon, the Creator.

Katherine fitted herself into Joshua's home like a square peg in a square hole. She was wonderfully sweet and good natured but with a clear steel core beneath the sweetness. She was always patient and soft spoken and any time Joshua needed assistance to move or change the position of his bed, Katherine was there. And most importantly, she did indeed live up to her billing as a pain management specialist. She administered her drugs almost as though by instinct. When Joshua wanted to try his wheel chair again, she gave him just the right amount of morphine to ease the pain of change and helped him to sit up. Joshua had been bathing himself with very little help from John, but Katherine took up the chore as if she had been doing it all along. She also relieved John of the cooking, at which he had been adequate but not great, and the house cleaning which had been hit or miss everywhere except in Joshua's room. She rather disappeared into the household like a super efficient servant.

"I never thought I would see the day when a beautiful woman could be in my bed room and I wouldn't even notice," Joshua said.

Fisher laughed ruefully, agreeing. "She seems to be everywhere."

Indeed her ubiquity was, at first, much appreciated, but after a little there was a kind of uneasiness between Joshua and John about her presence. Several times they came to the sudden knowledge of Katherine being in the room listening to the discussion and they had not even heard her come in.

Not that there was anything secret about the new book, but Joshua had always been rather secretive about his stories as they were being written.

He had brought John into the work only because he hoped to pass the story along to his protégé if and when he became unable to continue it himself. But there was a quality to Katherine's presence which began to make them both nervous.

They had taken to discussing the pages Joshua wrote and sent to John and those discussions were usually intense and exclusive. They spoke as though they both were living in the world Joshua was creating.

John still had dreams so real they frightened him. He began to doubt his own sanity as well as Joshua's assurances that he was not being drugged, but he continued with the experiment because, though the dreams were disturbing, they left in him a sense of power, a sense of need, and above all, a growing sense of love and care for the creatures in the dreams/story. He had also taken to adding ideas to the story as Joshua was writing it. Some of the ideas Gordon discarded out of hand, but some of them, like the death of the colonel, Joshua used.

"You two certainly are into what you are doing," Katherine said to John one late evening. The two of them were sitting at the kitchen table. Katherine had a cup of tea before her and John had Crown Royal whiskey. Fisher and Gordon had spent the early evening considering whether Captain Fay would have a yet larger role, and whether Fay would somehow be converted to a Fisherite. Occasionally the consideration had risen to a rather high volume.

"The boss and I," John laughed, "are like a couple of kids playing pretend, only we can't go out and use sticks as swords or handkerchiefs as flags so we sit in his room and play in our minds."

"It's almost as though you are convinced this *"fiction"* you are writing is real."

John felt a trickle of suspicion in his middle and it made him careful in his answer. "Do you read?" he asked.

"Read?"

"Yes, read. For pleasure or diversion or time wasting?"

"I did some when I was a child. I loved it, but when I grew up, I began reading for information's sake. School and such."

"Well it isn't as though you are so ancient you can't remember your youthful literary indiscretions," John said smiling.

Katherine smiled back at him and said, "Thank you--I think."

"When you read stories, did you become truly engrossed in them? Did you come to feel as though you were a part of the story in some way?"

She crinkled her eye corners in thought. "I do remember feeling I knew the people in the story, or the pig rather, in *Charlotte's Web*."

Fisher smiled. "How do you think the author felt as he wrote the story? He really did know the pig and the spider and those children. They were parts of him. Little pieces of his mind shaped and colored and laid on a page so other people could *"see"* them at least enough so they would read the story. Or, more important to the author, be willing to lay down hard earned cash to buy the book."

Katherine crooked her mouth and nodded her head to the side. "I guess I see, but what you and Joshua are doing...I don't know. It seems more...more. You talk about the characters as though they could walk through the bedroom door any second."

"Good. That means we have created something believable. Now all we have to do, or rather all the Boss has to do, is translate our discussions into characters on the page."

She ran her eyes over Fisher for a moment. "He modeled the character Fisher in the story after you, didn't he? I mean not just the name, but other things as well."

John sipped from his drink before answering. "The Boss asked if he could use me as a character and I said yes. I didn't know he was going to cut so close to the bone in the using." He smiled self deprecatingly. "I didn't know my savior complex showed so much."

She acted as though she hadn't heard. "And he has put himself in it too, hasn't he? I mean as more than the author. Gordon is a character."

"Gordon has been a character in all the Forneria novels."

"Rather egotistical isn't it?"

Fisher thought about the question and how it had been asked and decided it was not a condemnation just an observation.

"I suppose it is, but I seem to remember Ben Johnson or someone saying to think anyone would want to read your written words is the most egocentric thing a man could do. I don't think he said egocentric though."

Katherine laughed. "True I guess, but this seems like...I don't know...God Complex."

"Yeah, I guess, but have you ever considered the author as god?"

"Oh boy," she laughed. "I smell a philosophical tirade coming on."

John laughed. "It is a discussion the boss and I have had several times. It is something he has thought about a lot where the Forneria stories are concerned."

She stood, sipped from her tea cup and said, "I've never read any of them. Would you like a sandwich or something?"

"No thanks. I'll just finish this and put it to bed. This writing as a partner wears me out," he said and tossed the last dribble of the whiskey down.

"Especially when the working together goes on for 36 straight hours."

John shrugged. "He's running out of time and he knows it. I know it too, so I don't really mind."

"Even when he gets impatient and hollers?"

Fisher shrugged again. "This is important to him and he's a genius who is going to hand his baby over to me, so while I don't enjoy getting hollered at, I understand."

"Understand? What's to understand? They are just pulp stories."

He looked over her with barely controlled contempt before saying, "You should read the books. They might help you understand what is going on now. They are all in the library here."

"Maybe I will," she said. "Maybe I will."

John said good night and went to his room. He showered, climbed into bed and was almost asleep when the direction of his talk with Katherine seeped back into his mind for a worrisome moment, but he was too tired to consider the thought.

Eighteen

Ez, Mandy, and the other Traveler families crowded around and watched the dust cloud of the cavalry troop that had taken John Fisher grow smaller. They would reach Barstow in a few hours; the heavily loaded wagons would take a whole day. Unburdened droms could run as fast as a horse. Pulling loaded wagons eight-drom teams could barely move as fast as a man walking. "I don't know as we should foller them on to Barstow," Ez said. "Farther away from Fisher and cavalry we stay the better."

There was some muttered agreement. "We got Sweetening to sell, Ez," Jim Bitter said. Bitter, broad shouldered with sandy hair and beard, was an up-and-coming leader. He was less than half Ezra's age but his opinion was respected. "We have to go to Barstow, or else clear to Bakersfield, and I don't think the droms would make Bakersfield. They are tired and ain't been well fed in days."

"None of us been well fed," Bitter's wife Ruth said. She was holding a thin eighteen month old boy-child on her hip. She was dark haired and old before her time like most Traveler women. "Some of the children are starting to cry from loose teeth. We need fresh meat and vegetables."

Many of the women agreed with Ruth. They had been living on Traveler stew made with dried meat and shriveled or moldy vegetables for weeks. "Water tanks is full. Skins is full. Droms drunk 'til they swoll up," Mandy, standing with another group of women spoke up. "Maybe we oughta move on up to Copper seep and just sit tight a couple of days. We could hunt some and dig some roots if they's any left. They was prickly pears under the shade of the cliffs. Wait for things to cool down. Maybe send Bitter or somebody on a drom to scout Barstow before we go on."

Ez considered this for a moment then nodded his head. "I believe so. Anybody object?" he asked. No one objected.

The seep was dry. It never had been a preferred water hole, being very brackish, but water had continued to well out from beneath the mountain even when many other water sources had dried up. Desert dromules were not usually picky about the water they drank, but watering them from the seep was difficult and usually cost half a wagon load of sweetening so the Travelers generally avoided it. Dry or not the Travelers set up camp by parking their wagons in a U against the cliff where the seep was, with droms and the place where the water used to be at the center of the camp. They sent out hunting parties and gatherers to dig up the desiccated cattail root around where the seep had been. Cook fires sprang up, people rested, thinking and talking about what had happened in the past three days. The question on everyone's mind was how did Fisher bring water to Boron Springs?

"I b'lieve they was water in the pond but it was under the dried mud and when he walked across it, it broke the mud seal and let the water leak back out," Bitter said. He had been going fire to fire listening to what Traveler families were talking about as they prepared supper.

"D'you ever remember Boron Springs to be dry?" Ez asked. "An' do you ever 'member the water tastin' so sweet and cold? It was always warmish and not far from soured. Droms would only drink it if they was real thirsty."

Bitter grunted. "They's lots of folks remembering it so."

"Other question," Mandy added bringing her small three legged stool close to the two men, "was he *really* John Fisher and did Gordon *really* send him?"

"I never seen Fisher before, and I never seen a picture of him ner nothin', but what the hell would a man be doing to claim to be Fisher if he

103

ain't? Fisherites are having more trouble with Great Lucian's people than we are and that's saying something," Ez said.

"He come from Father Gordon and he really was Fisher," Em, short for Emmaline, said. "I knowed it from the first time I set eyes on him."

"And how'd you know?" Ez asked, not unkindly. "He was out yonder in the alkali pans without so much as a hat. Seems like Gordon would have give him more sense."

"I just knowed. I felt it in my heart." Em said.

"'Felt it in my heart,' she says. I felt like I was picking up a viper," Ezra said, but it was not true. He had felt some power in the man too, and now he wished he had not; wished he could shake off the ember of hope which had ignited in his middle when Fisher had said, "No one should ever thirst again."

Two days later in the still and sultry morning Jim Bitter saddled a nervous drom and prepared to head for Barstow. "I'll ask around about buyers. Maybe I can get a better price if the they think we are in no hurry to sell."

"Don't be too smart about it," Ez said. "Them buyers might decide they could get along without it."

Bitter grinned. "Gonna need sweetening until Great Lucian's Dry ain't dry no more."

"Didn't you drink outa the same pond I did? Fisher says the Dry is gonna be over soon."

Bitter stopped grinning. "I hope he's right." He turned to his wife who held the same solemn eyed child on her hip as the night before. She held another little boy by the hand. "You gonna be all right, Ruthie?" Bitter asked, concerned. She was so thin and fragile looking it seemed impossible she had the strength to carry the child. She smiled and the dark circles beneath her eyes lightened.

"We'll be fine, Jim. Mandy and Em are helping with the boys and Willy Mello can drive if need be." A little iron came into her look. "I want you to be careful though. We can get along without you for a while but not forever."

Bitter smiled and leaned over to kiss her gently. Then he kissed both the little boys before swinging up into the saddle. Mandy came around the wagon and handed an extra water skin up to Bitter. "Don't use it unless you really need it, Jim."

"I won't."

"May you never thirst," she said.

Ezra turned and looked at his wife. "You a Fisherite now?"

The droms, which had been nervous for days, heard or sensed the quake first, before there was any rumbling or ground trembling. Bitter's drom twitched its ears and snorted then reared, almost unseating its rider. The earth rolled and rocked like an angry sea, boulders and gravel rolled and sifted down the cliff against which the wagons were parked. The Travelers tried to hide inside the wagons, but Ez was not so foolish. He began shouting and running from wagon to wagon looking like a wobbling drunk because of the rolling earth. "Come out. Canvas ain't gonna stop rocks. Come out and come on away from here."

People began to come out and move down away from the cliff side and the wagons, looking over their shoulders fearfully. Inside the circle of wagons the dromules reared and snorted and brayed in terror. They ran down to the bottom of the circle and jammed themselves against the wagons trying to escape. Ez, noticing the panic in the animals, collared two other men as they ran by and the three of them tried to move one wagon in the bottom of the circle to let the dromules out and away from the cliff before it slid off and covered them, but by the time the wagon was beginning to move the quake was finished. The droms still bleated and crowded against the wagons, but when the shaking stopped, they seemed to get control of their fear some and began to calm down.

"Enough, enough," Ez shouted at the other two men. "If they'll stand quiet, we'll let 'em until we see what's what." The three eased their strain on the wagon wheels and turned to the group who had gathered a hundred meters down the hill from the wagons.

"Everybody here?" Ez asked in a loud voice. No one answered him directly, but since no one spoke up he assumed all were present or accounted for. "Anybody hurt?" he asked. "Anybody lost?" Again no one answered.

"Good." He looked around, assessing. "I think we oughta hitch up the droms and move down away from the cliff. It could come down anytime. Anybody disagree?"

"But where we gonna go?" a woman's voice asked. There was a murmur of agreement.

"For now we'll just move down the hill a couple hundred meters. Bitter can still go on to Barstow to see what's what. We'll just wait right here till he gets back." There was a buzz among the people which ended in agreement. "All right, let's go, but be careful hitchin' up the droms. They're still pretty spooked."

The group broke up and moved to their family wagons. In a few moments a wail went up from two wagons which had been near the cliff. Boulders shaken loose from above had fallen on the wagons. They weren't buried or totally destroyed, but a wheel on one was broken as was the rear axle on the other.

Ez sent the families from the broken wagons to help others to move the still whole wagons to safety promising the Sweetening and the household goods would be off loaded and the wagons patched back together once the other wagons were safe.

Aftershocks came an hour after the first quake. More rocks, gravel, and dirt dropped down the cliff face, but most of the wagons and droms were out of the way by then. The shaking made everyone more nervous while it did no real harm. A few men moved back under the frowning, earth-shedding cliff to unload the two broken wagons and set about repairing them. They quickly unloaded the Sweetening and household goods, stacking it all out of the way.

The sun was hot so people glanced at the water bags as they held their thirst in check by will power.

Jim Bitter, after hours of helping to move the wagons, re-mounted his drom and with only a wave, headed toward Barstow

Aftershocks continued as though the earth were shivering beneath the baking sun. At first, each tremor brought cries of alarm, but after scores of them the travelers began to have fear overload. They would simply stop what they were doing long enough for the shaking to cease then return to their business, so almost no one noticed yet more rumbling in the middle of the oven-like afternoon heat. No one from the group which had moved away from the cliff looked toward the seep. The men working on the broken wagons stopped and looked around so they might run if more rocks shook loose from above, and in looking around they saw the water begin to bubble from beneath the cliff. In moments it filled the slight depression which had been Copper seep and began to run a rill down the slope, filling water cut dry ruts which had not seen running water in a hundred years.

As the freshet continued to grow and run down to the reassembled wagons, the Travelers stopped. Every eye turned to the water. No one could believe what they were seeing. It was like Boron springs all over again. No one stepped forward until Em, not looking anywhere accept directly at the running water, began to shout, "It's Fisher. It's Fisher! He made the water to flow! Gordon sent him to make the water flow! Hallelujah! Hallelujah!"

Others joined Em's shouts and the echo of it rang from the cliff and across the desert, but not all the Travelers were as happy or as sure of the goodness of this water flowing in the desert. Ez watched his daughter rejoicing and rejoiced with her, but he was torn. He drank from the stream, dipped his hat full to pour it over his head then sat back on his heels and thought, *fresh water flowing everywhere means no market for Sweetening. We got wagon loads of worthless sticks.* And as the joyous noise rose and reverberated from the cliff face, he began seeking a way to profit from useless sticks and flowing water.

Half a dozen ravens rose from the top of the cliff, dived down, and began to drink from the running water.

The Travelers who had drunk from the stream grumbled. The ravens were birds of ill omen, but, remembering how Fisher had let Lucian's messengers drink, they made no move to chase the birds away.

When the ravens had drunk their fill, they flapped in the water with raucous cackles and clacking then flew away toward the west to carry news of water to their master.

Nineteen

"They are claiming exigent circumstances, Joshua," Ed Chance said. Balding and pale he held the telephone receiver which seemed too large for his head, tight against his ear. He listened to the hum on the telephone wire and Gordon's breathing as his client, his old friend, absorbed the information. He knew Joshua had taken to his bed and would likely never get out again. Chance listened for some rustle of bed clothes through the speaker phone but there was none. He knew then Joshua could hardly move.

"I'm dying too fast and not fast enough," Gordon answered after a little.

"That's about the size of it. They claim you have fallen under the influence of your assistant and are pissing money away like a drunken sailor at his behest. They are begging the court to expedite the case in order to preserve your estate."

"Such absolute bullshit would be funny if it wasn't so serious. John is getting room and board and three hundred dollars a week. He drives my car, what little driving there is to do, and I do most of the shopping on the internet. Katherine is getting a thousand a week and she's worth every penny. Course she orders drugs through the hospital, which costs a big chunk every week, for all the good it is doing me, but insurance pays for most of it and I pay for the rest. Which reminds me, my insurance company is threatening to cut me off. Could you look into it for me?"

"I'll get someone on it right away."

"Thank you, Ed. I don't know what I would do without you."

"Nothing to it, Joshua." There was a pause of commiseration between the old friends. After a little Chance said, "You know what I can't figure out is what Lucian is thinking. The more law he puts on this the more it costs him. Your legal fees are going to eat up the estate faster than anyone could steal it, and his attorneys sure aren't working for free."

"It isn't the estate he cares about, Ed. He offered to drop the law suit and give away all the rest of the estate if I would just give him the Forneria copyrights. He's nuts about them!"

"Um, hum," Chance said, having heard this before. "So why didn't you just turn the copy rights over to him? Save us all this grief."

"I'm not going to let anyone tell me what to do with my stories, damn it!" Gordon snapped.

"You're as nuts about those stories as Lucian is, and you know it," Chance said with a rueful laugh.

Joshua growled, "I suppose."

Chance drew in a deep breath and let it out slowly. "They are accusing John of funneling money out of your accounts into some off shore bank account."

"Ed, if he could manage such a thing, he would absolutely deserve whatever he could steal. He has no access to any account of mine. I have thought about setting up a special account for him and dumping a couple of my accounts into it, but it has just been more trouble than I can manage."

"Probably wouldn't be a great idea anyway, Joshua."

"Probably not, but Lucian is beginning to piss me off enough to do something provocative. What can we do, Ed? Can you tell 'em I'm too sick to come to court?"

"They have already stipulated any court action would come to you rather than the other way around. They are being the soul of reason in the most unreasonable ways."

Joshua thought for a moment. "Tell them I am a sick old man who is obligated by contract to finish this book, and I can't do it if I have to fool with them."

"Is it true?" Chance sounded concerned.

"It can be. I can have Dilton Publishing draw up a contract and pay me an advance. Bill Carney, my agent, will have a fit and probably sue me, but what's one more law suit?"

"I don't think it will help, Josh. They are going to have their day in court if they have to haul your casket in."

"Damn!"

There was another silent commiseration. Ed Chance spent it wondering if Joshua's breathing sounded more labored than the last time they had talked.

"All right, what happens next?" Gordon asked after a little.

"They are going to want to depose you and John and probably Katherine. Probably want you to submit to an examination by a psychiatrist."

"Didn't we just do that a couple of weeks ago?" Gordon asked rhetorically.

"You know they aren't going to accept any report from a shrink hired by us. And their shrink will not be as nice as ours. He'll be looking for any little eccentricity and God knows you have a couple of those."

"Hey, whose side are you on anyway?"

"Yours, God help us."

Gordon laughed. "Naw, God isn't going to help at this point." He fell silent for a few moments then said, "When you are writing a crap novel one of the standard ploys is to always make things worse before you make them better. And if this is a tragedy rather than the comedy, it looks like from here it won't ever get better. We'll just shuffle off with great weeping and wailing and gnashing of teeth."

"You are incorrigible," Chance said chuckling.

"No, I'm Episcopalian. Keep me informed Ed."

"Will do."

"Bye."

"Good bye, Joshua."

~*~

Gordon lifted his right hand as though it weighed a hundred pounds and poked the hang up button on the speaker box. "John," he called.

There was no answer.

"John." He called louder.

There was still no answer.

"Goddamn it, John, where the hell are you!" he shouted and with another part of his mind noted how his roar was weaker than it used to be.

Katherine came in the door from the hall. "He's asleep, Joshua," she said.

"Asleep?" Joshua growled. "It's 2:30 in the afternoon! Since when does my goddamn assistant take a nap in the afternoon? Get him in here."

Katherine's deep blue eyes blazed at him. "I'll wake him if you *really* want me to, but he's sleeping because you have been working him sixteen hours a day on an easy day, and by my count this is the first sleep he has had in more than forty eight hours, unless he dozed off in here, which I doubt."

Gordon glared at her for another moment then blew out his breath in defeat. "You're right. Just because I can't sleep doesn't mean you two shouldn't. When was the last time you slept?"

"I sleep when you are abusing John in here. And I could help you sleep if you'd let me."

"No. I don't have time to waste sleeping," he snapped.

"You are crazy. You are going to slip over into sleep deprived psychosis if you don't watch out. What is so damned important you have to beat yourself and John to death?"

"There are people depending on us."

"What people? You are the only one depending on you so far as I can see. John could do very well without you, and God knows I could get another job in a heart beat."

"Not you two, others!"

"What others?" she demanded.

Gordon glared at her for a moment then snapped, "Never mind. Can you give me another shot? I'm hurting."

Katherine looked at her wrist watch. "Yes," she said and went to the table where several ampoules and packaged syringes lay.

"Not too much," he said to her back. "I don't want to go dopy."

She opened a new syringe, loaded it from an ampoule, made sure the air bubble was out of it, and came to the bed. "I could set you up with a self-medicator, Joshua. All you would have to do is push the button when you hurt." She put the tourniquet above the elbow of Gordon's right arm and patted the bend of his elbow to raise a vein.

"I don't want a self-medicator. Too easy to push the button at the first twinge," he looked at the syringe as she stuck it in his vein.

"OK," she said as she released the tourniquet band.

The ridges of pain across Gordon's brow smoothed as the Morphine spread it's warmth through his body. His clouded eyes took on the artificial shine of the drug.

"Better?" Katherine asked.

Joshua managed a small smile. "Better."

Instead of going out as she usually did, Katherine pulled the chair from where John usually sat closer to the bedside and sat down. "You want to tell me what people it is you think are depending on you?"

The morphine, easing his pain, made Joshua light headed, and since the story was so close to his mind all the time, he said, "The people on Forneria."

"Forneria? You mean the characters in your books?"

"People. My creatures. I created them and I owe them my attention for as long as I can give it to them."

"You really think they are people?"

"Absolutely. I created them and I love them and they are people," Joshua slurred a little. "I think you gave me too much. I'm sleepy. I shouldn't be sleepy, I have work to do."

"Trust me Joshua. You need some sleep and God knows poor John does so just go to sleep for a little while. When you wake up, John will be awake and you two can work again."

Joshua's eyes rolled, out of his control for a moment. "You gave me too much," he said again.

"Go to sleep," she said. "Maybe you can dream of your people in Forneria."

He didn't answer this time. His eyes were closed and his breathing had deepened.

Katherine watched him sleep for a moment. She had grown very fond of Joshua in the weeks she had been in his employ and could not see anything of the ogre she had been lead to believe he was. He was sometimes snappish but that was because he was hurting and he always apologized afterward. She took a moment to smooth his ruffled beard and leaned over and kissed him lightly on the forehead then went out.

Twenty

Captain Fay who had returned to his patrol in the desert after handing Fisher over, brought his troop back to Barstow the instant the spooked horses could be re-gathered. He went directly to the headquarters building of the fort and found John Fisher and ten others digging into a pile of rubble.

Without dismounting he demanded, "You men, have you found any one? Colonel Barrie?"

Fisher straightened from his work and the others with him did the same. "Your Colonel is dead Captain." He indicated four covered bodies lying beneath the shade of a small section of uncollapsed wall. "He was crushed by the falling building."

The Captain looked at the bodies then glanced around the plaza where others were digging in other piles of masonry. His eye did not stop at the fountain which had continued to run, but after a moment he did a double take and came back to it. It had been dry when he had left Barstow two days before. "When did it start flowing again?" he asked. No one answered him and he said, "Some one answer or I will have you all flogged."

Noah, suddenly bold said, "It has flowed since John Fisher called to our Father Gordon the Creator asking for mercy." Fay put face and name together and looked to Fisher. "Prayers to any god save Great Lucian are forbidden," he said.

"If I had prayed to Lucian, would he have let the water return to the fountain?" Fisher asked.

The Captain blinked at the question then retreated into his orders. "*Great* Lucian, dog. And that other name is forbidden."

"Why should the son be called great and the father forbidden?" Fisher asked. Again the Captain blinked at the question and slowly reached for his side arm.

"Would you kill me simply because I speak truth, Captain?" Fisher asked. "Is Lucian so afraid of a name he bids you kill anyone who speaks it? Are you so foolish as to kill someone who wishes only to help those still trapped in the rubble?"

The men who had been helping Fisher dig murmured in agreement. The Captain brought his hand away from the pistol at his hip. "We will take this up later," he said. "For now continue what you are doing. I will be back after I organize more rescue parties."

"Are you thirsty, Captain?" Thomas asked. "The water is clear, sweet, and cool." Fay swept his eyes over the men, looking for the mockery he was sure was in the question, but he found none. After a moment he turned his horse sharply and trotted away with his troop behind him. Fay led his troop to the guard barracks and began putting together rescue squads. More than half the troopers from the barracks were dead or injured beyond helping with the digging out. Fay put some of the less grievously hurt to caring for the more severely injured and organized others into five man press gangs to patrol the town on foot.

"Begin by telling stragglers they have been pressed to help with the digging out," he ordered. "If any resist, use force. Shoot a couple if need be. Any looters you see order them to stop. If they run, shoot them. If not, press them into service. If you find organized civilian parties working, leave them to work. Pick up only the stragglers and looters. Also, send a couple of men to guard the water supply tank."

The first sergeant said "Yes sir," but continued standing before the Captain.

"Something else, Sergeant?"

"Sir, the horses have not been watered for hours. They are very thirsty. Permission to water them – and the men, sir?"

"Very well, go ahead. But be sparing. Water is tight and will get tighter."

"Yes sir. But there's no need to..." then the sergeant thought better and shut his mouth with a snap.

The Captain studied the sergeant a moment then said, "Sergeant? You were saying?"

"Sir, begging your pardon sir, but after seeing the fountain in the plaza some of the men checked the well beside the stable we used to water the horses. It's been dry for more than two years sir, but it ain't dry no more." The man closed his mouth and kept his eyes frozen straight ahead, unfocused, on the Captain's eyes.

"If there's water in the well, why didn't you just go ahead and water the horses and men?" the Captain snapped.

"Beggin' your pardon sir, I heard what you was saying to them in the plaza so I thought it best to ask before doing, sir."

The Captain let out a breath and kept his temper. "Water them and when they have had all they can drink, men and animals, keep drawing from the well until all the troughs and tanks are full. The well is going to dry up again any time."

The sergeant allowed a skeptical look to creep into his eyes but he clamped it down quickly, saluted, and went to carry out his orders.

Night brought out make shift torches and any lanterns still intact. Rescue efforts continued though at a slower pace. People who were digging had been at it since morning and were tired beyond thought and thirsty beyond measure.

Word of the running fountain passed through the rubble like a cooling breeze. Many exhausted rescuers found their way there to see if it was true. Most looked for a moment then hurried away to return shortly carrying anything which could hold water. Some came to see the fountain and when they discovered John Fisher was alive and was the reason the fountain ran, stayed to join the group around him. Many echoed Noah's earlier words. "I knew you were still alive. Lucian could not kill you or stop you. You have come to save us."

Sitting on the rim of the fountain for a moment of rest Fisher once more tried to bring the world into focus. It all seemed more real now than it had at first. *Earthquakes and death tend do make things feel more real, I guess. But I still don't know how I am supposed to save these people. I mean I guess I could just wander around making fountains flow and wells come back to life but just to do it in a thousand square miles would take years on foot, and I have no idea how big this world is.*

When the thought crossed his mind it made him frown. Why would he consider the size of this world? A world was a world. It would be roundish with oceans; the lands across the oceans would be different from this land, wouldn't they? But he could not bring any memory of having seen or heard of more than Los Angeles, Barstow, Tehachapi, and Boron Springs. He knew there were seas of some sort because the Sweetening the Travelers harvested and sold could even be used to make sea water potable, but Fisher could not remember having seen "a sea." He knew about them, and about worlds and cities, but it was knowledge from the shadow existence he remembered from some other place. From the place where Joshua Gordon was a person he knew. A friend. A man confined to a wheelchair or a bed with a dreadful disease.

But people here thought of Gordon as a god. They thought of him as the Creator who had for some reason abandoned them to another god's cruelty, but now had sent him, John Fisher, to defeat this cruel god and grant mercy to the people.

"John Fisher," a stranger from the rubble of Barstow asked "why did Gordon forget us for so long?"

Fisher looked at the man who was filthy with digging. His clothes were ragged and there was no excess flesh on him. His face was thin and leathery and looked shrunken. Suddenly the thought came to Fisher; *He would not seem so shrunken if he were not so dried out. There is not enough moisture in his body to give it even the least plumpness.*

117

"Father Gordon has never forgotten his children," Fisher began. "You are never far from his heart. He loves you and it gives him great pain to see his children suffer so. It near broke his heart when his children began to forget him as Lucian and his cruel armies marched. And it doubly hurt him because Lucian is Gordon's son whom he loves. Lucian betrayed Father Gordon and, knowing how precious were the creatures of this world, Lucian strikes at them in order to wound his father."

"But why does Great Lucian hate his father so?" another asked. A small crowd who had come to drink and draw water had stopped to listen.

"I do not know. I cannot see into the heart of Lucian or understand his cruelty, but he will be defeated. Gordon will not leave you, his dear creatures, to suffer."

"But how can Great Lucian be stopped, John Fisher? He is a god more powerful than us. We are only poor mortals. He has power over the earth and will do with us as he pleases."

~*~

"Worship and honor Gordon the Creator. Trust in him. Believe he will defeat Lucian. Put away your fear and your worship of Lucian."

From the back of the small crowd a voice called out, "Easy enough for you to say. You command water from dry fountains. Who are you to tell us to put away our fear?"

A soft rumbling suddenly came to the ears of the crowd and there was a united gasp and murmur of fear. There had been aftershocks of the quake all day, but this was a different sort of rumbling. Many thought it was another true earthquake come to claim the lives of those left from the first temblor.

A flash of heat lightening lit the sky, static discharge built up from wind and sand. There were no clouds, no forked lightening discharges, no threat of rain. Only the far off rolling of thunder; only the blink-of-an-eye flash lit up the whole sky for an instant and was gone, to be followed by another, and another, and another.

A gasp even more full of fear than the one a moment before went up from the crowd, and cries of "Look! He glows like a lamp! John Fisher burns, but is not consumed!" Others, including Noah and Thomas silently knelt on the dusty street, hands folded, eyes on the blue-white nimbus enfolded man sitting on the edge of the fountain.

The rumbling came again. Many from the crowd said, "It is true! Gordon has sent him! He is here to save us from Lucian's Dry!"

John stood on the edge of the fountain with the nimbus still around him. "Gordon has sent me with a message for you and every creature in this world," he said. "The Father wants you to understand. Lucian will never leave Forneria until you are no longer fooled by his lies. Lucian is the Father of Lies and every word which comes from him is a lie. Even those things seeming to be true are lies. Lucian wants only for this world and all the living creatures in it to die. To disappear. To become 'Uncreated.' Lucian, the son, is jealous of Gordon the Father. Lucian has tried to create, but he cannot, so instead he will destroy. Like a foolish child who cries because he cannot have a toy then steals the toy to break it so no one else may every have what he cannot.

"This is the war being fought here, but it is not the only war. In the other universe, the one from which I came, where Gordon has his existence, and Lucian has his other existence, there is another war. Lucian must be defeated there and here. This is why Gordon has sent me. And you, the believers in Gordon, the faithful who have resisted the blandishments of Lucian the Deceiver, must help me."

"But how can we help you, John Fisher?" several asked. "We are only people, not gods like Lucian. How can we battle a god?"

John looked out over the torch lit crowd. "With truth," he answered. "Every thought you think must be a question seeking the truth. Everywhere you go you must seek truth. Everyone you meet must be told the truth."

"Such truth will get me killed, John Fisher," a man's voice from the crowd called out. "It will get my wife and children killed. Great Lucian has forbidden the very name of Gordon and this truth you talk about is all about Gordon."

Fisher looked for the man and met his eyes. "You are right, friend. Truth is dangerous, but Lucian's lies are more dangerous. His lies will kill you and your wife and your children and all the rest of the world. And all you have to do to accomplish such death is nothing. You can kill your family by doing nothing, or you can take the chance of life by speaking truth."

The crowd murmured as its pieces talked one to another. Fisher, whose blue white nimbus had been fading as he spoke, waited. The words he had said were not precisely his own, yet they were. They had been put in his mouth by Gordon, but they were also words he believed.

"And how do we know you are speaking the truth, Fisher?" came a question from the crowd, followed by many voices of agreement.

"Have you drunk from the fountain? Or from one of the wells now full of water? Has Lucian ever given you anything? Even when he first came with his army, did he give to all or only to some?"

"Lucian gave only to those who helped him," a voice from the crowd's fringe answered. "But you, when you gave us water at Boron Springs you gave to all, even Lucian's messengers."

"And who might you be friend?" came the voice of the doubter.

"I am a Traveler who witnessed the miracle at Boron Springs."

Jim Bitter had arrived in the late afternoon and done what he could to help, and when he heard how the fountain now ran and the wells were filled by Gordon at Fisher's beseeching, he knew this was indeed one sent to save the world.

"The ravens had mocked us," Bitter went on. "And when the water bubbled up in Fisher's tracks, and we all drank, I wanted to chase the ravens away, but Fisher would not let me. He said *all* were Gordon's creatures and *all* deserved Gordon's mercy."

"And I have seen Fisher's mercy," Thomas who had been in prison and who had worked beside John said. "The colonel, who had ordered John Fisher to the dungeon, was trapped beneath the rubble. Fisher found him and when it was clear the colonel would die and was asking for water, John Fisher soaked his own shirt to bring water to the dying man--" A hush fell on the crowd. They could sense there was more and they waited for it. "--and wept when this man, his enemy, died. Is that not enough proof he is from Gordon the Creator?"

"This crowd will disperse now, or my men will fire."

Every head turned to see Captain Fay on his horse with his troops, rifles at post arms, ranged across the back of the plaza.

The Captain, with no fear, spurred his horse forward into the wall of people. It opened a way for the horse and some on the edges of the crowd began making their way down the rubble choked paths out of the plaza without waiting to see what would happen.

When the Captain reached the fountain, he drew his side arm and pointed it at John Fisher. "You are under arrest for violation of the decrees of Great Lucian, God Ruler of Forneria."

"Put up your pistol, Captain, I won't resist. And tell your soldiers to stand at ease. These people have done nothing, only listened to me."

Captain Fay studied Fisher's face, looking for some shadow of fear. He was disappointed when he did not find it. "Sergeant," the Captain ordered, "bring manacles."

"Yes sir!" the sergeant answered and came forward up the furrow in the crowd the Captain had made. He went directly to John Fisher and looked up at him, for Fisher still stood on the edge of the fountain. The crowd fell to dead silence. The slight clinking of the chains and the splashing of the running water could be heard all across the plaza. Fisher looked down at the sergeant then stepped down to the ground, extending his wrists for the manacles. The sergeant hesitated.

"Have you tasted of the fountain, Sergeant?" Fisher asked.

The sergeant's eyes opened wide then he looked from Fisher to the Captain.

"Get on with it, Sergeant," the Captain said.

"Yes sir, but, begging your pardon sir, it don't look like he's gonna resist. Do we really have to chain him? Seems--ungrateful--sir. I mean we all drank, sir."

Without hesitation the Captain turned his pistol from Fisher to the sergeant and fired.

The bullet made a small hole in the right side of the sergeant's head and blasted away a large piece of his skull and brain matter on the other side. He collapsed, dead before he hit the ground.

Twenty-One

The shot brought Fisher awake with a jolt. He was soaking with sweat, dislocated, and trembling with reaction. He sat up, breathing hard, his heart hammering. He reached out, found the bedside lamp, and turned it on. For the first moments the bedroom felt hostile and foreign then the yellow light and simple décor began to feel right so he relaxed a little. He drew several deep breaths to slow his heart then turned to sit on the side of the bed.

The dream had moved along well. It had not been as disturbing as some of the previous ones. It was as though the dream landscape were becoming familiar. In this one there was flowing water and thirsty people drinking when, from nowhere, had come the Captain bringing tension then panic. When he had fired the shot which killed the sergeant, Fisher had been torn from sleep.

John looked at the digital clock on the dresser. Three o'clock. But with the Venetian blinds and the drapes pulled he could not tell if it was three a.m. or p.m. He stood, pulled on his bathrobe and opened the drapes. The sun was bright. Three p.m. He went out and to Joshua's room. Without hesitation he opened the door, no longer worrying about whether Gordon might be asleep.

"Why did you kill the sergeant?" Fisher demanded.

Gordon who was sitting in his cranked power bed with his computer on a swing table across his lap looked up then glanced back at the computer screen. After a moment he said, "I didn't. The Captain did."

"Screw the Captain! He's your creature! You made him kill the sergeant."

Gordon started to shout back at Fisher but bit it off and regained control of his temper before asking, "You have never written a book, have you?"

John was thrown by the sudden change of direction. He had expected argument, or acquiescence, or denial, or something other than what he had got.

"What the hell does that mean?" he growled.

"I have never had a book effect me or anyone around me like this one has, but in other books I have had the interesting but uncomfortable experience of one or more of the characters taking themselves out of my hands and doing what they want, which is what happened with the Captain. He had done the deed before I knew what had happened and once it was done I just couldn't take it back."

Fisher blinked once, twice, three times before saying, "Just go back before it happened and delete back to there and start again. You are the author; you can do what you want. You're the Creator, for god sakes!"

"And I repeat, you have never written a book have you?"

"No!" John answered in exasperation. "I mean not exactly. I have tried to draw out some of my stories to book length, but they usually collapsed because the story was just too small."

"Have all of your attempts ended the same way?" Gordon asked. The avidity in his eyes sent a chill through Fisher. "Have they all ended because the story wouldn't support the length?"

Fisher stared at the other for a moment and finally said, "No. A couple of times it seemed like the story wasn't mine any more. Like it had gone places I didn't want it to go."

"Like the characters had minds of their own and wouldn't do what you wanted," Joshua said flatly.

Fisher opened his mouth but nothing came out. He closed it again and after some minutes of thought said, "I think maybe you *are* nuts and me too. We're talking about these scribbles on paper as though they are real."

"They *are* real." Joshua said, his voice passionate. "They exist. They live. They have being. They have minds of their own sometimes."

Fisher pulled the chair he usually sat in nearer to the bed and flopped into it. "So, the sergeant is dead and no help for it."

"I'm afraid so, and I really am sorry. I hate hurting them."

"You didn't balk when I wanted to kill the colonel."

"No, but he was such a minor character, and I saw how the death of a minor character could advance the story. So, though I don't like it when the characters are hurt, there are times when it is just unavoidable."

Fisher let out a disgusted breath. "Omelets and broken eggs?" he snorted.

Gordon widened his eyes in place of the shrug he could no longer manage. "I hate to say yes, but--yes. To get to where I want to go some of my creatures are going to die. Some by my hand--or yours, and some at each other's, like the sergeant. But something can be made out of it. We can move the story forward, I think. I don't quite see how right now, but it has to be useful or the book is done for."

Katherine came in without a knock and was stopped short by the tension in the room. Emotion was as palpable as the smell of disinfectant.

"What are you doing back in here?" she asked John. "You just went to bed a couple of hours ago."

"Couldn't sleep. The book has me in its grip." He smiled a goofy smile trying to dismiss his words as a joke, but the denial didn't quite fly.

Katherine looked from the younger man to the older. "You two look like conspirators caught in the act. What are you up to?"

"He's right Katherine, and you're right too. It's the book. Get a couple of authors collaborating on a book it is rather like a conspiracy," Joshua said smoothly.

She looked from the one to the other again and shook her head. "Crazy, is what you are, both of you. How do you feel Joshua? Do you need a shot?"

Gordon thought on the question for a couple of moments then said, "No. I've been so caught up in work I didn't notice when or if the last shot wore off. Natural high and stuff."

"All right. Then will you be OK while I go out for a little while?"

"Boy friend?" Joshua asked, smiling.

"You know you're my only love, Joshua," she answered with a smile dazzling enough to make any male heart trip over itself.

"Liar," Joshua said.

She blew a kiss and opened the door then turned her attention to Fisher. "Don't tire him," she commanded, reinforcing the words with a finger jabbed toward John. "And you could use a little more sleep yourself. I don't need you sick too. One crazy sick author is all I can handle."

"Yes, Ma'm," John said.

Katherine went out and they were quiet for a while as though savoring her memory.

"I wonder where she's really going?" Joshua asked.

"I don't know," Fisher said.

~*~

The Bright Spot cafe was a hole in the wall diner on Sunset Blvd and Katherine could not figure why Lucian had wanted to meet her there rather than at his house or office but he had insisted. When she went into the dimly lit place, she was even more uneasy than she had been. Katherine was not feeling nearly as chipper as she was letting on to Joshua and John. She was not looking forward to the meeting she was about to have. It gave her a funny feeling in the pit of her stomach. She had not stepped into her position with Joshua under the best circumstance, and she didn't feel any better now than when she had started. She had only taken the job because Lucian had begged

126

her. He had said that she would be protecting Joshua from the machinations of John Fisher who was dead set on robbing Joshua blind, but she had seen nothing to make her believe that John was anything more than what he claimed to be; an assistant and writing partner to Joshua.

Lucian Gordon sat in a back corner booth from which he could watch the door. He waved Katherine over and she sat down across the table from him. Without even a hello he said, "Do you have the disk?"

"Yes," she answered and dug the CD out of her purse. "I'm not exactly comfortable with this, Luke. I mean keeping an eye on your Dad is one thing, but this seems like stealing."

Lucian smiled indulgently. "I know, but it seems to me the only way to make sure there is another copy. Dad has always been a little nuts about protecting his work and not sharing it with anyone before it is done, but now...I just worry that this final work will be lost or stolen if Dad should suddenly die."

That didn't ring true to Katherine, but she let Lucian's smile and manner re-assured her, just as she had let him convince her there was nothing unethical about working for him and for his father at the same time. "I only want to protect him and make his last days as comfortable as possible," he said. "And I know you need the money so what difference does it make. I don't mind that you are being paid by Dad and by me. It is like a grant that you get even while you are working at some other job. "

"Isn't there some other way for you to get the material though?" Katherine asked. "This all seems really cloak and dagger and silly."

"It is cloak and dagger and silly, but Dad wouldn't let me have a copy otherwise. I mean, I would have just hacked into his computer but the one he is using is not hooked up to the internet so that idea wouldn't work. Besides, that really would have been illegal, not just a little sneaky or naughty like copying the stuff and handing it to me."

Katherine studied Lucian's face for a moment, still not convinced this was right.

"Something else bothering you, dear?" Lucian asked.

"No, not exactly--it's just that I was all prepared to hate John for being a con man or something but he is not oily or sneaky or anything. He and your father seem to genuinely like each other and they seem to be happy to be working together. I mean they fight sometimes but it is always about this story they are writing and the fights don't ever last long." What she did not say was that watching Joshua and John together reminded her of watching a father and son, and try as she might, she could not picture Joshua and Lucian working together like Joshua and John.

"A con man can only succeed if the people he is conning trust him," Lucian said.

"I suppose." She glanced up at the clock. "I really have to go. I have to be back to give Joshua his shot this evening." She slid out of the booth and stood.

"Call me when they have more pages done."

She nodded and turned away. Lucian watched the sway of her hips but nothing sexual crossed his mind. He only wondered if there was some way he could talk her into giving his father an overdose to shorten up the waiting time between now and eternity.

Twenty-Two

When the shot echoed sharply around the torch-lit rubble of the plaza, the crowd ducked as one man they screamed with alarm.

The pistol returned to aim at Fisher quick as a striking snake. "Put them on Fisher or I'll kill you."

A grumbling rose from the crowd. The fear of a moment before still lingered, but those who had not managed to get away through the wreckage reacted with the anger of unreleased adrenalin.

John, still with no sign of fear, squatted, but rather than pick up the chains he put his hand on the dead man's shoulder. "Forgive us, sergeant. Sleep well, and may you never thirst." Then he picked up the manacles, stood and snapped them onto his wrists.

"Where shall I go, Captain? The prison is gone," Fisher said.

The Captain gestured with his pistol toward the empty rift in the crowd where his horse had driven through.

John moved past the Captain's horse without looking up or around. He heard the grumbling of the crowd growing and felt them pushing in, filling in behind him.

The crowd slowly engulfed the Captain's horse and after a few steps the horse was forced to shoulder through the mob enclosing it.

"Open a path again or I'll shoot," the Captain threatened, moving his pistol from side to side. A moment of fear crossed his face, but he controlled it. "Corporal," he called, "prepare to fire on them."

There was a rattling as rifles came to the ready and it spurred the crowd toward panic. Those closest to the soldiers tried to push back away from them but succeeded only in causing the next layer of people behind them to panic and push back more. It set off a chain reaction which reached the horse and rider in only a moment, enclosing them tighter in the mob.

"Open a path or I'll shoot!" the Captain said again, his voice rising with his own fear. But the mob could not open. There was no place to go. The soldiers, with rifles aimed, were at the back of the plaza, the few street openings not choked by fallen buildings were jammed tight with panicky, angry people.

The Captain, eyes rolling like the eyes of his horse fired randomly into the crowd, but had no time for a second shot. His horse reared trying to find a way out and threw the Captain half out of his saddle. Hands from beside his horse reached up, grabbed him and pulled him from the horse onto the ground.

A hundred stamping feet and the flailing hooves of his horse battered the downed officer as he managed to roll himself to his side, cover his head, and pull his knees up to the fetal position.

When the Captain went down, the soldiers were left without a commander. Some fired into the crowd while others tried to turn and flee. All was chaos with screams of pain and shouts of anger and fear echoing through the ruins that were Barstow.

In the midst of it all John Fisher, hands still manacled, knelt beside the fallen Captain putting his own body between the Captain and some of the pummeling. "Move away!" He shouted into the legs of the mob. "Give him room!"

Suddenly someone was kneeling beside him. It was Noah. Fisher put both chained hands upon Noah's shoulder and said, "Protect him as much as you can."

Noah looked as though he would resist the idea, but after a moment he gave a curt nod.

Between mob and chained hands standing was not easy. John pushed his way the few steps back to the fountain. He stepped up on the rim again and shouted, "Enough! Everyone calm down. Soldiers, put down your weapons. Your Captain is alive. Put down your weapons."

Others in all areas of the crowd took up Fisher's pleas, shouting for calm and after a few moments, a reduction in noise, if not real calm, began to radiate out to those who had attacked the soldiers as they fired. The beating of them stopped, but the mob hung on to their captives.

Fisher and the others continued to shout. Soon areas of quiet grew and linked together. The roar of the mob did not cease but lessened. The flickering lights showed a sea of Hieronymus Bosch faces, many with mouths open in pain and in blood hunger.

"Enough," Fisher said more quietly. "There is no need to harm anyone else. Release your prisoners."

Some in the crowd shouted "No. These are Lucian's servants. They do not deserve to live! They fired on unarmed people. They are murderers!"

"They are creatures of Gordon and he loves them. He would not want them or any of his creatures harmed, even these who have served Lucian."

"Even this one, John Fisher?" Noah said, pulling the bleeding, battered Captain to his feet.

The crowd roared as one voice, like a great hungry beast after the Captain's blood. Blood spilled and had whetted the mob's appetite for more. Fisher stepped down from the rim of the fountain, his chains clinking. The power radiating from him now had no need of blue auras. People between him and Noah parted. He stood beside the bleeding Captain. "Even this one needs mercy," he began, his voice strong, and filled with emotion. "All who thirst after mercy may taste of it if they wish. Gordon, our Father, wishes mercy for *all*. He wishes us to be merciful toward one another. We must care for one another. But not only for those we love and who love us, but for those who do not love us and whom we do not love. Those who hate us must also be loved by us for how else can their hate be transformed." Fisher turned to Captain Fay. "It is up to you, Captain. You may gather up your soldiers and leave and continue to serve Lucian, or you may renounce Lucian and drink of the mercy of Gordon the Creator who loved you even before you were born. Y*ou* must choose."

The Captain looked into John Fisher's eyes and felt the power of them. He saw truth in them. After all he had done to harm this one, there was mercy if he wanted it. He could also walk away and not be harmed despite the mood of the mob. Fisher's power would protect him.

The depths of Fisher's eyes pulled Fay into them. They touched his heart and made the conscience he did not know he had awake to the pain he had created in his service to Lucian. "I'm sorry, John Fisher," he whispered, "I did not know."

His eyes fell on the crumpled and bloody shape of the sergeant whose life he had taken only moments before and the sorrow of his act cut his heart with a red hot blade. "What have I done?" he asked himself then looked again at Fisher. "What have I done?"

"What is done, Captain cannot be undone, but you can stop before you ever do anything like it again. Accept Gordon's mercy and change your heart. Serve him."

"I do not deserve mercy," Fay said and dropped to his knees.

"But it is yours, Captain. It is yours." Fisher laid his chained hands on the Captain's bowed head.

After a moment Fisher looked up to see half of the mob kneeling with the Captain.

"Release your prisoners," Fisher commanded. "Remember Gordon's love and mercy."

With a groan as though they were laying down heavy weights, the people began releasing the soldiers, many of whom joined those already on their knees.

Fisher turned back to the fountain where he found a wooden cup lying on the ground. He picked it up and dipped it in the pool. He carried the cup back to where the Captain knelt and held it out to the officer.

Fay looked up and his eyes fell on the offered cup. He received it in both his hands and drank from it.

"May you never thirst, Captain," Fisher said.

PART TWO

One

The letter for John came in the morning mail. No special delivery, no registered mail, just plain first class, hand addressed, with no return. When John held the unopened letter in his hand, he felt the malevolence in it. "Wonder what this is?" he asked with some apprehension, turning the plain white envelope over in his hands.

Katherine looked at it. "It's addressed to you, right?"

"Yeah."

"Who's it from?"

"Don't know. No return address."

"Then I would advise if you want to know what it is and who it is from, you open it," she said with a lifted eyebrow.

Fisher looked at her and said, "Yeah. Guess so." He turned the envelope to the side, tapped the letter inside down then tore off the other end. He blew in it to blossom it out and fished out the letter. It was hand written on Lucian Gordon's letterhead and said, *"I would like to meet with you at your earliest convenience. Please call the number above."* It was signed *"Luke."*

"Holy shit!" John breathed.

Katherine looked over his shoulder. "Wonder what he wants?"

"Good question."

"It has to be your call, John," Joshua said when John told him about the letter. He was hurting and uncomfortable and tired beyond words. He wanted desperately to sleep, but sleep came only in short snatches dictated by his myelitis and by his obsession with working. Katherine sometimes put on her stern nurse hat, forcing him to take a break, slipping him a little extra morphine occasionally to make sure he could rest.

"If you'll recall, our last meeting wasn't too cordial," Fisher said. "In fact I think it set all this law suit stuff off in the first place."

Joshua studied his protégé for a moment. "And it bothers you, doesn't it?"

"I told you then I felt like a rat coming between a father and son."

"And I told you it had damn little to do with you," Joshua snapped. "Lucian wants Forneria and I wouldn't have given it to him no matter what. You were just the proximate cause."

John had grown used to Joshua's shortening temper. He understood the pain and the obsession. He was feeling some of the latter himself. There were times now when he was unsure which world was dream and which real. "What do you think he wants, boss?"

Joshua turned the question over in his mind before saying, "In the gospels when it became apparent to Satan Jesus was going to be a tough nut to crack, he came to Jesus and offered him the world if only Jesus would serve him."

Fisher raked his bottom teeth over his top lip. Joshua had talked about gospel and Jesus before but such a comparison made Fisher uncomfortable. "You think he is going to offer me a bribe or something?"

"Probably. Bribes, or threats, or both."

Fisher again looked at the letter in his hand. "The difference between this temptation and that one is I'm not the man-god."

Joshua softened a little more. "I don't expect you to be, son. Go see what he has to say, and if he offers you something sufficiently tempting, take it."

John started to protest but Joshua cut him off. "You owe me nothing, John. You have been a great help with the book, but even so, because of the dreams and all, you can still walk away with no hard feelings. I told you participation was voluntary and I meant it."

After a time John said, "I have to think about this a little more." He stood and headed for the door but turned back before going out. "You're wrong you know. I do have a stake in Forneria, even if not another book ever gets published. I loved the stories before I ever met you, and now when I find myself in one, I have come to love it even more. The creatures there are important to me. I want to see how their lives finish up."

Joshua, his voice breaking a little, said, "I appreciate your saying so, son. Makes me think I might really have been an author once and maybe can be one more time."

Fisher handled the note so much in the next couple of days it was wrinkled and dog eared by the time he decided to make the telephone call. The phone rang twice before it was answered. "Mr. Fisher, I've been expecting your call," Lucian said, keeping it light.

"I'm not sure I am doing the right thing calling you."

"What could it hurt to talk, Mr. Fisher? I have a feeling many of our desires are parallel--anyway. I only want the best for my father." The statement rang false in John's ears, but he let it pass. He didn't know Lucian except from their one meeting, and though Joshua had told him very little, Fisher was wise enough to know anything Joshua said about his son might be tainted.

"Where do you want to meet?" Fisher asked.

"I think some neutral place would be best. Would Scandia Restaurant be acceptable?" Lucian asked.

"A little pricey for me," John said. "Joshua pays me, but not enough to eat at Scandia, if you know what I mean?"

"I do indeed. The dinner will be my treat. After all I am the one who asked for the meeting."

Fisher hesitated, thinking an expensive meal might compromise him somehow, but then discarded the suspicion. *If it's part of the bribe I can tell him to stick it, and walk away.* "Fine, Mr. Gordon."

"Please, call me Luke, or Lucian if you must." The phrase, so like Joshua, gave John pause. How could father and son be so alike, yet so different? "Lucian then," he said. "When shall we do this?" There was a moment's quiet as if Lucian was checking his watch or perhaps his calendar.

"Would tonight at seven be too early?"

John grinned and said, "No, no. Tonight at seven, at Scandia."

"Wonderful. See you then," Lucian said and hung up. Fisher said goodbye into the already dead receiver.

"Sounded very civil," Katherine said. She had come into the library unnoticed, leaning against a bookshelf.

"Yeah. Civil. 'Step into my parlor said the spider to the fly.'"

John considered wearing a coat and tie but settled on polo shirt and slacks. It was Hollywood after all. The Maitre d` looked at him as though he were a bug, but John figured he looked the same way at everyone not a film star or celebrity. "Mr. Lucian Gordon," the waiter repeated. "Yes, follow me, if you please." Lucian was in a very private banquette at the back of the restaurant. He rose when the Maitre d` handed John over and offered his hand which John gripped and released. They sat with the table between them. Lucian asked, "Would you like a drink, John? We have time before dinner. I took the liberty of ordering for us."

"Crown on the rocks?" John said. A waiter appeared as if by magic and Lucian ordered the drinks. Crown Royal on the rocks and Laphroaig with a splash of water. "Is dad treating you well?" Lucian asked.

"Depends what you mean. He hurts a lot and it pisses him off when he can't control his body any more, and he isn't sleeping very well so he's kinda cranky sometimes."

Lucian chuckled. "I can imagine. When he worked in the past, he was pretty much a bear to be around, and I can't see the situation being better with him sick."

"I think he does pretty well, considering."

Lucian shrugged. "Maybe it was just me," he said. The drinks came and John sipped his, watching Lucian over the rim of the glass. "Forgive me for being blunt, but why am I here?"

Lucian lowered his glass. "I had intended to wait until after we eat but, if you insist, I want to offer you a bribe."

Fisher shook his head a little as though to clarify what he had heard. He had not expected Lucian to lay it out so boldly. "Well, OK. Pretty straight forward. What kind of bribe and what do I have to do to earn it?"

"Hardly a thing. You will continue as Dad's assistant until his book is finished, or he dies, and you will sign papers vacating his bequest to you. I will give you two hundred fifty thousand dollars. Half at the time of signing, the other half after Dad dies when you deliver the Forneria copyrights to me."

John looked at Lucian's face, trying to read it. He couldn't. At last he picked up his glass and sipped again. "Lot of money. But the Forneria copyrights will probably be worth a lot more over the years."

Lucian put his hand out of sight behind the table and brought up a sheaf of paper held together with a big paper clip. He tossed it gently across the table and it landed in easy reach for John.

Fisher picked it up and felt a jolt as he recognized what it was. It was a copy of what he and Joshua had been working on. "Where did you get this?" Fisher asked.

Lucian did not answer but simply looked deeply into Fisher's face. "Do you really think this is ever going to be worth a quarter million dollars?" Lucian asked.

John looked from the manuscript to the man. "I don't know. Maybe. It is rough right now, but I think it has potential."

"And it will have Dad's name on it of course, which will make it worth something, but the reading public is fickle and books are expensive. Joshua Gordon's name not withstanding I don't think this..." he lifted his chin at the manuscript..."will sell out its first printing. Probably sell a few hundred in hard bound and maybe a few thousand in paperback, if it ever makes paperback. It isn't very good."

Fisher hesitated, studying Lucian's face before answering, "I disagree, but one way or another what does it matter if it sells ten million or two hundred? What difference would it make to you? Why do you want the copyrights so much?"

Lucian picked up his glass, swirled the amber liquid then sipped and set the glass down. "My mother died alone on a kitchen floor because my father was too busy to have taken her to a doctor to find out she was sick. She died, no doubt calling his name because she adored him, but he was half a continent away selling a book--the first of the Forneria books. Over the years those stories have been more important to him than anything else in life. More important than my mother, more important than me, more important than anything. I left home as soon after college as I could and made my fortune, but never once, *not once* has he ever said so much as 'I am proud of you,' let alone 'I love you.' I want the copyrights because they are the only things which really matter to my father."

Fisher rolled the statement over in his mind for a moment before saying, "Joshua told me a variation of the same story, but I didn't believe him. I thought he was just too close to the thing to see the reality of it. Turns out he was right." He fell silent, thinking then said, "It's crazy you know? I mean obsessive compulsive nuts."

Lucian's face became red. "Any crazier than his leaving everything to me except those copyrights, which he leaves to a total stranger?"

John shrugged. "They are his to do with as he wishes. After all, they protect his creation."

Lucian's face moved from red toward purple. "Not only his creation. Mine too. He has pulled me into it therefore I have more stake in this one than in all the others.

John frowned, not understanding what Lucian meant, but before he could ask, Lucian continued. "One way or another I will have those copyrights. I had hoped to avoid some of the mess involved, but I see there is going to be no help for it."

Fisher finished the last of his drink and slid out of the banquette. "Under the circumstances I think maybe I'd better decline dinner after all. Thank you for the drink."

He turned away then thought of something and turned back. "Where did you get those pages anyway?"

Lucian sat still as a statue studying Fisher's face, as though trying to decide whether or not to actually say what was apparently burning on the tip of his tongue. At last he said, "My father not only loves Forneria more than he loves me, he takes pleasure in using it to torture me. He emails the pages to me a few at a time as they're finished."

Two

The Travelers spent the rest of the day and the night at the restored spring called Copper Seep. Somehow *Seep* did not seem an appropriate name for the flowing stream rolling from beneath the cliff and down the water course which had been dry for all memory of even the eldest Traveler. "Maybe we'll meet Bitter on the way back to us," Ez said, sitting on the high wagon seat with the droms' reins separated between his fingers in preparation for leaving.

Mandy, who sat beside him said, "Maybe we oughta just wait here. They's plenty of water."

"But they ain't plenty of feed. The droms et most of the greasewood bushes naked and a lot of the cactus. They gonna start wandering off looking for more if we don't get on."

There was also the fact the foraging parties had found little to feed themselves save some scrawny rabbits and desiccated cat tail roots. The prickly pear was long gone. After more half-hearted discussion it was decided they would move on the following morning. Barstow, if it was still there, was more than a day's travel from Copper Seep. The surfeit of water made the time seem negligible. Even the sun felt cooler to begin with, but as midday approached, it stole any imagined cool from the Traveler's minds. Thirst once more set in, but years of habit kept them from drinking though their barrels,

tanks, and water skins were full. It was easy to forget the flowing water of the
seep and the bubbling water of Boron Springs when the parching wind rose
and blew sand into their faces. Mandy and Ez were three from the end of the
column of wagons today. There were ten wagons so "lead" and "drag" of the
column changed every day. The head wagon after a day of leading fell back to
the end or drag position and day by day worked its way back to lead. This was
done so everyone had to suffer all the hardships of every position and reap
any benefit any position in the column had. Drag was often the worst of all
because the dust of the column rolled back and enveloped the drag wagon in
gritty yellow clouds. However, if the wind blew from either side or from the
rear of the column drag was not so bad.

Lead had its problems too. The front wagon was required to pick the
best route which was not always easy. The never still wind of the desert blew
dust, tumble weeds and even small stones across the already faint tracks.
Earthquakes small and large were frequent, and might suddenly make a piece
of the ground which had been flat yesterday jut up several inches like an
escarpment. If the column was head up into the wind, the lead wagon took
the brunt of the wind and anything carried in it. All in all, the best position
in the column was somewhere in the middle.

In the afternoon, shortly after the noon stop to water droms and
people, word began to pass from the drag wagon about a huge dust devil
which appeared to be following them.

Mandy stood up on the wagon seat and leaned way out, but she could
see nothing except the towering top of the spinning wind. She watched for
several minutes before saying, "I never seen a dust devil so big, Ez. It goes
way up in the sky. Must be as big around as a wagon on the bottom 'cause it is
broad as the full moon on top."

"Is it really follerin' us?" Ez asked.

"Seems like."

"Mamma, I'm scared," Em said from inside the wagon.

"What fer?" Mandy asked. "Ain't nothin' but a spinny wind." She turned around and sat down beside her husband. "It'll be gone in a little bit," she said, but her voice betrayed her own uneasiness.

Worried murmurs whispered up and down the train. Children too small to understand the tension felt it none the less and began whimpering.

As the day trickled on toward evening the murmuring grew louder and soon could be heard over the jingling of the harness chains. The dust devil still followed them and the head on wind which should have broken up the twister, or at least made it move some other direction, grew stronger. Heavy grit blew like tiny bullets into the faces of the lead wagon and it grew so strong the droms were forced to turn their heads aside so they could breath. This forced the teamsters to saw at the reins to keep the column moving forward.

It was still early when word passed down the column they would circle for the night and sit out the storm.

Behind them the dust devil appeared to stop and stand still even as it continued to spin.

With practiced efficiency the wagons turned left and right and formed the night circle in a few minutes. They unhitched the droms and moved them into the center of the circle where they turned their backs to the wind which continued to tear beneath and between the parked wagons.

When the camp was set several men walked out toward the dust devil.

"It just ain't natural," Ez said, looking back and shaking his head as the worm of cloudy yellow dust extended and danced high into the air.

"What you think is going on?" a Traveler named Joe Birdwell asked.

"I don't know, but it can't be good," Ez said and turned back to the wagon circle. "Reckon I'll go get me some coffee and think about it."

The others looked from the dust column at Ez's retreating back then turned and followed him to the wagon circle.

When the sun went down behind the western mountains and the sky deepened toward black, the wind suddenly stopped. A still heat, more uncomfortable than the wind, settled over the desert. The towering whirlwind continued spinning in the stillness then it seemed to lean forward moving straight at the Travelers camp. A ripple of fear mummered. "Thing might tear us up," Birdwell said.

"If it comes on," another answered.

"And it might just pass on by or disappear before it reaches us," a man called Max Burden said.

"It ain't collapsed all day. Don't know why it would now," Ez said.

"Well, what are we gonna do?" several people asked.

"Too late to do much of anything but pray now," Max Burden said, and as if his words were their cue, many of those who had rejoiced at the stream from Copper Seep began to cry out for Gordon the Creator, who had sent water to them when they thirsted, to save them.

The chorus of wailing and prayers rose as the whirlwind drew closer and closer, rising to an almost deafening pitch when it was only a few yards away, yet no breeze stirred the oppressive heat which blanketed the camp.

"You ask mercy of the wrong god, Travelers," The booming voice of Lucian said from the depths of the wind column. The voice made the ground shake. "Gordon does not hear you. He does not live in this world. I, Lucian, am the god of Forneria. From me comes any mercy you may be shown."

The Travelers all fell silent as if cut off by a switch.

"Kneel when you ask mercy of me," Lucian commanded.

The Travelers, confused and buffeted by fear began dropping to their knees, but they remained quiet.

Ez, nearest to the wind and on his knees said, "What will you have us do, Great Lucian? We worship and fear you, but when we were thirsty, the man John Fisher brought us water."

"Fisher is no man. He is a demon sent from the hell where Gordon dwells. He wants only power. He cares not at all for you or for anyone."

Mandy, kneeling beside her husband gathered up her courage and, despite the chill of dread in her stomach and the shaking of her bones with fear she said, "But the water, Great Lucian?"

"I released the water to you. In the same way I now take back my largess. Boron Springs and Copper Seep are dry as of now."

"But, Great Lucian, why?" asked Birdwell.

"Because, despite my mercy toward you all, you failed to worship me. I am the god of Forneria. Worship other than me and all my mercy dries up."

"We will worship you Great Lucian, god of Forneria," a voice from the back of the group called out and others echoed it and echoed and echoed until all the Travelers were chanting, "We will worship Great Lucian, God of Forneria."

The towering whirlwind swayed to the rhythm of the Travelers voices. "My people," said Lucian after a time. "My creatures. Hear me now. The demon John Fisher must be stopped. If you meet him, kill him. I would see his body stretched upon the sand."

Did not the cavalry take him to Fort Barstow? But he did not say it, only agreed along with all the others to kill John Fisher if they found him again.

Lucian's voice became sweeter. "There will be great reward for the one who kills the demon. I will bring the servant of truth, who destroys the liar Fisher, to my great fortress to the north and make him the child of Great Lucian and give him his heart's desire."

Ez heard the promise and began calculating. "Great Lucian," he asked with fear in his voice, "when we kill the demon, how shall we collect our reward?"

"Bring his body to me at the northern fortress. When I have seen his body you will have your reward."

"It will be so, Great Lucian," several voices called out.

The column of dust swayed for a moment then suddenly lunged forward and swallowed one of the wagons.

The Travelers gasped. "What's happening?" they asked as they rose from their knees and scuttled away from the roar and crunch of the wind as it engulfed and chewed the wagon.

It was done in seconds. Bits of crushed wagon, torn canvas, chewed possessions and splintered sticks of sweetening whirled and climbed the column of wind where it was spit out in a rain of shrapnel to fall upon the fleeing Travelers. Some of the debris struck the running people, knocking them to the ground.

Ez turned back to see if the tornado would go on to destroy all the other wagons, but when the single wagon was chewed to splinters, the funnel wind stood still. Lucian's voice came from it again. "I am Great Lucian, God of Forneria. Worship me and your rewards will be great. Call upon the name of Gordon and your destruction will be total."

The column straightened itself as though stiffening, and in an instant the wind was gone leaving the previously trapped dust and dirt to collapse in a heap. The dirt fell in a mound like a fresh grave for the destroyed wagon.

Three

Fisher's mind whirled as he drove home from Scandia. He didn't know who to believe any more, and a quarter million dollars, while not really a huge amount, was more money than he had ever seen in one place. When all he had to do was sign over something he didn't even have, might never have. He had no proof at all that Joshua had really changed his will. He had never seen a copy, nor had anyone sworn to the changes under oath. It could all be lies to keep him in the dark, helping Gordon with this last book. Pie in the sky. And Lucian might have been right. The book they were writing might not be any good. It might never sell a copy. Hell, it might not ever be published for all Fisher knew. He hadn't seen any contract or talked to any publishers' reps. It could all be the delusion of a sick man trying to stave off death with work, and eternity with words on a page. But if all the negatives were true, then why would Lucian want the copyrights so much? Did he really think--really think--the Forneria stories were the only way to do it? *But it can't be! It can't be true because if it is, it is totally stone nuts, insane, rubber room, straitjacket crazy!* Yet he had heard the same story, in two variations, from Joshua and Lucian. Each side of the conflict told roughly the same story, so it might even be true, one way or another.

Adding to the growing whirl inside Fisher's brain were the dreams and the plot, the getting-fuzzier-all-the-time line between dreams and reality. *What the hell was that? How was it happening?* Joshua had sworn he was not drugging

146

John or hypnotizing or mesmerizing him, but the assurances didn't make the dreams seem any less real when he was in them or any less weird and scary when he was awake. It didn't make him feel any less for the creatures he met in the dreams or for them when he was awake either. Sleeping and waking he loved the creatures of Forneria, from the dromules--so like camels but not--to the ravens both red and black, and especially, to the people. He couldn't even think of them as "characters" any more! They were fully realized to him, and even when they attempted to hurt the other creatures of the dreams, John Fisher cared. They were creations of his partnership with Joshua Gordon, and now he cared for them. "Which is just as nuts as all the rest of it, John!" he said aloud to the traffic. "It is Napoleon factory crazy!"

Then there was Lucian in Forneria and California. Lucian seemed to think he was somehow involved in the creation of this new book. What was it he said? *"He pulled me into it..."*

So what do I do? Do I just keep on keeping on? Or do I take the money and run? Or do I just run? None of this other mess really concerns me! Unless it is all true. Which was the thought rolling up next on his mental consideration screen as he rolled the last few yards up the drive of Joshua Gordon's house.

He didn't put the car in the garage as usual, but only cut off the engine. Jumping out of the car, he strode into the house. He did not stop until he burst into Joshua's room.

Gordon and Katherine were both startled. She was bending over him listening to his heart through her stethoscope. A blood pressure cuff was on Gordon's left arm. A tray with an ampoule and a hypodermic needle sat on the bed side table. Gordon lifted an eyebrow and said, "Must have been a short dinner."

"Katherine, I need to talk to Joshua--"

"So talk," she said going back to her business of checking heart rate and pumping the blood pressure cuff.

"Alone."

She looked back at Fisher and became the stern nurse. "You can talk to him when I'm finished. I'll give him his shot, and when I am finished I'll leave. Not until. If you want to wait five minutes, OK. If not, leave or go ahead."

Joshua glancing from Fisher to Katherine and back and said, "Never mind, Katherine. I can wait on the shot. I'm not hurting too bad yet. Leave us alone."

Katherine gave John a poisoned dagger look then turned the look on Joshua. "You two deserve each other," she said as she draped her stethoscope around her neck and went out.

When they were alone, all the questions in John's mind jumbled together. He could not sort them out enough to know where to start. At last Joshua asked, "Well, what happened?"

Fisher pulled his chair close to the bed and sat down. "Just like you thought. He offered me a bribe."

"Umh. How much?"

"Two hundred and fifty thousand dollars."

"Is that all? The copyrights alone are worth three or four times as much, plus what ever this new book is worth. I didn't expect him to be a piker. Did you take it?"

Fisher studied Gordon's face. It was grayer now than a few weeks before and the lines in his forehead and beside his nose were much deepened by pain. All the things John had thought about in the car swirled together again. "Not yet," he said.

Now it was Joshua's turn to study the younger man. "Holding out for more money?" he asked but didn't mean it.

"Joshua, I am one confused son of a bitch," Fisher began. "I am having trouble telling lie from truth and real from--not real. I don't know what, or more especially who, to believe. I mean everything you've told me could be lies. I have no proof of the change in your will. I have no proof this thing we are working on will ever be published. I don't know anything! Couple of months ago I was a starving artist driving a cab to stay alive, but my life was my own! Now I don't know who I am."

Without a word Joshua pushed a speed dial button on his telephone. After two rings there was the click of an answering machine and a rich baritone voice said, "You have reached the law offices of Whittaker, Belhaven, and Chance. Our offices are closed. Our regular office hours are nine a.m. to six p.m. Monday through Friday and nine a.m. to two p.m. Saturday. Closed Sunday. Please leave your message, including your telephone number after the tone..."

After the beep Joshua said, "Ed, this is Joshua Gordon. I need you to bring me a copy of my will--certified copy please--tomorrow morning as early as possible. Thanks." Then he hung up. "I don't have Dilton Press on the speed dial but their offices are closed until tomorrow anyway. We could call Bill Carney. He's probably not in his office either and I hate to call him at home, but if you want I'll push the button."

Fisher slumped in the chair and studied Gordon for a few heart beats. "No. No need," he said. "I can wait until tomorrow. Sorry about the trouble, but Lucian really turned my crank."

"You can still call back and tell him you'll take the money. If I were you, I would call him back with a counter offer. Ten million to renounce and take a powder."

"He'd never pay that much."

"You sure? This is about more than money."

"He did get a little purple when I turned him down." John sat quietly studying Joshua for a few more moments then said, "Lucian had copies of all the pages we have, or at least it looked like it. It could have been a Kansas City roll I suppose, I didn't look at every page, but I don't think it was."

Joshua looked troubled by this.

"He said you emailed him the pages every day--to rub his nose in it."

Gordon let out a sigh. "Luke, Luke."

"I take it you didn't send him the pages?"

"I didn't. I wouldn't ever and especially not to rub his nose in it." Joshua looked sadder than John had ever seen him. His son hating him was a thing which he had learned to live with, but it still hurt him deeply. "If you are satisfied, could you send Katherine in on your way out?"

Fisher hesitated a moment then stood. "I'm sorry boss. I should've had more faith in you."

"No, you shouldn't have. I wouldn't."

John nodded and turned for the door but turned back a second later. "If you didn't send him the pages, and I didn't send them, how did he get 'em, if it really was them?"

"Something to consider," Joshua said.

They looked at each other for a time as though trying to read what the other was thinking. At last John said, "Why did you put Lucian in as the antagonist? You could have used any other name or force you wanted to, but you chose Lucian. He said something about you having dragged him into this."

Joshua tried to shake his head but succeeded only in making a twitch of his chin. "That's a hell of a good question, John. A hell of good question, and I wish I had a hell of a good answer, but I don't. I swear to you it was unconscious on my part. Maybe it is some kind of special trick played on me by the Great Author of this novel of a life we both are in."

"Could we change the name?"

"It is something else to consider--later. Go away now. I need a shot.

John stood and headed for the door. He was not satisfied with Joshua's explanations, but at the same time he was so deep into Forneria that he could not see himself letting go of it now, no matter what. Send Katherine in."

"Yeah, sure," he said and went out.

Moments later Katherine came in and began to examine Joshua's eyes and color and feel his forehead like a mother with a sick child. "You look like hell, Joshua. Are you hurting?"

"Yes. Give me an extra big shot please. I crave oblivion, at least for a little while."

Katherine looked for a moment as though she might cry, but she controlled it by assuming her nurse persona. She filled the needle, wrapped the tourniquet, brought up the vein, and injected him without another word.

She stayed until Joshua drifted off to sleep then hurried out and to her room. She needed to think. She had listened at the door to most of what Joshua and John had said and listening to them talk about Lucian and about the pages she had taken to him, made her stomach turn over.

After more than an hour of wondering what to do, she called Lucian at the private number he had given her.

"Things are not going well here, Lucian," she began. "When John returned from your meeting this afternoon, he practically accused your father of lying to him. He said you told him Joshua was sending the pages to you."

"Take it easy, Katherine, I just did that to knock Fisher off balance."

"Well you succeeded! He was practically raving when he got back. He stirred your father up so much I thought he would have a heart attack!"

Lucian chuckled. "Good. Maybe he'll really think about taking the money now."

"It all calmed down in a few minutes and they went back to talking about the book. They were talking about how and why you wound up as a character in the book. It was as though they thought you and John were really in the book."

Lucian was silent for a long while before Katherine heard him take a deep breath that might have been either a sigh of satisfaction or resignation. Then he said, "It sounds like Dad has slipped over into obsession and Fisher is feeding right into it. That bastard is going to rob Dad blind. He already has the copyrights, and it is just a matter of time till he has all the rest to."

"I have heard Joshua say that he gave the copyrights to John so that you wouldn't destroy Forneria. He seems to think you will pull all the books off the shelves and throw them into a big bonfire or something."

"That's all part of the obsession."

Now it was Katherine's turn to be silent. She thought about all she had heard and seen at Joshua's house and what she had been told and was being told by Lucian and she was confused. She had grown to like Joshua and, despite Lucian's belief that John was some kind of a heartless con man, she just could not see him as anything other than an unremittingly kind and helpful fellow who practically worshiped Joshua.

"Lucian, I really--I've never been comfortable with this arrangement, but after tonight I think maybe it is time for me to quit. I mean you father needs a nurse but ...I just feel like such a traitor.

"Katherine you are not a traitor! You are a protector of a sick old man, and I am happy to have you there."

"But you must understand. I feel like I have to put Joshua's care ahead of everything and this arrangement between us makes me feel like I am betraying him."

"Would you be doing anything different as far as treating my father if I hadn't offered you money?" Lucian said, trying to sound both officious and persuasive at the same time.

"No. I'm his nurse and I would do what I am doing no matter what."

"Then I think you have answered your own problems. All you have to do is continue to be the exceptional nurse you are, doing everything in your power to protect and ease the pain of your patient, and we will continue with our arrangement."

"Yes, I suppose so," she said.

Four

The Travelers saw the cloud of carrion birds rising and circling like smoke long before they could see the city. Birds, jackals, coyotes, flies, ants, and death beetles told the story of the fifth day after the Barstow earthquake. Tens and perhaps hundreds had been trapped when the buildings fell. No one had a truly accurate count, but five days in the heat without water left no one in any doubt the last rescues had been made. The cemetery on the north side of the city had many fresh graves. And as the Travelers wagon train went past, they saw several burial parties at work. Jim Bitter looked up from the work of burying the dead, saw the Travelers column, and strode toward the wagons. He lifted his hand in greeting then stopped, looking puzzled. After a moment he walked on. As he approached the lead wagon he saw Ruth, her bonnet hanging down her back, her hair wind-tangled, climbing down from their wagon and walking toward him.

Bitter smiled and waved to her, but continued to the lead wagon. "Where's the other wagon?" he asked.

"We'll talk about it later," Birdwell who was in the lead wagon answered. "How's it with you?"

Bitter shrugged. "Some good, some not. Lots of folks dead and lots hurt. Fisher and Fay got the place organized so them was alive been dug out. They's still some dead under the mess--as you can see." He glanced up at the circling ravens and vultures. "But they's water. Just like at Boron Springs.

Fisher filled up the wells and the fountains. All running and all cold and sweet."

"Still?" Birdwell asked.

"Well, I reckon. They was a little bit ago. What do you mean?"

Ruth Bitter, smiling like sunrise came up and received a kiss and a quick hug from her husband, but Jim's attention was mostly reserved for Birdwell. "Remember how Copper Seep started running a river after the quake? Well, when Great Lucian come visitin'..."

"What?" Bitter asked sharply, "Lucian come visitin'?"

"Great Lucian come in a whirlwind yesterday evening," Birdwell explained as though to a slow child. "Destroyed Gillem's wagon; dried up the seep again and Boron Springs. Said everything was dry until he said otherwise."

Bitter narrowed his eyes then shook his head. "Wells is filled here. I just drew water an hour ago."

Ez had jumped down from his wagon and come forward. He shook hands with Bitter and said, "Did I hear you right? You said Fay and Fisher? You mean the cavalry Captain what took Fisher from us?"

Bitter nodded and there was a strange look on his face. "It was amazing! Half the town was on their knees. Fisherites everywhere now--"

"Includin' you?" Ez asked.

Bitter hesitated a few moments, looked down at his wife then nodded his head. "Reckon I am," he said. "I never seen anything like it. Never felt anything like it!"

There was a glow on Bitter's face as though a sun beam focused strictly on him. He went on with awe and happiness. "It was as though Gordon himself had come down to speak to us. Fisher stopped a mob from killing Captain Fay and stopped 'em killing the soldiers what fired into the crowd. Just talking to them he stopped it all. Said we all of us need mercy from Gordon and all we had to do was ask for it to have it granted. The Captain all of a sudden knelt down and Fisher brought him a cup of water-- said something to him, but no one except them was real close could hear. Then Fay bowed all the way to the ground, but Fisher bent down and made him stand up. In a few minutes them as heard Fisher's words to the Captain started offering each other drinks of water and saying 'May you never thirst.' But they wasn't talking about water I'm pretty sure."

Bitter suddenly laughed. "Somebody offered me a big ole iron pot with water in it and said the words. Took all I could do to lift the thing to my mouth, but I did it and drank and I was all of a suddenly cool and--I don't know what. Content I reckon. Like everything was gonna be right from now on."

Ruth gripped his arm. She could see his joy and feel the changes in him, but she shivered with fear at not knowing how those changes were going to affect the family.

Ez and some of the other Travelers glanced over at the fresh graves and the burial parties working at new ones and wondered at Bitter's talk of everything being all right.

Bitter noticed. "Look, I know it sounds crazy, but I think everything *is* gonna be all right. John Fisher is come to help us remember Gordon the Creator and free us from Lucian's Dry."

Birdwell studied Bitter for a few heart beats before saying, "Great Lucian told us anyone brings John Fisher's body to the Northern Fortress will be rewarded."

Bitter heard the words and shook his head at them. "I wouldn't say nothing about it here abouts," he said. "Fisher has a lot of friends in Barstow now. He mighta stopped the mob from killing the soldiers, but he might not be around to stop somebody what's drunk from one of the wells or fountains."

"We'll keep our council," Ez said.

"Where can we circle up, Jim?" Birdwell asked.

"West of town. You'll have to go around. Streets are still full of tumbled buildings. Places you can't hardly walk."

"You coming with us?" Ruth asked hopefully.

Bitter looked back at the burial party which was still working then at her again. "I'll be there after while. I hafta finish helping them. I promised."

She did not look displeased, but clearly she wanted to go with him. He stopped her. "Go on with the boys," he said. "I'll be over with you in a little while."

She studied his face for a moment then said, "All right, Jim," and accepted another quick kiss before heading back toward the Bitter wagon.

The crowd of Travelers regrouped themselves into family wagons and turned west to go around the ruins.

Bitter helped the burial party for a little while, but after a time he asked if they could handle the job without him. When they said yes, he looked toward the still rising dust of the wagon train but turned toward the plaza.

John Fisher looked around for the red bird but it was no where to be found. He felt he needed some clarification for what was going on after the night mob in the plaza. Fisher found himself the center of Barstow's army of displaced people. All seemed to look to him for instruction and comfort. He did not feel competent for the position, but failing to find help from the bird, he did what he thought best. He sent Captain Fay to continue the search parties, though hope of finding anyone still alive was all but gone. He put Noah Simons and Thomas Pitney in charge of surveying the food situation, and some whose names he did not know in charge of burial parties. When it became too dark to continue searching, the exhausted population gravitated to the Plaza as if to draw comfort from John Fisher, from the still flowing fountain, from being together. Their lives were gone, changed forever by the earthquake, by John Fisher's restoring the wells, and by the sharing of water in the plaza the night before.

After a time Fisher called for more torches to be brought near him. He stood on the rim of the fountain. "Soon you must make some decisions; whether to stay here and try to rebuild Barstow or to go to the west over the mountains to Bernardo City. I must go elsewhere."

There were protests from the crowd. "We cannot live without you, John Fisher. Lucian will come and destroy us. He will dry up the wells once more and leave us to die of thirst because we have called upon Gordon."

"Gordon, my father, has other duties I must accomplish before I can return to him."

There were groans of fear, and of sadness that they would be left to themselves once again, but Fisher went on. "Remember this, children of Gordon's mercy. Because you have shared the water of life with me, Gordon our father will not desert you. He gives you power through me to resist Lucian. All you need do is call upon Gordon in my name and he will grant what you ask."

"But the wells, John Fisher," a voice from the crowd called. It was Jim Bitter. He had told John of the price on his head, but had not said anything about what Birdwell had told him about the water. He did not want to believe it, but at last the doubt festered like a sore and had to be answered. "I have heard the water at Boron Springs has dried up and a stream which flowed from Copper Seep flows no more."

"Did you drink from the pool at Boron Springs, Traveler?"

"Yes sir."

"And was the water cold and sweet?"

"Yes sir."

"Then I ask *you* to tell me, has the spring the water of Boron opened in you dried up?"

There was a grumbling from the crowd. They did not understand what Fisher was talking about, but it made them worry the respite from the Dry might come to an end.

"Does the feeling of joy and content and surety which came to your heart when you drank from the spring remain? Does the knowledge of Gordon the Creator and Father of us all still dwell in your heart?"

Fisher stopped speaking and cast his eyes over the crowd in the plaza. The people fell into a breathless anticipatory quiet, waiting for Fisher's next words, almost holding their breaths, and in the pregnant silence the musical trickling of the fountain seemed to grow louder and louder until every ear was attuned to it. The sound brought the taste and the feeling of the water shared the night before; the feeling of oneness with one another and with Gordon the Father.

"The spring still flows," Bitter answered. "It flows in me and it flows in Boron."

Fisher nodded. "The water does flow and will continue. Gordon is faithful and will keep faith with his people--so long as they keep faith with him. Lucian is the King of Liars. He is not ever to be trusted. And you who have shared water with me and with one another have power against him. Lucian has only the power which you grant him. Do not grant him power over you."

"Does it mean we will never be thirsty again, John Fisher?" a reedy voice from near the front asked. Fisher turned to a little boy standing near the fountain. The boy knew thirst intimately. His face had the same dried, sunken look John had seen in almost all the people he had met in Forneria. Even the days of plentiful water from the wells had not erased the memory of thirst

Fisher stooped to look into the child's brown eyes. He put his hand on the boys shoulder. "No, my son, you will drink every day from the wells of the earth, but so long as you trust the Father of us all, your heart will never thirst again."

"I understand," the boy said.

Fisher smiled and ruffled the child's hair then stood. He lifted his hand in a benediction and said, "May you never thirst," and stepped down.

Not many of the Travelers were in the plaza to hear Fisher. Jim Bitter brought the news to the wagon train. Squatting beside the center fire, with Ruth and his eldest son Willy beside him, and the youngest, little Jake, on his knee, he told the gathering what he had heard.

"He said the water still flows at Boron and if it flows there, I'd bet it flows at Copper Seep too," Bitter said.

"Great Lucian--" Birdwell began.

"John Fisher says Lucian is the King of Liars," Bitter said.

"And what is to make us believe Fisher is not a liar?" a voice grumbled.

"Have you already forgotten the water of Boron, or the stream pouring out from under the cliff at Copper Seep? The water in the wells here? The fountain? The trickle of water was loud as a shot when the people fell quiet to listen to John Fisher." Bitter hesitated, considering whether to say what he was thinking, but after a few moments he went on. "And I believe him because of what happened in the plaza two days ago. The Captain what brought Fisher here to Barstow was changed. After killing one of his own men for disobeying him, he was struck down with the power of John Fisher's words; the power of his eyes. Captain Fay fell to his knees and wept for what he had done, and when Fisher helped him up, he was a different man." A strange look came over Bitter's face as he continued. "He was changed and I was changed. I trust John Fisher. If he says there is water, there is water."

"Trust Gordon the Creator, through whom all power is given."

The Travelers who had been listening to Bitter turned around to see John Fisher, Captain Fay, Noah, and Thomas standing between two wagons at the edge of the crowd.

"May we come to your fire, Travelers?" Fisher asked.

"Please come share our fire," Bitter said eagerly, going to the four with little Jake still in his arms. "Have you eaten, sir? Captain? I am sorry I don't know your names. We have plenty."

"Thank you, James," Fisher said, but did not move to accept the invitation. "And you Ezra," Fisher asked without moving. "What do you say? Can I share your fire and your food?"

Ez pulled at his beard and studied Fisher as though he stood alone. Ez could almost feel the sweep of Fisher's eyes over him. It was as though Fisher could read his thoughts. This was not the same man Ez remembered from the first day. "Come, John Fisher," he said. "It's just Traveler stew and sage tea, but you're welcome to join us."

John stepped over the wagon tongue followed by the other three and came to the fire. They stood for a moment holding their hands out to warm them, for the night was desert cold. "Lucian offered a great reward for me, did he not?"

There was a gasp from the Travelers. Mothers pulled their children closer to their skirts. Fay, Noah, and Thomas all turned to look at Fisher.

Ez remembered the rapport which had developed between Fisher and himself when they rode together before Captain Fay...

And now the Captain stood with the man who had been his prisoner. Now the Captain was prisoner but of a different kind.

"Great Lucian said he would reward anyone who brought your body to his northern fortress," Ez said. Now the Travelers gasped at the completely truthful answer.

Fisher smiled. "Do you believe Lucian's promise?"

"No!" Bitter and others answered.

"Ezra," Fisher asked again "do you believe him?"

The Travelers looked to Ez and held their breaths for what he would answer.

"I believe Great Lucian wants you dead," Ez said. "And I think he would pay almost anything to have you so."

Fisher smiled again. "Will you kill me then, if I spend the night beneath your wagon?"

Now it was Ezra's turn to smile. "No, John Fisher. I owe you for a drink of water you once gave me. It would be inhospitable of me to kill a man while I still owe him. And, while I believe Great Lucian wants you dead, I am not so sure he will really pay."

"Then I think we should go north and find out if Lucian is as good as his word," Fisher said.

Ez and others shook their heads with confusion. "What do you mean?" Ez asked.

"I am going to seek Lucian tomorrow. These three will not let me go alone."

"Nor I, John Fisher," Jim Bitter said, stepping forward. He turned and handed Will to his mother, who took the child with an open mouthed look of shock.

Fisher caught his eye, just for a moment, nodded his ascent then went on, "Ezra, you first gave me water when I thirsted--I think you should sell me to Lucian, but I prefer you not kill me before the deal is made," Fisher said and looked steadily at Ezra.

The Traveler scratched thoughtfully beneath his beard then tipped his wide brimmed hat to the back of his head. "I thought you was a heat wiggle or a demon or a fool when I first seen you," Ez said. "Now I know I was right about the fool part. I think Great Lucian will eat us alive, me included, but if he don't eat me, I'd like to be there to collect after he eats you." His crooked smile was lost beneath his beard, but everyone could hear it in his voice.

For the first time since he had come to in the desert heat, John Fisher laughed.

Five

Katherine had never been a "reader" as such. She had read text books and as a teenager had a fling with paperback romances, but she found the romances silly and repetitive after she had read a dozen or so of them. She thought these Forneria stories were probably much like some romances-- written in a repetitive formula which kept only the simple-minded amused. But day after day she watched John and Joshua labor and argue and talk as they worked on the last--or what Lucian had told her would be the last-- Forneria story and she thought if she had been the one sweating over a story like the two of them, she would certainly want someone to read it, even if that someone was a spy.

Besides, she *was* curious about what made these books a prize for which Lucian was willing to spend a fortune to get the copyrights to. And by the converse, what made them so dear that Joshua was willing to spend a fortune and risk the approbation of his son in order to hand them over to a relative stranger. Joshua's library had several volumes of each of his books in several languages. The books had every sort of binding. As she looked more closely, wedged in among a dozen matched volumes hand bound in leather, she found a cheap paperback. She pulled this book from the shelf and flipped the cover open to the title page. She was surprised to find a hand written note on the page opposite the title. It said:

"*Joshua,*

You are the epitome of what I was talking about in this. I wanted to be what you have become. I wish you joy in your creation and peace in your life."

There was no signature, but below the note in sloppy lines of hand print was a poem.

SCRIBBLER

I want to be a Creator--
A god whose word calls from the void, solidity--
Who from the lifeless dust may call
The very spark which animates--
Whose thought doth life impassion--
Whose whim can make the very stars bow down.
And yet, I cannot lift my hand to create life--
Not e'en the smallest cell.
Nor make dust more than lifeless mud
By watering it with foolish tears.
But my conceit will not allow
That I am less than God,
And so I scratch out words,
Pretending they are living things.
And so, by scratching words, create the worlds
I cannot call to be.

The poem was not signed. Katherine read the note and the poem through several times wondering who had written them. She decided to ask. She quietly slipped into Joshua's room, hoping not to disturb him if he happened to be asleep. He seemed to be growing worse much more quickly now. In the last week he had had more bad days than good, and he had asked for morphine enough to knock him out more frequently. He had worked less on the book. John often came in to talk with him, but it was not always about the story. When she had first come to work, Joshua and John had been more like mentor and student. Now it seemed as though they were friends finding solace in one another.

"What time is it, Katherine?" Joshua asked, though there was a clock sitting on the table so he could see it.

She glanced at it and said, "It's two o'clock."

"A.m. or p.m.? I can see it's two o'clock, but with the curtains pulled tight, I can't tell morning from night," he said with the cranky sound of a sick child.

"It's afternoon."

"Is John here?"

"I don't know. I think so. Shall I get him?"

"Just tell him to find me a twenty-four hour clock."

"I could open the drapes."

"No!" he snapped. "I don't want to see outside! I just want to know what time it is."

"Sorry."

He sighed and said, "No, I'm sorry. I hate whiners! And now I am one."

"More like a grouch than a whiner," she said lightly and came to fluff his pillow. In order to do it she had to put the book down. She laid it on the swing table almost beneath Joshua's nose. He looked at it but did not even try to pick it up. His hands seldom worked to his brain's specification any more.

"What's the book?" he asked.

"It's one of the Forneria stories." she said as she picked it up again. "John suggested I read it so I could maybe understand why you two are so intense about this new book."

"Which one is it?"

"*Angels of the Coast.* It was strange the way it was stuck in with all the beautifully bound volumes. I haven't actually started it yet. I wanted to ask what the writing on the fly leaf was."

"This paperback is as precious to me as any of the leather bound volumes, so please be careful with it."

"I will be careful. What is the writing? It isn't signed."

"It came from a friend, another writer. He's dead now. He bought it somewhere overseas and sent it to me." Joshua's voice choked up with emotion.

"Are you all right Joshua? I didn't mean to..."

Joshua painfully lifted his hand and wiped at his eyes. "I'm all right. Just old man's tears. He never got much ink himself, but he always seemed happy about my success. Breaks my heart he isn't better known."

"I like the poem. It reminds me of you and John."

"Lloyd would be happy with that. He always said poetry was when the poet opened his heart to let the reader look in."

"I like that."

Joshua looked at Katherine silently for too long. "Why did you do it, Katherine?"

She turned to answer his look and decided to do him the courtesy of not denying her duplicity. "I needed the money. Lucian called me and offered me fifty thousand dollars for what he said would be a few months work, with another fifty if it stretched more than six months."

"You don't strike me as the type to be much swayed by money."

"My mother was sick for a long time. Even with me there to care for her, the bills stacked up. When she died, I barely had the money to bury her. With fifty thousand dollars I can pay off a big chunk of that debt."

"Not all of it?"

"About three quarters."

"You should have held out for more," he said. "He offered John a quarter million for the copyrights."

"Quarter million. Lot of money for something as intangible as copyrights."

"Not intangible. The Forneria books will probably go on to make thousands more dollars for as long as they are in print. At least the quarter million, and probably more. And the key words in my sentence are, *as long as they are in print.*"

"Lucian told me you would say something like that. He said you were obsessed with some idea about if the copyrights went to him, he would pull the books off the shelves."

Joshua laughed but the taste of it was bitter. "He told you, huh?"

"Yes. He said you were..." she trailed off.

"He said I was crazy. Non compos mentis."

"Well, yes."

"And I'd bet my last buck he had big crocodile tears in his eyes when he told you, didn't he?"

She blushed. "No, he didn't. He just..."

"Doesn't matter what *he just*...He is a skillful liar. You believed every word. Add belief to the money and you become a loyal minion."

The idea of being a *loyal minion* stung Katherine. "It wasn't a lie! I've seen and heard you and John plotting. You are going to give the copyrights to John and cut Lucian off completely."

"Not so. Luke will get all the rest of my estate, whatever is left after all the bills are paid. It may not be much, but he will get the rest. Just not Forneria. John will get Forneria."

"To keep Lucian from somehow destroying your pretend world," she said with flat disgust in her voice.

"He would!" Joshua said intensely. "He can never expect to sustain Forneria. Never create anything like it. But he can destroy it, and he will. If I let him."

"Why would he, Joshua?" she asked skeptically. "It makes no sense at all. They are just pulp fiction with potential to make him some more money. Why would he want to do hurt to himself?"

Joshua blinked at her a few times. He could have told her the same thing he had told the "tame Shrink" but he decided against it. Instead he said, "At the risk of giving you ammunition when it comes time to judge my competency, have you ever read the Bible?"

"No, not really. I wasn't raised in a church."

"A shame. Not the church part. Most churches--maybe all churches, I don't know--are havens for bigots or idiots, but the Bible is a book full of great tales to teach us great lessons. The one I am going to tell you now isn't just a straight ahead lesson. Some of it is implied, but it's still there. In the Bible Satan is the bad guy, but if everything comes out right at the end, Satan is going to be defeated. That's fine, but if everything is predestined to happen, why should anyone worry about the end? Satan is going to lose, but only if he lets the game continue to the end. But he won't let the game end. He can't win and he knows it, but he can destroy everything so no one wins. He can wipe all the pieces off the board like a child throwing a tantrum. He still loses, but now he can go sulk and tell himself the big lie--I WOULD HAVE WON IF ONLY THE GAME HAD FINISHED! It's the way children behave. It's the way many adults behave. Hitler told his generals to destroy everything in their paths as they retreated. Completely scorched earth. He couldn't win and he knew it, but he could destroy so much no one else could win either. Once he issued that command his generals knew he was nuts and knew they were defeated, so they were not so foolish as to destroy everything. Sometimes even fanatics have moments of sanity, though they seem to be few and far between."

"Are you saying Lucian is some kind of satanic evil guy because he wants the copyrights to your books? If you believe that you truly are insane," Katherine said shaking her head.

"I told you would think so, but ask Ed Chance what he knows about it. Or better yet, next time you see Lucian tell him the little story I just told you and see what kind of reaction you get. Now get out of here and leave me alone."

Katherine blinked back the mist from her eyes. She had come to like Joshua and did not want to see him as insane, or evil, or deluded, but it seemed those were the only choices left. Besides she had been found out as a spy which left only one choice. She sighed and stiffly said, "I'll have my stuff packed in half an hour and be gone. You can keep last week's salary."

"I didn't say you were fired!" Joshua snapped. "If you want to quit, go ahead and quit, but if you want to stay--for the sake of the money Lucian promised or any other reason--you can stay. But whatever the decision, make

167

it somewhere else. I'm tired and sick and I want you out of my sight for a little while."

Katherine was confused. "I don't understand. You want me to stay?"

"Replacing you would be a bigger pain in the ass than I need right now. You are a competent nurse. Besides, I know you are a spy. I couldn't be sure about anyone new. Now get out. And send John in."

Katherine turned away then turned back and held out the book she had brought in. "Shall I leave this here or return it to the Library?"

"If you're leaving my employ, please return it to the Library. If you are staying, I think you should read it and read Lloyd's poem again too. Maybe you'll begin to understand what this business with Lucian is really about."

Katherine looked at the lurid cover of the book with its background of billowing sails and it's foreground of a hero defending a damsel from slavering, evil pirates. She looked up at Joshua and thought how much more shrunken and ill he looked than even the few weeks before when she had first come. "I guess I'll stay, Joshua," she said. "I have to see how all this comes out." She turned and walked out the door.

Six

John Fisher sat on the pile of rubble that used to be Barstow watching the daylight grow in the east. He had not slept and the lack was making his whole body feel heavy. He wondered why he had decided to go north to Lucian, but it seemed the right thing to do. One way or another, saviors did battle with oppressors, whether they were demi-gods or conquerors. Fisher did not like the idea of doing battle with Lucian, but it appeared there would be no other way.

"You are right. There is no other way," the voice of the red bird agreed with his thought. Fisher focused his eyes through the dim dawn and saw the bird sitting a few feet away. It looked scruffy. Patches of feathers were missing and other parts were ruffled as though they would soon fall out.

"You don't look well," Fisher said.

"I'm not. I don't believe I will last all the way through the book. Doesn't matter. You are looking triumphant. You did well even without my help."

John thought he detected a note of change in the bird's tone. Maybe it was a note of regret. "Why are you here?" he asked. "You don't usually appear unless something is about to change drastically."

"Something is about to change drastically. Go on with your plan to face Lucian in his home. It is the only way you will ever reach the end."

"What is the end?"

"I can't tell you."

"Figuring out what to do would be much easier if I knew what the end was going to be."

The bird bobbed its head. "No doubt it would, but it would also make you some kind of seer, but you aren't a seer. You are a doer."

Again Fisher felt the bird was not telling him everything. "You have some idea about the end don't you?"

"Somewhat, but you will have the final word of it."

"Me? How? I can hardly make it from day to day. All these things are happening around me, but I don't feel as though I have any control of them at all."

"At this point you have only the barest control, but you have more as things go along. By the end you will have more control than any other human in Forneria, but don't expect it to mean you will be in total control. Right now I, in my Joshua form in the other world, am controlling many things, but I will hand control over to the other you before long."

"The other me did not know what he was getting into, did he?"

"Most times none of us do." The bird bobbed its head and flapped away toward the west.

Fisher watched until it disappeared and thought for a bit longer about saviors. There was something else about them he could not quite remember; something which slipped off the edge of his brain like a drop of water sliding down a windowpane. He looked around and saw there were many shiny black ravens who'd been watching him speak with the red bird. Now they watched him as he sat thinking. He could not tell if they had seen the red bird or not, nor did it really matter if they had. Idly he picked up a pebble, tossed it in his hand, threw it toward four or five of the birds who had been sitting in a row watching. The birds lifted lazily, not really threatened by the pebble. Circling as they had been for days, their search for carrion resumed.

Watching them lift on rising air, Fisher caught the liquid thought which had been escaping him. Saviors tended to die pretty often. As he watched the birds, a shiver which had nothing to do with the dawn breeze ran down his back.

"Beg pardon, John Fisher," Noah Simons interrupted his thoughts. "The droms are ready. We need to get on before the sun is up and it starts really getting hot."

"Thank you, Noah," Fisher said. He stood, shoving his thoughts to the back of his mind.

A dozen dromules stood ready beneath the faded blue desert sky. Six were saddled for riding and six loaded with food and water. Captain Fay had protested riding a drom. "A man looks like a crow standing on a manure pile riding a drom," he said.

Ezra and Jim Bitter, who had been handling droms their whole lives, laughed and agreed with him. Dromules were ugly, evil tempered, stubborn beasts which could try any man's patience, but they could go days without water and subsist on what little living plant matter they could find along the road. "Your horse wouldn't live a day without us pulling a water tank, Captain." Bitter said.

"But droms are gaited like three legged dogs! They'll rattle your bones loose in no time!"

"Yes sir, but they can outrun a horse over broken ground."

Fay snorted and gave in. He hated to admit anything was faster than his gelding.

Two groups of people stood waiting to say good bye, and twenty ravens watched and waited with them.

The Travelers kept together and separate from the Barstow survivors. Among the Travelers, Ezra and Jim Bitter shook hands and embraced family and friends. Ruth Bitter did not try to hold her husband from going.

"I hate to leave you, Ruthie, but I just feel like I have to." He looked worried.

"We'll be fine, Jim," she said. "We'll bring Gillem and his family into our wagon until they can get another built."

"And we'll all watch out for 'em, Bitter," Mandy said. "Just like always."

Bitter nodded his acceptance then leaned down and kissed his wife.

Ez listened to all this, apparently unmoved. After thirty years of marriage, he and Mandy were both more like two pieces of leather than a man and a woman.

"You be careful, old man," Mandy said. "You ain't as tough as you think you are."

Ez, his face stolid, nodded. He did not speak for fear his voice would break.

When Noah and John Fisher approached, all eyes turned to them. Many from the Barstow survivors murmured they would like to go with the six.

Fisher, hearing this, shook his head. "You cannot come with me. I would leave these five behind, but I do not know the way. I do not know what I am going into and would not want to take anyone more than these into danger. If you do not think you can stay here in Barstow, go over the mountains to Bernardo City or even into Los Angeles." He stopped and looked from the Barstow survivors to the Travelers and back. "I am sad to see even the sharing of water has not made one people of two. I ask you Travelers to stay in Barstow to help the townsmen rebuild. And you, townsmen, I ask you to help the Travelers as they recover from Lucian's destruction of their wagon and water tank. This world is too hard a place for us to be divided because of different lives. Now we must learn to trust and help one another."

Fisher turned to one of the droms and set his foot into the step stirrup.

"John Fisher," Emmaline, the daughter of Mandy and Ezra called and John turned back.

Emmaline held out one of the broad brimmed Travelers' hats. "To keep the sun off."

"Thank you, Em," he said, smiling as he put the hat on. Then he surprised the girl and himself by leaning over and kissing her on the forehead. "Remember me when I am gone, Em. Never let anyone forget."

"No one could ever forget you John Fisher," she said.

"If they could forget to worship Father Gordon, who created all, how could they not forget me?"

He turned back to the drom, put his foot in the step stirrup then lifted himself into the high-pronged saddle. The others mounted and when they were all balanced in their saddles, Fisher lifted his hand, "Tell everyone the time of Lucian's Dry is coming to an end. Share water with all who thirst..." He pointed at the ravens who still watched, "...even those who serve Lucian. And, may none of you ever thirst." He turned to Captain Fay and said, "Lead on Captain."

Seven

"I like the way you left Barstow," Gordon said. His voice was heavy, burdened with unremitting pain. "The kiss was a nice touch." He was sitting cranked up in his bed with the computer screen before him. John thought he seemed a little better today, despite the sound of him, but he also realized it might be wishful thinking. "It seemed like the right thing to do."

"Remember our little talk about characters doing what they do without your volition?"

"Yeah, I remembered." John fell silent and sat, eyes unfocused, chin balanced on his thumb, teeth gnawing at the side of his wring finger.

"Something bothering you?" Joshua asked after a while.

Fisher continued to gnaw at his finger for a moment before answering. "I don't think I am still comfortable with using myself as savior in this. It was one thing when you were doing most of the writing. It was kinda fun, and funny, but now I am doing a lot...I mean...it seems the height of hubris."

"I didn't do it to make you uncomfortable."

"I know, I know. You did it to pull me into the story--which I still don't understand."

Joshua, whose eyes were continually blood shot, now with drugs and with lack of sleep, looked into Fisher's eyes as though to communicate telepathically. "I'm not sure how I did it either, or if I did it. One school of thought says if you know a person or a thing's true name, you can control it utterly. I think I know your true name, but then again, I think such stuff is

174

nonsense. I think we only do what we allow ourselves to do. I think you believed all along Forneria was real, and when you began to be named as part of it you willingly went there. It is a sort of conspiracy of creation between us. And as for hubris, perhaps it is." He drew in a labored breath and let it out again. "Perhaps you'll have to pay for what I have made of you. If you continue with it. Perhaps I am paying right now for my own arrogance in ever having thought to try creating a world like Forneria."

John harrumphed. "Whom the gods would destroy they first make arrogant?" His mouth corners turned up in a knowing smile. "Apologies to Shakespeare," he said.

"Shakespeare created worlds too," Gordon said, "but he put them on a bare stage and hypnotized London into believing they were seeing Verona and Venice and Scotland."

"Yeah, but he never put himself into his plays, and he never even thought of making himself the savior of any of those worlds he created."

The two were quiet for a time, sitting like men who had been friends for fifty years, men who had no need to fill silence with pointless conversation. "There is a poem by a friend of mine… came back to my memory the other day," Joshua said. "Katherine found it in the flyleaf of the paperback edition of *Angels of the Coast*."

"I've seen it."

"I think Lloyd hit it on the head, and whether it is hubris or not, anyone with our kind of hunger for creation can't help themselves. They will find a way to create and they will battle to save their creations. Did you know one of Hemingway's wives once lost the only copy of a manuscript of his? She lost it on a train in Europe. It was never found again. It wasn't long after that he divorced her."

"I doubt if a lost manuscript was the only reason."

"No, probably not, but I'd bet my last buck it had a lot to do with it. And the moral to this story is, screw with a Creator's creation at your own peril."

175

John rubbed his fingers across his forehead and closed his eyes. He was incredibly tired. *And if I am this exhausted, what must Joshua feel like.* "By the way," he said, eyes still closed, "Katherine is the one who sent the manuscript to Lucian."

"Glad you figured it out. Lucian said it was you. Said you wanted to rub his nose in it, but I couldn't buy that. I'm arrogant enough to think I have come to know at least a little of what you will and won't do."

"Maybe you don't know me as well as you think," Joshua said softly, more as though he were talking to himself than to John.

"Meaning what?"

"I had a feeling she was a spy from the beginning. I mean look at her. All the other people off the list of nurses were trolls. Why would Doc Erdinger send nine trolls and a beauty? Didn't make sense. I just wonder how Lucian managed to put her on the list to begin with. Maybe Erdinger is working both ends against the middle. No matter. Anyway, I could have said no, and when I figured out she was sending him the pages, I could have fired her, but I didn't. And as far as I know she is still sending pages to him. She sneaks in here, downloads the pages onto a disk when she thinks I am knocked out. So maybe I *am* rubbing his nose in it. I wouldn't put it past me. I've known me for a long time, and I can be a whirling son of a bitch sometimes."

"Ah come on, Joshua, don't go getting all down on yourself now. You're human and humans make mistakes."

"Yeah, I suppose, but when I think back, I was about as lousy a father as you could hope for. I didn't beat Lucian, or lock him up in a dark room, or sexually abuse him, but I was a lousy father. Hardly available to him when he was a kid. He mostly was raised by housekeepers and babysitters. Abuse of a different kind, but it's abuse all the same."

"All right, enough of that crap," John growled. "Even if it was true, which I'm not agreeing with, it is long past fixing, and if you intend to stay sane, you have to get on with the present."

"What's the point of staying sane when I'm a dead man anyway?" Gordon said with a finality which was new. Until today Joshua had always been as upbeat as his pain would allow, but today there was a darkness to his spirit, and it spread through the room.

"Ah Shit," John said and stood up. "You can wallow in past mistakes all you want to, but you'll do it without me." He headed for the door.

"John"

Fisher turned back.

"I'm not going to live to finish the book," Joshua said. "My motor control is all but gone. I won't be able to lift my hands at all pretty soon. I have almost no control of my bowels and bladder. Forneria is about to fall on your shoulders completely. You know more or less where we were going with the book. Keep it alive for me; it's all I can ask."

John didn't trust his voice to say yes so he just nodded his head and went out.

Eight

Three weeks out from Barstow, John Fisher and company, weary, hot, and thirsty stopped for the night beside a spring where two, sun-blasted cottonwood trees grimly clung to life. The spring was called Tuchinara for the ancient abandoned city which could be seen on the mountains far away to the east.

They watered the droms and started a cook fire. When they sat down to rest, they looked toward the eastern mountains.

Tuchinara, set high above the desert floor, could be seen for miles. It gleamed red-gold like fire in the western sun, drawing the eyes of the six like magic. A half dozen moving black silhouettes crossed the reflective city. ravens circled, watching all.

The travelers were so used to seeing the gleaming black birds they no longer noticed them.

"It is very beautiful" Captain Fay said staring at the gleaming city. "I have seen it several times before, but I have never been closer than this. I would like to go there and see if it as beautiful close up as it is from afar."

"Wouldn't go in there was I you," Noah Simon said. "I've heard it's haunted."

"Bah," Thomas said. "No such thing as haunts. Probably just wind moaning around the buildings."

"When I was young and dumb we used to cut Sweetenin' up round yonder," Ezra said. "Bitter's Pa and some others dared me to go in."

All eyes turned to Ez.

"Did you go?" Fay asked

"Yep. Shook like a leaf the whole time." He laughed at the memory. "Didn't find no ghosts, but it is a strange place. Made outa worked stone from a big quarry back from the city. No small stones neither. Some of 'em bigger than a Traveler wagon. An' they ain't stuck together with nothing. No cement or mud or nothing. And them stones is just smooth as glass.

"I heard the buildings were round," Noah Simon said.

"Some of 'em. Some more oval than round. Ain't no corners no where for sure. Even places kinda look square ain't got no sharp angles."

"Wonder who coulda built such a place?" Bitter asked rhetorically. John Fisher looked at the city fading into night and remembered who built it. "The Tuchinar were once the servants of Gordon in a war among the stars," he began. "And when the war was through, Gordon made Forneria for them as a reward. He made all the mountains and valleys and animals and Forneria was paradise. And he gave paradise to the Tuchinar to live and grow and prosper forever."

The others all looked to Fisher expectantly. "If Gordon gave Forneria to them forever, where are they?" Captain Fay asked.

Fisher, remembering, but not as though he had been there, said, "After a thousand years some of the Tuchinar were no longer happy. They envied Gordon his power and wanted to be Creators themselves, but rather than ask Gordon for the power to create, they said, "We are powerful. We can make even the air serve our purposes." They began to seek ways to create without their Creator's help. First they built machines to control the earth and air, to control the sea and rain, but it was not enough. They were not satisfied with controlling the world Gordon had given them so they took some of Gordon's creations and used the power of their machines to change them. Dromules came from those changes. The Tuchinar mixed animals which would not ever have mixed and using their power created Dromules.

"But some of the Tuchinar did not use the machines to make good and useful beasts such as the Droms. Some made loathsome and dangerous animals. They delighted in the harm these beasts could do to others. They would set the beasts to battle one another to death, and this did not please Gordon, but he had promised Forneria would be theirs forever and being a kindly Creator, he did not punish the Tuchinar.

"Not all the Tuchinar believed the few were doing right to so cruelly use Gordon's creation so they began to chastise those who had strayed into cruelty saying, 'This is evil. It is not what Gordon wishes--for you to use his creations for such perversion.'

"But those who had strayed laughed at the others. 'We will do as we will do. We are gods on Forneria. Our will is supreme.' Still, Gordon was loathe to punish the Tuchinar; he looked away from the evil. He asked those who still served him to continue to speak with those others, to persuade them of their evil and change them back to the true ways of Gordon, and the true servants did as they were asked. After a time the evil Tuchinar grew tired of the reasoning of Gordon's servants and began to strike them down and kill them, but not satisfied with the mere debasement of Gordon's creation by murder, they used their knowledge and the power they had gained from their perverse deeds to bring their victims, whose souls had returned to Gordon, to life again as monstrous slaves. These soulless beasts could only be sustained by the life energy of those still possessed of souls. The carnage was horrible.

"Gordon then repented of having given the Tuchinar Forneria for their own. He called to those still faithful to him saying, 'Go to the Valley of the Great Trees, and I will bring you home to me, and give you a new place, where you will live forever in peace.' So the faithful did as they were told, gathering in the Valley of the Great Trees to wait upon Gordon. When the evil Tuchinar saw the others departing they were angry and fearful of their soulless slaves, afraid those might turn upon them, having no other sustenance. So they set their slaves to hunt after the faithful who had departed the city.

"But Gordon would not let the soulless ones harm the faithful. He protected them and made them so the beasts could not see them. When the last of them were inside the Valley of the Great Trees, he sent an earthquake to make a landslide which closed the pillars of the Valley. The soulless ones were defeated and turned again on their Creators. Those evil Tuchinar then cried out to Gordon in their fear and asked Gordon to have mercy on them and save them from the evil they themselves had created. Gordon, hearing their cries, relented from his vengeance, and bound up the abominations the evil Tuchinar had created. And the evil Tuchinar asked to be taken home like their brothers, but Gordon would not take those who had thought themselves better than their Creator. Instead, he scattered them over the universe to live alone in eternity."

When Fisher fell silent, the sounds of the night filled the camp, sounds making the five look around them nervously and move closer to the fire. After a little, Thomas Pitney, who did not believe in ghosts, asked, "Is it true, John Fisher, or is it just a tale to frighten children?"

"It may frighten children but it is true," Fisher said.

"But why have I never heard this before, my Lord?" Captain Fay asked. Others agreed. The only thing they knew about the abandoned city was its name, Tuchinara.

"When Gordon created the new people of Forneria, the ancestors of us all, he left nothing save the name for you to know. He has sent me to tell you the rest."

"But how do you know, John Fisher?" Ezra asked skeptically. "You was born in Forneria just like the rest of us warn't you?"

Fisher nodded. "But before I was a man of Forneria, I was with Gordon my Father. I knew the battle among the stars. I knew the Tuchinar. I *was* before Forneria, and I will continue *after* Forneria, not as you see me, but in my true form."

Noah, with a troubled look, asked, "But how do we know this is true?"

Fisher looked from man to man and opened his mouth to speak but, Jim Bitter spoke first with absolute conviction. "We know it is so because John Fisher has told us it is so. If it were other than this, he would have told us."

Fisher smiled. "You were truly changed in Barstow, James. Gordon has given you understanding beyond what your eyes can see. When I am gone, you must remember this day and tell others." The five who had accompanied Fisher looked at one another. All had heard what he had said, but none of them understood what he meant. Thomas asked, "When you are gone?"

"Some day I will be called back to my Father Gordon. When I am, you must remember me."

"But John Fisher, you...you have power," Noah protested. "You are taking us to challenge Lucian. If you die, Lucian will destroy us all. No one will be left to remember you."

Captain Fay, military still, despite having been so changed in the plaza said, "Lucian will be defeated. You must believe it, Noah. I believe it is Gordon's will that Lucian, who is his son, also will not destroy Forneria with his Great Dry. I can believe nothing else. John Fisher calls water from dry wells and breaks hearts only to make them whole again. Lucian will be defeated."

John Fisher nodded his agreement, but then said, "Even so, no man is promised tomorrow. Not even me. All who live do so at Gordon's behest and Gordon can require his gift of life of anyone at any moment. "The six fell silent thinking their own thoughts in the flickering firelight. At last Bitter and Ezra rose and dipped stew from the pot which had been warming on the fire and, as though their movement had freed the others, they all rose and took food. They returned to their places, eating in the continuing silence. The first sliver of the new moon rose and shed its silver glow on the desert. Tuchinara seemed to gather the feeble light to itself. Its presence was felt by all the men though none of them looked up to see the pearlescent glow.

"John Fisher," Thomas asked after a while. "Has one of the Tuchinar machines caused Lucian's Dry? Is Lucian a Tuchinar?"

Nine

John slouched in his usual chair in Joshua's room as he watched the boss sleep. Joshua was shrunken to a bundle of sticks wrapped in parchment. John held a piece of paper in his hand. The paper had been courier delivered an hour before. It was a new offer from Lucian. He was offering John a half million dollars now. Half to be paid for a signature on the enclosed agreement and half to be paid after Joshua's death at Lucian's receipt of the copyrights.

Half a million dollars was more money than John had ever thought of possessing, especially all at one lump--or two lumps. If he signed the paper in the presence of a notary, the first half of the money could be his in twelve hours. It was tempting. But then John remembered the look on Emmaline's face when he kissed her on the forehead. The look of all the people in Barstow. He held each of their lives in his hands. He could bring an end to the world of Forneria just by signing the papers.

For the hundredth time the thought pulled him up short. The line between the "real world" and Forneria seemed to be getting fuzzier as the days passed. There were moments when John *knew* he had fallen into some kind of psychosis, but a moment after, he knew clearly the difference between Forneria and California. Joshua had pulled him into Forneria with his fascination of creation; fascination for the creating of Forneria which more and more had fallen to him as Joshua grew weaker; had pulled him deeper into the creative process.

And now Lucian had added to the pressure and incipient confusion of creation with a simple way for John to unplug himself from it all. Just sign the paper. No more worries. No more dreams, no more Forneria--which thought brought him up short yet again--back at the beginning of the cycle he had been running through since the first time Lucian had offered him money.

Fisher was so caught up in his thoughts the noise of the opening door as Katherine came in startled him. "I wondered where you were," Katherine said in a half whisper. "I thought you would be at your computer."

John delayed a moment. "Courier delivered this a while ago."

He held the papers out to Katherine who took them, looked over them, and handed them back. "Lot of money," she said. "A little more than thirty pieces of silver."

"Lot more, and I don't even have to kiss someone to betray them all. To collect I just sell out a world."

Katherine turned, glanced at him, and understood this was a real and troubling decision to him. John's brow was more furrowed than usual and he looked more tired. "You're buying into all of Joshua's nonsense, aren't you?"

He turned his eyes up to her and didn't turn them away. At last she broke off the contact, turning her eyes down.

~*~

Katherine felt Fisher's belief in Forneria like a flash of heat. Two weeks before she probably would have thought the whole question silly. Now she had read *Angels of the Coast,* was reading *The Miners,* and though she did not believe as Joshua and John seemed to that Forneria was a real place with real people, she understood how much these stories could affect the reader. She had almost come to think of the Forneria books as histories of some foreign land, not actually fiction.

"I think," Fisher began after a little. "I think I am going to go on finishing it, at least until Joshua is beyond being betrayed."

Katherine smiled with some cynicism. "And maybe Lucian will jack up the price some more," she said.

John stood. "Yeah, maybe he will," he said and walked to the door. "Let me know when the boss wakes up. I'll be in my room."

~*~

In his room John flopped into the desk chair. He tapped the computer mouse. The screensaver blinked off to reveal what he had been working on when Lucian's offer was delivered. Forneria and his--or rather John Fisher's--departure from Barstow. He had written it from a half remembered dream, and as he had tapped away at the keys, the dream came more and more clearly until it felt as though he had been there to taste the water, to smell the sweat of the crowd, and feel Emmaline's smooth forehead with his lips. *If I continue the story, if I end up as the publishing author, I'm going to change the name of the savior. It's just too egocentric to go on using my name in the book when my name will be on the cover along with Joshua's.*

He looked at the offer from Lucian again. He considered how much money a half million dollars really was. *Even if I actually finish the book, even if it gets published, I might never see anything like this much money. How much are the copyrights really worth? Will I ever realize this much from them if I do get to keep them?*

There was also the subject of his own work. If he continued with Forneria, a world not of his own creation, what would it do to the worlds he might someday create in his own work? This was a creative swamp full of quicksand and alligators. If he took up Joshua's world, it might swallow him. Already he had tried to break free enough to write a story of his own, but Forneria would not let go of his mind long enough to even begin another story.

The phone beside the computer rang and John answered it.

"He's awake," Katherine said.

John dropped the phone back into its cradle without a word. After a moment he hit the button and sent the computer file to Joshua's computer, picked up Lucian's offer, and headed for Joshua's room.

Katherine was still in the room going about her nurse business or at least pretending to.

"How you doing, boss?" he said sitting down.

"Been better."

Joshua's voice which had been a strong, pleasant baritone was now whispery thin.

"Stupid question. Sorry."

"How long have I been out?"

"Couple or three hours."

"Have you been working?"

"Before. I just sent the stuff to you. Some small changes on the exit from Barstow. You can read it when you feel like it. In the last couple hours I've been cogitating on this." He held it out toward Joshua, but most of the control of Gordon's hands was gone now. He could hardly lift his arms.

"What is it?" he asked.

"Temptation. Lucian has upped his price for the copyrights."

"How much?"

"Half a million."

Joshua ran his eyes over Fisher's face. "Considering it?" he asked.

Fisher raked his bottom teeth over his top lip in the silence then said, "Yeah. Considering it. Lot of money."

"Not enough. Call him back and make a counter offer. Tell him ten million," Joshua said with tiny twist of bitterness which strengthened and sharpened his voice.

"He'd never go for that. It's too much."

"Don't you believe it. He has it. He can replace it by looting a couple of medium sized companies, and he won't hesitate to put widows and orphans on the street if it will destroy Forneria."

Katherine stopped pretending to be busy and turned around, her face red with indignation. "What an awful thing to say about your own son!"

Joshua turned his head enough to see Katherine. "You think I'm exaggerating? Lucian has no conscience when it comes to getting what he wants. He hasn't since he was a child. He's made a fortune by being ruthless and he hates me enough to do whatever he has to. You don't believe me, call him. Go ahead. Put it on the speaker phone. Let John make the offer and see what happens."

"He gives his time and money to every good cause in the world," she protested. "He's on the boards of three hospitals I know of. He cares about people. He helps people."

"He does so to make sure eyes turn away when he guts companies and breaks them up, laying off the people working there." Joshua was breathing hard to put all the strength he could muster into what he was saying. "Call him. If you want to know the real Lucian, call him!"

Fisher looked from Katherine to Joshua to the paper still in his hand. "What if I do and he says OK?"

"Then take it and be damned. I'm too tired to care any more." He closed his eyes and continued to breathe, wheezing asthmatically.

Fisher breathed deeply himself, as though trying to get more air into Joshua's lungs then he turned to the phone. He picked up the receiver and dialed the number on the letter in his hand. When the phone rang, he pushed the button for the speaker and hung up the hand set.

Lucian answered with a curt "Yes."

John, hesitated a moment then said, "Lucian, this is John Fisher. I received your offer."

Now it was Lucian who hesitated. "Very well. Have you called to accept?"

"No, I want to make a counter offer."

They could hear Lucian take a breath and let it out slowly. "And what is your counter offer?"

John looked at Katherine who waited with her mouth slightly open. He looked at Joshua whose eyes were still closed. "Ten million," he said. "I want ten million dollars. Half now and half when I hand over the copyrights."

Almost before the words were gone from the room Lucian said, "Done. I'll have papers to you in an hour."

Katherine's mouth fell open. "Oh my God," she said. "Oh my God. You are as insane as your father."

"Who's that?" Lucian snapped.

"Katherine, the spy you sent to be my nurse," Joshua said. "She didn't believe you would pay anything to destroy Forneria. I think she does now."

"Fisher, do we have a deal or not?" Lucian demanded. "You made the offer and I accept. We have a deal!"

John blinked and started to say something, then thought better of it and said, "No. No deal."

"I accepted your offer! We have a deal!"

"I didn't say I agreed, and there is nothing on paper. I don't agree and there is no deal. There never will be a deal. Forneria will live as long as I can keep it alive."

The silence coming through the phone was viscous, thick with malice, flowing like toxic syrup. At last, with tight control, Lucian said, "You will never get those copyrights. Never." And the phone disconnected.

Joshua's labored breathing was the only sound in the room. "Thank you, John," he said between gasps. "Thank you."

Katherine, who had been frozen in place, recovered her nurse essence and crossed to her patient. She picked the oxygen mask from the regulator and placed it over Joshua's face. She lifted the stethoscope from around her neck, put it in her ears, and pressed it to his chest. After listening for a few moments, she straightened and pumped the blood pressure cuff.

"Call an ambulance, John. His heart is laboring and irregular and his lungs are rattling."

"Joshua," Fisher said, "Joshua?"

Gordon opened his eyes, focused on Fisher for a moment then closed them again.

John Fisher turned and dialed 911.

Ten

The droms plodded along six abreast in their ragged gate, and all six men riding them pondered Captain Fay's opinion of droms. All were sore from the shaking the beasts gave them. By comparison, the rough bump and rattle of a hard wooden wagon seat began to be remembered for its surpassing comfort. The riders rested their aching bones by walking and leading the droms. It was hot work to walk, but walking a part of the day was the lesser discomfort.

Above them five ravens circled and rode the up drafts from the heated desert floor. They did not swoop down close, but they stood out against the clear heat-faded blue of the sky. They circled and watched as though the little troop were carrion, or would be soon.

Fisher saw the shimmer of a mirage in the heat of the afternoon, but he disregarded it. There were mirage lakes all over the desert of Forneria. He had seen hundreds since leaving Barstow so another one was nothing to be noticed, except every time he looked up, the mirage was still there. Usually they made a brief appearance, disappearing with just the slight change of angle brought by the movement of his drom, but this lake continued shimmering at the edge of the world and growing. In fact, it appeared to have towers sprouting from it. At last he asked if anyone else saw the massive towers above a lake ahead of them.

"You ain't crazy, Fisher. It ain't just a heat wiggle. They really is a big old lake up yonder. Some might even call it a sea," Ezra said.

"It is Lake Mono," Bitter said. "About deep as the knuckle of your finger. Four five inches maybe."

"Mono? Never heard of it," Noah said.

"No reason you should have," Captain Fay said. "This place is so desolate Lucian's army doesn't even patrol it. There is nothing here. How do Travelers know about Mono?"

"We harvest Sweetenin' and go where it grows," Ezra said.

"Nothing grows here!" Fay protested.

"Not now. Sweetenin' grows near places where the water's gone brackish, and Mono is 'bout as brackish as they come," Bitter answered.

"Sweetenin's been gone since Bitter was a child," Ezra said. "Used to grow on the West side of the Mono, but between Travelers and no rain at all making the lake get thicker, don't grow no more."

"Are there buildings in it?" Thomas asked.

"No. Alkali and salt pillars. They ain't as big as they look from here. Tallest one's maybe twice as tall as a man."

"And the water?" Fisher asked.

"So much alkali in it now a wagon load of Sweetening won't make a cup of it fit to drink. Way more salty than the ocean," Bitter said. "So thick now you can float a rock on it," Ez said, a smile tugging at the corners of his mouth beneath his beard. "If it's kinda flat. Rounder one'll sink--but slow."

Fisher glanced at the older Traveler. "You wouldn't lie to a stranger now would you, Ezra?" He asked with a laugh.

"Never would, John Fisher. Never would."

"He might stretch the truth a little though," Jim Bitter added with a laugh.

"I suspected as much," Fisher said.

They rode on into the fading afternoon. The heat seemed to grow more oppressive as they drew closer to the alkali lake. The desert wind, which always seemed to move across the ground, blew less and less. Sweat usually evaporated in the wind, but now in the still air it rolled down the faces of the

men. The humidity made it difficult to breathe as did the alkali fumes rising from the lake. When the sun reddened and moved down to touch the far away mountain range, Ezra called a halt among the first of the salt pillars. "I believe we need to rest a bit, eat something, sleep a little and go on when the moon rises. I hate being down here by the Mono. Always so sticky it's miserable, and the alkali stinks and burns your throat. We'll get out of here as soon as we can."

"So the alkali is what smells?" Noah asked.

"I think maybe they used to be fishes or something lived in there. The smell always reminds me of spoiled fish," Bitter said.

"Ain't been nothing living there for a thousand year I'd bet, 'cept a little Sweetenin," Ez said. "Takes a long time for water to thicken up like that. Even sea water."

They climbed off their droms to sit down in the shade of some of the salt pillars. They drank sparingly from the water bags and gave the droms a little also. They had to be wary watering the droms because the animals were clever. They would drink the whole bag given the chance. "It'll be a couple hours till dark and an hour more till moonrise, so get some sleep," Captain Fay said. Bitter and Ezra agreed and when the saddle cinches were eased on the droms, the men tipped their broad brimmed hats down over their eyes and slept.

John Fisher did the same though he knew he would not sleep. Sleep was something which had deserted him. He could rest with eyes closed but did not even doze. The lack of sleep was really not much of a bother to him now. At first he had felt heavy and tired without it, but now his mind and senses seemed to be sharpened to a realm of hyper-sensitivity. Every place, every thing, even the smallest detail of the trek, was etched into his mind. When he closed his eyes, he could recall everything. He almost felt he could remember each grain of sand, each withered leaf, each cactus barb which had crossed his vision. Forneria seemed to be more and more within him as well as around him.

A sound of wind stirred but not a cooling breeze. This turn of air brought a sudden thick wash of the alkali stink up from the lake. The smell,

sulfurous like the stink of a sewer, caused Fisher to gag and brought him from his thoughts. He sat up, pushing back his hat from his eyes. The sun was down but complete darkness had not come, only deep dusk which obscured but did not hide a thing. Fisher turned his eyes toward the direction from which the wind blew trying to see what was causing the stink but saw nothing. He turned his head trying to shield his nose in the crook of his elbow but it was no use. The stink seemed to thicken.

The sound of wind rose. Out in the center of Mono Lake what looked like a shining ribbon of light rose and grew. It illuminated the pinnacles sticking up from the shallow lake. Fisher narrowed his eyes trying to make out more detail, but the shining ribbon was no more than a twist of light whirling like a dust devil with a hazy veil made of water vapor rather than dust. As Fisher watched, the spinning water spout grew and moved toward the shore where the six rested.

Fisher stood and walked through the deepening twilight toward the edge of the water never taking his eyes off the expanding waterspout. He stopped with his boot toes in the alkali water. It was difficult to tell how large the rotating column was, but it seemed perhaps three times the height of a man. It was moving swiftly toward the shore now, toward where he stood waiting.

The moon began to rise and the golden light of it glinted off the whirling water like a mirror reflecting lamplight. Suddenly, the glow of reflection formed itself into a shape Fisher had seen before. He had seen it when he read *TUCHINARA,* the first of the Forneria stories. It was a man dressed in full Tuchinar armor. A corner of Fisher's mind noticed how, even in the first creation of Gordon's mind, the Creator had borrowed ideas. The huge man reflected in the water spout would have been called a conquistador in other contexts. He wore a bucket shaped helmet with a brim, pointed at the front and back, a shining steel breast plate and shin guards. His boots had pointed steel toes so they could be used as weapons in close fighting. But more than recognizing the model for this reflection, Fisher recognized the man wearing the armor. It was Lucian, or rather the model of Lucian Joshua had built in the story. This Lucian wore a

pointed beard and while this model's eyes were more piercing than the real Lucian's, Fisher saw the same fire in those eyes he had seen at their first meeting.

The whirling water stopped a few feet away from Fisher as though it could not leave the lake. The stench of the wind maintaining the column was over powering. "Why did you not die where I left you?" The Tuchinar said, its voice huge and echoing, though the nearest reverberating surface was many miles away.

"If you had only knelt to me, we could have saved so much trouble. It was why I brought you to the desert from Fort Bouchet. If you had bowed your will to mine, you could have had all the riches of Forneria for yourself and in that other world too."

Suddenly Fisher remembered: this was how he had come to be in the desert where the Travelers had picked him up. Lucian had taken him from his prison and offered him riches and power and luxury here in this world. If only John had done nothing--but go to the mansion Lucian had promised, and amuse himself with all the riches, servants and concubines--nothing else. Only bow.

"Lucian, you know I could not simply let you have Forneria. It is too precious to your father. It has become too precious to me."

"ARRGH!" Lucian roared, as Fisher felt the concussion of the sound. "If I must be confined here, why can I not rule here?"

"Because you would destroy what your father created."

"What I created! Did I not make the droms which serve these creatures? Did I not change the birds to be my messengers? Did I not create...?"

"No, you did not create!" Fisher contradicted. "You and the other Tuchinar only stole what your father had created and changed it. Then those power greedy ones, the ones like you, perverted even the little good you had done."

"Lies! I create all, I control all, I will destroy all! This place, these creatures so precious to Father, I will destroy. They will die slowly of thirst and heat. I will make this paradise Joshua took from us an everlasting hell of blazing sun and melting stone and sulfurous wind where no creature may ever live again."

"This is not victory, Lucian. It is a tantrum. To destroy all is not to win."

"By torturing his creatures, by unmaking his world, by living beyond Joshua I am victorious."

Fisher reeled back. The hate was the overwhelming stench which rolled out of the fetid alkali lake. What Lucian had said implied he knew there was the other world where Joshua was sick.

"You are surprised, Fisher? You think I am only of the world my father has made? Like you, I have one foot in the other world as well. Gordon wanted me here as well as there so I came, but not to play the puppet, and soon I will control. Soon I will destroy in Forneria and in that other world."

John was having trouble breathing. He had thought his was the only power from the world of the Creator, and the belief had made what must be done seem doable. Once he had begun to know Forneria, truly know it, he had felt that simple perseverance would bring him to the successful conclusion; simply plodding on through whatever adventures Joshua's mind had devised was all John was required to do. Now the surety with which he had spoken to the crowd in Barstow seemed hollow. It was not just a matter of continuing to share water among themselves and treating one another with mercy. There was more; there was harder; there was more dangerous; there was possibly defeat.

Fisher's mind spun wildly with these realizations, finding nothing to brake the chaotic careering. There must be something. Joshua would not have built a story without the possibility of victory for himself and his creatures.

Suddenly his mind stopped whirling as though a brake had been applied. He thought he saw it. The possibility of survival. "If you are so powerful Lucian, if you are truly 'Great Lucian,' why did you not simply kill me when I refused to bow to you?"

"ARRGH!" Lucian howled again. "Because *he* would not let me!" The misty whirling conquistador shot out his arm and pointed.

Fisher looked where Lucian pointed. Sitting atop one of the alkali towers in silhouette against the now risen full gold moon was Joshua's avatar, the red bird.

"He controlled. He still controls," Lucian hissed. "But soon, soon he will not. Soon my father will be dead and you will be left alone. You will be meat for my messengers!"

The Tuchinar lifted its arms and threw back its head with a howling laugh which made the Mono towers tremble. The demonic laughter echoed back from the far mountains, so loud it made Fisher's head feel as though it were crushed.

Lucian disappeared and with him the waterspout. A thousand times quicker than it had formed and come to the shore it disintegrated, dropping the stinking alkali water down on Fisher in a pounding rain. The volume of water was so huge it drove Fisher down onto the sand as though thrown there by an ocean wave. He lay on the gray-white sand gasping for breath. A copper salty taste was in his mouth. He raised his hand and found blood flowed from his nose and ears. His eyes ached as though some one had tried to pry them out of their sockets.

"I am sorry, John," the red bird wheezed. It had flown down to make a barely controlled landing beside him. It was terribly ragged now with many patches of feathers gone. Fluid ran from the black bead eyes and the voice, once so quick and clear and sassy was a thin creaky whisper. "I can not help you any more. Now Forneria is yours. Save it. Save my creatures" the bird begged. "Save my children. Please."

The bird cocked its head in an echo of its previous pert manner and disappeared into the stinking night.

Eleven

Joshua was taken directly to intensive care. Katherine was allowed to go with him because she was his nurse, but John had no visitor's rights at all. Literary assistants were employees and employees were not allowed into intensive care units to see their bosses so John was stuck in a medium sized yellow walled waiting room parked on an uncomfortable couch. Others in the waiting room were clumped together in small groups, held to each other by the glue of their own concerns. There was a bank of telephones marked with the numbers of the ICU units, but he did not know which unit Joshua was in. Besides, whoever answered probably would not have told him a thing anyway. Almost an hour later, Katherine came out to the waiting room. John went to her when she was barely in the door. "So what's happening? How is he?"

Katherine, nurse face firmly in place, said, "He is doing as well as can be expected. He has some fluid in his lungs and his heart seems to be laboring. They have him hooked up to a heart monitor and oxygen and saline drip."

"Is he conscious?"

She hesitated then said, "Not really. He seems delirious. He doesn't seem to be aware of what is around him, but his eyes are open part of the time and he keeps mumbling. Nothing much coherent."

"Nothing much? What is he saying?"

She swept her eyes over his face as if deciding whether or not to tell him and Fisher finally grabbed her arm above the elbow and commanded, "Tell me!"

"He keeps saying the names of the characters in the story you two were writing." Her self-control suddenly slipped a little. "After what Lucian said on the phone...Oh God! This craziness has hurt Joshua so much! It may have killed him."

"Stop it," Fisher said. "The boss isn't dead yet. He's stayed alive by force of will. I can't think his will has deserted him now." She heard the slight, flat note of hopeful fear in what John said and wondered about it. The way he said *Boss* sounded like *Dad.* After a moment of silence John asked, "Has anyone called Lucian?"

Katherine's mouth opened a little in surprise. "But..." she began.

"Somebody needs to call Lucian," he said vehemently.

"They hate each other," she protested. "Why should Lucian care?"

"I don't know if he does, but if it was my father, I'd want to know no matter how much I hated him. Besides, it isn't for Lucian, it's for the boss."

"Joshua? Why would..."

"Lucian may hate him, but the boss still loves and cares about his son. You should have listened in on more of our conversations and worried less about getting Lucian the manuscript," he said with a little acid. Katherine's face reddened. "Call him," John said. "He needs to know."

After a moment she pulled her cell phone from her pants pocket and hit a speed dial button. In a moment she said, "Hello, Lucian?" She paused to listen then said, "Your father is at All Saints Hospital in intensive care. He's...Lucian? Lucian?" She folded the phone and put it back in her pocket. "He hung up," she said.

"OK. We've done all we can do. Now we can only wait. Can you get me in there to see him?"

"It's restricted to family."

"I am family. He's the only father I've ever known."

Katherine was taken aback by the look on John's face. She had seen it on family members of the desperately ill. John had known Joshua only for a little more than a year. He had lived with him four months. Yet when John said he was family, she believed it. "I'll see what I can do. Wait here."

Fisher nodded. "Before Lucian gets here if you can. He won't let me in. I'd bet my last buck on it."

"He may not come."

"He'll come. I promise you, he'll come."

She nodded. "I'll see what I can do." She turned away and Fisher went back to perch on the edge of his couch. She was back in the waiting room doorway in a few moments waving him to come on. John was up and at the door as if by teleportation and Katherine lead him down a hallway whose yellow painted walls were supposed to be soothing and cheerful. They stopped at the double doors identified as Intensive Care. The doors opened into a huge round room lined with glass windows all round. In the center was the nursing station and monitor station.

"Joshua is there in number four. There's no one with him now, but the nurses are in and out all the time. I'm going to the desk to get them looking the other way. You get across the room into number four and be quick about it. These people are used to watching three or four rooms at once."

John nodded his agreement and did as he was told. As soon as Katherine distracted the nurse at the desk he went.

Joshua looked like a dead man. Only the slight movement of his chest with each breath said different. His longish hair was sweaty lank and the gray showed more than ever before. His skin was gray and clammy looking. His eyes, though open, were not seeing anything in this world. His nose and mouth were covered by a clear bubble oxygen mask. It did not fit well because of his beard. John was surprised they had not intubated him, but they had not. John Fisher, literary assistant, pseudo-son, savior, held Joshua Gordon's right hand in his own and said, "I'm here, Boss."

Joshua blinked for the first time since John had come into the room and his eyes turned and focused. "I had hoped to live long enough to finish," he said, voice muffled by the clear plastic oxygen mask.

"You will," John said, but didn't believe.

"No. I'm tired. It's on you now, son. You can do it."

"OK, I will."

"Good. Good."

"Are there any notes I haven't seen? Any plot plans?"

"On you now. Did somebody call Luke?"

"Katherine did a little while ago. He'll probably be here in half an hour."

"I may not make it another half hour."

"Ah cut it out, boss," John said, his eyes stinging.

"He won't believe me," Joshua gasped, "but tell Luke I do love him. I wanted so much for him. I wanted...doesn't matter. Save Forneria from him. Destroying it will destroy him too. Don't let him hurt himself because he hates me."

"I'll tell him, boss, I'll tell him." Joshua's grip suddenly tightened, crushing John's fingers. The steadily beeping heart monitor suddenly went into spasmodic rhythm and a screamer alarm went off. In an instant the small glass walled room boiled with people dressed in various color scrubs. John was shoved out as the crash cart was shoved in and he stood watching through the glass wall as they first massaged Joshua's heart with chest compression then brought out the defibrillator paddles.

"Are you a family member?" someone asked John.

"He's my father," he answered.

"You're Lucian?" the nurse asked, disbelief clear in her voice.

"No, John."

"Well, whoever you are you better get out of here. You're not supposed to be here and they don't need help."

John turned, feeling lost. He saw Katherine beside the entrance doors and went to her. "He's gonna die. He's tired of fighting. He's gonna die," he said. The loss in John's face was clear. Katherine read it and it cut at her heart. She opened her arms and pulled John to her. There was nothing she could say so she just held him for a time then walked with him back to the waiting room.

Lucian, impeccable in a three piece gray suit, came into the waiting room drawing hospital administrators in his wake. Even visibly in a hurry, he seemed very much in charge. He stopped a moment in the waiting room and saw John and Katherine sitting side by side. Ignoring John he asked Katherine, "How is he?"

She shook her head. "They had to bring in a crash cart a few minutes ago. We haven't heard since."

"What room is he in?"

"Number four."

Lucian went to the telephone marked with a four, picked it up and after a moment said, "How is my father?" He listened for a moment then said, "Can I come in?" Apparently the answer was negative for Lucian's color darkened. "When can I see him?" Again he listened then said, "Very well. I'm in the waiting room. Please let me know as soon as I can come in," and hung up.

"He wanted to see you," John said. "He told me he wanted to see you."

Lucian blinked as though trying to determine where the sound he had just heard was coming from.

"He told me to tell you he loves you no matter what," John said.

Lucian could not ignore that. A shock of outrage brought his gaze to lock with Fisher's eyes. "Loves me? He told you to tell me he loves me! What crap!" It was said loud enough to cause every eye in the waiting room to turn toward the three.

Katherine's face which had been set in sympathy with John's sadness, hardened. The man she thought she knew, whose image had begun to crumble with the phone call which had set off this crisis, fell several more notches. She could not believe it. How could she could have been so wrong? "You can't even accept a dying man's confession?" she said.

"There was nothing about being wrong anywhere in it," Lucian said. "He loves me? Crap! He loves those scribbles on paper more than he ever loved me or anything else."

Katherine did not understand, nor did John, and Lucian saw they did not.

"Don't you understand?" he asked. "I am the Prince of Darkness. Dad cast me as Lucifer from the moment I was born. I was the serpent in the Eden of him and my mother. He was so afraid a child, me, would steal my mother away from him he made me the bad guy. He even named me for the Satanic Majesty. Lucian! Then he wrote *TUCHINARA* with devils who were sons of the Creator, and went away from Eden to tell the world about it. He loved mother, but he couldn't stay with her while I was there. And when Mother died, he blamed me--blames me even now!"

Lucian's face had gone from tightly controlled placidity to rage, from smoothly handsome to deep scarred ugliness as the pain and hatred flowed out.

"And then you come along. Worshipful and awed by the great literary genius and he takes you in. And do you know why? You have the right name! FISHER! John Fisher, after the Christian symbol. It made you his fair haired boy. Your name! He has us cast as Lucifer and Jesus here in this world and in Forneria. I know it. You know it. He knows it. And he wants to make damn sure everybody else knows it. He is God in all the books he has written and now with his dying breath, he wants you and me to know he is God in this world too!"

Telephone number four rang then rang again. No one in the waiting room moved. It rang again and Lucian drew in a deep breath and blew it out, gaining control of himself. It rang the fourth time and Lucian, his savoir faire mostly restored, answered it.

"Yes." He listened. "Very well. I'll be in." He glanced at John and Katherine standing expectantly beside the couch. "Can we all come in?" He listened then surprised John when he said, "Three of us." He listened again then said, "Well what the hell difference does it make now? He's dead isn't he?" He listened. "Fine then. We'll be right in." He hung up the phone and turned to them. "They stopped trying to resuscitate him five minutes ago. Said his heart wouldn't respond, probably because of the Myelitis. We can go in." Without waiting for an answer he turned on his heel and went out with an air of noblesse oblige. John and Katherine followed a moment later.

In the glass room Joshua had been laid out more neatly. Drip lines, monitor lines, and oxygen mask were gone. His hair and beard had been hastily combed and a sheet had been pulled up to the top of his chest. His arms lay outside the sheet at his sides. Lucian, as though he were a dutiful son hosting the viewing, had moved around to put the bed between him and the door. He stood with hands folded in front of him looking down at the body. He looked up when Katherine and John came in. His face was hard, but they saw what seemed to be tears, shining but unshed, in his eyes. "Did he leave any instructions about burial?" he asked.

"I don't know," John said. "He talked about being cremated, but I don't know if he set anything up. Ed Chance will know."

Lucian looked as though he had smelled something a little foul. "I'm sure he will. I'll find out. We'll do whatever is called for before we read the will. My attorneys will file to have it overturned as soon as it's read."

"Let it go, Lucian," John said. "He's dead. You can't hurt him any more."

Any unshed tears which had been in Lucian's eyes were suddenly gone. "He's not dead until Forneria is dead, and I won't rest until he is well and truly dead."

"But why?" Katherine asked.

"Because I am tired of being Satan in two worlds!" he said and walked out.

PART THREE

One

Ezra woke and shoved his hat back from off his eyes. Bright gold moonlight nearly as bright as day softened the stark desolation of Lake Mono. He rose, had a small sip of water from his water bag, corked it tight again then went to wake the others. He walked along kicking the bottoms of the feet of the sleeping men, not noticing one of them was missing until they rose and began milling around. "Where's Fisher?" he asked. The men looked at one another and no one answered.

Captain Fay looked from man to man then turned to face the lake and in a voice tinted with worry called out, "John Fisher, where are you?"

"Here," a small voice answered.

The five ran and found Fisher still sitting where he had collapsed beneath the weight of the downpour of alkali water. Blood still flowed from his nose and ears and his eyes were red and irritated, but his breathing had eased. Seeing him by the gold light of the moon they all asked at once, "What happened?"

Noah, who still carried his water bag, knelt beside Fisher and uncorked it. He spilled a little onto the sleeve of his shirt and used the baggy cloth to wipe some of the blood from Fisher's face. "Lucian," Fisher said weakly. "He came out of the lake like a waterspout. Didn't you hear him talking? Did you not hear him laugh before he went away? His laugh was so huge it stole my breath away."

The men looked at each other questioningly then looked around as though the whirlwind of water might come out of the lake again.

Ez remembered another of Lucian's spinning winds and he was not surprised no one save John Fisher had heard the words of the god.

"Are you much hurt, John Fisher?" Noah asked, once again wiping his wet sleeve over John's face.

"I think I am all right. There is an ache deep in my skull, but it is less than it was a few moments ago." They stood silently for a few moments each man wrapped in his own thoughts "He is a Tuchinar," John said. "Lucian is a Tuchinar. He showed himself in the water column."

Ezra, still haunted by memory of the whirlwind said, "I would like to move away from here while it is still dark, like we planned, but it depends on you, John Fisher. There is a spring called Ivy which I have never seen dry. There is shade and a Traveler's cache of supplies. I had intended to rest the animals there for a day. If you can stand to travel fast, John Fisher, we can reach it by tomorrow afternoon."

Captain Fay assessed Fisher's condition and said, "Ez is right. We must go now. This is no place to recover. There is no water and no grazing for the animals. We must go on. We will help you, John Fisher."

"You are right. We must go." Fisher tried to stand but could not until Thomas and Noah grabbed him under each arm and helped him. He was wobbly, but after a moment his legs steadied and he released himself from Thomas and Noah. He made a step, then another, gaining strength.

"You two stay with him," Captain Fay said. He gathered Bitter and Ez with a look, and they went to get the droms' saddle girths tightened. Noah and Thomas steadied Fisher as he climbed into his saddle and settled himself then went to their own animals.

"Always have mistrusted the Mono," Ez said, looking across the lake which was like liquid gold beneath the full moon. He turned his drom and the little caravan north into the night.

~*~

The ragged gait of the drom did not help Fisher's headache or his abused body, but those were not the things his mind dwelt upon. Gordon's avatar had said he could be of no more help. Lucian had battered Fisher seemingly at will, though John was sure Lucian did not yet know Gordon's protection was gone. And anyway, what did that mean?

Gordon's protection gone. Fisher tried to remember the other world where Gordon had been a father in a wheeled chair. There he had been the Great Creator of this world where every jarring step of the droms shook Fisher's very bones. And Lucian. He remembered Lucian as a tall handsome man who resembled Gordon. The true son of the father, not Fisher. Did Lucian know more about the other world, the other home, than John knew? The Tuchinar from the lake had said he had a foot in both worlds. That was more than Fisher could be sure of. His hold on the other world was tenuous at best. There were so many blank spots! They left him wondering if perhaps the other world was not some delusion created out of his own bruised mind. Yet it seemed real to him. He could remember so much, sights and smells, things he knew he had never seen or done here in Forneria. He could half remember his childhood in the other world before he woke in the desert.

His earlier memories of Forneria were like things he had learned; history which was known but had not been experienced directly. *And I am going toward some confrontation with a power I do not understand and which is probably much stronger than me. Why am I doing it? Why is it I am so beset? I am afraid. Oh God, oh Gordon, deliver me from this! I don't know what to do. Have mercy on me! I cannot do this.*

Fisher hardly noticed when the sun came up. He might never have noticed if Bitter had not ridden close and pulled the Traveler hat which dangled down Fisher's back on a thong up onto his head. "Are you all right, John Fisher?"

Fisher did not answer the question but said, "Thank you, James," and continued in his dark reverie.

~*~

Bitter continued to examine the other for a moment, a worried look on his face, but when no other words were forthcoming, he heeled his drom and moved up beside Fay and Ezra. "I don't think he even knows where he is," Bitter said.

Those two looked back at Fisher who swayed back and forth, barely staying in the saddle. Thomas and Noah rode behind and at either side so they could heel up to steady him if need be. "If nothin' don't happen, we'll be at Ivy by this afternoon," Ez said, turning back to the front. "He can rest there and we'll get a better look at how he is."

"What do you think happened back there?" Bitter asked of anyone who might have an answer.

"John Fisher said Lucian came up out of the lake," Fay said. His military mind caused him to add, "They must have battled and John Fisher must have driven him off."

Bitter looked at Fay for a moment. "Maybe, but why did Great Lucian choose to attack now? Why hadn't he come before when Fisher was fillin' up wells and springs and stuff? Seems to me like then would have been the time for Great Lucian to show up."

Bitter's use of Lucian's honorific was not lost on Fay. "I don't know, but I do know in the plaza in Barstow John Fisher changed me, and I will serve him so long as he lives. So long as I live. Aren't you the one who said he was Gordon's own son?"

Bitter thought about what the Captain was saying. He had been so sure then. He had known in his heart he was speaking truth, but now?

From the corner of his eye Ezra studied Fay's face, set in surety, then Bitter's scored by doubt. He turned, looking ahead once again. "Looks like I may collect my reward up north," he said quietly, but could not tell if the others had heard him or not.

Far away, just above the horizon, Captain Fay saw something against the heat-bleached blue of the sky. "What is that?" he asked of no one in particular.

"Looks like smoke," Bitter said.

"T'ain't smoke," Ez said. "Too broken up." He looked up and across the sky above them. There were no ravens. He looked back at the horizon. "Betcha it's carrion birds."

"Messengers?" Fay asked.

Bitter searched the sky above them. "There's been birds with us since we left Barstow, but I don't see any now."

"What would they be doing up there ahead," Fay asked, "circling like there's something dead on the ground?"

"Wouldn't be Ivy, would it?" Bitter asked.

Ez considered for a time, ticking his teeth together like a clock working. "Might be. Can't tell yet. "No one said anything more, but the three all privately wondered if the ravens might be waiting for the travelers to see what was dead at Ivy.

Fisher continued to be present in body only as they plodded along. His thoughts ran over and over the same ground, always ending with thoughts of his inability to continue, without Joshua's help, with what Joshua had sent him to do. Raucous cawing brought him out of his thoughts and made him look up. Ravens had followed him almost since the first day he remembered, but always in flocks of ten or fewer. Now, above them, circling and cawing, there were a hundred or more. The other pilgrims pulled their mounts to a stop and looked up with apprehension. They had watched as a part of the column of birds broke away and streamed toward them like a twisting black piece of the night's fabric. Ez, Bitter, and Captain Fay drew pistols to fight if need be, but the birds stayed high enough not to pose an imminent threat so the men did not fire. It was as though Lucian's birds had come to give them an escort.

Thomas heeled his drom and rode up to the three who still held pistols, though they were pointed down now. "What is happening? Why are there so many above us now? There were only three or four."

The other men simply shook their heads and continued to look up. "Should we stop here? Go no farther? Maybe change direction or something?" Thomas asked.

"Ivy is the closest water," Ezra said. "Unless he," Ez indicated Fisher with a bob of the head, "Unless he can pull water up outa the ground in a place where it never flowed." There was perhaps a little contempt in the words but it was hidden beneath a real puzzlement. "We stop here we don't even have protection of rocks to hide behind."

"I say we go on so long as they just stay up there and nothing else," Fay said.

"Maybe we ought to see how convinced they are we're harmless," Bitter said. He cocked his pistol and raised it toward the flock of ravens. A hand reached out and pulled Bitter's arm down.

While the others had been looking up, concerned with the birds, Fisher and Noah had ridden up. As he forced Bitter's arm down, Fisher said, "They are Gordon's creatures, too. Put up your pistols! They have done nothing so let them be. Let's ride on."

Fay was first to holster his pistol, but soon Ez and Bitter put theirs back in the drom side packs. "I'm gonna leave mine loose enough to get out in a hurry all the same," Ezra said, then heeled his mount and moved forward.

Fisher, now very much in the world of Forneria, glanced up at the flock of ravens again, wondering if he had done right. Then the thought, *not to take life is always the best choice,* passed through his mind.

Two

Joshua had arranged his funeral well in advance. He was cremated and his ashes placed in an air tight, water tight canister in the Gospel side wall of the stone chapel of Rathmer College. This had taken a little doing since technically the chapel was not allowed any funerary rights, but with a donation and a specially procured permit all gathered and in place months before his death, Joshua was placed beneath a one foot square brass plaque which simply gave his name above years of birth and death. The service was supposed to be private but word leaked out somehow. The chapel was packed with some forced to stand outside. Many of the mourners carried a Forneria novel.

John was taken by surprise when Lucian asked if he would like to sit on the pew set aside for relatives of the deceased. To himself, John questioned the gesture, but rather than tempt Lucian to rescind it, he kept his mouth shut and sat. He thought perhaps Lucian was trying to maintain a public persona of equitable sanity which was fine. This was the day to bury the dead. The fighting and bitterness would come tomorrow. He asked if Katherine could join them and Lucian, still gracious in public, gave his permission. Katherine started to refuse. She wanted nothing more to do with her former employer. John had had to advise her to accept the certified check for fifty thousand dollars that had arrived the day after Joshua's death. "You earned it. Just because you didn't know what you were doing, doesn't change that fact. Take the money and you are completely quits with Lucian. No obligations either way."

"But it feels like dirty money."

"Your creditors don't care dirty or clean. Take the money and pay your debts." She had at last taken his advice, but when she sat down on the pew at the funeral, she was very careful to place John between her and Lucian, as though mere proximity would somehow drag her back into Lucian's orbit.

There was no official wake. Rumors of several gatherings passed around, but John and Katherine went home to Joshua's house. Again Lucian had been gracious, telling them they could stay in the house as long as they wished. "Why is he suddenly being so nice?" Katherine asked John as they sat in the living room before the cold empty fire place. They were still dressed in their funeral clothes, she in a dark blue linen suit with a ruffled white blouse, he in the same clothes he had worn the first time Lucian had tried to bribe him. She sat with primly crossed ankles, he slouching with tie pulled askew.

"I don't know. I think he is trying to maintain a public face on all this. I think he knows how crazy-obsessive all this mess is and doesn't want crazy-obsessive to somehow get in the way of his winning the law suit. And there is the possibility he is nice in a lot of ways," John said. "He just has one blind spot where he won't see reason."

"How could he ever think he could kill Joshua's work? Did you see all the people carrying Forneria books at the funeral?"

"He thinks so because in his way he is as nuts about Forneria as Joshua," John said rubbing his eyes. He had not slept much in the last three days, partly because there were a lot of things to do, though busy-ness was more excuse than reality. Joshua had made all the arrangements and Lucian carried them out precisely. Actually, he was afraid to sleep. The last dream trip to Forneria had not gone well. By the end of it John had known Joshua was going to die and known the burden of continuing the story was about to fall on him completely.

"How about you?" Katherine asked, watching him closely. "How crazy obsessed with Forneria are you?"

John met her eyes then looked away and laughed ruefully. "You are a very astute lady."

"What are you going to do?"

He shrugged. "Just what I promised the boss I would do. Keep on with the story. I think the book is already sold. I don't know if there was an advance or not, but no matter what, I feel like I have to finish it. Beyond that..." he shrugged, "I don't know. Lucian is going to challenge the will. Papers probably already delivered. I'll find out tomorrow at ten."

"And what if Lucian fails to overturn the will?" she asked.

John drew a deep breath and seemed to sink lower in the arm chair. "I don't know. I think maybe me winning scares me more than if he wins.

At quarter of ten the next morning John, once again wearing his only suit, walked into the well-upholstered office of Whittaker, Belhaven, and Chance, Attorneys at Law. The beautiful red haired receptionist knew who he was though John could not remember ever having met her and was sure he would have remembered meeting so lovely a woman. She ushered him, without a knock, into Ed Chance's office.

Lucian, and another man John supposed was his attorney, was already seated before Chance's desk. Chance stood, offered his hand across the desk and said, "Have a seat, John." He indicated a large wing back leather chair beside Lucian's attorney.

The man stood, offered his hand and said, "Arthur Drew, Mr. Gordon's attorney."

The two sat and when they were comfortable, Chance said, "Shall I read it or do you just want the highlights?"

Lucian said, "For the sake of knowing exactly where this all stands please read it."

Chance nodded then opened the legal folder and began at page one. Ed Chance was named executor and a requisite fee was named. The rest was just as John expected. Everything, save a couple of small bequests to charities and the Forneria copyrights, went to Lucian. When Chance reached the part about the copyrights, he stopped for a moment and said, "Since this section was the bone of contention, I encouraged Joshua to set it in stone by saying something like the copyrights will remain with the legatee and cannot be sold or given to anyone else for the life of the copyright, but he wouldn't do it. He said he trusted you, John, to do what was best."

John swallowed, thinking how his life would have been much easier if he had never met Joshua or Lucian Gordon. He wished Joshua had listened to Chance and made it impossible to sell or give away the copyrights, but since he hadn't, John was stuck with any decision which had to be made.

"Can you give us an approximation of the value of the estate, Mr. Chance," Lucian said, pronouncing the attorney's name as though it had a nasty taste.

"It will be strictly a guess."

"An educated guess. How much?"

"After fees and taxes, if it was all liquidated, in the neighborhood of five million dollars."

Lucian nodded. Five million dollars was not negligible to him, but it was not a huge amount of money either. He nodded and after a moment turned to John. "Mr. Fisher, since my father has left the choice in your hands I am going to make you an offer here in the presence of witnesses. I will turn the estate over to you completely and add the ten million dollars we talked about on the phone if you will..." Attorney Drew handed Lucian a piece of paper. "...if you will sign this agreement to relinquish all claim on the Forneria copyrights. It means fifteen million dollars give or take, and all you have to do is sign your name to this." Lucian placed the paper on Chance's desk.

John blinked. He felt as though he had been hit with a hammer. Fifteen million dollars was a huge fortune. It could set him up to write what he wanted and never worry again about publication or anything else for the rest of his life. His children and probably his children's children could live on it if he made a few wise investments. All for a signature. He smiled wryly. *And I don't even have to sign it in blood?*

"And if I say no?"

"Then we move to the next step..."

Chance interrupted before Lucian could name the next step. "Challenging the will is going to be very tough, Lucian. I don't think there is a judge in the system who would overturn it. You would have to prove your father was non compos mentis when he had it written, and that would be very difficult. You could perhaps get some forensic psychologist to make that diagnosis, but I have Dr. Erdinger's statement. I am sure he would testify as to Joshua's stability, as would John and probably Katherine as well."

"Mr. Drew told me the same things, and upon further consideration, I see you are correct. Therefore we will go at this from a different direction." He turned to Drew again and was handed a small tape recorder Drew had taken from his brief case. He set it on Chance's desk and hit the play button.

John's voice said, *"I received your offer."*

Lucian's voice answered, *"Very well. Have you called to accept?"*

"No. I want to make a counter offer."

"And what is your counter offer?"

"Ten million. I want ten million dollars. Half now and half when I hand over the copyrights."

"Done. I'll have papers to you in an hour."

Lucian pushed the stop button. "You made the offer and I accepted it. There is an implied contract."

John's mouth opened but nothing came out then he closed it and tried again. "You taped the conversation illegally. You did not inform me you were taping it. Besides, if you recorded it, you should play the rest of it. The part where I say "no deal" which came next."

"The contract was implied as soon as I agreed to your offer," Lucian said coolly.

"No money ever changed hands!" John felt certain desperation.

"There was no time. That was the day, in fact the moment after the phone call, if I understand correctly, when my father went into intensive care. Exigent circumstances dictated we delay the contract. Now those circumstances have changed." Lucian once again turned to Drew and was handed a cashiers check. "Here is the agreed upon first installment. Five million dollars." He extended it toward John.

John looked from the check into Lucian's eyes. The other had gone through the business calmly, as though nothing out of the ordinary were happening, but behind those eyes John could see flames like those he remembered from the eyes of the Tuchinar who had risen from Mono Lake.

"Ed, do I have to take it?" John asked.

"Are you asking me to represent you in this matter, Mr. Fisher?" Chance asked formally.

John looked at the attorney with a sinking feeling. Was Joshua's friend and lawyer going to betray him after his death? "Yes I am. Will you represent me, Ed," he asked.

"Do you have a dollar?"

John drew his wallet from his jacket pocket, fished out a one dollar bill, and held it out. Chance took the dollar. "I am now on retainer to John Fisher in all legal matters."

"Do I have to take the check?"

"No."

"We have a deal," Lucian said, his face darkening as his control slipped just a little.

"We do not..." John began, but Chance held up his hand to quiet him.

"My client disputes the claim, and you will be required to prove it in court," Chance said.

Lucian, the fire in his eyes more apparent than a moment before, handed the check back to Drew. "Arthur, put it in an escrow account."

The lawyer received the check, but before he could get it into his brief case, Lucian stood. The veins on his neck and his deepened purple color showed his anger and frustration. "This is foolish, Fisher. You should have taken the money." He turned and stalked out.

Drew, having gathered himself, stood and offered his hand first to Chance then to Fisher. "Gentlemen," he said, "we'll see you in court," and followed his client.

Three

The flock of ravens above the six men grew larger as they continued toward Ivy, and it was soon apparent what they had first observed to be hundreds did in fact become thousands of the blue-black birds circling in a rising plume above the oasis. As with the whirlwind which had followed the Traveler caravan, Ezra watched the whirl of birds saying, "It ain't natural."

"And it's Lucian's doing, sure as I'm born," said Bitter.

"Is there some way we can turn aside, Ez? Captain?" Fisher asked.

"We have water for a couple more days," Ezra said. "We could go east into the mountains to Bear Wells, but it's a hard trip and the wells might be dry. They wasn't much reliable before Lucian's Dry."

"There is no way we can fight," the Captain said. "They could overwhelm us with numbers until our ammunition is gone then tear us apart at will."

"And even if we turn toward this Bear Wells," Thomas said, "the birds would just follow us and do what they will."

Fisher thought a moment and looked up at the raven darkened sky. He was more afraid than when Barstow was falling around his head. The headache from his last encounter with Lucian had reduced from its skull splitting intensity, but it was still there. And most important was that there was no longer the red bird avatar of Joshua to advise him. He was on his own; did not know if he still maintained any power, but seeing no other choice, he said, "Then we will go on into whatever Lucian has planned for us."

Very soon they came within sight of Ivy. There were several palm trees and some nearly dead cottonwood trees so black with sitting ravens it seemed as though the leaves had been replaced with black feathers. "Never seen nothing like it," Ezra said in a hushed tone. The men rode on into the oasis nervously looking up at the waiting birds. They stopped at the edge of the pool, made a deep blue by the fact it bubbled up from hundreds of feet below the desert, slid off their mounts, and knelt beside the droms as they began to drink. The men nervously avoided putting their heads down to drink. All of them dipped water with their hats and poured it over themselves before dipping hands into the water to bring it to their mouths. The ravens in the trees suddenly began to make the rattling-bones sound Fisher had heard before. A thousand birds in the trees rattling together sounded like a graveyard of suddenly risen skeletons while the flock of birds above Ivy dimmed the light to a funereal dusk as they soared lower. The men, startled to their feet by the sound and the sudden dimming of the light, cast looks at the threatening ravens. They instinctively grouped themselves back to back. Fay and the two Travelers who had taken their pistols from the side packs lifted the pistols to fight, knowing full well they did not stand a chance if the birds attacked.

As suddenly as the sound had begun it was gone, and into the nervous silence a single raven's voice spoke. "Help us, John Fisher," it said, after which the rattling bones clatter began again.

The men were stunned. They straightened and lowered their pistols, looking at one another over their shoulders.

Fisher looked up at the birds seeking the one who had spoken, but, save for size, each bird looked like the other. Finally his eyes settled on one bigger than the rest. "How may I help Lucian's messengers?"

The birds fell quiet again and the large one John had addressed said, "Our mothers from before memory of the first egg have told us of the Tuchinar who made us. We were made to serve. But when the Tuchinar went away, we were free to fly where we would. Then Great Lucian came from the south and we were no longer free. His was the power of the Tuchinar, and to prove it he killed us by the thousands. So, to live, and because Great Lucian was Tuchinar, we served. Now you say we are created by Gordon, not Great Lucian, and though we have served Great Lucian against you, you allow us to drink when we thirst. Those who serve you also allow us to drink. If Great Lucian is not our Creator, but only one who kills us, we need not serve him. If Gordon is our Creator, and if you are Gordon's son, then we would serve you who could have caused us to suffer but did not."

Fisher considered a moment, "I cannot free creatures who will not be free," he said. "You are already free, if only you wish it. You only serve Lucian from fear. If you defeat your fear, you will be free indeed."

The rattling-bones sound rose to a clattering roar. After a time the ravens fell silent again. "Can you not protect us, John Fisher? If we serve you, can you not save us from Great Lucian's wrath?"

"Upon the shores of the Mono I could not so much as protect myself."

"But you did not die."

"True, but it does not mean I will not. I go to confront Lucian now, but I do not know what the end will be. I *am* Gordon's son, but I am still only a man. "

For a time the birds were silent then the clatter rose again and fell in a moment. "We would serve you, John Fisher. Though Lucian may kill us, we will serve you."

Fisher's voice suddenly choked and would not come out. The thought of these creatures willing to die to serve him was more than his battered emotions could take. Tears mixed with regret, admiration, and sorrow for the pain to come welled up in his eyes and began slipping down his cheeks.

At last he managed to gain control of himself and said, "The service you can do for me is to be free. If, in your freedom, you fly to all corners of Forneria, tell those who listen to be merciful to one another and to all creatures of Gordon's creation. Live in peace and never forget you are Gordon's children whom he loves." A chorus of caws and clicks followed by the rattle of raven conference erupted then was succeeded by the rasp of feathers rubbing against feathers as wings sliced through the air. In moments, Ivy, which had been black with ravens, was empty of the birds; none rode the desert air currents above, none remained in the trees, none hopped upon the ground or ticked their beaks to drink.

The six men, still standing back to back first turned toward one another then the five all looked to John Fisher who held his hand to his forehead to shade his eyes from the sun. "Let's get into the shade," he said moving toward the sparse protection of the cottonwood trees growing beside the pool.

The five hesitated a moment then Captain Fay holstered his pistol; the Travelers went to put their pistols away before following Fisher into the shade. They rested and when the sun passed behind the rim of the world, they all lay down.

John Fisher could not remember when he had ever been so tired. He had not slept in many days. What with the hard travel in the scorching sun he had given up what little reserve strength he had left. Now he lay down, knowing he would not sleep, but needing the relief of laying down whether sleep came or not. To his surprise he found himself growing drowsy in the relative cool of the darkness, and after a little he fell into a sleep filled with jumbled dreams. There were ravens and droms and people and earthquakes. There was bubbling water. And mixed in with the visions of Forneria were visions of the other world. He saw Gordon and felt the life go out of him. He heard the last words spoken and felt the loss. Lucian, the man, was there too, along with a beautiful blond woman. At last his dreams settled and a pair of hands filled his mind. They were set with fingers cocked upon a keyboard, familiar, yet somehow unknown. The fingers held in position were not moving. On a lighted screen a little above the hands were lines of words which he could not quite read. He knew they were important; his very life was in those words, but he could not make sense of any of the squiggles. Suddenly the hands lifted from the keyboard and the perspective of the dream changed.

He was looking at his own face, his own body seated before the keyboard and he knew the frustration of his other self--knew the pain through which the other he was battling. Knew the loss and...

John Fisher sat up with a cry. The dream was gone and he was once more in the oasis called Ivy. Other men, good men who had been created by Gordon slept on around him, so weary they were not disturbed by his cry. They were his creatures too, and he knew the love and longing of a Creator for his creatures as he passed his eyes over the sleepers. And suddenly he was shaking. Despite the desert heat still lingering, Fisher trembled as though touched by a polar wind. The bitter cold radiated from within him. It was an arctic knowledge that paralyzed his other; the knowledge that all the world was in his hands and in his charge. He had no idea in Forneria or the other place what was to happen next.

Four

John stared at the glowing computer screen displaying a few lonely lines of words, the same lines, in fact, as the previous half hour. Those were the last lines he had written before Joshua died. John knew roughly how the book was to end, but between where he was and the final page, there were some difficulties to be gotten over. His staring at the screen did not seen to be helping him. He wished he could empty his mind, concentrate on the task, but that was beyond him--the words may as well have been translated into Sanskrit for all the depth of understanding them he could manage.

His mind would not land anywhere, but replayed the scenes of months past; not memories of working in this house, at this desk, but of Joshua as friend and mentor, the times before John had come to live in his house when they had sat in the Student Union coffee shop talking about nothing in particular as they sipped long since oxidized coffee out of paper cups.

But the way Joshua had immersed him in the creation of Forneria! John thought he should be really angry with Joshua as the victim of his blatant manipulation, near to being drowned actually, but then again how else could the boss have managed? How else could he have brought someone into such intimate contact with his creation save by sucking him directly into the imagining of it. But when Joshua died, the dreams stopped. The boss had sworn that he was not manipulating him or drugging him or hypnotizing him but the dreams were gone and without them John could not find a way back into Forneria.

Joshua had been in Forneria too, granted in the shape of the red bird, but John had no doubt the boss had been with him in Forneria—*really there*, just as he had been *really there*. How had he done it? How had Joshua made himself really a part of his creation?

John did not consider this account had to be tainted with madness, being teleported physically into literary creations solely by the will of the Creator. It did not cross his mind that his dream life, his life in Forneria, might be psychosis. It had become the ending desired by Joshua Gordon, the Creator, the ending John had entered into and lived throughout. Now John was an embodied part of Gordon's creation. Now Forneria was his world to protect, to save, both there and here.

That thought jolted out of his reverie. John tried to bring his mind back to the task only to find Lucian had crept into his thoughts like a trickling stream of sewage. How, how, how could a son hate his father so? How could a man so rich want something so trivial as control of a few stories his father wrote? Wanting them only to destroy them. How could a man famous for his philanthropy conceal such a bitter, vicious, loathsome obsession? How could a man who had what John had longed for his whole life, a father who loved him, be so bent as to try to destroy his father's beloved life work? Fisher heard the echo of Lucian, "He loves those stories more than he loves me."

Was it true? Had Joshua loved the creatures of Forneria more than his own son? Was that why Joshua had used Lucian as the satanic figure in the book? Did Joshua think he had somehow spawned a ravening monster and feel so sure of it that he felt compelled to expose the monster in his last book?

Through the offers presented by Lucian before, John had not really been much tempted. But now as he sat knowing he was in control of everything in Forneria, that he was the new God of Forneria, he was truly tempted. *Why don't I just let him have the damned things? They are just scribbles on paper! I am so tired! I am so disgusted with this fight that wasn't even mine before and needn't be mine now!*

Unexpectedly the computer screen blurred and John found his eyes full of tears. Grief overcame him and he sobbed, bringing his hands to his eyes. Joshua, who for good or ill, had become the father he had never known, was gone almost before John had learned to love him, and the pain of loss crushed his heart.

But as he sat, the grief turned to anger; anger at God or the universe or the great author of all, whatever one wanted to call the power which held humanity in time's toils. Why had Joshua been taken from him so soon? Why had they not had years to know one another? Years to work together, so John could smoothly and gently take over the creation without the pain and death and thirst?

Now John truly understood what Joshua meant by "The Great Author." Author-Creators did what was necessary to finish and protect their creations, just as Joshua had with Forneria. Just as Joshua would expect John to carry on.

If he could.

But here you sit. Crying like a baby, not able to find one lousy word! Fine Creator you are! He snuffed up his running nose then went to the bathroom for a tissue to blow it. When he could breathe again, he went back to the computer but did not sit down. It was useless to sit there with nothing but storms in his mind. He turned and headed for the Library where the liquor cabinet was, thinking perhaps a drink would steady him down.

Or knock me out. Either alternative would he acceptable.

He found Katherine sitting on the large leather couch in the library, legs folded beneath her. The copy of *Tuchinara* she had been reading lay forgotten on the cushion beside her. She looked up at the sound of John's footsteps and hurriedly snatched a tissue from the box wedged between her body and the arm of the couch.

"You too, huh?" John said.

She chuckled ruefully. "I was just reading along and all of a sudden I started crying." She shrugged. "You?"

"Trying to work and not succeeding since I couldn't see the screen anymore. I'm getting myself a drink. You want one?"

"Yes. Whatever you are having."

John opened the bar, brought out a bottle of Canadian Mist whiskey and two glasses.

"Ice?" he asked.

Katherine shook her head.

He poured two fingers of liquor into each glass and brought one to her then sat down on the other end of the couch.

"I keep expecting him to holler for me," she said and took a sip.

"Yeah. Place is really empty."

They sat quietly, folded into their own thoughts. John glanced up and noticed Katherine was crying again. He moved the book which was between them and scooted over to her. "You OK?" he asked.

"If he had just died from heart failure or a stroke or an aneurism, I wouldn't have felt bad. I mean it was inevitable. He knew it. We knew it. And he was hurting so much. If it just happened..." She sighed and didn't finish.

"Yeah."

"I feel as though I'm partly responsible. If I hadn't doubted him about Lucian, maybe he wouldn't have called and gotten so upset." She cried harder and leaned forward to hide her face against John's shoulder. He put his arms around her.

"If he hadn't called and you hadn't heard Lucian, you wouldn't have believed Joshua. I think he wanted you to believe him more than anything else. Not that I blame you for not believing him. Hell, I had dealt with Lucian in his obsessed mood and I didn't believe he would take the offer."

"And he offered even more?" she asked pulling away so she could look into his eyes.

John nodded. "And since I didn't take it, we go to court anyway."

"He's crazy. He really is obsessed."

The telephone rang. John untangled himself from Katherine and answered it. It was Ed Chance. "We need to have a meeting, John. I don't know how Lucian managed to do it, but he persuaded a judge to be ready to hear preliminary arguments day after tomorrow."

A sick chill of dread went through John. "Just shows you what money can buy."

"I try not to be cynical, but yeah. Would it be convenient for you to come down here now?"

John glanced at the grandfather clock in the corner. It was one p.m. "Sure. I'm not doing anything but feeling sorry for myself anyway. I'll see you in half hour or forty five minutes."

"Fine. Is the nurse, Katherine, still there? She heard the whole thing didn't she?"

"Yes, she's here. Want to talk to her?"

"Yes, please."

John handed the receiver to Katherine and she said, "Hello."

After listening for a few moments she said, "Yes, of course. No trouble." She listened a moment more then said, "See you this afternoon. Bye." She handed the receiver back to John. "He wants to see me too."

John studied her speculatively. After what they had been through together in the last few days, he was beginning to feel somewhat different about Katherine than he had when he found out she was a spy. "We have to win this, you know?" he said.

"A couple of weeks ago I would have thought it was nonsense. But you're right. We have to win this." She picked up *Tuchinara*. "I don't know if I can believe Forneria is a real place out there somewhere, but it needs to continue to exist right here."

Traffic was brutal, but they made it to Chance's office in forty five minutes and were seated with drinks in hand a few moments later. Chance, most unusually, poured himself a drink. "I don't usually drink at the office, but it has been one of those kinds of days."

"Several of those kind of days," John said.

Chance sipped quietly then set his glass on his desk blotter. "You said Lucian didn't finish playing the recording..."

"I assume he recorded the whole conversation, but maybe not."

"What was the rest of the conversation?

""I don't remember exactly," John answered and looked the same question at Katherine who said she didn't either. "Can you get a copy of the recording in discovery, if there is such a thing in civil court?"

"There is and I should be able to, but what if Lucian is crazy enough to edit the tape and still swear it was the end?"

"But I heard it too," Katherine said.

"All right. Tell me about it. Just you, Katherine."

She blinked thoughtfully, gathering her story and said, "I really thought Joshua was just being cynical when he dared John to call Lucian, but John made the call. When Lucian answered, John put it on the speaker so we could all hear and when John said ten million, I almost laughed it was so ridiculous. But then Lucian said "Done!" and he would have papers to John within an hour. Joshua said something, but I don't remember what. Then John said the whole thing was a joke and they didn't have a deal and would never have a deal. Lucian began shouting they did have a deal and he was going to hold John to it. He was in a screaming rage, and that was when the call ended. I don't remember if John hung up first or Lucian did."

Chance nodded. "Fine. Fine. Is it the way you remember it, John?"

"More or less."

"Did Lucian know you were all listening in?" Both of them thought for a moment then said yes they thought he had known. Chance nodded again. "Then this is all going to depend on whether the judge believes Lucian or you two."

"Is that good?" John asked. Chance hesitated then shrugged. "Depends on the judge."

John studied the attorney's face for a couple of beats longer than would have been necessary for a simple answer then asked, "It depends on whether the judge will stay bought, doesn't it?"

"Again, I try not to be cynical, but yes."

Katherine looked distressed. "Do you really think Lucian has bribed the judge? I can't believe..." she stopped and thought further. "After all this I suppose I should believe Lucian is capable of anything."

All three sat silently for a time before John said, "I don't know how I am going to be able to pay you for all this, Ed. The buck I gave you was a considerable chunk of my fortune. I'm a complete pauper. The only money I had was what Joshua was paying me. As is I'm stony broke. I can't even pay for an hour of your time much less all the time this is going to take."

"Don't worry about it. Given the notoriety of this case--and I'll make sure it gets some notoriety--when you get the copyrights we'll talk about my fee."

"But what if we lose?"

"We'll cross that bridge when we come to it"

Five

The six rested two full days at Ivy then traveled again under the waning moon. They continued to travel in the relative cool of the night so long as there was light to do so, but when the moon waned to a thin sliver then disappeared all together, they were once more faced with traveling by day. They tried to find shadow to rest in at high noon, but often as not the longest shadows were made by the men on their droms. A week passed before they began to climb from the blazing desert into the cooler foothills of the Mountains of the King. There the land was not quite so sere and became more forgiving. Water was still in short supply, but the cooler air at the higher altitudes diminished their thirst.

Trees appeared and after a few days the men were traveling through a forest, its trees growing ever more closely spaced. The dappled light of the Ponderosa forest closed in and turned to crepuscular, but the darkening forest, while much cooler, made them nervous. They peered into the foliage as though they felt eyes watching them. Every noise made them snap their heads around, eyes and ears seeking the source.

The droms, perhaps reacting to their riders' anxious movements, became skittish and tried to bunch up. At first the riders held them back, but soon there was no stopping them, and the six men were forced taking comfort in riding closer to one another. Ezra and Jim Bitter once again dug out their pistols. Captain Fay had been resisting the urge to do the same, but when he saw the Travelers arm themselves, he drew his own gun.

The dusk thickened toward night and though they were all loath to stop in such dense forest, they were left with no choice when the dark became so ebon they could hardly see one another. They stopped in the middle of the pine-masted trail they had been traveling, not even moving to the side, and armed teams of two, went seeking windfall wood to build a fire. Thomas and Fay went together; Jim Bitter and Noah went too. Back with the droms Ezra and Fisher stayed close to one another with firm grips on the animals' reins.

"What is it we fear, Ezra?" John Fisher asked.

"I don't know. I only felt like this one other time in my life. I told you I went into Tuchinara and shook the whole time. Well, I felt just like this. Like they was something watching me. Somethin' hungry."

A few moments later when Ezra heard a crunch of some fallen branch he almost shot Captain Fay and Thomas coming back with their load of wood. "You boys should have hollered or been singin' or something," Ezra said. A scream diverted their attention. It was not a sound a human voice could make even in the most extreme agony. The sound sent chills of horror through the four and a moment later Ezra and the Captain whirled, pistols at the ready when Bitter and Noah came running. "Did you see something?"

"We heard the scream and ran back here," they said.

"Get a fire started, Thomas," Fay commanded. "Ezra, watch to the east. Jim to the west."

The Travelers did not hesitate to take the Captain's orders arranging themselves so Thomas and the others were in the center of their triangle. "There could be a hundred men ten steps from me and I wouldn't be able to see 'em," Bitter groused, but he didn't stop scanning the blackness against whatever made such a blood chilling scream.

When the fire began to blaze, Thomas fed fuel into it to make it bright.

"Bitter, Ezra, keep your backs to the fire so you'll still have some night vision," the Captain said and took his own advice. The other three set about making hot food and drink.

"This wood is not going to last long," Thomas said.

Noah, disgusted with himself said, "I was so scared I dropped all the wood I gathered."

"Well then, you need to go back and get it and maybe more besides," Ezra said. "I'm just hopin' what ever made that howl is afraid of fire."

"Wonder what it is?" Noah asked.

"I think I don't want to know," Thomas answered.

Fisher felt a sudden chill of knowledge. He did not know what was in his other mind, the mind in the other world, but in the pit of his stomach he felt the knowledge. When the fire was burning well, Bitter and Noah walked in the direction from which they had run looking for the wood Noah had dropped. They found the armload just outside the wavering light the fire was throwing through the trees. They wasted no time picking it up and hurrying back toward camp and firelight. They were hardly back inside that range when another scream reverberated through the forest, only to be instantly echoed by another from the opposite direction. Bitter and Noah ran the rest of the way to the fire and Bitter returned to his place near the fire, again facing away from the light with pistol drawn.

"'Cept the sound ain't right, I'd say it was a hunting pair of mountain cats," Ezra said.

"Build up the fire some," Fay said.

"Wood won't last long as is, Captain," Noah answered.

Fisher, who had been crouched by the fire lost in thought, stood up. Without a word he stepped away from the fire and walked toward the edge of the wavering light. No one noticed him at first, but when they did, they began calling him back to the protection of the fire and the triangle of drawn weapons. He did not stop until he was only the dimmest of figures among the trees. Then the five saw him lift his arms as he had done at the fountain in Barstow, but his prayer this time was different.

"Creatures of the Tuchinar, come to me," he shouted. Then he added an extraordinary few words. "Do not be afraid. We will not harm you nor will you harm us." Fisher lowered his arms and turned back to the fire. When he reached the men, he said, "Put up your pistols. They are useless. These creatures are not like any other." He turned and looked out at the dark forest, waiting for what the others could not even guess.

In moments a scream came from the north and it was echoed one after another until the nerve stripping sounds were a hellish cacophony which pounded upon the men like a furious tide. So horrifying was the sound it stole all courage from the five. First they shook as though naked and cold then cowered, covering their heads as though to ward off blows, making themselves smaller and smaller before falling to the earth in the fetal position. Only John Fisher stood and watched as the loathsome creations of the Tuchinar came forth from the forest.

The creatures were human in shape with head, arms, and legs, but they were not human. Some were immense with monstrous arms and legs but only tiny heads. Many were stooped beneath the weight of massive shoulders. Some limped on unevenly sized legs; some were covered with scabrous disease; all were filthy with the stench of death upon them thickening the air around Fisher. He did not flinch nor look away nor gag no matter how stomach turning was the smell, even though as they came forward he could see all the gaping mouths drooling with hunger. As the vile creatures crowded closer and closer to him, Fisher felt pity for these accursed beings like a spike driven into his heart. *Even these Abominations were Gordon's creatures and now are mine.* The beasts fell silent and the silence was as oppressive as the cacophony had been.

"Who calls us and tells *us* not to be afraid?" asked a monster whose skin was pale gray and covered with oozing sores.

Fisher ignored the question and asked, "Why has Lucian released you?"

"To eat the cherished of Gordon..."

"And of Fisher," another added.

"Why have you obeyed him?"

230

"We were hungry and Great Lucian is our Creator and our master."

"Lucian is no Creator. He is a destroyer. You are creatures of Gordon and when the Tuchinar perverted his creation to make you, it broke his heart."

A hum of voices rose among the monsters. Some though laughed at the thought of being Gordon's creatures. "If we are children of the other, why are we thus? Why do we hunger so? Why were we imprisoned in Tuchinara?"

There was bitterness to the question, which wrung Fisher's heart. "When Gordon called the Tuchinar home, those who perverted his creation could not come. Instead Gordon, the merciful, sent them to all parts of the universe so they might never again do harm to his creation. He could have extinguished you, but instead he pitied you because, though you are loathsome beasts now, you were not always. He closed you into Tuchinara where you could not hurt any thing he had created, but also so you might be a warning to any who came near the city and as a reminder. Gordon is merciful; no one should ever again pervert his creations."

"And how do you know the heart of Gordon? You who are meat for our hunger."

Fisher lifted his arms as though to embrace the whole foul gathering. "I am John Fisher, sent by Gordon to free Forneria of Lucian's curse, and to free those imprisoned from the first creation. Gordon and I are one."

"To free the prisoners?" some asked. "To free us?"

"We are free now!" The first monster growled. "Great Lucian has freed us from Tuchinara. How can Gordon or Fisher make us more free?"

"By taking you home as he took the righteous Tuchinar. By transforming you from this," Fisher waved his hand at the stinking mob, "back to what you would have been had the Tuchinar not to tried best their Creator by perverting his creation."

"And what if we do not want to be changed?" asked the first monster.

"Then you will again be bound in Tuchinara, perhaps until eternity."

"Who will bind us?" sneered a giant who had four flipper-like arms.

"I will bind you," he answered softly. "Gordon and I are one."

A great muttering growl rose and grew to nearly as loud as had been the noise of the first gathering. "And how will you manage it, Fisher? We are

231

legion, you are one." The flipper-armed giant lunged from the mob and threw its crushing appendages around Fisher.

Others of the monsters looked as though they would have joined the giant had there been room, but the giant had pulled Fisher to its chest in a vice like grip. Some stood back noncommittally to watch the uneven contest, but some of them cried out against the killing saying, "He has come to help us! Let him help us if he can!" The giant ignored the pleas. It continued to smash Fisher against its wide bony chest. After a time the monster released its prey, thinking to find a pile of flesh crushed to anonymity, but instead Fisher, with not a bruise on him, stood where he had before.

"Kneel and call out to Gordon if you wish to be free," Fisher said quietly. A moan of submission rolled from the outermost ring of monsters to the inner most and nearly all the loathsome beasts knelt. The few left standing growled and threatened, but none made another attempt to harm Fisher. "You few," Fisher said. "You may still kneel and be freed."

No others knelt. Fisher sighed. "Gordon will love you forever, as will I, but you have chosen imprisonment. I am sorry, but you leave me no choice. Be gone!" And they were.

After a moment a gasp rose from the monsters, but it was not a gasp at the disappearance of their brothers. The five men who had been overcome with terror were getting to their feet though they were still in the grip of the fear. They shook and gaped with it, but their eyes were open to witness what would come next. "I wish I could transform you all in this instant," Fisher said to the horrific, kneeling legion, "But your transformation must wait until Lucian is defeated. Meanwhile you must return to Tuchinara, but as free beings, not as prisoners."

"But what shall we eat John Fisher?" one monster asked.

He was answered by cries of "Yes, John Fisher. We hunger beyond bearing, but we wish not to harm those cherished by Gordon or by you. How can we live?"

"You will have no need, for you will sleep until I return." Fisher for the third time raised his arms to embrace the horrific beings before him and said, "Gordon sent me to save the innocent, to free the slaves, and transform the Abominations. Go and sleep now. I will return soon." He lowered his arms as the beloved Abominations disappeared to await his return. Fisher turned to the five who faced him. Those could not take their eyes off him. Even Ezra, who had still been skeptical of Fisher's power, felt the awe of that which he had witnessed and when the others knelt he did too. "You five must tell all what has happened here when I have gone. You must tell everyone why I came just as I told the Abominations."

"But you cannot leave us, John Fisher," Noah said.

"We need you." The others agreed.

I cannot stay forever. Soon I must go, and when I do, you must be my witnesses."

Ezra said. "We will tell all truly."

"It is all I can ask."

Six

Katherine sat in the big armchair in John's room in her usual comfortable pose, legs folded under her. She had a strong light on so she could read. John had been sitting at the computer until a few moments before. He had been laboriously finishing his current chapter and when he closed it up, he hit the print button and lay down on his bed. Katherine retrieved the newly printed pages in a few moments returning to the chair to read them. She had not begun reading the manuscript of the new novel when she would copy it to send to Lucian. Then she had popped the disk into the machine, copied it to a new disk then mailed it off to Lucian. It wasn't until just before Joshua died that she started reading it as well as *Angels of the Coast*. She hadn't asked permission, though she knew Joshua was always rather secretive with his work until it was at least roughed out, but when no one seemed to mind, she continued. Then when Joshua died and all the lawsuit mess came to a head, she went back to the beginning of the manuscript and started again. It meant a lot more the second time through.

Everything in life seemed to mean more now and she did not quite understand why. To be near John also meant more now. Since the day they had comforted one another after Joshua's funeral, she found she continued to seek him out.

John had noticed Katherine hanging around him more. He really didn't wonder about it much, thinking she was feeling lost without Joshua to care for, but for whatever reason she was hanging around, he was happy she was. When he saw she was reading the manuscript, he had some mixed feelings at first, but decided what the hell; she was nearly as deeply involved in the lawsuit as he was so she might as well know what was really at stake. The copyrights were important, but because his possession of them had been challenged, the manuscript of the new novel was more important. While he had immersed himself in the earlier Forneria stories when he read them, this one was a part of him, part of past and future. It was immersed in him rather than the other way around and he felt, no matter what, this story had to see publication no matter what happened to the copyrights. The thought of losing this story to Lucian made him sweat.

Katherine laid aside the last page and leaned back to let it settle.

After a little John opened his eyes and, seeing she was finished, said, "Well?"

She looked at him. "I don't see how you write at all when there is all this court business hanging over you. I would be so distracted and nervous I couldn't begin to concentrate."

John sat up and shrugged. "It's a good place to go hide from the real world. Sorta like meditation. And you didn't answer my question."

"Which one?'

"Don't be a pain in the ass! Do you like it or not?"

"Does it matter?"

"Hell yes it matters! If you hate it, I'll probably finish it anyway because I can't do anything else, but I won't be as happy or satisfied with it. And--I feel like I owe Joshua something. He wrote some stories which are *beloved,* for lack of a better word. I don't want to finish up what he started by turning it into some kind of unreadable crap in the process. That's why this last chapter was such a bitch. I was afraid, I'm afraid I'm departing from his original idea."

"No, I don't think you are. And I do like it."

"Thank God! I'm really hung up on where it is going, though. Joshua and I talked about it from the beginning because there were several places I didn't understand why he had done what he had done. But when I asked, he always said the characters in the story had done it; he was barely in control. I thought that was nonsense, but I'm beginning to understand what he meant now. The last chapter--if I was in full control, I would never have set it up like it is. I mean, the way it is running there is going to have to be some kind of a sacrifice at the end, and we all know who the sacrifice is going to be. It is built into the set up and has been from the beginning, but the trick is going to be to make the sacrifice seem real."

"Real? I don't understand."

"OK, in case you hadn't noticed, this thing is pretty much stolen from the New Testament. I mean with salvation and miracles and evil, we haven't even bothered to try to disguise it. But the thing which always bothered me about the story of Jesus was, here was a guy--assuming the story is more than some alternate version of a creation myth. Anyway, Jesus is this guy with power. I mean he turns water into wine and heals the sick and raises the dead. He even says he could call an army of angels to protect him if he wanted, but at the end he gets crucified. He lets them kill him. With a couple of words he could have had it all end without the pain and blood, but he didn't. Why?"

Katherine narrowed her eyes in thought. "I'd say because it *had* to be. I mean, what kind of a story would it be if Jesus just ran around doing miracles and ended up as some kind of conqueror? He'd just be a kind of comic book Alexander the Great with super powers. But the story's real point is the man who has all these powers sacrifices himself, lets the very people he has come to help, come to save if you will; he *lets* them kill him because it is the way it *has* to be. It's what makes that comic book story human rather than comic book."

John nodded. "Yeah, you're right, but in this story I'm not set up for the people to kill him, but for Lucian to do it--I think. I mean I don't exactly know yet! The Boss and I talked about it, and it is the way the story is set up. It is inevitable, but...I don't know."

After examining John for a time, Katherine unfolded herself from the chair and came to sit beside him. "Maybe you should stop worrying about it for now. If Lucian wins, you may not get to finish it let alone publish."

John glanced at her and felt a sudden warmth to have her sitting beside him. It felt *correct* to have her leg pressed against his; not particularly sexual, although there was some sexuality too, but as though it was proper-- inevitable.

"Right again," he said. "And if I could put it away and not worry about it, I would, but I can't. It is constantly on my mind so I can't help worrying about it."

"I suppose I don't really understand the *creative mind,"* she said with comic emphasis on the last part, "but I don't see why this book is so important. The world will keep clanking along whether you finish it or not." She felt him go chilly the instant the words were out of her mouth.

"It matters," he said with instantly boiling passion. "Maybe not to you or anyone else, but it matters to me, and it matters to those creatures who live in the pile of paper over there." Katherine's mouth fell open. She closed it and studied John's face. The smoldering eyes, pale cheeks, and straight line mouth told her he wasn't kidding. Like Joshua, he had come to believe in the life of the creatures he was creating.

"I'm sorry, John. It didn't come out like I meant it too, exactly."

John relaxed some and said, "I'm sorry too. It's just...I don't know. I used to think Joshua was sort of agreeably crazy to believe in Forneria. Now I'm as crazy as he was. These people inhabit me. I inhabit them." The passion of his voice ratcheted up as he continued.

"We dwell blended together as parts of one another. I live..." he touched his chest, "...they live." He pointed at the stack of manuscript. "I die and, at least until they are whole within their world, they die. If I make them whole like Joshua did, then while their world may not continue through an open ended universe, at least they will be alive within the closed universe which was finished when their stories were finished. And they will continue to stay alive in their closed universe so long as people, readers, continue to know them."

John turned and put the heels of his hands to his eyes. The tension in him was like a burning fuse. "Forneria, my Forneria, is just so real to me I hardly know which is the real world and which is the world I am creating. I know it sounds completely egotistical, but I think I know how God feels, at least on the limited scale of my own heart. I understand the otherness yet oneness of it. I don't know how to explain it to you without sounding like some mystic nut case, but Forneria lives in me and I live in it."

Katherine put her arms around him and pulled him to her. After a moment he relaxed and put his arms around her too. The solidity of her brought his whirling mind back to the room where they were sitting. She became an anchor connecting him back to the reality of the bedroom.

John, still pressed close to Katherine, said, "I don't know if I can do this tomorrow without coming apart. Will you come with me?"

"I have to go anyway. I'll be there."

He leaned back so he could look into her face but did not let her go. "No, I don't mean just be there. I mean be close to me. Hold my hand. Help me not to flip out and go after Lucian."

"You won't," she soothed. "You didn't at the hospital."

"I was in shock. Tomorrow I'll just be angry--and protective. You saw how I was with you a few minutes ago. What am I going to do if Lucian makes some crack about Forneria or Joshua? What little perspective I have will evaporate."

She touched his face and pushed back the lock of hair which had fallen over his forehead like a mother soothing a child. "All right, I'll stick with you if the people in the court will let me."

John pulled her to him again saying "Thank you, Thank you!" He pulled away from her to look into her eyes then, without a thought, he kissed her.

Katherine tensed, pulled her mouth away, and looked into his eyes. The gold flecks in the green seemed to spark and to draw her in, ease her apprehensions. She leaned in and kissed him back..

Seven

After dismissing the Abominations of Tuchinar, Fisher walked away from the five at the fire. They looked at one another, questioning whether they should follow him out into the darkness, but though they had lost their dread of the forest, they knew Fisher needed to be alone. After a moment of consideration, they sat down around the fire, not even bothering to preserve their night vision. What they had seen had squeezed their hearts with terror and torn their hearts with pity for the tortured horror of the monsters. What they had seen swelled their hearts with hope. Such awesome power, such merciful grace, had never been witnessed in Forneria. Each man turned silently into his own thoughts to understand what he had seen.

For John Fisher the terror of the forest was gone, but there was still a deep, aching fear in him. He walked into the darkness so his companions could not see him trembling and sweating. The fear which Lucian had planted in him at Mono grew even as knowledge of his power grew. *This is all in my hands. I am now the God of Forneria, but even though I am the Creator in the other universe, I do not know what will happen here, exactly.* There was some tenuous connection between his Forneria self and the other self, the Creator-self, which allowed him to see some shadow of the future, but not a clear sight. Never a clear sight.

At the back of his mind he began to feel he knew what must happen. He did not like this feeling, accompanied as it was by ominous dread and vain resentment. There might be another self elsewhere, but *this* Fornerian self could bleed and hurt and feel love for these people; this living-self felt pity for the sad, loathsome creatures of the cruel Tuchinar; this self had no illusions about suffering and pain, it knew the fear of death. After Mono he knew he was as subject to them as any creature in Forneria. He knew at some point his story, his life, would come to an end, in fact had to come to an end because he knew his death was the only way he would be able to do for the beloved Abominations what he had promised them he would do; take them home. But it did not make the fear less or the dread of pain less.

As night dragged on, the five witnesses began to feel a despair they had never known before. They felt the loss of Fisher. He had walked into the darkness, separating himself from them, his absence like a growing hollow in each of them. They remembered how he had stood fearless before monsters that had completely unmanned the five of them. How he had spoken the truth to Lucian's messengers, telling them they were free, but that their freedom would cost them.

All the witnesses had tasted the water, which renewed itself at his behest, and had been changed by it. They knew how they had changed by being with this man and they felt the dread of the departure of which he had spoken.

At the same time they were glad to be separated from him because clearly he was more than human, and his ultra-humanity frightened them. Such a being had never before been born and they felt the end of this more-than-human being would be their end as well. They were bound up with him now and could not get free except at his behest.

Night passed. At dawn Fay said, "We should find out where he went."

"I think we should leave him alone. He walked away and will be back when he gets back," Noah said.

"Fay is right. We need to know where he is. We won't disturb him, but we need to know where he is," Bitter said.

Ever pragmatic, Ezra said, "We need to prepare some food for him and for ourselves. And look for a spring. The water bags are less than half full, and the droms are gonna need more forage soon."

Thomas stood and started to walk away.

"Where are you going?" Fay asked.

"The fire needs wood if we are going to cook. I will look for John Fisher while I look for wood."

The idea was so practical the men looked at one another and smiled then stood and went in different directions seeking wood and Fisher.

Thomas found Fisher a hundred steps away. He sat with his back against a tall straight pine tree, his eyes closed as though he were asleep. Thomas did not approach but continued to pick up windfall sticks. When he was loaded down, he went back to the fire, dumped the wood and fed some into the fire. He reported to the others as they came back.

They made up some gruel and pine tea and ate quietly.

The morning passed into afternoon. Ezra dipped a bowl of the gruel and asked where Thomas had found Fisher.

"I don't think we should disturb him," Noah said.

"I'll just put the bowl near him. He can reach it if he wants it."

The others nodded their agreement and Ezra went.

Fisher was still sitting as Thomas had found him. His eyes were still closed, but the look of him had none of the peace of sleep. His brow was furrowed with what could have been worry or pain and drops of sweat out of proportion to the heat of the forest dotted his face.

Ezra approached quietly. Fisher did not open his eyes or give any acknowledgement he was aware he was no longer alone. Ezra put the bowl beside him, hesitated a moment then walked back to the others.

The others looked anxiously to Ez, but he just shook his head and sat down again.

In the dusk Fisher came back carrying the still full bowl of gruel. He looked stooped and tired and his eyes were like hollow black holes. He passed his eyes over the five of them. He wanted to tell them to go home, go back to their families, go back to their lives, but he knew their old lives were gone, changed forever. At last he breathed out and said, "I must go on. I will not ask you to go with me for I do not know what else will happen. Lucian's fortress is only a few more days' travel, is it not?"

241

Fay, the only one who had actually been in the Northern fortress, said, "Yes, about a week."

"Then I can go on alone."

"No," Fay said. "I cannot let you. I am a poor servant at best, but please allow me to continue with you. I may be of some use yet."

"Nor can I," Noah said.

"We have come this far with you," Thomas said "and we will go on."

The others agreed with him. Fisher cast his eyes over the five again and almost wept in fear for these dear creatures. "As with Lucian's messengers, you are free to go as you will, but if you come with me, there may be death at the end. I do not wish you hurt."

"Sir," Ezra began then stopped at the sound of his own voice. It sounded strange to him to call this man 'sir,' but it also sounded right. "Sir, if we go back--if I go back, I ain't gonna be the way I was. I'm changed. I don't believe I can keep living in the world unless I go with you."

The others murmured their agreement. Fisher slumped beneath the burden of their devotion then nodded his understanding. "I hope you do not live to regret your decisions."

Before dawn the next morning, while the six were still rolled in their blankets sleeping, the attack came. With shouts and shots into the air for the sake of surprise, a dozen of Lucian's cavalry fell on them. The soldiers had been sent with specific orders to take the men alive if possible, but should any of them resist, they could be killed, except for Fisher. Fisher was to be brought to Lucian alive, no matter what.

Captain Fay, Bitter, and Ezra had been sleeping with their pistols near at hand for days, and the shooting and shouts brought the three of them up armed and ready. Not knowing the cavalry was firing into the air, they began answering fire with better aimed shots of their own. The light was too little for truly well aimed shots, but with blue and yellow muzzle flashes flaring like deadly fireflies, someone was bound to be hit soon if the firing did not stop. John Fisher stood, still wrapped in his blanket and began shouting "Stop, stop shooting all of you! We surrender! We give up! Stop firing!" He threw off his blanket and stood full height with his hands in the air.

Noah saw Fisher and did the same, also throwing his hands above his head.

Bitter, firing at the dimly seen figures of the soldiers, saw Noah and Fisher surrender so he did the same, but his pistol was lifted high above his head.

Lt. Banning of Lucian's cavalry recognized the pistol as a weapon and fired. The bullet spun Bitter around and dropped him to the ground. Captain Fay saw Banning fire and Bitter fall. Trained in the arts of war he brought his own pistol around and fired without a thought. The shot caught the Lieutenant square in the chest. He went down like a stone.

"Noooo!" Fisher cried and his voice was like thunder. All the shooting stopped at once as though all of them had come awake from the nightmare at the same instant.

"Enough," Fisher shouted. "No more shooting. We surrender. If you are sent to kill us all then be about it. We will not resist any more." He turned his eyes to Fay then to Ezra and both lowered their pistols. A moment before they would have killed for Fisher, now at his command they were ready to die.

The troopers did not know what to do. They had seen their commander go down and now they stood weapons at the ready waiting for some command. A company sergeant knelt beside the wounded Lieutenant. In the growing light the troopers saw the sergeant's shoulders slump, a man who had seen too many dead comrades. After a moment he stood and came toward the five who were gathered around Bitter as he lay on the pine mast.

The grizzled sergeant stepped to Captain Fay, who still wore his uniform though the badges and insignia had been stripped from it. The soldier saluted. The emotion on his face twisted Fay's conscience. The last time the Captain had killed had been in Barstow on the night his heart was changed.

Fay, his voice choked and quiet said, "I am not a soldier any longer, Sergeant. I serve John Fisher."

The Sergeant looked confused and lowered his hand. "Which one is Fisher, Sir?"

"The one kneeling there, beside the wounded man."

The sergeant turned to Fisher and said, "Sir, we are commanded to bring you and these others to Great Lucian. Do you surrender?"

Bitter lay on his back. His chest was covered with blood and more blood was leaking from the wound high on the left side of his chest. He breathed in great gasps and with each breath more of his life pumped forth.

Fisher looked up at the sergeant then looked back to Bitter. "Why did you shoot? He had his hands up. Why did you shoot?"

Not their fault, John Fisher," Bitter gasped. "I still had the pistol."

"Sir, do I have your surrender?" the sergeant asked again, his voice tight.

Fay stepped to the soldier.

"We surrender, Sergeant. We will go to Lucian without any more killing."

Bitter lifted his hand and gripped Fisher's arm. "Tell Ruthie..." he gasped.

Tears came to Fisher's eyes as Bitter struggled to say his last good bye. They ran down his face and dripped onto Bitter's wound. "You can't die, James," he said. "You can't die. I won't let you die." He looked up at Fay and the sergeant. "Bring me water. Bring me water quickly," he commanded.

Noah heard and brought a water bag to him.

Fisher drew out the stopper then lifted the bag to the light of the coming dawn. "Great Creator," he said through his tears. "Make this the water of life."

He lowered the bag and let the limber neck of it down so the water spilled into Bitter's mouth. "The water of life, James. Drink and be whole."

In the blink of an eye the blood stopped pumping from Bitter's chest, and in another moment he sat up. As Fisher had commanded, he was whole.

The grizzled sergeant gasped, and the other troopers lowered their weapons and stepped forward to see if what their eyes had told them, what could not possibly be true, was indeed true.

Bitter, who had *known* he was a dead man, cast his eyes around at the soldiers and at the world which was as new to him now as to a newborn. He looked down at his still torn and bloody shirt then brought his hand up to where the wound had been. He tore the shoulder of the shirt off and ripped open the torn place so his bare chest could be seen. There was no mark on him in the place where the bullet had penetrated. The flesh was whole and smooth in the growing daylight. In less than a heart beat the sergeant dropped to his knees and threw off his cap.

"Sir...John Fisher," he began. "The Lieutenant....sir, he's my son..." his voice choked and he could not go on. Fisher stood. He looked down on the bowed gray head then put his hand upon it.

"Come, Sergeant."

The man turned his face up and the look of hope was brighter than the new day. He stood and walked beside his prisoner. The other soldiers still stood, awestruck, with their weapons forgotten though they were still in hand. The sergeant said, "Order your arms. Put 'em away. We don't need them any more."

The troopers hurried to do it and turned to follow Fisher and the Sergeant to where the Lieutenant's body lay. Fisher still held the water bag and when he approached the body he turned the limber neck down and dribbled some water into his hand. He knelt beside the body. Fay's shot had taken the young man high in the center of his chest, destroying his heart as it tore through his body. He had been dead before he fell.

"What is your son's name," Fisher asked. "Benjamin, sir. Ben. "This is the water of life, Benjamin," Fisher said dribbling the few drops of water from his hand onto the young man's slightly parted lips. "Drink and be whole."

Many of the troopers surrounding the body thought, how can he drink? He is dead. But when the water had trickled into the young man's mouth they saw the spark come back to his dead, staring eyes, and in a moment he who had been dead drew in a breath. In another moment he sat up and the radiance of his face was like what had been on Jim Bitter's face a few moments before. Though he had been dead, now he lived.

Eight

Ed Chance considered calling a press conference, but he was afraid no one would show up. Instead he made a few phone calls to friends in the media letting it be known that Lucian Gordon--Yes *the* Lucian Gordon--was about to be in court. And yes, Chance did think Josh Gordon's son would be present at the trial because this was in the nature of a personal thing.

"Personal?" Anthony March, columnist for the Times asked. "What's personal about it?"

"He is trying to get the copyrights to his father's work."

"His father? And who is his father...Oh wait, the Forneria series, right? He just died a couple of weeks ago didn't he? What, his father cut Lucian out of the will or something? I wouldn't think there was enough in the estate for him to bother with."

"There isn't. Besides, Tony, you know I wouldn't try to sell you on anything so ordinary. See, Joshua left his whole estate to Lucian, except for the copyrights. Those he left to a young guy named John Fisher."

"Hum," March grunted. "Kinda strange I guess, but there's a lot of *so what* in it. Who cares?"

"Anyone who ever read a Joshua Gordon novel is who. Didn't you notice how many people showed up at the funeral? It was like Joshua was a movie star or something."

March grunted again. "And I still say so what? I mean Gordon wasn't Hemingway."

"Something a little quirky goes along with it. See, Lucian only wants the copyrights so he can let the books die, Tony. It is his stated purpose to bring an end to all remembrance of his father's work."

March was quiet for a moment then said "OK, a little strange, a little better. Kinda like book burning."

"Which is why I called you. I know you are very big on freedom of speech and anti-suppression of any kind of words in a line so I thought you might be interested."

"Maybe I am, a little. I don't remember ever reading or at least finishing any of Gordon's books. If I remember, they were a little pulpy for my taste."

"Tony, you are a snob. Just because a book comes out in paper back first and has a picture of a buxom wench on the front, you think it is pulp crap..." March laughed."...and won't read it."

"I always wondered, if they were so good, why somebody didn't make a movie out of one."

Now Chance laughed. "For a man who earns his daily bread with the written word you are also a remarkably lazy Philistine. A Philistine snob, God help us."

March laughed again. "I guess so, and I still wonder why no movie."

"I think they actually tried a couple of times and I think they brought one out based on *Tuchinara,* but it didn't do well. To much of the ethereal flavor of it got lost when they just used the story. You oughta try reading a couple of them."

"Maybe I will."

"In any case, you might do well to make a couple of calls to check this out. I mean, if I were you, I would want to know a little bit more about why a man famous for his wealth and for his charity work would want to kill off some moldy pulp fiction series written by his own father."

"Maybe I will give it a look. I take it you are involved in this lawsuit some kinda way?"

"Right you are. So, if you do decide to dig into this a little, I'd appreciate your forgetting my name. It might get a little sticky if you don't."

Now March sat forward in his chair. "Are we talking violation of a gag order here, Ed?"

"Tony, I would never violate a gag order--especially since one hasn't been issued yet. I expect it tomorrow, so if you want any information about the case I'd hurry."

"Who is the judge?"

"McSweeny."

March's garbage heap of a mind instantly shoved a fact to the top of the pile. "Didn't Lucian Gordon have something to do with getting him elected?"

"Why Tony, you wouldn't be thinking Lucian used some kind of undue influence would you?"

March thought about it. A lot of big political stories had started with just such little things as favors called in because of election contributions, and with Lucian Gordon in it..."Might be a dangerous idea, Ed."

"Yes, indeed it might which is why I would appreciate your not mentioning where the idea originated."

"OK, you got me. I'm curious enough to at least make a couple of phone calls."

"All I can ask."

"It may be all you get, too. See ya, Ed."

"See ya, Tony."

Chance was gratified to see reporters waiting on the courthouse steps the next morning to greet his arrival with client in tow. He was a little surprised to find Katherine, stunned to find her holding John's hand. He had asked her to be there *just in case'* but he sure had not expected hand holding.

"What makes Lucian Gordon want these copyrights so much, Mr. Chance?" one reporter asked.

Ten microphones were stuck in the lawyer's face to hear the answer.

"Mr. Gordon's stated purpose is to erase the memory of his father's books from the literary memory of the world," Chance said.

"Why? What's in them?"

"Read one and see. They're all still in print."

"Is that why his father left them to someone else?"

"Yes. Joshua wanted his literary legacy to live on so he left the rights to the books and stories to my client."

The reporters turned to John. Katherine stood close by, his shoulder still holding his hand, grave concern in her eyes.

"Mr. Fisher, why did Joshua Gordon leave the copyrights to you?"

John was astonished by the amount of attention suddenly poured out on him, feeling a tiny kernel of fear sprout and take root inside himself. He had never been particularly afraid of crowds, but all the microphones bristling and the avid faces of the reporters made him break out in a sweat. Katherine squeezed his hand and he was glad she was there. After hesitating he stammered, "Joshua wanted me to take over the world he had created and keep it alive."

"And are you keeping it alive?"

"I'm trying. I'm working on the book Joshua and I were writing together when he died."

"A new book? When will it come out?"

Again John hesitated, but this time Ed Chance jumped into the silence. "Impossible to say. It will depend on the results of this case--which we need to get to, so if you ladies and gentlemen will excuse us."

He turned and put a sheltering arm around John's shoulder which should have seemed ludicrous since John was considerably taller than Chance, but the gesture achieved its purpose; John became the beleaguered innocent. With Chance on the right and Katherine on the left they climbed the stairs with camera flashes following them.

The court room, which for a civil trial would ordinarily have been nearly empty, was jam packed with on lookers. As at the funeral, many of the spectators carried copies of one or another of Joshua Gordon's books.

Chance, Fisher, and Katherine worked their way through the crowd to the table at the front left of the room. Katherine, not really being a party to the proceedings, would ordinarily have sat in the hall waiting to be called to testify But when Chance tried to leave her outside, John said, "No, Ed. Can't she stay with me? I really need her."

Chance saw the pleading look of his client, thought for a moment, and said, "If this works, we won't need her to testify today, and if it goes against us, I'll be in jail. Since we won't need her for a couple of days any way, all right." He turned to Katherine, "But you better do your best to be invisible."

She nodded and they elbowed their way in.

They looked for a place right by the rail in the gallery where she could sit and still be close to John, but every seat was full so she hung on to Fisher's hand and sat down at the table with him.

John had never been in a court room before; he remarked how it looked a lot like the ones on TV.

"Art imitating life--or maybe the other way around," Chance said.

"I can't believe how many people there are. And all those reporters! I never expected anything like this."

"Had to make sure this whole thing didn't end up on page nine of the business section. With the full glare of publicity focused on this room, maybe the judge will be less likely to rule in Lucian's favor even though he owes Lucian."

"Can't we get a recusal? Isn't it illegal for a judge with direct ties to one of the parties to preside?"

Chance examined his young client with newfound, but somewhat amused respect before saying, "Ah. But the ties between him and Lucian aren't direct enough to make it an obvious call." I intend to remind the judge of their combined histories, but I don't think McSweeny will sit still for a recusal.

A stir at the back of the court room made heads turn. Lucian Gordon and his lawyer were making their way through the spectators. When they had elbowed their way to the front, Gordon glared at them with a special acidity reserved for Katherine. Arthur Drew sent a watery smile their way.

"I don't think he ever liked me," Katherine said.

"All rise," came the bailiff's call and the courtroom quieted as everyone stood.

Judge McSweeny came in, looked over the packed courtroom and blinked in surprise before he sat down. "Counselors approach, please." he asked, seating himself.

Chance and Drew went to the bench amid the rustle and clatter of the courtroom gallery seating themselves.

"What is all this?" the judge began. "I thought I would be presiding over a business hearing. The courtroom looks like the OJ trial!"

"It was supposed to be a simple matter of contract enforcement, your honor," Drew said.

Looking with disgust at Chance the judge said, "Is this your idea, Counselor?"

"Not exactly, your honor. Joshua Gordon has a lot of fans, so when they heard Mr. Gordon's son was suing to try to pull Joshua's work off the shelves, they naturally became interested."

"Your honor, such a claim is not any part of why we are here," Drew said. "We are charging Mr. Chance's client offered to sell the copyrights to my client who, in good faith, agreed to the arrangement only to have his good faith abused by Mr. Fisher withdrawing the deal and we believe therefore Mr. Fisher is in breach of contract."

"Your honor that is not--"

McSweeny held up his hand. "I don't want to hear arguments, gentlemen, I just want to find a way to get some of this mess cleared out of my courtroom."

"The simplest way would be to recuse yourself, your honor," Chance said almost casually.

Drew shot him a disbelieving glance and McSweeny's glare could have cut sheet metal. "Step back," the judge said. The counselors returned to their tables and sat as McSweeny shuffled papers. After a moment he said, "I'll entertain motions, gentlemen."

Chance came quickly to his feet. "Your honor, since you have close and well known ties to one of the parties to this suit, we would move you recuse yourself from this trial."

There was a hum of talk from the spectators as McSweeny rapped his gavel and said, "I'll have quiet in my court room or I'll put all spectators out." They quieted and he went on, "Your motion is denied, Mr. Chance."

"Exception your honor," Chance said.

"Noted."

"In which case, your honor," Chance turned and picked up a packet of papers from his open brief case, "may I approach?"

"What is it, Mr. Chance?"

"Your honor, since my motion for recusal has been denied, I have here a motion to make this a jury trial rather than a summery judgment."

Drew was on his feet. "We object most strenuously, your honor. Matters such as this are handled by summery judgment, not juries. This is a civil matter in which my client is not seeking damages, only the enforcement of a contract."

McSweeny gave Chance another hacksaw glare and said, "Mr. Chance, you aren't implying this matter might not be decided fairly by me are you?"

"No your honor--not precisely."

The judge first paled then reddened. "You are treading very close to contempt, Mr. Chance."

"Begging the court's pardon. It was not my intent to impugn the court's impartiality. I only meant to say my client disputes the existence of any contract and, while I am sure your honor would make an absolutely even handed judgment, I do not believe the weight of such a judgment should fall solely upon your shoulders." Chance smiled winningly.

McSweeny wanted to wipe the smile off Chance's face, but he was a political animal who recognized the danger of this small case. On the one hand, he had Lucian Gordon, the goose that laid the golden egg of campaign finance. On the other hand he had--he was not entirely sure what he had, but it smelled dangerous.

After a moment the judge decided the best thing to do was to postpone any decision.

"Gentlemen, I will have to think about this."

Drew was once more on his feet. "But your honor, we were hoping to-_"

"Sit down, Mr. Drew. It isn't going to happen today. I will give you my decision tomorrow morning at nine o'clock. Meantime, I am issuing a gag order regarding this case. There will be no further talk to *anyone* about the matter before this court. Do I make myself clear?"

"Yes, your honor," Both lawyers said in unison.

"Goes for you two as well," McSweeny said, glancing from Fisher to Gordon.

"Yes sir," John said. Lucian only nodded, looking stunned at the prospect of delay.

"Very well, we are in recess until tomorrow morning," the judge said. He quickly left the bench disappearing into chambers.

Chance turned and winked at Fisher. Lucian saw the wink and turned purple. He stood, spun on his heel, and elbowed his way out through the departing crowd.

Nine

Lieutenant Banning, for long moments, could say nothing. Astonishment at being alive gripped his restored heart and paralyzed his voice. He had only just realized he was dead when John Fisher called him back to life. Banning's face radiated light and eyes of the company drank in the sight until there was a reflective glow in them.

Nor could Sergeant Banning speak for a long time, but his voice was choked off with grateful tears. His face reflected the living light of his son's countenance as he continued to kneel beside him. When Fisher rose, the sergeant grabbed his hand and kissed it. "Thank you, sir. Thank you for my son's life."

Fisher smiled and pulling his hand out of the sergeant's grasp, he laid it on the sergeant's grizzled head. Ezra and others recognized the look upon Fisher's face. They had seen it on the faces of doting parents whose children had done particularly well at something. It was the heart wrenching adoration of a father who had just rescued his child from a burning building.

Bitter, who was also aglow with renewed life, was still surrounded by those who were his traveling companions. He rose to his feet and removed his bloody shirt. He had no other to put on, but the lack did not bother him. All the four others kept looking from him to John Fisher and back. Bitter continued to glance down to the place where the bullet had torn his chest.

There was nothing there. No scar, no bruise, no mark of any kind, only smoothly muscled flesh.

The dozen soldiers who had witnessed all felt the power of restored life in Bitter and their Lieutenant, but they still did not understand what had just happened. They thought they had seen a man wounded unto death healed. They thought they had seen their Lieutenant return whole from the grip of death, but they looked at one another and each could see questions in the eyes of his compatriots. Did we really see this? Does this John Fisher, whom we have been sent to bring to Great Lucian, really have power over death? They had heard it whispered he could call water from dry wells and change men's hearts with his words, but on the heels of those whispers, Great Lucian had said repeating any such rumors would be punished harshly, perhaps even with execution.

Fisher went to the fire, now more ash than fuel, and stirred it with a stick. He found some still red coals, fed some small wood onto them and blew on the little pile. The kindling burst into flame and Fisher began adding bigger sticks. He felt the eyes on him and looked up from the fire.

The Lieutenant stood beside his father. The resemblance between them was remarkable. He too had taken off his bloody shirt and held it in his hand. Those who had been under his command now stood near him as though drawing the strength of life, as well as it's reflected glow, from him into themselves.

"We must prepare something to eat and move on," Fisher said, adding more wood to the fire. "Lucian will be anxious."

"Sir," Sergeant Banning said, "you should not go further. Great--" he stopped and started again. "Lucian wishes you harm. He sent us to bring you and we were told to kill everyone except you if necessary."

"I know, Sergeant. But I must go to meet him if Forneria is ever to be free of his Dry. Free of him. Had he been patient, I would have brought myself to him and saved you the trouble of finding me."

"But, sir," Lt. Banning said, "Lucian will kill you."

Fisher shivered though the morning was now very warm. "I still must meet him."

"Then we will, if we may, accompany you, sir." the Lieutenant said.

Fisher had tried to leave his little company behind but they would not stay; now he had a dozen more ready to follow him--perhaps follow him into death.

"Benjamin, I go someplace none of you can follow me. I *must* meet Lucian, but you and these others do not have to. You can stay here or go back down the mountain and anywhere else you want to go. I do not want you dead again," he smiled gently.

The Bannings, father and son, looked crestfallen. The elder said, "Sir, please let me come with you. It doesn't matter if my life is forfeit, my son is alive."

There was a general sound of agreement through the group and several said they would prefer to go with him no matter the danger.

Fisher examined all of them before saying, "I think you do not know what you are getting into, but if you are determined, I cannot stop you. You are free people."

The Bannings looked over the troop and Ezra looked over the pilgrims. All were ready for whatever came, be it life or death.

Fisher saw it too, but shook his head. He hated the idea of any of these creatures being in danger because of him, but, at the same time, his quailing spirit was comforted by the fact he would not be alone. "Very well," he said at last. "We will go as soon as we have eaten."

They made a considerable troop once the cavalry with their horses and pack droms were joined to the six with their mounts and pack droms. The day was hot and sere, but beneath the pines they were out of the sun. The air was scented with the exhalation of warm pine needles and resin of the trees. Captain Fay spoke with Lieutenant Banning and they decided to let Banning and half his troop, pennants flying, ride in front. The other half, under Sergeant Banning, rode at the back. So, looking more like a guard of honor than a custodial company, they started for Lucian's stronghold.

The Northern Fortress was located inside the walls of a monstrous ancient volcanic crater long since extinct and overrun by pine forest. The troop stopped as it crossed the rim of the crater to look down into the bowl.

The fortress was cut into a basalt face on the west side of the crater and was reached by a switchback road chipped out of the cliff. The magnificence of it was indescribable with its tall black turrets and its massive black stone walls, but it shrank into insignificance before a colossal lake at its feet. The crater was so wide the far side was misty with distance. It looked like a mere black line between water and sky.

"It is wider than the Mono," Ezra breathed.

"Is it fresh water?" Noah asked of anyone who could answer.

"It is fresh," Lieutenant Banning answered. "Clear, cold, and sweet, with fish looking as though you could reach down and touch them, but so deep you could not begin to go down to them on one breath."

"It seems to be closer to the foot of the palace than it was when I was here last," Captain Fay said.

"Yes sir, it is," Sergeant Banning explained. "Few weeks ago it started rising. Still is. Been coming up a little until the warden in the fortress has started worrying it may over flood the road."

"It started to rise the day John Fisher opened the fountain and the wells in Barstow," Bitter said without any doubt and others nodded their agreement

"I did not open the waters of the earth," Fisher said with quiet authority. "You all seem to think I am more than I am. Gordon the Creator released the waters of the earth. The Creator freed the Abominations, and the messengers and restored Bitter and Lieutenant Banning. I was only the vessel. Remember when I am gone, he who made the world and who made you, listens to your prayers as he did to mine, and he will heed them. He wants you to be well and not suffering and only asks that you in return remember him and treat every living thing with mercy and respect, even those that sustain you."

There were nods of acceptance all around, but no one truly understood yet. Fisher could only hope they would remember his words tomorrow and in days after.

A far away echo of a bugle call reached them.

"A look out has spotted us, sir. The garrison will turn out to see us come in."

Fisher nodded. "It is time to go on, Lieutenant. Lucian waits," he said, and as he said it the others saw him shiver as though brushed with an arctic wind. When the little troop approached the base of the mountain, people from the garrison came outside the fortress lining the road as they passed. The people stood quietly looking at the cavalcade, asking one another, "Which one is he? Which on is Fisher?" Most had heard the name whispered, but almost none had seen him.

As the cavalcade, looking still more like a triumphal procession than an escort for prisoners, made its way up the crowd-lined path to the palace gate, Ezra thought about the last time he had met Lucian. Then the god of the world had been a whirlwind, but clearly a whirlwind did not need a fortress.

In a widened landing at the top of the road but outside the courtyard gate, the troop dismounted. They turned their mounts over to waiting grooms then formed up a proper escort to enter the fortress precincts.

The courtyard was dominated by an image of Lucian which was carved into the face of the cliff. The courtyard was filled with soldiers of the garrison and servants from Lucian's dwelling. There was a rustle and buzz of anticipation as the escort arranged itself in a box around Fisher and his followers. The guard detail came to attention and marched their charges through the crowd to the foot of the stairs which swept down from the palace door to the courtyard. They stopped at the bottom step just as two trumpeters came out onto the broad staircase landing from the huge main doors. They stopped, lifted their trumpets to their lips, and blew a fanfare that was both an introduction and call to arms.

All eyes turned to the sound. At the top of the broad staircase stood Lucian in Tuchinar armor. Tall and handsome with a pointed beard like

Satan's, Lucian looked every inch the conquistador of Gordon's first book. Blinding light reflected off his highly polished armor and helmet. There was a magnetism in this being. Power radiated from him in a near visible aura. Here was the Being who demanded worship and cruelly controlled life and death through thirst and pain; and to add to his god-like appearance, above his head, unlike any human likeness, a halo of shining, obsidian black. He casually held a conquistador's broad sword with a jeweled handle and sheathed in a jewel encrusted scabbard as though the magnificent artifact were a walking cane.

Everyone looked from Lucian's high magnificence to John Fisher, automatically comparing the two. Fisher was dressed in the same dirty, sweat stained clothes he had been wearing for weeks. He was as sun-browned and leather-dry as any other dweller in the desert of Forneria. His wide Traveler hat hung down his back on its cord showing his hair and beard, dusty and ragged. No more ordinary looking man had ever walked in Forneria, yet all had heard he commanded the waters of the earth and some had seen him command monsters and call men back from the dark heart of death.

Lucian paused at the top of the staircase, looking over the crowd and especially examining the escort he had sent out to bring John Fisher to him. With a nod he gave permission for the detail to march their prisoners up the stairs.

There was no hesitation to obey the command, but some glance or grimace told Lucian these men were lost to him. When they halted on the broad landing, Lucian said, "I see you have turned my soldiers against me, Fisher." His voice echoed from the monolithic building behind him so everyone in the courtyard could hear. "How unfortunate for them," he continued. "They will have to die, of course."

The crowd gasped. Though they had seen many of Lucian's lethal tantrums, they still were not hardened to his bloody cruelty.

"Can't have traitors going about preaching mercy now, can I?" He asked Fisher as he lifted the sword still in its scabbard and showed it to Fisher. He lifted the sword and swept the point toward the escort. Everyone in the courtyard felt the tide of evil intent wash over them, but only the soldiers who had escorted Fisher stiffened and fell.

Fisher glanced around at the still forms, apparently unconcerned. "Stop it Lucian," He said quietly. "Release them. We both know the Tuchinar machine you disguise as a sword controls the weather, but it has not the power of life and death."

Lucian laughed. It was an echo of the booming laugh Fisher had heard from the waterspout at Mono. The Tuchinar stepped to where Lieutenant Banning lay. "This is the one you called back, is it not?"

"Yes."

"You are wrong, John Fisher. The Tuchinar machine may not command life and death, but when I draw it forth--" he pulled the gleaming steel from its sheath, cast the sheath aside and lifted the slightly curved blade above his head "--and strike off the lieutenant's head, he will be quite dead." Lucian began the downward swing.

"Enough," Fisher said, raising his voice only a little. "The one you want to kill is me, not poor Benjamin."

Lucian stopped his downward swing and looked up, grinning. The jet colored halo gleamed. "Yes," he said, "you are right. I do want you, but since I cannot have you, what with your now being the Creator since my father is dead, I'll have to settle for these." He raised the sword again, a smile of relish on his face.

"What will you gain by killing them, Lucian? You can no longer hurt your father. You can not gain power in Forneria by killing them. Why bother?"

An acid smile crossed Lucian's face. "It will give me joy to steal them from *you*, Creator. Spilling their blood hurts you, and *that* gives me joy. I told you at Mono, destruction is power and control. I will have power.

"And those," Lucian said with relish, riposting the point of his sword at the five who had traveled from Barstow with Fisher. "I will enjoy having their blood as well, and though you are the Creator now, you cannot stop me."

The five could almost feel the edge of the sword as if it marked them; understanding very little of what they were hearing. They, the soldiers lying as though dead were not dead, and though John Fisher had stopped Lucian from killing them, all their lives still hung in the balance.

"But why, Lucian? Why? You could have been the divine caretaker of Forneria. Your father wanted more than anything to hand the world over to you so you might care for its creatures. Why would you want to destroy what he created?"

"Why would I want to take my father's cast-offs?" he sneered. "And why would I want to preserve this--" he turned around indicating the whole world. "--for one who had no time and no love for me in the other world? One who used me as the evil balanced against you?" Lucian shook his head with what might have been disappointed sadness then looked up at Fisher.

"My father loosed me here for the sake of his story. As the beast who threatened to destroy his creation. Very well, I will destroy it, beginning with these," He once more pointed with his sword. "I will be the beast my father designed me to be and you cannot stop me. You cannot cage me because I am not in any way your creation." He laughed but now it was like his laugh at Mono. The sound of it rang from the castle walls and out across the lake.

The crowd of soldiers and servants who watched covered their ears but still crumpled with the pain as did Fisher and the others, the barrier afforded by their hands was not enough to buffer the power of Lucian's voice. Blood sprang from their noses and ears, and many cried out in pain.

"You see," Lucian went on. "Even my laughter can sweep them away." He raised the sword again preparing to slash down on the unconscious Lieutenant.

"But it cannot sweep me away," Fisher said, staggering to his feet. He straightened himself, drew in a deep breath and the blood from his nose and ears dried up and disappeared. "I am the creation of both your father and myself. I will not be swept away. I will stand and you cannot destroy me."

Lucian lowered the sword-machine and leaned on it as he studied Fisher. After a little he nodded and the acid smile returned to his face. "I cannot destroy you, but I can tear the heart out of you," Lucian said. "You can continue to live and play with the water of the world. Perhaps you can run about reanimating those I kill, but I will control. I will control. I will destroy Forneria here," he jabbed the sword at the earth, "and I will destroy Forneria there," he jabbed the sword at the sky. "You will never stop me."

"Wouldn't it be more satisfying to destroy me?" Fisher asked. "I am the one you envy. I am the one you hate for stealing your father's affection. Wouldn't you rather kill me?"

Lucian stopped jabbing at the sky and stared at Fisher, intrigued by the question. "You just said I could not destroy you. Now you ask if I wouldn't like to. What foolishness! You are trying to stall me with your foolishness. You tell me I can't, very well. I can't, so I will kill off your creatures."

"But what harm have these creatures done you? Why should you destroy them just to hurt me? Why not leave them in peace? Take me instead."

Lucian lowered the sword. "Take you? And how can I? You are the Creator. In Forneria you are eternal."

Fisher shook his head slowly. "Not eternal," he said. "Only so long as I wish to live. You may have my life if you will spare these now. Let them live and you may have my life."

Lucian leaned on the sword. "Are these creatures truly so dear to you, Fisher? Is it worth your life to see they die of old age rather than by the edge of my blade?"

"They were very dear to your father, and they are very dear to me. I will trade my life for theirs."

Lucian smiled and the black halo over his head sparkled with fiery delight. "Done," he said and came toward Fisher.

"But first, you must release them. I must see they are alive and well or the trade is off," Fisher said.

"But of course, oh great Creator!" Lucian said with sarcastic pleasure and a mocking bow. He picked up the discarded scabbard, thrust the sword into it, and touched some of the jewels. All of Lieutenant Banning's men woke and began shaking their heads to clear them of the cobwebs left by the Tuchinar machine.

"And all those," Fisher swept his arm back to indicate all in the court yard who, still bleeding and stunned from Lucian's hellish laugh, were staggering to their feet.

Lucian nodded.

"And these?" indicating Ezra, Fay, Bitter, Noah, and Thomas.

They will all have to heal on their own," Lucian said with another biting smile.

"So long as they live to heal," Fisher said.

"You have my word."

"And all the rest of Forneria? Will you spare it?"

Lucian studied Fisher for a time. "I will not turn my blade or my army on any of the creatures of this dung heap if you give me your life."

"No, John Fisher! Do not believe him," Thomas cried, and the others raised their voices to agree with him.

"If he is not true," Fisher did not turn his eyes from Lucian's, "he will not have power to take my life."

Lucian, smiling like a cobra about to strike said, "I am crushed. These creatures do not trust the very son of their Creator. I have given my word."

Fisher nodded his assent. He drew in a deep breath and let it out. He was afraid. He had reached the place he had known he must reach since Joshua's Avatar had told him he could not help any longer. He knew it was the only way, but he was still afraid of the pain. He had helped to create life on this world and in so doing he had helped create death. He knew it was only a door to be stepped through, but the part of him which was a human of Forneria was afraid.

Lucian lifted the sword and placed the point just a little toward the center below Fisher's left breast. He pushed it enough to break the skin and Fisher winced with the pain. A scarlet stain dotted Fisher's dirty hunting shirt.

"Does it hurt, Creator? Are you afraid?"

Fisher said nothing.

Lucian pushed the blade a little harder and was gratified to see the blood stain widen and the muscles of Fisher's jaws tighten as he fought the pain.

"A shame this moment cannot be much prolonged, Creator. Some hours of New Testament agony would bring me great joy."

Those who had traveled with Fisher had watched and listened, understanding very little, now saw the blood and knew John Fisher was about to trade his life for theirs. Almost as one man they stepped forward to stand beside Fisher. "Please, Great Lucian," they begged Lucian. "Do not do this. Take us instead. The world needs him."

Lucian lowered the sword and studied the men. "Would you die to save him?"

None answered him. He lifted the sword point. "Are you sure you would take his place?" He jabbed the sword a little into Noah's breast. Noah gasped with the pain of it. Lucian chuckled then moved the sword point to Fay's breast and jabbed him too.

Fisher stretched out his hand and grasped the blade, slicing his palm and fingers. Blood began to seep down the blood groove of the sword. "I will not allow it. Even if they will, I will not allow it. In this the Creator and I are one. Take me or take none, but you cannot take them without my let."

The five, though they were as afraid of the pain as Fisher said, pleading, "But the world needs you."

"I cannot stay. I told you before I could not. Now let me go. You live on. You must be my witnesses."

The hope vanished from the men and they sank into silence.

Lucian drew in a breath of satisfaction. "Now can we get on with this?"

"Remember your word Lucian," Fisher said, his voice losing its command and quivering a little.

The quiver drew a great smile of anticipation onto Lucian's face. The black halo burned now like a fiery coal. "It is a fearful thing to die here, is it not Creator?"

Without waiting for an answer he threw all his weight against the sword hilt and drove the point through John Fisher's breast and through his body.

Fisher cried out with the pain of it. He reflexively grasped the sword blade near the hilt and the edges sliced his hands more so the blood dripped onto the glassy black floor. He staggered and went to his knees, gasping. His fall wrenched the sword's hilt from Lucian's hand.

Lucian squatted down before the kneeling Fisher. "I gave my word I would not kill them, and I will not, but with you gone, and with this," he gripped the hilt of the sword-machine, "I will call back all the waters. Forneria will dry to a cinder and every creature from the least mouse to the tallest tree, from child to crone, will dry up with it. They will die as surely as if I had hacked each one to death with this sword." He stood, put his foot against Fisher's chest and, with a great tug, he wrenched the sword free. His laughter grew and rose and echoed from the mountains and once more swept all within hearing to the ground.

Ten

Katherine and John did not talk about the trial as they drove home except for John to say, "Thank you for sticking with me."

"I had to," she answered. "I don't know why, but I felt Joshua would have wanted it Guess I'm still his nurse even after he is gone."

"You're his nurse and I'm his voice, and I feel like he is standing right behind me most of the time."

Katherine, who was driving glanced away from the snarl of sunlit traffic at John who was slumped in the passenger seat. "You're not the only one. I could have sworn I heard him calling me a couple of nights ago. I was so sure I actually got up and went to his bedroom to check."

"He keeps whispering in my ear how I need to hurry and get the book done, but he doesn't say why."

Katherine glanced at him again. "Do you really hear him?"

"No, I'm as nuts as he was, but not hearing voices and invisible friends kind of nuts. It's just a feeling I have. Like maybe he wants this thing done so quickly so as to take advantage of the publicity from the trial."

"A little mercenary isn't it?"

"Joshua could be mercenary. He liked to sell books and it sorta bothered him. He thought maybe his attention to writing and the business of selling books had made him a lousy father. It was on his mind right to the end."

They fell silent and Katherine maneuvered through the freeway traffic and off onto the surface streets. "You hungry?" she asked.

"A little I guess." Since they seemed to be on the same wave-length, John knew she meant to stop at a restaurant. "We have food at home," he said.

"Yeah, but at home someone has to fix it before we can eat it." She turned into the parking lot of a "better" chain diner.

"I don't have any money," he said.

"I'll get it. After all, my ill gotten gains from Lucian should be used for something worth while, like feeding his opposition."

John studied Katherine's profile as she parked. Her nurse-short blond hair curled around her ear and made it look delectable. He suddenly sat up, leaned across the seat and kissed it.

She turned and ran her blue-eyed gaze over his face then she smiled dazzlingly. "That was nice. I liked it. I hate how we wasted so much time before finding one another."

The joy he had felt a moment before was suddenly gone. "I liked it too. But I worry it is just some kind of reaction to Joshua's death and all the crap that has come with it. I don't want it to be just comfort in time of trouble."

Katherine stroked his face. "Doesn't really matter does it? I think we ought to enjoy it while we have it. If it turns into something else--something more--good. If not, we have each other to lean on for a while anyway. Come on. Let's eat." She opened the door and slid out into the noisy, smoggy air. After a moment John followed. They sat across the table from one another and made small talk as they ate.

Finished eating, John sat tearing a piece of bread into fragments. His mind, following a labyrinthine subconscious logic, suddenly clicked onto what he was doing. "This is my body," he began, "Which is broken for you and for many. Do this in remembrance of me." He put the small piece of bread in his mouth.

"You can't do the rest of it though," she said after watching him for a moment. "No wine."

"Yeah, I guess." John continued tearing at the bread and his mind continued running on what was never far from his consciousness. "You know, there's no sacrament in the book, exactly. Joshua didn't set anything up and neither did I. Maybe we should have. I mean, if you're gonna steal, you oughta steal the whole thing."

"I think a Last Supper would be too much. You have used the New Testament, but you haven't taken it word for word. And in a way I think you did set up a sacrament. Sharing water."

"Yeah, I guess we did. We stole it from Robert Heinlein."

Katherine looked blank, not understanding the reference.

"*Stranger in a Strange Land*. Valentine Michael Smith. Human kid raised by Martians who value water because they don't have any. Gets brought back to earth and establishes a religion based on everyone being god and sharing water."

"Never read it," she said.

"No real loss. Not one of his best. Too full of high school philosophy."

"I was never much of a science fiction kind of a girl. I liked mysteries."

"Romances?" John asked with bated breath.

"No," she answered with a little disgust in her voice. "I read a few, but they were just too sloshy and had too many holes in the plots."

"Thank God. I wouldn't want to fall in love with a girl who reads romance."

Katherine blinked at him. "Fall in love?"

"Yeah, fall in love. It's what I'm worrying about," he said, looking deep into her eyes.

Katherine shivered, not sure if she wanted to pursue the turn the conversation had just taken. "Maybe we need to ignore our feelings for each other," she said with more practicality than she really felt. "At least until after this court business is finished."

He studied her face for several moments before he said, "Maybe you're right. Let's go home."

~*~

John sat down before his computer screen and called up the last chapter he had been working on. He was not happy with it. It did not go where he wanted it to go and he was worried about some of it being too maudlin. But he didn't trust his judgment anymore, at least not at the moment. There was too much else on his mind to make it easy to look at his own work and say it's good or it stinks. He was tempted to throw out the whole last chapter and go at it again but something stayed his hand. *Must be Joshua holding me back,* and then hurriedly discarded the thought. He had never been a believer in ghosts, and he didn't intend to become one now.

Katherine tapped at the door which was open. John turned to her and said, "Come on in. I need an excuse not to write."

"Then I think you should not try to write tonight," she said. "I think we should go to the living room and sit down in front of the TV and let our brains turn to oatmeal."

John noticed for the first time how she was dressed. She had on a soft, silky looking house robe over satin lounging pajamas.

"I think your point is well taken," he said, standing up. "Oatmeal brains, here we come." He came to her but didn't go past. He stopped, grabbed her by the shoulders and kissed her hard.

They didn't make it to the living room.

~*~

Even Ed Chance was surprised at how many people were outside the courthouse the next morning. He had known Joshua's books were popular, but he had no idea those who spent a few dollars on a paperback book would care enough to come out to the courthouse carrying signs. Most of the placards said "LET FORNERIA LIVE." There were a few which said, "LUCIAN GORDON = BOOK BURNER."

He frankly had thought his calls to the media would perhaps stir up a little attention but figured it would fade fast. Publicity was what he'd hoped for when he had tried to bully Judge McSweeny into throwing him in jail for contempt. Lawyers who tick off judges and get thrown in jail are good newspaper grist. Dead authors aren't. Usually. *But then again I could be wrong.* He turned back to looking for Fisher and Katherine.

They came pushing their way through a knot of reporters fending off shouted questions. Chance made his way down the courthouse steps and shoved through the crowd to John who smiled in relief to see him.

"Now folks," Chance said, "you know Judge McSweeny issued a gag order yesterday. My client can't answer any of your questions, and neither can I. Ask us again after court today. Perhaps we'll have something for you then."

Chance hooked his arm under Fisher's left arm and pulled him on up the stairs. John barely had time to grab Katherine's hand to pull her along too. The courtroom was as crowded as it had been the day before. Chance tried again to leave Katherine in the hall, but like the day before, she and John seemed welded together, so he left off trying. "If anybody asks, you are my assistant," Ed told her.

"What's going to happen?" John asked.

"The judge is going to say whether or not we get a jury trial."

Lucian and Drew, his attorney, came into the room and sat at the plaintiff's table. Lucian glared at John, Katherine, and Chance then turned to say something to Drew.

"All rise," the bailiff called and the court room fell quiet as the judge came in.

Judge McSweeny looked as though he had not slept. He had dark circles under his eyes and furrows more deeply etched in his forehead than the day before. He scanned the crowd then sat. The courtroom sat.

"I..." McSweeny began hesitantly. "...I have decided, in view of my connections with one of the parties of this suit that, though I believe I could be perfectly fair in my judgment, I have chosen to avoid even the appearance of a conflict of interest. Therefore, rather than try to patch together a trial by bringing a jury into it, I will recuse myself."

The room was suddenly abuzz with talk.

McSweeny rapped his gavel. "Order," he said sharply. "This is still my court room and I will have it cleared if I don't get silence."

The room quieted again, though not completely. John glanced at Lucian and noted his color had gone from its ruddy normal to purple. A vein in the temple visibly throbbed.

The judge continued. "I have asked Judge Arthur Fugard if he will preside and he has agreed. Therefore, this hearing will re-convene at Judge Fugard's earliest convenience. Counsel may contact Judge Fugard for a new trial date. Until such a date is established, the gag order on this matter will continue in force." He rapped his gavel and said, "This hearing is adjourned."

Lucian was on his feet with Drew hanging on to his arm like a terrier, but Drew could not stop him. "You can't do this to me, Bill! You owe me! I put you in that robe and I'll take it off you next election." Drew was shushing Lucian and trying to calm him--and having no luck at all. The color of Lucian's face had gone from purple to a plum color so deep as to look almost black.

Ed Chance could only lean back in his chair and shake his head in disbelief. "I did it to stall. I never figured he would actually recuse."

"Well, is this good?" John asked. "What happens now?"

"Now I get time to really prepare a case. I think maybe we can even get this thrown out with a non-biased judge," Chance said, a little doubtfully.

Katherine threw her arms around Fisher hugging him fiercely. "It is better than good. It is wonderful!"

The commotion at the other table altered suddenly. Lucian's voice gave way to Drew shouting, "Call 911 someone! Call 911! He's collapsed!"

Lucian Gordon lay on his back. Drew was loosening Lucian's tie, pulling frantically at the collar button. People were crowded around trying to see.

Chance, Fisher, and Katherine were on their feet and beside them in a heart beat. Chance started motioning the crowd away with "OK, back up, people. Back up! Give them some room. Has anybody called the paramedics?"

"I did," The bailiff said.

Katherine was down on her knees beside Lucian whose eyes were closed. His color was still more purple than pink and his breathing was very ragged. She leaned down and put her ear to Lucian's chest.

"Heart sounds pretty good. A little thready...whoa!" She sat up. "It stopped!"

She grabbed the front of Lucian's shirt and ripped it open, measured with her fingers up from the point of his sternum and thumped his chest as hard as she could then started chest compressions.

"Either of you know how to do CPR?" she asked.

"I do," John said.

"Get at it," she commanded, all her nurse training coming to the front.

John positioned himself on the opposite side of Lucian's body, tilted Lucian's head back and made sure his air way was clear then sucked in a deep breath. He clamped his finger and thumb over Lucian's nose and began mouth to mouth, one breath per thirty of Katherine's compressions.

In minutes the paramedics arrived. They lifted Lucian onto their gurney and swapped out the CPR with John.

The courtroom had been a noisy, busy place until the bailiffs cleared it to let the paramedics in. Then it was over; the paramedics gone, a thick quiet fell. In a moment only Chance, John, and Katherine were left in the room.

John shook his head in confusion. "What happens if he dies? Where are we then?"

"One thing I have learned in years of dealing with the law," Chance said, "sufficient unto the day is the evil thereof."

Katherine and John both looked puzzled.

"Don't worry about what you can't control. Tomorrow is soon enough."

"I thought Lawyers were always in control?" Katherine said. "Do they ever ask a question they didn't know the answer to already?"

Chance smiled crookedly. "In the best of all possible worlds, which this ain't. Shall we go?"

The bailiffs had shooed all the reporters out of the hall, but they couldn't shoo them off the courthouse steps. There were several waiting there when the three appeared and they began throwing questions instantly.

"Now you people know," Chance began, "we can't answer any questions pertaining to the case so just give it up."

"Can't you tell us your thoughts about what happened in there?"

"Not if it pertains to the case."

"How about if it pertains to Mr. Gordon's health?"

"We have no idea what happened. I'm sure Mr. Drew will hand out a press release of some sort."

The three continued to push down the steps through the reporters as Chance fielded questions. John was busily watching his step so as not to take a header down the stairs. Katherine still hung onto his hand and there was a sudden electric feeling which jumped between them and made him look up at her. Her eyes were directed at the bottom of the steps where the people with signs had been standing earlier. Now there was only one person, one sign. His sign was not a protest but a statement. It said, "Forneria Lives."

A shiver ran up John's back.

Eleven

Until the moment Lucian pulled the sword from John Fisher's heart, only drops of blood escaped the wound. When Lucian wrenched the blade free, Fisher's blood poured out front and back like cascading fountains. Lucian laughed in delight with the brilliant red streams.

Fisher swayed but remained on his knees for a moment. "Your time is passed, Lucian." He said through teeth clenched against the agony. "Forneria lives."

Lucian's laughter continued as he shook his head in disbelief. Even now this minion of his father might refuse to believe he had won at last. "Your time is passed, savior," He shouted and shoved Fisher down the stairs with his foot.

Fisher's blood spun out in great drops spattering each step as his body rolled down the stairs. He ended face to the earth at the bottom of the stairs, his blood soaking into the dry ground of the courtyard.

A shadow passed, the day darkened imperceptibly.

Those struck down by Lucian's laughter were staggering to their feet and trying to staunch the blood from their noses and ears. Many were looking at Fisher's lifeless body at the bottom of the stairs as they felt the new hope he had given them flee in the face of this cruel death.

The sun seemed to blink as though it could not stand to look at what had occurred below. Those whose eyes were still on John Fishers body thought the shadow was the universe mourning the death of the Creator's son,

274

but Sergeant Banning, a man who had seen too much death himself, looked up. "It's a cloud," he said.

Clouds were gathering from all over the horizon. The heat-faded blue of the sky disappeared in the space of a few minutes as thunder rolled.

Lucian's face lost its satisfied smile as he looked up at the darkened sky. He snatched up the jeweled scabbard and thrust the bloody sword into it. With the two halves of the Tuchinar machine reunited, he began touching the jewels in sequence from top to bottom. The scabbard's jewels glowed and winked as he touched them, but the sky continued to darken and more thunder rolled.

Sergeant Banning, Ezra, and the other elders of those in the courtyard recognized what was happening. The last rain had fallen from Forneria's skies when the elders were young, but they remembered what it had been like. They remembered the cool wind and the sweet smell of the wet plants.

"What is it?" Lieutenant Banning asked his father.

"Rain storm," the sergeant said, not taking his eyes off the lead colored sky.

Ezra brought his eyes down from the clouds to fix on Lucian who still frantically touched the glowing gems of the Tuchinar machine.

"Even your Machine can't stop the rain now, Lucian," he said. "John Fisher has brought the end to your Great Dry. You spilled his blood and he is spilling the rain."

As though in answer to Ezra's words the first fat drops pattered into the dust.

All eyes turned to Lucian whose hands had stopped playing up and down the machine. He flung away the scabbard and ran down the stairs with the naked sword in his hand. The five could only watch and turn their faces up into the slowly increasing rain.

At the bottom Lucian viciously kicked his shiny boot toe beneath Fisher's body and turned it over. He turned the blade down, gripped the sword hilt with both hands, and falling to his knees, he began stabbing

275

Fisher's body over and over screaming, "You lied! You lied! You cannot have Forneria! It is mine! I will destroy it! It is mine!"

"It was never yours," Captain Fay raised his voice over the sound of the strengthening rain. "We all were foolish enough to forget. Gordon was the Creator, and we let you rule for a little while, but John Fisher told us we need only remember we are Gordon's children, and he spilled his blood to prove to us it was so. Your time is finished."

Thunder reverberated from the mountains and made the walls of the black fortress vibrate. Pitchforks of lightening flashed and the thunder that followed rolled before the flashes had faded.

Lucian, drenched to the skin by the rain, wrenched the sword from Fisher's body, staggered to his feet, and turned toward Fay brandishing the naked blade. Step by step he began to climb toward the five.

Fay, shining blue white with the ambient electricity of the storm, watched Lucian's ascent without fear. "Kill me if you will, Lucian," he said. "Kill all who witnessed Fisher's death, but all over Forneria people are turning up their faces into the blessed rain..." he lifted his arms up as he had seen Fisher lift his, "...saying John Fisher has ended Lucian's Dry."

Lucian stopped a step away from the Captain. Rainwater poured in rivulets from the brim of the Tuchinar's helmet and dimmed the gleam of his armor, but the black halo blazed like a burning coal. "I will mix your blood with this filthy wet!" he screamed and drew the sword up and back to strike off Fay's head, but as the sword reached the top of its arc, a blue white bolt sizzled from the heavens and engulfed him from the point of his upraised sword to his boot heels and passed through to crack and melt the black stair on which Lucian had stood.

Standing only a step above Lucian, Captain Fay was thrown down, insensible. Others nearby were also thrown down, but many others dropped to the ground to hide their faces from the fury of the heavens.

After a moment of shock, Ezra, Bitter, Noah, and Thomas recovered themselves and ran to help Fay who was stirring.

"I'm all right," Fay said when they reached him and helped him rise.

The rain poured down, making radiant auras about all the men where they stood on the steps. Thomas looked toward Lucian's smoking corpse. His armor was blackened by the lightning and the Tuchinar Sword was shattered into a thousand lightning blued shards; the hilt had melted in Lucian's hands.

Noah's eyes passed over Lucian's corpse and on down the steps seeking John Fisher's body.

"Where is he?" Noah asked. "Where is John Fisher?"

All eyes turned to the bottom of the steps but Fisher's body was no longer there. A few minutes more and the rain eased to a slow, steady drizzle. Those in the courtyard did not try to get out of the wet. They sat in the warm rain as though to let it soak into their parched bodies. Many times they turned their faces up and opened their mouths to let the drops fall in.

As the rain slowed some of the soldiers and servants who had served Lucian approached the five and asked, "What shall we do now?"

The five looked at one another and said at last, "We will tell you all what we think you should do in a little while. Go now to everyone and tell them we will speak to them all in a little while."

Those who had asked departed and passed the word.

Among themselves the five asked, "What should we do?"

"When people in Barstow asked what to do," Bitter said, "John Fisher told them to go if they wanted to go and stay if they wanted to stay, but many of those had lived in Barstow all their lives. Here, no one has lived more than a few years. Everyone here is from somewhere else."

"Perhaps we should tell them just to go home," Noah said.

"Yes. We should tell them all to go home," Thomas said. "We all should go home."

All agreed home was best. So when people gathered at the foot of the broad staircase to the black fortress as day was drawing to a close, Captain Fay, who had been elected by the others to speak, stood on the landing at the top lifting his arms for quiet. When he had the attention of the crowd, he said, "We five have discussed what to do next and we think all who lived and worked here should return to the people from whom you came. Go home, and when you meet others tell them what you have seen. Tell them John Fisher has shown Forneria the true mercy of the Creator."

Fay stopped and passed his eyes over the crowd to make sure all were listening. "The Creator was so merciful. John Fisher came and sacrificed himself to bring the rain back to Forneria, though we had forgotten Gordon. Tell everyone Lucian is no more. And remember to give mercy to all as it has been given to you."

The gentle rain tapered off as the following dawn lightened the east. When the sun rose, it turned the remaining clouds gold as those who had been in service in the black palace departed for their homes.

The five reclaimed their droms, headed south, and as they passed through the conifer forests, they noticed the trees seemed more alive, more up-thrusting, and the wind which had been hot and withering was now cool. The resinous aroma mixed with the deeper, richer aroma of wet pine mast and the sharper fragrance of mountain laurel.

When they crossed down into the flatter land, which had been sere, punishing high desert, they smelled the reborn greasewood, sage, desert cypress, and other dry land plants wakened by the rain. What had seemed desiccated and dead had been reborn in days with the coming of the rain. The silver green of the desert plants shown as far as the eye could see.

All the water holes they had used were flowing full again. What had been dry arroyos now had trickles of water in their bottoms. When the five stopped to water their droms and rest beside one of the resurrected streams, they found it already inhabited. Tadpoles hatched from eggs deposited years before in the sand and among the rocks now quickened by the rain water flowing over them. Tiny fish with sharp spines along their backs hovered in the deeper parts of the stream awakened by the return of the water. And birds! A hundred different kinds dropped to drink and bathe in the pools and streams and feed from the newly born aquatic richness.

Mono was still much the same as before. It would take much more rain than had yet fallen to make a noticeable difference in the vast stretch of alkali water, though the air, which had been so heavy and filled with the nose burning bitter dust of the alkali towers, was clear.

Rain fell off and on as they traveled. Hours of rain would be followed by days of brilliance with air so pristine it gave radiance to every rock and bush. During those rains the travelers would put on their wide hats and the water would run down the broad brims like waterfalls, and as they looked at one another they would smile through the rivulets--until they suddenly remembered what this delight had cost and then the smiles would flee from their faces.

At Ivy the pond had become a lake. Many of the cottonwood trees had water a foot up their trunks now.

The travelers found some dead fall wood which was not too wet and, with persistence, started a fire. As evening thickened, Bitter noticed there were ravens circling the oasis. In moments three of the great black birds had circled and landed first in the trees then on the ground near the men.

Bobbing and bowing the ravens came close and, turning their heads first one way then the other as though to make sure these were really the men they sought, the larger one said, "Greetings, servants of John Fisher."

The men glanced questioningly at one another then at the ravens. "How do we greet you now?" Captain Fay asked. "Once you were messengers, but now you are free."

The ravens clicked, rattled, and squawked between themselves before the spokes-raven said, "You may say Messengers. We are free, but we are Messengers still."

"Of whom?" Ezra asked. "Lucian is no more."

"We serve him who told us we were free."

"John Fisher said he did not need your service when you met him here, nor does he need you now," Thomas said. "Do you not know Fisher's spilled blood has brought back the rain?"

The ravens laughed in almost the same raucous way they once mocked humans when they were servants of Lucian.

The five were pricked to anger by the mocking caws. "Why do you laugh when he who freed you spent his life not only to free you but to save you? Lucian would never have let the rain fall again until Forneria was a dried up cinder. Why do you laugh?"

The birds bobbed and bowed and clacked then laughed again. "We know all. John Fisher's death, Lucian's death, the rain returned, and the message we deliver to you."

Still angry with the irreverent birds, the five demanded the message, whatever nonsense it might contain, be delivered and the birds depart.

Laughing at the men's anger, the ravens flapped their wings wide and lifted onto a nearby tree branch. "We are commanded," the spokes-raven began, "to tell you to come to the city of the mountain."

"Which city of what mountain?" Captain Fay asked.

The ravens clacked and rattled among themselves then said, "The city whose name is forbidden to us. Where our kind began."

The men frowned, not understanding then it dawned on the only one who had been into the city. "Tuchinara?" Ezra said. "We are to come to Tuchinara?"

The ravens flapped and quivered the feathers all over their bodies then clicked and squawked agitatedly. "You have said," the spokes-raven answered.

"Why should we go to Tuchinara?" Thomas asked. "It is filled with ghosts. Even you said so, Ezra."

"Who sent this message?" Bitter asked.

Now the ravens laughed and squawked mightily, opening their wings. "We serve John Fisher," they all said and lifted into the darkening sky.

Twelve

"They aren't exactly forth coming about his condition," Ed Chance said into the phone. He was sitting in the intensive care unit's waiting room at All Saints Hospital and had been for nearly three days. As he talked to Fisher, he thought how ironic this was for him to be needed here again. Less than a month ago Joshua Gordon had been in the same ICU. Chance had sent John and Katherine home after the first few hours because they both showed signs of coming apart at the seams. He had stayed pretty continuously, trying, without much success, to get information out of nurses or doctors.

"What does it mean, Ed? Where are we with the law suit?" John asked with a little desperation in his voice.

"I don't know. I'm gonna try to get hold of Drew to see if he knows anything."

"He isn't there?"

"No. He was for a little while yesterday. He was talking to the guy in a white coat I think is Lucian's doctor, but I don't know for sure. After they were done, Drew turned around and looked at me then left without a word."

A nurse stepped into the waiting room obviously looking for someone, but when her eyes fixed on Ed Chance, who still had his cell phone pressed to his ear, she frowned and headed for him. "Could you please put your cell phone away sir?" she said not unkindly, but firmly. "We have rules against their use in the waiting rooms. They can sometimes interfere with our monitoring devices."

"I'm sorry," Chance said, folding his phone. An idea occurred to him and he put on his most harried face. "I was just trying to find out what is happening in there," he lied. "No one will tell me anything about my brother and I'm worried sick."

The nurse softened. She saw distraught people every day and could sympathize with their frustration. "Well," she began, "I'm not really supposed to tell you anything, but--who is your brother."

Chance looked relieved and said, "Thank you so much. Lucian Gordon."

The nurse narrowed her eyes. "Lucian Gordon?" she was suddenly skeptical and the hardness she had shown before returned. "Mr. Gordon doesn't have any brothers. I've known him for years. He is on the board of this hospital. Who are you really? Press?"

Chance reddened. "No ma'am...not a reporter. An attorney."

"A lawyer?" she said, rolling the word around in her mouth as though it tasted nasty.

Chance decided to throw himself on the dubious mercy of this woman. "I'm representing John Fisher in the lawsuit between Lucian Gordon and Joshua Gordon's estate. I am just trying to find out what is happening with Lucian so I will know how to advise my client."

She studied his face closely, and for a moment Chance thought she was going to call security to frog march him out of the hospital, but instead she said, "The business with the books isn't it?"

"Yes Ma'am."

"I never heard Mr. Gordon say anything against his father, but it was pretty clear to me there was some ill will between them. Then with Joshua dying here not long ago and now this trial--I don't understand it."

"I don't understand it either, and I am in the middle of it. Can't you please just tell me how Mr. Gordon is?"

The nurse glanced around as though checking who else might be listening. There was only one other small group of people across the room and they were very intent on the conversation they were having. "I don't really know much, but an aneurism caused his collapse. I can't say what kind or where or anything else. It's not uncommon. Mr. Gordon is on life support."

Ed waited for more, but when nothing more was forthcoming he said, "Thank you for that much anyway." His cell phone rang and the noise erased what little good will he had built up with the nurse. He fumbled the phone from his pocket and answered it.

"Take it outside," growled the nurse.

"Yes ma'am," Chance said, then into the phone he said, "Hang on. Let me get out of here," and headed for the door. He felt the nurse's eyes boring into the back of his head. At the end of the hall he stepped out a door onto a balcony which looked over the city. "OK, go," he said into the phone.

"This is Arthur Drew. I'd like to meet with you and your client as soon as possible."

Chance was silent, thinking about what he had just heard for a moment. "Where?" he said at last.

"My office."

"Can you give us a couple of hours? I need to clean up a little. I'm still at the hospital."

"Five o'clock this afternoon?"

Chance looked at his watch. It was a little after ten a.m. "Fine. We'll be there."

~*~

Drew's office was a somewhat more classical version of Ed Chance's. When the three walked in, a receptionist was waiting for them and showed them directly to a conference room. Drew, with the appearance of infinite patience, already sat at the broad mahogany table. He stood when the three of them entered, shook hands all around, and asked if they would like coffee or something else.

Chance, wanting a few moments to study his adversary, said yes, they would have coffee. John almost protested; he didn't want coffee, he just wanted to get on with this, but Ed had instructed them both to keep their mouths shut unless he told them to talk so John bit his tongue and possessed himself in patience.

When coffee was delivered, Drew said, "Let me summarize the situation here, Mr. Fisher. I think we all want this lawsuit to go away, and perhaps I have a solution that could satisfy everyone."

Chance looked at Fisher who gave a noncommittal shrug so Chance said, "Won't hurt anything to listen, I suppose."

"First, let me bring you up to speed on Mr. Gordon's condition. Like his mother, a blood vessel in his brain has ruptured. An aneurism the doctor called it. Unlike his mother's event, however, your quick thinking and prompt action have saved Mr. Gordon's life."

John didn't quite know how to feel about this. If he and Katherine had been a little less prompt--but Drew was continuing. "Unfortunately, saving his life was not quite enough. The ruptured vessel caused extensive brain damage leaving him comatose. This condition appears to be permanent..."

Katherine gasped.

"....however Mr. Gordon's doctor tells me this is an area of medicine which is rather obscure so they will not say for certain whether Mr. Gordon will continue in this vegetative state. They have relieved the pressure on his brain and he might wake, but the doctors are not hopeful."

"So where does that leave me," John began.

Chance said, "Hang on, John."

Drew held up his hand to quiet them both and continued. "Since Mr. Gordon has no living family, my law firm has been left in a rather peculiar position. Mr. Gordon made us, made me the executor of his will--which would be a completely straight forward proposition under other circumstances, but his will cannot be probated unless Mr. Gordon is actually dead, which he isn't. Instead, another codicil in the will leaves Mr. Gordon's estate under the conservatorship of my law firm, again meaning me. What it boils down too is I am in a position which requires me to manage and care for Mr. Gordon's estate so as to preserve it in case he either recovers or dies."

"Legal limbo," Ed Chance said.

"Unfortunately. I am going to begin proceedings to have Mr. Gordon taken off life support, as per instruction in Mr. Gordon's will, but I already know it is going to be a long battle, instruction not withstanding, since the doctors caring for him--well, let us say they will oppose me."

"Which means this case is going to be stuck in limbo," John said. He leaned forward and put his head in his hands. *My God, Joshua, what have you gotten me into?*

"Perhaps not," Drew said. "Life or death would not really matter to the lawsuit. It will continue unless some rapprochement can be reached."

John looked up. Chance said, "Rapprochement?"

"Since I am the conservator of the estate, I have the power to complete this suit either in court or by some agreement reached here. I personally would prefer to resolve it among us."

Chance raked his upper lip with his bottom teeth, considering. "I think you know this suit was snake bit from the beginning, Arthur. There is no way a judge is going to rule there was a binding agreement. Even a tame judge like McSweeny, which is why he recused himself."

"I'm not entirely convinced on that point, and oral agreements can be as binding as written, but I am hoping to avoid having to find out. I'd like to offer a compromise." He waited to get some indication he should go on, but saw only the open confusion of all three of the others. "All right, fine. Here it is. You will take the last offer Mr. Gordon put forward--the ten million dollars in cash plus the rest of Joshua Gordon's estate. In return for which you will sign over the copyrights to Lucian Gordon's estate..."

"That is no compromise at all!" John scooted forward in his chair and almost shouted.

"Hang on a second, John," Ed said as Katherine put a restraining hand on John's arm. "Let him finish."

"Thank you. I have no instruction as to what should be done with the copyrights should they come into the estate's possession. Lucian had been making noises about buying up books and letting them fall out of print, but I have no instructions about that and, since I am charged with *conserving* his estate, it would seem madness to do anything which would clearly damage the estate. Therefore, if you agree to the terms I have put forward, I, as conservator of the estate, will sign an agreement to the effect that Joshua Gordon's books will continue to be produced until such time as they no longer sell or the copyrights lapse. The agreement will also say under no circumstance will the estate ever make any attempt to destroy the Forneria stories until and unless I have specific instruction to do so from Lucian Gordon himself."

The three sat in silence as they considered what they had just heard. After time Ed Chance said, "What about the last book? The one Joshua and John were working on?"

"The copyright will come with the others."

"But it isn't published yet. It isn't even finished," John said. "It is at least half my creation and I want it published. Will this deal stop publication?"

Drew thought for a moment then said, "I believe it can be published if you have or can find a publisher, and it will fall under the same agreement."

"And what will John get out of it? After all it is half his, or more," Chance asked.

"Mr. Fisher will be awarded a *royalties only* contract for half the royalties of the book. The rest will go into the estate."

"And, if I sit down and write another book set in Forneria?"

"The estate will grant you a license to use the name and you will hold the copyright on the book or books subject to the license agreement."

John looked to Ed Chance but could read nothing in his expression. He asked with his eyes if he could talk and received a nod but nothing else. Chance was keeping his cards very close to his vest and waiting to see what John would say.

"I don't like it..." John began.

"It will wind up with you getting a great deal of money and still having access to the rights you sought," Drew said.

"But what if Lucian wakes up?"

"Realistically, Mr. Fisher, the chance of Lucian coming out of his coma with anything like enough mental capacity to make decisions about anything is vanishingly slim."

"I don't know," John answered. "It feels like I'm bailing out on Joshua."

"Let me lay your situation out for you, Mr. Fisher," Drew said, steepling his finger tips together, "you are, for all intents and purposes, penniless. When you agreed to help Joshua Gordon work on this final novel, you were on the verge of being evicted from your apartment and you were barely making eating money driving a cab. Joshua paid you fairly well, but most of the money went to pay various debts. You have approximately eight hundred dollars in a checking account and the clothes on your back. Is this substantially correct?"

John suddenly felt like a bug under a magnifying glass. "It is probably about right," he said glumly.

"You owe Whittaker, Belhaven, and Chance a considerable sum for handling this suit, do you not?"

"I am not going to push for any money from him, Arthur."

"Consequently, your firm finds itself in the position of being out quite a large chunk of money which it can't really afford."

John turned to Chance. "Are you in trouble because of this mess, Ed?"

Chance shrugged. "It's a temporary problem."

"Unless your partners decide you are a liability and ask you to either put up some earnest or leave the partnership," Drew said flatly.

"Could they do that, Ed?"

"They probably won't."

"But they could?"

Chance tilted his head in acknowledgement.

Katherine, who had been listening quietly said, "I think you should do agree to it, John."

"But..."

"No. I think you should do it for the same reason you told me to take the money from Lucian. You earned it and the compromise leaves you with almost everything you wanted plus a whole lot of money. Sounds like you have a chance to have your cake and eat it too."

John turned to Ed Chance. "You're my attorney, what do you say?"

After a moment he answered, "If we go to court, we are probably going to win, but it could take another year, maybe longer. Meantime you and Katherine will have to find some other place to live because the house belongs to Lucian and I assume Arthur would want to rent it out for the sake of the conservatorship, and I know you two can't pay the kind of rent the house is worth. Then there is eating, and your eight hundred bucks ain't gonna go far toward feeding the both of you. I think it is a good compromise. Having your cake, like Katherine said."

John sat quietly for a time, thinking. It did seem to be the best outcome he could hope for – and fifteen million dollars.

"Well, on the advice of council--for which I have yet to pay--I think it's a deal."

Drew nodded his head and gave a satisfied smile. "Wonderful," he said.

"We'll want to see this in writing as soon as possible, Arthur," Chance said, standing and extending his hand.

"I'll have the papers drawn up and in your hands before the weekend." Drew stood and shook Chance's hand. He turned and did likewise with Fisher and Katherine.

As the three were about to leave, John turned back.

"Mr. Drew, whatever made you come up with something like this?"

Drew smiled somewhat enigmatically. "I read *Tuchinara* my first year in college. Joshua Gordon was a relative unknown then, but the book moved me--made me wonder about...a lot of things. I just couldn't bear the thought of not having it and the other stories out there for other people to find."

John smiled, nodded his understanding and the three left.

Thirteen

John Fisher jolted awake and sat up with a gasp. He was totally dislocated. Memories of both worlds were jumbled together not making cohesive sense. He blinked and turned his head side to side trying to reunite his scattered consciousness--the agony of Lucian's having driven the sword through him--in a panic he looked down at his bare chest; he saw multiple scars. Gingerly, he dragged his finger tips over the scar ridges. They were not at all tender, but the memory of the pain was as though it had happened only a moment before. But had he not been stabbed only once, not multiple times?

He remembered Lucian's taunt as he, John Fisher, had knelt, mortally wounded. He was defeated, after everything he had gone through, after Joshua's death, after Lucian's collapse--and those memories stopped him. In his mind he had two incompatible images of Lucian. One, the sneering demigod with a sword; one the business-suited man lying on a floor with...Katherine. He shook his head to try to separate the two sequences but succeeded only in making his head ache as though his brain were sloshing back and forth in his skull. He looked around, seeking something solid to settle his eyes and his mind on. He was seated on a large smooth red stone shaped like a chaise lounge. The stone bed was in the middle of a small marble enclosed rotunda.

Looks like a mausoleum. His mind still not firmly set in his head. *Where else would a dead man be but in a mausoleum?* "But I'm not dead," he said aloud, so

289

the sound of his own voice could reassure him. The marble walls gave back the comforting reverberation of sound bouncing so he turned himself and put his legs down, noticing for the first time he was naked. And it was cool. One of the main memories of his previous life in Forneria was heat. Dry, oppressive, desiccating heat, which was only marginally less at night. But this place was cool and – mausoleum like.

Fisher shivered looking for an exit. He slid from the stone couch and stood cautiously. He did not see a way out; that caused a dribble of panic, but he controlled it by taking two deep breaths, letting his mind coast for a moment. Knowledge came to him like dawn coming to the world. *I am John Fisher. I am the Creator now. Joshua Gordon is dead. I woke in the desert. I rode with the Traveler's wagon train. I was in the earthquake in Barstow. I...sought out Lucian who held Forneria in pain and drought and would have held it so until everything...*A flash of Lucian lying on the floor with Katherine kneeling above him pressing his chest came into Fisher's mind.

Not here. There. Here Lucian is--was--was...Lucian was dead here.

Fisher recalled creating a storm in the other world to be used in this one; remembered calling it from his mind and filling it with lightening. Lightening--and it was all clear. He remembered and melded the two worlds in his mind. In the other world he had created this world and Lucian was dead here. The drought was broken. He had allowed Lucian to spill his blood in order to prime the creative pump of Forneria. The blood had drawn the rain and the storm to itself. He had filled the storm with lightening which waited only on some error by Lucian to close the trap. Lucian had lifted the sword and the lightening had killed him and destroyed the Tuchinar machine he had been using to control the weather.

Unconsciously Fisher had walked across the rotunda as his two minds fused and found he was standing before what looked like a firmly closed double door, but both his minds knew what to do now.

"Open," he said aloud and the doors rumbled open. Tuchinara greeted his eyes. It was just as Joshua had created it so many years before with its rounded corners and soft geometric shapes, all made of natural stone with nothing of the coldness of stone. These buildings were like living beings

290

sleeping peacefully beneath a beautiful blue sky. The air was fresh and sweet with a new smell of blooming plants. Without hesitation Fisher stood in the midst of the central plaza and lifted his arms. "Awake, my children," he commanded. "Your hearts are paid for with my life. Now you are changed. No more soulless Tuchinar monstrosities. Now, servants of the Creator."

With slow timidity the beings which had been Abominations came forth from the buildings around the plaza. No more were they scarred or ill or disfigured. Now they were beautifully made with flashing eyes and beaming smiles. "We waited as you told us, Creator, and you have honored your word," the first one to reach Fisher said. "We are your servants forever."

The Creator looked over his new creation and was pleased with what he saw. "I have made you new," he said. "Now I must present you with a choice. If you would return with me to the other world to serve, you may. But you may also serve me here by watching over this world so no more of the Tuchinar may arise to plague Forneria."

A rumbling of conversation passed through the massed beings. *Angels. This is my angel army. My heavenly host.*

After a moment, or perhaps an hour--time seemed to mean nothing anymore--one of the angels said, "Command us Creator, so we can do your bidding."

John looked over the host and thought of Joshua's first creation of Tuchinara. His heavenly hosts had been given free will and their will had brought the world to grief. Yet could Fisher do less for his creatures than what the father of all had done? "No, you must choose," he said. "Decide among yourselves. Those who wish to go with me I will take, those who wish to stay here, I will leave. You are free to decide, each for yourself. Now go. I have other business which must be finished soon."

The new-made angels bowed and departed. Fisher turned to a building on the plaza. Inside he found what he knew he would. A robe of bright saffron yellow waited, placed there long ago by Joshua Gordon. It was the robe of rulers and the last noble ruler of Tuchinara had taken it off and hidden it away on the day he left to go back to Gordon. No other had worn it since long ago in Forneria. As Fisher put on the robe and closed it with the magna-touch fasteners, he understood how in Forneria time had no meaning for him. Forneria was forever, so long as even one person remembered Joshua Gordon and John Fisher, Forneria was endless. Gordon was eternal; Fisher was eternal, regardless of life in the other world. *I wonder if the other world works the same way. Can God be God forever in the other world where I exist? Regardless of life or death in whatever other place he might exist? I would certainly like to kick the idea around with Joshua.*

The melancholy of loss touched Fisher and choked him for a moment, but he shook it off and stepped into the lift. It whisked him up to the orbiting observation platform Joshua had placed above Tuchinara in the first book. Around Fisher was the spangled blackness of space. Stars and planets in the unfathomably distant cosmos created by Joshua, or perhaps by the other Deity and borrowed by Joshua for his own creation. Fisher smiled at the thought and looked down on Forneria. From the platform he could see from sea to desert to northern and southern ice. He could see the cities of the coast and the green cover of the eastern mountains. Roiling rain clouds drifted in waves from the northwest to bathe the land below. Of course the rain would never get out of hand in Forneria. It would soon return to its normal cycle and never again pound and join together in floods to plague the people, at least not now. Perhaps in some later creation, flood and fear and pain would be necessary, but for now the rain was soft and soaking. The desert would drink up the water and blossom for a time. The Travelers would have to find a new trade-- in the next book. In the next book.

Fisher rode down from the orbiting platform to the top of the tallest tower in Tuchinara and stepped out. A little above him he saw three ravens riding on the thermals as they sought carrion to feed themselves. He lifted his hand above his head and without hesitation, the three birds tilted and came to land on the guard rail around the top of the tower.

"I would ask a favor of you, Messengers."

The ravens bobbed and bowed. "We heard Lucian had killed you as you had killed him," the largest raven said.

"He spilled my blood, to his grief. My life bought back Forneria."

292

The ravens considered this silently for a little. "What favor would you ask of Free Ravens?"

"Go to the oasis at Ivy and tell those you find I would see them here."

The ravens bobbed and rattled their bills. "We cannot speak the name of this place. You have made it so, Creator."

"It doesn't matter. They will understand."

After a time the birds laughed. "We will tell them," they agreed. They opened their wings and cast off from their perch, gliding west toward Ivy.

In a moment of non-time, Fisher set aglow the monument at the center of the plaza; a great stylized fire-fountain made of alabaster; a beacon to those who would soon reach the spring below named after the city above. Tuchinara.

~*~

The five spent the evening asking themselves and each other if they had all heard what the ravens had said. "John Fisher sent them?" Thomas asked as much of himself as of his friends. "How can it be? John Fisher is dead, isn't he? Did we not see Lucian drive a blade through him, roll his body down the stairs then stab him a hundred times as he lay on the ground?"

All agreed they had seen exactly that.

"But then his body was gone, leaving only his blood," Bitter said, and they all nodded agreement.

"Could it be some trick of Lucian's?" Noah asked.

"I helped carry what was left of Lucian away from the courtyard," Captain Fay said. "I have seen dead men before. Gordon and Fisher forgive me I have created many dead men myself. I tell you, Lucian was dead. If this has anything to do with him it is some trick of one of his servants."

"And what could they gain?" Bitter asked.

Then Ezra asked the question which had been bothering all of them. "No matter what or who, more important is the question: Why Tuchinara? Nothing is alive there. Even the ravens don't go there."

The gentle rain began to fall again, hissing in the fire and pattering on their wide Traveler hats.

The question none of them were ready to address was: *Shall we go to Tuchinara?*

They drank their tea quietly looking into the hissing fire, and each man kept his own council. They rolled into blankets against the rain without an answer.

Rain continued off and on as they traveled to the oasis called Tuchinara. It fell with a steady monotonous drizzle, slowly soaking into the still parched desert on the day they tied their droms beneath the now bright sycamore trees. Each one of the five stole a glance up at the abandoned city, though none looked long at it. They felt a visceral foreboding in staring at the place that had given birth to Lucian. John Fisher had sent the monsters to sleep in this city, now gleaming like pewter, when they had crowded around the six in the mountains. Fisher had told them to go to Tuchinara to sleep until he called for them. These monsters had once fed on human flesh; might they now be waiting for a dead man to wake them? Or when John Fisher died did they wake to stalk the five who had traveled with him?

Bitter built a fire with damp wood, hooding it with a windbreak of large rocks and green branches pulled and hacked from the trees. Talk had mostly died after the visit of the ravens and over the days the quiet had grown. Their silence reverberated loudly now as the wet dark enclosed them. The men did not look at each other, but into the fire. They did not try to preserve their night vision for nothing would creep up on them in the night. All they feared was in the city above them. Anything which might seek to hurt them from there could not be stopped by the ability to see it coming.

One by one the men quietly rolled themselves into blankets for the night. Ezra was last. He went out into the darkness to relieve himself before sleep and as he cast his eyes around the dark, he looked toward the heavens. The rain had stopped and through the spotty clouds the stars were multitudinous in the black sky. There was no moon. He looked back toward the mountain his eyes had passed over. There was a light.

Ezra studied the light for minutes. It was not a light like the lights in the sky, but more like the glow, as of a fire, seen from a distance.

After a little he went back to the others and said, "They's someone up yonder."

Faces peered out from under blankets and looked at the elder Traveler. "What you mean?" Bitter asked.

Captain Fay, freeing himself said, "Show me."

The others all threw off their blankets and Ezra lead them out into the night.

"There, on the left," Ezra pointed.

They looked at the pinkish glow quietly for a long time before Fay said, "Is it actually in the city or outside it?"

"Don't know. In the city, I think. They's a big open square where you can look out over the valley down here. I believe that's where the fire is. Course, it has been a lot of years since I was up there so I may disremember a little.

"Well, let's go see," Thomas said.

Noah said, "It's too dark now."

"Is it a signal in answer to our fire?" Asked Bitter.

"Maybe," Fay said.

"Well let's go see," Thomas said again, a bit more exasperation in his voice.

Ezra said, "Tomorrow is soon enough."

"Soon as it's light," Fay said.

No one hurried back to the fire. Eventually Fay rolled again into his blanket. Bitter returned to camp for his and Ezra's blankets. The Travelers sat leaning back against back, eyes unwavering on the pink glow. Noah and Thomas lay down where they were without blankets and watched as well.

After midnight the patchy clouds closed up and rain began to mist down once more.

The rain was like a silvery fog when light rose in the east, and the light was hardly started when the camp was broken, the droms packed, and the five started with some trepidation toward the dimly seen outlines of Tuchinara. The ancient city loomed above them as they rode up the switchback road toward the entrance. Leaden clouds made everything dreary though no rain fell.

Ezra tried to remember how he felt when he had gone into the city as a young man. He could recall terror growing as he went closer to the city, but now, while there was apprehension, there was not the bowel tightening fear of the earlier time.

"Maybe 'cause I'm older or something," Ezra said, "but it don't feel the same as last time. When I was a kid it, felt like every building was full of hungry eyes all looking at me. Now it just seems lonely, like a single grave beside the road."

What little talk there was tailed off to nothing as they came through the switchback gate into the city itself. The clop, splotch of the droms feet and the sighing of a breeze around the buildings were the only sounds.

At the edge of the wide plaza the men stopped. All thought they had seen something across the open area, but the misty drizzle made clear sight impossible. As if by the very hands of the Creator, a wide rent opened in the clouds. A beam of sun so brilliant it made the men squint speared down like benevolent lightening and they saw John Fisher, aglow in his saffron robe standing below the Tuchinar monument; a gigantic stone flame coruscating and incandescent as if it were real fire.

They had seen this man die! They had seen a sword driven through his breast. They had seen the blood pour out and soak into the thirsty earth. How could this be? They sat upon their animals looking toward the stone flames torn between hopeful awe and fear.

As if he had read their minds, John Fisher lifted his arms in welcome and said, "I am he who was dead and am now alive."

Noah, who had been a Fisherite longer than any, reacted first. He threw himself down from his Drom's back and ran to Fisher. At the base of the monument he fell to his knees then bowed his face to the paving stones.

"Stand up, Noah. It is time for you to stand. Since before I was in prison in Barstow you believed, now you can see that you have not believed in vain." Noah stood as the others arrived, babbling their amazement and joy.

"Is it truly you, John Fisher?" Captain Fay asked.

Fisher smiled. He gripped the sides of his robe and pulled the magna fasteners open. In the brilliance of the sun the men saw all the scars on his chest and especially the widest one under his heart. "And now Forneria is free," he said. "Lucian is finished here. But there is another place I must go now. Lucian is only dead here. In the other place I go to continue the battle, and these go with me." He turned his left hand palm up and a multitude of beautiful beings dressed in white and wearing shining breast plates appeared on the left side of the plaza. "These are the beloved Abominations, now transformed to angel warriors. They have decided to accompany me." He turned his hand over and the bright host disappeared. He lifted his right hand palm up and another host of angel warriors appeared to the right side. "These have chosen to remain here. They will continue as guardians so no evil may come from outside to harm Forneria. They will maintain Tuchinara as their dwelling place." He turned his hand over and the host was gone.

"Now I must leave you too," Fisher continued. "I live, and because I live, Forneria lives. I leave this world in your hands. My angels will keep away all evil from outside, but you must keep away the evil from within. I leave you to make Forneria a heaven or a hell. The choice is up to you. Never forget Gordon was your Creator. Never forget what you have seen in these last months. Tell everyone I was dead but am now alive, and remind them to be merciful to one another as I remind you to give mercy to every creature forever."

Fisher looked into the eyes of each of the men then lifted his arms to the heavens and was gone.

297

Fourteen

John entered the chapel, pausing a moment just inside to let his eyes adjust to the light. He looked around him at the plain and simple interior and at the altar, covered by an altar cloth woven of gold and linen threads. The tall candlesticks were wonderfully worked bronze twists topped with rich looking white bees wax candles. The tabernacle in the back center of the altar was a carved marble house with a wrought gold door. Inside the door an already blessed wafer of communion bread was held safe and its presence was given witness by the lit sanctuary candle hanging to the left of the altar. Above the tabernacle, between the two candles, was a baroque crucifix of carved ebony, the cross edged with beaten gold. The Christos wore a gold crown of thorns.

John steeled himself with a deep breath then went forward.

At the front John, while not having been raised in any church, felt he should obey the tenants of this church since it was Joshua's place of worship, so he knelt and crossed himself in front of the altar rail. He stood, turned to the left, and sat down in the front pew nearest to the plaque marking the resting place of Joshua's ashes. *The boss is probably laughing right now,* John thought as he remembered talking with Joshua about what happened after death. *He would have said what was behind the plaque was just some ashes which might be good for adding lime to the soil if they were spread in the garden, but nothing else.* The real Joshua was long gone from them. If there was an afterlife, of which John was not sure, Joshua would be there. Still it seemed right to come here to have a talk with him.

John looked at the plaque and said, "Boss I'm sure you know without my telling you I finished *World Without End.* I did the best I could with what we had talked about and the few notes you left. But I had hell's own time figuring out how to put myself into the story the same way you did. When you died, I stopped dreaming and I...I really hated you then for getting me into this to begin with, but I kept asking myself how you did it. How did you put yourself into the story? And then it came to me--maybe it was you whispering in my ear or that Great Author you used to talk about, or the muse, or something, but whatever it was, I suddenly realized that all I had to do was convince myself it was true history!

Believe that this had all happened just like people believe all the stuff in the Bible happened even if they weren't there to see it all. Faith, I guess you'd call it. "The belief in things unseen..." When I realized *that,* I found out I could control the story, even though I couldn't exactly control the characters. Not that it was easy, but I did it, and that's how it came out. It turned out ok, I think. Anyway, it's out and selling great. All the publicity from the trial and Lucian and all, and they are sending me on a book tour besides; TV and radio and such. They're already flying off the shelves. I guess I feel ok about it, but I don't know. I still feel like I bailed on you when I agreed to the compromise, but it is too late to back out of it now, so..."

John stopped and took a couple of breaths before continuing. "They are still arguing about pulling the plug on Lucian. He doesn't seem to be any better, but the doctors keep saying he could come out of it. I personally think they see a cash cow and can't help milking it, but maybe I'm just cynical. But the reason I'm telling you this, which again you probably already know, is, if you have any influence with the way the universe wags, maybe you oughta throw a little weight behind letting Lucian die. It would be a mercy to him and I know how you felt about mercy. I also know how you felt about Lucian. I just wish you two could have worked out your differences here in life, but you didn't, so maybe if he crosses on out of this world to the next, you can reconcile there. Anyway, it's something to think about, if you have anything to say about it."

John paused again, shifting gears. "I asked Katherine to marry me, and foolish girl that she is, she said yes. I guess I have you to thank for her along with a lot of other things. Without you I have no idea where I would have wound up. You saved me. I guess in another way you used me too, but it's ok. It came out all right at the end. Better than all right.

"Boss, I couldn't have asked for anything better if you had been my father. In a lot of ways I think of you as my father since I never really knew mine. I just wish--but wishes...Ah well."

John sat silently for a long time then, looking at the plaque and at the crucifix then turning inward to look at his own heart, "I want you to know I'm going to take care of your creatures the best I can. I have started a new Forneria book. I hope the great author of this world will take care of his creatures long enough for me to finish it. I'm gonna give you credit too. It's gonna be, *"Next in the series of Joshua Gordon's Forneria stories,"* right under the title. By and bye I'm gonna write other stuff too, not just Forneria stories, but not for a while. I want Bitter and Ezra and Fay and Noah and Thomas to get used to thinking of me as the Creator too, but then I want to create some worlds of my own. Guess I'm like your friend's poem in *Angels of the Coast*.

"...By scratching words, create the worlds

I cannot call to be."

John smiled, but his vision was so blurred he had to wipe the tears from his eyes. "Anyway, Boss, thanks for everything. Rest in Peace. I love you.

The End

ABOUT THE AUTHOR

G. Lloyd Helm has been writing for 30 years, having published poetry in a wide variety of magazines and newspapers including: "The New York Poetry Anthology," "Stars and Stripes News," "The Los Angeles Times," "The Antelope Valley Press," and "The Antelope Valley Anthologies," among others.

He has published short stories and memoirs both in the US and in England in such journals as "Pligrimage" which published the memoir "Football" in Spring 2005, and a second memoir "4 April, 1968" in the winter of 2008. He has published short stories in "Citadel" the literary magazine of Los Angeles City College," "Delivered Magazine," which is based in London, "Short Story Library," The University of S. Illinois' "Eureka Literary Magazine," "Tales as like as not," and London's "Black Gate Magazine."

Helm has published two novels in the F&SF field: *Other Doors*, From MousePrints Publishing and *DESIGN*, from Publish America.

VISIT OUR WEBSITE
FOR THE FULL INVENTORY
OF QUALITY BOOKS:

http://www.roguephoenixpress.com

Rogue Phoenix Press

Representing Excellence in Publishing

Quality trade paperbacks and downloads

in multiple formats,

in genres ranging from historical to contemporary romance,
mystery and science fiction.

Visit the website then bookmark it.

We add new titles each month!